STARLIGHT 1

STARLIGHT 1

EDITED BY

PATRICK

NIELSEN

HAYDEN

A TOM DOHERTY
ASSOCIATES
BOOK

NEW YORK

STARLIGHT 1

A Tor Book
Published by Tom Doherty Associates, Inc.
175 Fifth Avenue
New York, N.Y. 10010

Tor Books on the World Wide Web:
http://www.tor.com

Tor® is a registered trademark of Tom Doherty Associates, Inc.

Design by Lynn Newmark

Library of Congress Cataloging-in-Publication Data

Starlight / Patrick Nielsen Hayden, editor.—1st ed.
    p. cm.
   "A Tom Doherty Associates book."
   ISBN 0-312-86215-6 (v. 1 : pbk. : acid-free paper).—
   ISBN 0-312-86214-8 (v. 1 : hardcover : acid-free paper)
   1. Science fiction, American.   2. American fiction—20th
century.   I. Nielsen Hayden, Patrick.
PS648.S3S655   1996
813'.0876208—dc20   96-8454
                                    CIP

First Edition: September 1996

Printed in the United States of America

0 9 8 7 6 5 4 3 2 1

COPYRIGHT ACKNOWLEDGMENTS

CONTENTS

INTRODUCTION

YOU HOLD IN YOUR HANDS THE FIRST VOLUME OF THAT RARE THING in modern SF, an original anthology series. Not a theme anthology, not a collection of reprints—but a collection of new stories, never before published, spanning the range of SF today.

Short fiction is, of course, the R&D laboratory in which SF constantly reinvents itself. Novels are all very well—I make my living editing them, and you won't hear me gainsaying their pleasures—but short fiction is where SF writers take chances, stir the pot, kick out the jams. It's no accident that short fiction has been crucial to each period of major ferment and invention in the modern history of the field. It is, if you will, the garage rock of SF.

And of course much of that short fiction has appeared in the SF magazines, from the ravishingly vulgar pulps of the 1920s and '30s to the more dignified magazines of today. But since SF book publishing got going after World War II there's been a parallel track of original anthology series in book form, among them, notably, the several volumes each of Frederik Pohl's *Star Science Fiction*, Damon Knight's *Orbit*, Robert Silverberg's *New Dimensions*, and of course

Terry Carr's *Universe*. At their best, these series and others like them brought short SF and fantasy to a broader audience. Moreover, unconstrained by a magazine's monthly schedule, these anthologists and writers were able to nudge and develop each story into its own best proper form, however experimental or conventional that turned out to be.

We liked those anthologies. We think there should be more of them. And we have made some assumptions in the course of putting this one together.

First, we assume we don't have to give you a song and dance about the potential merits of SF. This is 1996. Our culture is saturated with SF, both good and bad. We don't have to tell you about it.

Second, we believe there are plenty of readers looking for the excitement, warmth, and unpredictability that were characteristic of SF storytelling before it got chopped and fine-tuned into precisely calibrated dosages for hypothesized niche markets. Before we—all of us in the SF business—decided that we knew in advance exactly what you want and what you don't.

Second and a half: Niche precision is boring. Someone once asked Damon Knight what kind of stories he really wanted for *Orbit*. He replied, "I'm trying to keep you confused about that." So are we. Which is why here you'll see science-by-god fiction, blatant fantasy, "magic realism," and who knows what else. Starlight shines down on everything: spaceships, Elfland, and the mysterious things humans do in the dark.

Third and finally, we think that despite decades in the ghetto and millions of words of defensive rhetoric and our chronic dreadful ingroupishness and the fact that the *New York Times Book Review* still doesn't review Gene Wolfe or Stan Robinson on Page 1 (weep wail), the self-conscious, self-aware SF field—the commercial genre—still has vigor, relevance, juice, and surprises left for us at the century's end.

Every project like this has debts to discharge. For this first volume, I am grateful to Lenny Bailes, Neil Gaiman, David Hartwell, Don Keller, Tappan King, Jonathan Lethem, Beth Meacham, Joel Richards, Sarah Rudolph, Martha Soukup, and Terri Windling for support, help, encouragement, and crucial information. Were I to thank every employee of Tor Books whose efforts contributed to *Starlight* I would have to list the whole company, but I want to single out publisher Tom Doherty, editor Claire Eddy, art director Irene Gallo, and marketing director Linda Quinton for special thanks. Without the giant short-SF brain of Tom Weber it is doubtful this book would exist. And finally, without Teresa Nielsen Hayden, wife and colleague, none of the stars would be in their places at all.

I hope you enjoy *Starlight 1*, and I hope you'll join us again in 1998 for *Starlight 2*.

—Patrick Nielsen Hayden

MICHAEL SWANWICK

THE DEAD

THREE BOY ZOMBIES IN MATCHING RED JACKETS BUSSED OUR table, bringing water, lighting candles, brushing away the crumbs between courses. Their eyes were dark, attentive, lifeless; their hands and faces so white as to be faintly luminous in the hushed light. I thought it in bad taste, but "This is Manhattan," Courtney said. "A certain studied offensiveness is fashionable here."

The blond brought menus and waited for our order.

We both ordered pheasant. "An excellent choice," the boy said in a clear, emotionless voice. He went away and came back a minute later with the freshly strangled birds, holding them up for our approval. He couldn't have been more than eleven when he died and his skin was of that sort connoisseurs call "milk-glass," smooth, without blemish, and all but translucent. He must have cost a fortune.

As the boy was turning away, I impulsively touched his shoulder. He turned back. "What's your name, son?" I asked.

"Timothy." He might have been telling me the *specialité de maison*. The boy waited a breath to see if more was expected of him, then left.

Courtney gazed after him. "How lovely he would look," she murmured, "nude. Standing in the moonlight by a cliff. Definitely a cliff. Perhaps the very one where he met his death."

"He wouldn't look very lovely if he'd fallen off a cliff."

"Oh, don't be unpleasant."

The wine steward brought our bottle. "Château Latour '17." I raised an eyebrow. The steward had the sort of old and complex face that Rembrandt would have enjoyed painting. He poured with pulseless ease and then dissolved into the gloom. "Good lord, Courtney, you *seduced* me on cheaper."

She flushed, not happily. Courtney had a better career going than I. She outpowered me. We both knew who was smarter, better connected, more likely to end up in a corner office with the historically significant antique desk. The only edge I had was that I was a male in a seller's market. It was enough.

"This is a business dinner, Donald," she said, "nothing more."

I favored her with an expression of polite disbelief I knew from experience she'd find infuriating. And, digging into my pheasant, murmured, "Of course." We didn't say much of consequence until dessert, when I finally asked, "So what's Loeb-Soffner up to these days?"

"Structuring a corporate expansion. Jim's putting together the financial side of the package, and I'm doing personnel. You're being headhunted, Donald." She favored me with that feral little flash of teeth she made when she saw something she wanted. Courtney wasn't a beautiful woman, far from it. But there was that fierceness to her, that sense of something primal being held under tight and precarious control that made her hot as hot to me. "You're talented, you're thuggish, and you're not too tightly nailed to your present position. Those are all qualities we're looking for."

She dumped her purse on the table, took out a single-folded sheet of paper. "These are the terms I'm offering." She placed it by my plate, attacked her torte with gusto.

I unfolded the paper. "This is a lateral transfer."

"Unlimited opportunity for advancement," she said with her mouth full, "if you've got the stuff."

"Mmm." I did a line-by-line of the benefits, all comparable to what I was getting now. My current salary to the dollar—Ms. Soffner was showing off. And the stock options. "This can't be right. Not for a lateral."

There was that grin again, like a glimpse of shark in murky waters. "I knew you'd like it. We're going over the top with the options because we need your answer right away—tonight preferably. Tomorrow at the latest. No negotiations. We have to put the package together fast. There's going to be a shitstorm of publicity when this comes out. We want to have everything nailed down, present the fundies and bleeding hearts with a *fait accompli*."

"My God, Courtney, what kind of monster do you have hold of now?"

"The biggest one in the world. Bigger than Apple. Bigger than Home Virtual. Bigger than HIVac-IV," she said with relish. "Have you ever heard of Koestler Biological?"

I put my fork down.

"Koestler? You're peddling corpses now?"

"Please. Postanthropic biological resources." She said it lightly, with just the right touch of irony. Still, I thought I detected a certain discomfort with the nature of her client's product.

"There's no money in it." I waved a hand toward our attentive waitstaff. "These guys must be—what?—maybe two percent of the annual turnover? Zombies are luxury goods: servants, reactor cleanups, Hollywood stunt deaths, exotic services"—we both knew what I meant—"a few hundred a year, maybe, tops. There's not the demand. The revulsion factor is too great."

"There's been a technological breakthrough." Courtney leaned forward. "They can install the infrasystem and controllers and offer the product for the factory-floor cost of a new subcompact. That's way below the economic threshold for blue-collar labor.

"Look at it from the viewpoint of a typical factory owner. He's already downsized to the bone and labor costs are bleeding him dry. How can he compete in a dwindling consumer market? Now let's imagine he buys into the program." She took out her Mont Blanc and began scribbling figures on the tablecloth. "No benefits. No liability suits. No sick pay. No pilferage. We're talking about cutting labor costs by at least two thirds. Minimum! That's irresistible, I don't care how big your revulsion factor is. We project we can move five hundred thousand units in the first year."

"Five hundred thousand," I said. "That's crazy. Where the hell are you going to get the raw material for—?"

"Africa."

"Oh, God, Courtney." I was struck wordless by the cynicism it took to even consider turning the sub-Saharan tragedy to a profit, by the sheer, raw evil of channeling hard currency to the pocket Hitlers who ran the camps. Courtney only smiled and gave that quick little flip of her head that meant she was accessing the time on an optic chip.

"I think you're ready," she said, "to talk with Koestler."

At her gesture, the zombie boys erected projector lamps about us, fussed with the settings, turned them on. Interference patterns moiréd, clashed, meshed. Walls of darkness erected themselves about us. Courtney took out her flat and set it up on the table. Three taps of her nailed fingers and the round and hairless face of Marvin Koestler appeared on the screen. "Ah, Courtney!" he said in a pleased voice. "You're in—New York, yes? The San Moritz. With Donald." The slightest pause with each accessed bit of information. "Did you have the antelope medallions?" When we shook our heads, he kissed his fingertips. "Magnificent! They're ever so lightly braised and then smothered in buffalo mozzarella. Nobody makes them better. I had the same dish in Florence the other day, and there was simply no comparison."

I cleared my throat. "Is that where you are? Italy?"

"Let's leave out where I am." He made a dismissive gesture, as if it were a trifle. But Courtney's face darkened. Corporate kidnapping being the growth industry it is, I'd gaffed badly. "The question is—what do you think of my offer?"

"It's . . . interesting. For a lateral."

"It's the start-up costs. We're leveraged up to our asses as it is. You'll make out better this way in the long run." He favored me with a sudden grin that went mean around the edges. Very much the financial buccaneer. Then he leaned forward, lowered his voice, maintained firm eye-contact. Classic people-handling techniques. "You're not sold. You know you can trust Courtney to have checked out the finances. Still, you think: It won't work. To work the product has to be irresistible, and it's not. It can't be."

"Yes, sir," I said. "Succinctly put."

He nodded to Courtney. "Let's sell this young man." And to me, "My stretch is downstairs."

He winked out.

Koestler was waiting for us in the limo, a ghostly pink presence. His holo, rather, a genial if somewhat coarse-grained ghost afloat in golden light. He waved an expansive and insubstantial arm to take in the interior of the car and said, "Make yourselves at home."

The chauffeur wore combat-grade photomultipliers. They gave him a buggish, inhuman look. I wasn't sure if he was dead or not. "Take us to Heaven," Koestler said.

The doorman stepped out into the street, looked both ways, nodded to the chauffeur. Robot guns tracked our progress down the block.

"Courtney tells me you're getting the raw materials from Africa."

"Distasteful, but necessary. To begin with. We have to sell the idea first—no reason to make things rough on ourselves. Down the line, though, I don't see why we can't go domestic. Something along the lines of a reverse mortgage, perhaps, life insurance that pays off while you're still alive. It'd be a step toward getting the poor off our backs at last. Fuck 'em. They've been getting a goddamn free ride for too long; the least they can do is to die and provide us with servants."

I was pretty sure Koestler was joking. But I smiled and ducked my head, so I'd be covered in either case. "What's Heaven?" I asked, to move the conversation onto safer territory.

"A proving ground," Koestler said with great satisfaction, "for the future. Have you ever witnessed bare-knuckles fisticuffs?"

"No."

"Ah, now there's a sport for gentlemen! The sweet science at its sweetest. No rounds, no rules, no holds barred. It gives you the real measure of a man—not just of his strength but his character.

How he handles himself, whether he keeps cool under pressure—how he stands up to pain. Security won't let me go to the clubs in person, but I've made arrangements."

Heaven was a converted movie theater in a rundown neighborhood in Queens. The chauffeur got out, disappeared briefly around the back, and returned with two zombie bodyguards. It was like a conjurer's trick. "You had these guys stashed in the *trunk?*" I asked as he opened the door for us.

"It's a new world," Courtney said. "Get used to it."

The place was mobbed. Two, maybe three hundred seats, standing room only. A mixed crowd, blacks and Irish and Koreans mostly, but with a smattering of uptown customers as well. You didn't have to be poor to need the occasional taste of vicarious potency. Nobody paid us any particular notice. We'd come in just as the fighters were being presented.

"Weighing two-five-oh, in black trunks with a red stripe," the ref was bawling, "tha gang-bang *gang*sta, the bare-knuckle *brawla,* the man with tha—"

Courtney and I went up a scummy set of back stairs. Bodyguard-us-bodyguard, as if we were a combat patrol out of some twentieth-century jungle war. A scrawny, potbellied old geezer with a damp cigar in his mouth unlocked the door to our box. Sticky floor, bad seats, a good view down on the ring. Gray plastic matting, billowing smoke.

Koestler was there, in a shiny new hologram shell. It reminded me of those plaster Madonnas in painted bathtubs that Catholics set out in their yards. "Your permanent box?" I asked.

"All of this is for your sake, Donald—you and a few others. We're pitting our product one-on-one against some of the local talent. By arrangement with the management. What you're going to see will settle your doubts once and for all."

"You'll like this," Courtney said. "I've been here five nights straight. Counting tonight." The bell rang, starting the fight. She leaned forward avidly, hooking her elbows on the railing.

The zombie was gray-skinned and modestly muscled, for a

fighter. But it held up its hands alertly, was light on its feet, and had strangely calm and knowing eyes.

Its opponent was a real bruiser, a big black guy with classic African features twisted slightly out of true so that his mouth curled up in a kind of sneer on one side. He had gang scars on his chest and even uglier marks on his back that didn't look deliberate but like something he'd earned on the streets. His eyes burned with an intensity just this side of madness.

He came forward cautiously but not fearfully, and made a couple of quick jabs to get the measure of his opponent. They were blocked and countered.

They circled each other, looking for an opening.

For a minute or so, nothing much happened. Then the gangster feinted at the zombie's head, drawing up its guard. He drove through that opening with a slam to the zombie's nuts that made me wince.

No reaction.

The dead fighter responded with a flurry of punches, and got in a glancing blow to its opponent's cheek. They separated, engaged, circled around.

Then the big guy exploded in a combination of killer blows, connecting so solidly it seemed they would splinter every rib in the dead fighter's body. It brought the crowd to their feet, roaring their approval.

The zombie didn't even stagger.

A strange look came into the gangster's eyes, then, as the zombie counterattacked, driving him back into the ropes. I could only imagine what it must be like for a man who had always lived by his strength and his ability to absorb punishment to realize that he was facing an opponent to whom pain meant nothing. Fights were lost and won by flinches and hesitations. You won by keeping your head. You lost by getting rattled.

Despite his best blows, the zombie stayed methodical, serene, calm, relentless. That was its nature.

It must have been devastating.

The fight went on and on. It was a strange and alienating experience for me. After a while I couldn't stay focused on it. My thoughts kept slipping into a zone where I found myself studying the line of Courtney's jaw, thinking about later tonight. She liked her sex just a little bit sick. There was always a feeling, fucking her, that there was something truly repulsive that she *really* wanted to do but lacked the courage to bring up on her own.

So there was always this urge to get her to do something she didn't like. She was resistant; I never dared try more than one new thing per date. But I could always talk her into that one thing. Because when she was aroused, she got pliant. She could be talked into anything. She could be made to beg for it.

Courtney would've been amazed to learn that I was not proud of what I did with her—quite the opposite, in fact. But I was as obsessed with her as she was with whatever it was that obsessed her.

Suddenly Courtney was on her feet, yelling. The hologram showed Koestler on his feet as well. The big guy was on the ropes, being pummeled. Blood and spittle flew from his face with each blow. Then he was down; he'd never even had a chance. He must've known early on that it was hopeless, that he wasn't going to win, but he'd refused to take a fall. He had to be pounded into the ground. He went down raging, proud and uncomplaining. I had to admire that.

But he lost anyway.

That, I realized, was the message I was meant to take away from this. Not just that the product was robust. But that only those who backed it were going to win. I could see, even if the audience couldn't, that it was the end of an era. A man's body wasn't worth a damn anymore. There wasn't anything it could do that technology couldn't handle better. The number of losers in the world had just doubled, tripled, reached maximum. What the fools below were cheering for was the death of their futures.

I got up and cheered too.

In the stretch afterward, Koestler said, "You've seen the light. You're a believer now."

"I haven't necessarily decided yet."

"Don't bullshit me," Koestler said. "I've done my homework,

Mr. Nichols. Your current position is not exactly secure. Morton-Western is going down the tubes. The entire service sector is going down the tubes. Face it, the old economic order is as good as fucking gone. Of course you're going to take my offer. You don't have any other choice."

The fax outed sets of contracts. "A Certain Product," it said here and there. Corpses were never mentioned.

But when I opened my jacket to get a pen Koestler said, "Wait. I've got a factory. Three thousand positions under me. I've got a motivated workforce. They'd walk through fire to keep their jobs. Pilferage is at zero. Sick time practically the same. Give me one advantage your product has over my current workforce. Sell me on it. I'll give you thirty seconds."

I wasn't in sales and the job had been explicitly promised me already. But by reaching for the pen, I had admitted I wanted the position. And we all knew whose hand carried the whip.

"They can be catheterized," I said—"no toilet breaks."

For a long instant Koestler just stared at me blankly. Then he exploded with laughter. "By God, that's a new one! You have a great future ahead of you, Donald. Welcome aboard."

He winked out.

We drove on in silence for a while, aimless, directionless. At last Courtney leaned forward and touched the chauffeur's shoulder.

"Take me home," she said.

Riding through Manhattan I suffered from a waking hallucination that we were driving through a city of corpses. Gray faces, listless motions. Everyone looked dead in the headlights and sodium vapor streetlamps. Passing by the Children's Museum I saw a mother with a stroller through the glass doors. Two small children by her side. They all three stood motionless, gazing forward at nothing. We passed by a stop-and-go where zombies stood out on the sidewalk drinking forties in paper bags. Through upper-story windows I could see the sad rainbow trace of virtuals playing to empty eyes. There were zombies in the park, zombies smoking blunts, zombies driving taxies, zombies sitting on stoops and hanging out on street corners, all of them waiting for the years to pass and the flesh to fall from their bones.

I felt like the last man alive.

Courtney was still wired and sweaty from the fight. The pheromones came off her in great waves as I followed her down the hall to her apartment. She stank of lust. I found myself thinking of how she got just before orgasm, so desperate, so desirable. It was different after she came, she would fall into a state of calm assurance; the same sort of calm assurance she showed in her business life, the aplomb she sought so wildly during the act itself.

And when that desperation left her, so would I. Because even I could recognize that it was her desperation that drew me to her, that made me do the things she needed me to do. In all the years I'd known her, we'd never once had breakfast together.

I wished there was some way I could deal her out of the equation. I wished that her desperation were a liquid that I could drink down to the dregs. I wished I could drop her in a wine press and squeeze her dry.

At her apartment, Courtney unlocked her door and in one complicated movement twisted through and stood facing me from the inside. "Well," she said. "All in all, a productive evening. Good night, Donald."

"Good night? Aren't you going to invite me inside?"

"No."

"What do you mean, no?" She was beginning to piss me off. A blind man could've told she was in heat from across the street. A chimpanzee could've talked his way into her pants. "What kind of idiot game are you playing now?"

"You know what no means, Donald. You're not stupid."

"No I'm not, and neither are you. We both know the score. Now let me in, goddamnit."

"Enjoy your present," she said, and closed the door.

*   *   *

I found Courtney's present back in my suite. I was still seething from her treatment of me and stalked into the room, letting the door slam behind me so that I was standing in near-total darkness. The only light was what little seeped through the draped windows at the far end of the room. I was just reaching for the light switch when there was a motion in the darkness.

Jackers! I thought, and all in panic lurched for the light switch, hoping to achieve I don't know what. Credit-jackers always work in trios, one to torture the security codes out of you, one to phone the numbers out of your accounts and into a fiscal trapdoor, a third to stand guard. Was turning the lights on supposed to make them scurry for darkness, like roaches? Nevertheless, I almost tripped over my own feet in my haste to reach the switch. But of course it was nothing like what I'd feared.

It was a woman.

She stood by the window in a white silk dress that could neither compete with nor distract from her ethereal beauty, her porcelain skin. When the lights came on, she turned toward me, eyes widening, lips parting slightly. Her breasts swayed ever so slightly as she gracefully raised a bare arm to offer me a lily. "Hello, Donald," she said huskily. "I'm yours for the night." She was absolutely beautiful.

And dead, of course.

Not twenty minutes later I was hammering on Courtney's door. She came to the door in a Pierre Cardin dressing gown and from the way she was still cinching the sash and the disarray of her hair I gathered she hadn't been expecting me.

"I'm not alone," she said.

"I didn't come here for the dubious pleasures of your fair white body." I pushed my way into the room. (But couldn't help remembering that beautiful body of hers, not so exquisite as the dead whore's, and now the thoughts were inextricably mingled in my head: death and Courtney, sex and corpses, a Gordian knot I might never be able to untangle.)

"You didn't like my surprise?" She was smiling openly now, amused.

"No, I fucking did not!"

I took a step toward her. I was shaking. I couldn't stop fisting and unfisting my hands.

She fell back a step. But that confident, oddly expectant look didn't leave her face. "Bruno," she said lightly. "Would you come in here?"

A motion at the periphery of vision. Bruno stepped out of the shadows of her bedroom. He was a muscular brute, pumped, ripped, and as black as the fighter I'd seen go down earlier that night. He stood behind Courtney, totally naked, with slim hips and wide shoulders and the finest skin I'd ever seen.

And dead.

I saw it all in a flash.

"Oh, for God's sake, Courtney!" I said, disgusted. "I can't believe you. That you'd actually . . . That thing's just an obedient body. There's nothing there—no passion, no connection, just . . . physical presence."

Courtney made a kind of chewing motion through her smile, weighing the implications of what she was about to say. Nastiness won.

"We have equity now," she said.

I lost it then. I stepped forward, raising a hand, and I swear to God I intended to bounce the bitch's head off the back wall. But she didn't flinch—she didn't even look afraid. She merely moved aside, saying, "In the body, Bruno. He has to look good in a business suit."

A dead fist smashed into my ribs so hard I thought for an instant my heart had stopped. Then Bruno punched me in my stomach. I doubled over, gasping. Two, three, four more blows. I was on the ground now, rolling over, helpless and weeping with rage.

"That's enough, baby. Now put out the trash."

Bruno dumped me in the hallway.

I glared up at Courtney through my tears. She was not at all beautiful now. Not in the least. You're getting older, I wanted to tell her. But instead I heard my voice, angry and astonished, saying, "You . . . you goddamn, fucking necrophile!"

"Cultivate a taste for it," Courtney said. Oh, she was purring! I doubted she'd ever find life quite this good again. "Half a million

Brunos are about to come on the market. You're going to find it a lot more difficult to pick up *living* women in not so very long."

I sent away the dead whore. Then I took a long shower that didn't really make me feel any better. Naked, I walked into my unlit suite and opened the curtains. For a long time I stared out over the glory and darkness that was Manhattan.

I was afraid, more afraid than I'd ever been in my life.

The slums below me stretched to infinity. They were a vast necropolis, a neverending city of the dead. I thought of the millions out there who were never going to hold down a job again. I thought of how they must hate me—me and my kind—and how helpless they were before us. And yet. There were so many of them and so few of us. If they were to all rise up at once, they'd be like a tsunami, irresistible. And if there was so much as a spark of life left in them, then that was exactly what they would do.

That was one possibility. There was one other, and that was that nothing would happen. Nothing at all.

God help me, but I didn't know which one scared me more.

ANDY DUNCAN

LIZA AND THE CRAZY WATER MAN

SHE WAS LONG DONE SINGING, BUT THE SCHOOLHOUSE WAS STILL full of her voice. It flowed into the corners. It washed along the ceiling and the floorboards. It surged against the backs of the farmers and mill workers as they shuffled out the door. It claimed all the space they had occupied. It crowded them, ready to pour out, into the cool night, and roll freely across the face of the mountain.

The woman who owned the voice sat on the edge of the little stage and shook out her hair of silver and gold, raked her fingers through it once, twice, as she sweated in the lamp's kerosene glow. I stood there in the dimness, sweltering and damp, my tie undone. The people leaving whooped and laughed, but I feared to say a mumbling word. No room was left in that place for my voice.

So, wordlessly, I stepped into the circle of light, and held out my business card. It was all the offering I had.

Alvin Pleasants, Charlotte office
CRAZY WATER CRYSTALS COMPANY
Of Mineral Wells, Texas

"Making weak men strong since 1880"
Sponsor of "CRAZY BARN DANCE"
Saturday nights on WBT

She read the card gravely and thoroughly, as if it were bad news
from far away. Then she handed it back and smiled. "Thank you,"
she said, "but Aunt Kate and I have no need of laxatives. Thank you
again, and good night."

"It's not a laxative," I said. "It's an all-purpose tonic."

"Is it, now? That sounds much more interesting. If you'll excuse
me?" She picked up her guitar case, hoisted it onto one hip to get a
better hold, then swung it between us and headed for the door. I
followed and matched her stride, for she was as tall as I was. I had
not driven halfway up the mountain called Yandro just to go back
to Charlotte empty-handed, however pleasant the drive in spring-
time.

All my other leads had come to nothing: a mandolin player in
Blowing Rock, a gospel quartet in North Wilkesboro, two fiddling
brothers in Boone. None wanted to be broadcast all over the Carolinas on a fifty-thousand-watt station in between advertisements
for Crazy Water Crystals. None wanted to pick up and move to
Charlotte and become famous, like the Monroe Brothers and the
Delmore Brothers and Fiddlin' Arthur Smith. None even wanted
a steady radio salary. The year was 1936, and I apparently no
longer could get 1931 mileage out of the phrase "ten dollars a
week."

I kept right alongside as she swept through a knot of people on
the porch. "Good night, fellas," she said. "I'll see y'all in church."

"Evening, Liza."

"Good night, Liza."

"Take care, Liza."

They stared at me as I kept pace, nearly at a trot, down the steps
and into the parking area. She walked right through the middle of
a terrible snarl of wagons and shying mules and Model T's that
churned around in circles slinging gravel. She looked neither to left
nor right, as if charmed. I had seen this in mountain women before,
this grim set of the jaw, this purposeful, loping gait, as if all slopes

were steep. But I soon stopped comparing other mountain women to Liza Candler.

I tried my usually surefire sales pitch: I told the truth. "You have a voice like the voice of the mountain," I said, panting. "I want to put that voice on the radio. I don't want to sell you anything. I just want people to hear your voice."

"They hear me now," she said.

"Not many, though. How often do you play a dance like this? Once a week? I doubt it. Once a month, more like? And always for the home folks. The same people, month after month, year after year."

"Don't you like the same people, month after month, year after year? Do you change the people you like every month, like shifts at the furniture plant? And do you aim to run alongside me all the way home like a haint?"

I stopped and watched her stalk on down the road. "No, I thought you'd stop and talk to me, so I could offer you a ride."

"I ain't stopping," she said, her checked dress indistinct in the dark, "but if you drive up alongside me and open the door I might get in."

I ran back for the Packard.

"And then," she called after me, "we can see what Aunt Kate has to say."

All the way up the road, I worked on her.

"You could come to Charlotte, stay for a week, visit the studio, get to know people, do a Crazy Water show on Saturday night, see how you like it. See how much mail comes in. Heck, I know people at RCA Victor. I could set up a recording session for you while you're in town. Do you know that Mainer's Mountaineers made eighteen thousand dollars last year for a half-hour's work in Charlotte? Just for 'Maple on the Hill'? They earned a half-cent in royalties off every record sold. How about that?"

Liza had her eyes shut and her head out the window, so that her hair streamed out behind. She had a profile like a cameo brooch. "A lot of people must have no music of their own," she said, "if they'll pay good money to try to hang on to somebody else's."

In the front parlor of the Candler place sat an ancient woman in a rocking chair, her feet propped on the grate of a cold iron stove. We walked in as she pushed a pinch of snuff into her mouth with one hand and snapped shut a small pouch with her other. She wore a tattered sweater, a gingham bonnet, and square eyeglasses as thick and grimy as windshields. Behind her, a gleaming shotgun leaned against the wall.

"Hello, Aunt Kate!" Liza cried, so loudly that I jumped. "This is Mr. Alvin Pleasants, from down in Charlotte."

Aunt Kate tucked the pouch into an apron pocket, pulled her eyeglasses down to the tip of her nose, and tilted her head back to look at me. Then she grunted and leaned sideways, slowly reached out behind, groped the air in the vicinity of the shotgun.

"No, Aunt Kate!" Liza yelled. "He ain't a fella! He wants to put me on the radio! He works for WBT!"

"Actually, I work for the Crazy Water Crystals Company, but I do have an office at WBT. And I know the Monroe Brothers personally." I sat on the edge of a horsehair davenport, which pricked me something awful, and handed Aunt Kate a brochure. "Here's a copy of WBT's Official Radiologue, the seasonal programming schedule, compliments of Crazy Water Crystals." Aunt Kate bent over the brochure and scanned it with the tip of her nose. Liza looked at me meaningfully. Her eyes were gray. "Oh, I'm sorry," I said, and I began to yell, too. "It's a copy of the station's schedule! A gift for you!"

Aunt Kate slowly looked up at me and asked, very quietly, "Who in the world raised you to holler inside the house any such a way?"

I glared toward where Liza had been. I heard her bustle around the next room, humming. "I'm sorry, ma'am. Your niece gave me the impression that you were deaf."

Aunt Kate swatted the air. "Shoot. Ain't no telling what that gal will come up with. But if you know so much about radios, how 'bout turn on that one over there?" She pointed at a cathedral set across the room. "It's time for my story."

I turned the knob, heard a familiar click, then felt the vibration as the tubes started to warm up. As Liza walked in, tying back her hair, the radio started that slide-whistle sound that said the station would arrive in just a few seconds.

"Aunt Kate," Liza asked, at a normal volume, "haven't you wanted to visit Aunt Oese in the TB sanitarium in Charlotte?"

"You know I have, honey," Aunt Kate said. "Just been waiting on you to take a notion to come with me."

"Then I reckon I might as well come do your program," Liza told me. "Just for one show, of course."

The station faded in on a commercial: "If you care for your loved ones' laundry, banish tattletale gray with Fels Naphtha! Yes, banish tattletale gray with Fels Naphtha!"

"Good night, Aunt Kate," Liza said, and kissed the old woman on the cheek. "Mr. Pleasants said he'd be happy to keep you company while you listen to your story."

"I did?"

"Good night, Mr. Pleasants," Liza said, standing in the doorway. "I hope that laxative company pays you well to drive around the countryside and bother people."

I enunciated carefully. "It's an all-purpose tonic."

"Is that so? Good night to you once again. I do hope you enjoy the program." She watched me through the narrowing crack, and I watched her, until the door thunked shut between us.

"And now—'The Romance of Helen Trent'! The real-life drama of Helen Trent, who, when life mocks her, breaks her hopes, dashes her against the rocks of despair, fights back bravely, successfully, to prove what so many women long to prove in their own lives: that because a woman is thirty-five—or more—romance in life need not be over. That romance can begin at thirty-five!"

As the organ music trilled, Aunt Kate leaned forward and puckered, sucked in her cheeks, squeezed a big dark drop from between her lips, and let it plop into a half-full Kiwi shoe-polish tin at her feet. She daubed her lips with a corner of her apron and sat back. The rocker and a floorboard creaked in harmony. The horsehair in the davenport worked its way a little further into me, as if to seize and haul me down into the brocade, fix me in that parlor forever.

Two months later, on the afternoon I met Liza and her aunt at the train station, my boss was pan-fried drunk. Had I known that, I might not have been so eager to drop Aunt Kate at the boarding-house and whisk Liza immediately up to the station, hell-bent to show her the glories of radio. As I threw open the door to Mr. Ledford's office, I realized my error.

"Oh, dear," I said.

Empty bottles of Crazy Water's chief competitor, Peruna, formed three rows of pickets that guarded three sides of his desktop from all comers. Despite the mutter and jerk of the electric fan atop the file cabinet, the office was sweltering, and Ledford's ever-present homburg sagged over his ears like a deflated pudding. He gazed sightlessly forward, his expression placid, mournful, and expectant of all bad things. I timidly introduced Liza, and in reply his bullfrog voice rasped even more than usual.

"Good afternoon, Miss Candler," Ledford said. "Please forgive me, but I am drunker than Cooter John."

"There is no need to apologize," Liza said, "but who, pray tell, is Cooter John?"

"Cooter John does not exist," Ledford said. "He is a mythic figure, a wraith with a legendary capacity for drink."

"Thank you," Liza said.

I cleared my throat. "Probably we should come back later," I said. "Mr. Ledford sometimes likes to sample the competitors' products, just to, uh, investigate the market."

"I no longer wonder that Peruna sells so well," Ledford said. "It virtually sells itself, in all its smoothness and guile." He lurched sideways, rummaged in his trash can, and came up with a clutch of empty Peruna boxes. "If you will excuse me," he said, "I have box tops to redeem."

"You can talk to Miss Candler later," I said, hastily. "Maybe I could show her around downtown? Come back here just before 'Briarhopper Time,' so she can watch the broadcast?"

Ledford flapped a hand at us, and we fled.

Out on the sidewalk, we walked into a hot breeze of exhaust fumes. We had to raise our voices to be heard over the rattles and growls of the Model T's and Model A's and the clangs of the streetcars that slid along the tracks in the middle of the traffic. Many of the Ford drivers seemed to keep one hand on the wheel and one on the horn, judging from all those honks and bleats. Drivers clawed at their collars, mopped their faces with handkerchiefs, wriggled out of suit jackets as their mindless automobiles rolled forward. Businessmen with briefcases, farmers in overalls, packs of dirty-faced children jaywalked at will, trotted from sidewalk to sidewalk, dodged the three streams of vehicles. Kids skipped merrily in front of the streetcars as the cowcatchers jabbed their shins.

"I am so sorry," I said for about the fifteenth time.

"I quite understand," Liza said.

"I handle all the talent—the singers, musicians, specialty acts. I don't have anything to do with the business side. But Mr. Ledford spends all his time dealing with the head office in Texas, and all he hears from them is sell, sell, sell. He gets discouraged. Me, I just listen to a lot of music. Good afternoon, Mr. Jennings!" I waved at the portly, gray-haired man at the rolltop desk in the lobby of the Union National Bank. He just glared back.

"Not very friendly," Liza said.

"He can't afford to be. He's the president of the bank. After the Crash, when so many other banks closed their doors, he moved his desk into the lobby and started handling all withdrawals personally. That's what kept him in business, probably—bullying people into not withdrawing their money."

On the next corner, a skinny young man with an open valise at his feet held swatches of cloth draped across his forearms. Around his neck dangled a ribbon of measuring tape. "Made-to-measure suits!" he cried. "A complete suit for a five-dollar deposit! Sir, that's a fine suit you have—couldn't you use another just like it? Have a good day, sir. Made-to-measure suits! Hi, Alvin, how's the boy?"

"Can't complain, Cecil, can't complain. Wife and kids all right?"

"Just fine, Alvin. That job lead I had last week went south, but hey, something will turn up. No, no need to linger, Alvin—you bought three suits off me last month, and I know you haven't worn through the pants yet. Beg your pardon, ma'am."

"Come by the station sometime, Cecil. We'll go downstairs and get a bite to eat. The family, too, if you like."

"I appreciate it, Alvin. I'll see you. Made-to-measure suits! Just like mine, only twenty-three fifty! Nice cool seersucker, only eight ninety-five!"

We crossed the street in silence. I felt that if I looked around at Liza, she simultaneously would turn to look at me, and the thought made me flush as if it had happened. Instead, I waved at Mr. Tate, who draped a towel across a customer's face as we passed his shop— five white men in tilted chairs, five Negro men in a row behind. Mr. Tate grinned and ran his hand through his nonexistent hair, a visual reminder that I should come in for a trim.

Finally Liza asked, "If you own so many suits, Mr. Pleasants, why have I seen you in only one?"

I jammed my hands into my pockets. "Maybe some people need new suits more than I do," I said. I watched the cracks in the pavement go past.

To my surprise, Liza cut in front of me and walked backward for a few paces, so that we faced each other. She studied my face the way a fiddler studies the bow, the way a mill worker studies the thump of the shuttle and loom. Then she whirled and dropped back alongside me.

"Mr. Pleasants," Liza said, "I'd be honored if you were to buy me a cup of coffee."

The Star Lunch had only a couple of other patrons—wrong time of day—and so Ari Kokenes gave Liza the royal treatment. He poured her coffee and fussed over her. Up front, I leaned over the display case and peered at the pastries, but my reflection got in the way. I rubbed my chin. I thought I had shaved myself raw that morning, but now my face felt and looked like an empty burlap sack.

"How about some of the baklava, Illona?" I asked. "And two forks, maybe?" I looked up. Ari's daughter shrank from the counter, dark eyes wide as she looked past me. I turned just as Earl Gillespie seized my shoulder and breathed Sen-Sen into my face.

"Cheer up, Alvin, you'll curdle the cream." He slapped my back and barked a laugh. "Just a joke, pal, just a joke. Hi, Illona, how's my ready steady?"

Illona silently busied herself with the baklava and a small square of wax paper. She wrapped and unwrapped and wrapped it again, her eyes downcast. She moved her body as little as possible. If Earl watched her long enough, she'd dwindle down to nothing.

"Wait up for me, willya, Alvin?" Earl asked. "I need your help, okay? Great." Earl blew a kiss at Illona, winked at me, and barreled onward past Ari, who stood at attention at the end of the counter. "Use your phone, Ari? Great," Earl said, without a glance at the man.

"Sure, Mr. Gillespie, whatever you say," Ari said without enthusiasm. He slapped the countertop with the end of his towel and looked at me fast and blank, as if I had been replaced by a stranger.

I paid Illona and smiled at her until she flashed one in return. As I turned away, she had a hurried conversation with her father in Greek, maybe one sentence apiece, and then dashed into the back. The beaded curtain danced behind her.

As Earl watched my progress across the room, he rocked on his toes, jingled change in his pockets, and shouted into the telephone's mouthpiece as if the nearly empty Star Lunch were Grand Central at noon. "Get me WBT, please." I shoved my chair around between him and Liza, with my back to the phone. As he blew a long wolf whistle, I tipped my hat up and tried to square my shoulders to make them wider.

"Who's that," Liza stated.

"The announcer who says, once a week, 'For fifty-six years, Crazy Water has come to the aid of the weak and ailing, and it has made them men and women ready to face life's hardships.' "

"He does have that look about him," Liza said.

"Damn these people!" Earl cried. "Can't anyone answer a phone anymore? Can't anybody do an honest day's work? Has the whole world gone union?"

"Who's he calling that's so important?"

"Himself," I said.

Adelaide must have picked up, finally, because Earl dropped his normal deep radio voice and went into an exaggerated nasal twang. "Yes, please, is Mr. Gillespie in? Mr. Earl Gillespie? No? Could you please ask him to call Monica at Metro-Goldwyn-Mayer as soon as possible?" I pictured Adelaide at the other end as she rolled her eyes and drew shaded triangles on her blotter. "I'll be on the lot until three, West Coast time. Tell him I'm at the bungalow. Yes, he has the number. Thank you so much." He hung the earpiece back on its cradle and walked over, showing Liza all his teeth and slicking back his hair with one hand.

"You aren't fooling anybody, Earl," I said. "One day while you're busy chasing shopgirls at the five and dime, you're gonna get a real phone call, and Adelaide will just think it's you and laugh and hang up."

He didn't look at me. "You forget your manners, Alvin. Aren't you going to introduce me to your friend?"

I sighed. "Earl Gillespie, Liza Candler." Liza nodded just enough to acknowledge her name. "Liza Candler, Earl Gillespie." Earl bowed with an Errol Flynn flourish. "What do you need, Earl? We got to go."

"Now where in the world did Alvin Pleasants, of all people, find a pretty gal like you?" Earl turned a chair around and straddled it, his arms crossed over the back, and fished in the little jar on the table for a toothpick. "I've seen him drink coffee with street peddlers and hillbilly bands and nigger barbers, but never with anyone as high-class as you."

"I reckon you don't know him too well, then."

Her gaze would have frozen a smarter man, but Earl, like any mule, sometimes needed an ax handle. He just looked her over and shoved a toothpick into his mouth and chewed it with slow relish. "Yes, indeed. Alvin's outdone himself this time. Let's see now. You surely aren't a nigger barber. I don't see you carrying anything on your person to sell. So I'd say you must be a singer. And if you sing as pretty as you eat that pastry, why then I bet they've already put you on a record or two, am I right? I sure would like to hear one. Oh, yeah, that's it, I was right. See her blushing, Alvin, you see that?"

I saw it, and I was surprised. "Miss Candler? Are you all right?"

"I *tried* recording before," Liza blurted. "It didn't work out, that's all."

"What do you mean it didn't work out?" I asked. "They didn't *like* you?"

She stabbed me a look. "I'll have you know Mr. Peer said I could sing the clouds across the sky." Right then, her voice was almost as flat as Aunt Kate's. Almost.

Earl grinned as he watched us go back and forth.

"Peer?" I repeated. "Ralph Peer? You recorded for the top field producer in the country?"

"Oh, I was just a youngun," Liza said, laughing a little. "It must have been five years gone." She stabbed a stray pistachio with her fork, glanced at me, sighed and went on. "I was visiting some cousins down here in the flats, and we saw the ad in the paper, and we just went over there and sang and that was it. Just some giggly mountain gals out having fun, clomping around in our brogans, tracking in mud. Mr. Peer was just being nice to us 'cause it was the end of the day. They were glad to get rid of us, I bet." She smiled real quick at me and then at Earl and then at me, and then she let it go and turned to look at something on a shelf that had all of a sudden become plumb fascinating.

Earl cleared his throat. "You ever met a real-life radio star before, Liza honey? Why don't you come up to the studio while we do the Briarhopper show this afternoon? Just tell 'em you're there to see me, they'll let you right in."

"C'mon, Earl," I said, "save it for the bungalow. And if you've got a favor to ask me, ask it."

"Oh, it's not big, Alvin," Earl said, swiveling his head around at me like a turtle. "Not worth interrupting a nice conversation. You need to slow down and enjoy yourself more. But since you asked, I'm working on next month's banquet for the Alf Landon campaign at the Hotel Charlotte. I thought it'd be nice to have some local musicians perform before all the speeches. Might help people's dinners set better. You suppose some of your hillbilly friends would be interested in that? I figured I'd ask you before I asked anyone else, just as a favor."

"I seriously doubt it, Earl. How much you gonna pay?"

"Now, Alvin. Remember, this is a benefit. Everyone's donating their time and energy. I am, and Colonel Macon, and Mrs. Steere, and everyone else. It'd be a little unfair if the musicians wouldn't donate their time, too."

"They make little enough money working for Colonel Macon and Mrs. Steere in the mills all day long," I said. "Now you want 'em to work for those same people at night, and do it for free? Forget it, Earl. Besides, I don't know any hillbillies, myself included, who would donate to the Landon campaign so much as a—a cold cup of coffee."

That said, I drank the rest of mine, flustered again. Both Earl and Liza looked at me. So did Ari, in a sense, even with his back turned. He stayed scrupulously within earshot and rearranged bottles of olive oil with great industry.

"Why, Alvin," Earl said. "I'm surprised at you. Saying such anti-American things in front of this impressionable young woman. You don't want her to think you've bet on a losing horse, do you?"

It was like batter turning golden in a pan. Liza suddenly beamed at Earl as if his mask had dropped off and revealed Clark Gable. "A losing horse, Mr. Gillespie?" She reached across the table and touched Earl's forearm, just long enough to rivet his attention.

"There's no doubt about it, young missy," he said. "All the papers say it's over, it's Landon over Roosevelt two to one." He proceeded to tell us how much better off the mill workers would be without government meddlers and Communist labor agitators, and how the Democrats in Washington kept finding new ways to pick an honest man's pockets. "Do you know they plan to assign a number to every worker in America, and fingerprint everybody, and issue dog tags? It'll be just like prison. Just like Russia."

"That sure is scary, Mr. Gillespie," Liza said. "In fact, I'd say you're the scariest man I've met in Charlotte. I believe we've got to be going, isn't that right, Mr. Pleasants? But I wish you and Governor Landon luck, Mr. Gillespie."

"Thank you, thank you, Miss Candler," Earl said, and rose with us. "Hey, Alvin. Alvin! About that banquet—"

"I already told you to forget it, Earl."

"Did I forget to mention," Earl said, as he examined the frayed end of his toothpick, "that the performers would be welcome to help themselves to the buffet? Prime rib? Shrimp cocktail? Peach melba? All the trimmings?"

I stood there, my hat halfway to my head. Ari waited, holding open the door.

"Can they take home leftovers?" I asked. I looked not at Earl but at the tiles beneath my feet.

"I don't see why not," Earl said. "No sense in it going to waste."

"I'll ask around," I said. "I'll see what I can do."

Outside, the three smallest Kokenes kids jumped rope on the sidewalk. Patent-leather shoes smacked the pavement to the rhythm of a singsong chant:

"Roosevelt's in the White House, waiting to be elected, Landon's in the garbage, waiting to be collected, Alf Alf Alf Alf Arf Arf Arf Arf, Roosevelt's in the White House . . ."

Earl glared at Ari, who shrugged broadly and smiled. One gold tooth sparkled in the sun. "Who knows where kids hear such things?" he said, and lifted his hands in resignation.

Earl grunted, tipped his hat to Liza, and strode away. He gave the jump rope a wide berth.

"We'll see you later, Ari," I said. I walked off in the opposite direction from Earl, even though he was bound for the station like us.

Halfway down the block, I said, "I'm sorry about that, too," assuming Liza was beside me. She was. I added: "I guess I'm sorry about everything today. Earl sure pushes my buttons, though. He knows my weaknesses."

"I'd call them strengths," Liza said. As she walked, she traced the brick wall alongside with her finger.

"Briarhopper Time" aired live each weekday afternoon right before "The Lone Ranger." Although their sponsor was Crazy Water's chief competitor, I had to admit that the Briarhoppers were one of the most popular bands at WBT, among the staff as well as among the public. When Liza and I got back to the station that evening, just as the show began, we joined about a dozen people gathered in the cor-

ridor outside the studio to watch the show through the soundproof
plate glass.

From the loudspeaker above our heads came the familiar opening—"Do y'all know what 'hit is? 'Hit's Briarhopper Time!"—and
then the first licks of "Hop Along Peter." Eventually, Earl Gillespie,
on the other side of the glass, stepped up to the microphone, and
Liza watched him attentively.

"Have a nice walk?" asked Ledford, who gnawed the tip of a new
cigar beside me. He looked considerably more focused.

"Mr. Ledford," Liza asked, "could I please borrow your lighter?"

"But of course," Ledford said, and handed it over.

"I didn't know you smoked, Miss Candler," I said.

"I don't," she said, and walked away with the lighter.

"Hey," Ledford said. She disappeared around the corner. He
looked at me like he expected me to sprint after her.

In the studio, Earl had launched into a commercial. His lips
moved on the other side of the plate glass; his dulcet voice crackled
through the loudspeaker. "And now a word from the Consolidated
Drug Trade Products Company of Chicago, Illinois, home of the
wondrous laboratories that gave the world Radio Girl perfume,
Kolorbak hair dye, and Zymole Trokeys cough drops."

The studio door in the far wall opened, and Liza sashayed
through, ushered by a smiling security guard who held the door and
waved to get Earl's attention. Liza high-stepped over microphone
cords as she approached Earl, the hem of her dress swinging.

Ledford's cigar drooped in his mouth.

Earl beamed at Liza and glanced up from his script at every
other word to mug and preen. She smiled and waved, wiggling her
fingers like a little girl.

"Friends, does your medicine chest include a bottle of Peruna?
Yes, I said Peruna—that's P-E-R-U-N-A, the all-purpose wonder
tonic that so many of your friends and neighbors rely upon when
they feel under the weather."

Liza stood directly in front of him, still smiling. Earl winked at
her, oblivious as she slowly raised the lighter.

"I'm sure all you Briarhopper fans out there don't need a re-

minder that for each Peruna box top you send in, you get a photograph of everyone's favorite hillbilly band—the Briarhoppers!—
absolutely free and suitable for framing."

Liza flicked the lighter aflame, and apparently jammed an
important cog in Earl's mind.

"But right now I want to address the, the medicinal benefits of—
of Peruna, which is safe and effective for adults as well—I mean, for
children as well as adults."

Liza set the top of Gillespie's script on fire and walked away,
smiling and waving at me. What else? I waved back. The paper
rushed into flame like it was soaked in Peruna, and Gillespie desperately tried to speed up his last few lines.

"Mothers and fathers, when your little ones wake up with a
stomach ache or a chill you'll want a bottle of Peruna on hand won't
you?" He held a torch by his fingertips. "Of course you will! Sleep
better tomorrow night because you have Peruna in your medicine
chest that's P-E-R-U-N-A just-ask-for-it-by-name-and-now-we-
return-to-the-Briarhopper-show! Shoot!" he hissed, and dashed his
flaming script to the floor as the band solemnly stepped forward and
began "More Pretty Gals Than One." A technician ran over and tried
to kick apart the ashes quietly, like a soft-shoe dancer in a medicine
show.

"What a pro," Ledford said. "Note how he said 'shoot' and not
'shit,' and turned away from the microphone just in case? Read all
the copy before it burned up, too. He does have talent, the son of a
bitch. Thank you, ma'am," he told Liza, and accepted his lighter with
a little bow.

"I just set your announcer on fire," Liza said. "Aren't you mad?"

"No, ma'am," Ledford said. "He's our announcer only on Saturday nights. On weekdays he works for the competition, and I happily consign him to the flames."

I watched through the glass as Gillespie bolted. "On the other
hand," I said, "this might be a good time to go out and get a sand-
wich." I hustled Liza toward the elevators as Gillespie charged into
view around the corner, holding his hand and cursing.

"Hold the car!" I cried.

As the door on the cage slid shut, I heard Ledford say: "You hush that bad talk, Earl. No one buys tonic off a cussing man."

Half a floor down, I asked Liza, "That damn fool stunt was for me, wasn't it?"

"You can have it if you like," she said with a grin.

I laughed. "Okay, I'll take it, then."

"Done."

"Done." We shook hands violently, as if pumping water, and then hollered laughing like younguns. The operator gripped the handle and shook his head.

I showed her around town, what town there was. The old U.S. Mint had been moved out to Eastover and reopened as an art museum, of all things, the first in the state, so I took her there out of civic duty. I showed her that the eye of the eagle above the door was really the taillight off a Ford, and she agreed that was the best part of the museum. We watched airplanes land and take off at Douglas Field, and I told her how Mayor Douglas made a big speech at the dedication about the brilliant future of air travel and then, when invited to go up in one of the things, replied, "Thank you, no." We went to the kiddie matinee at the State Theater, the New York Grand before talkies, because Johnny Mack Brown was signing autographs in between episodes of "Rustlers of Red Dog." Those younguns were screaming wild, and if their popguns had been loaded, why I wouldn't have given you a nickel for the life of Johnny Mack Brown. Then we ate fifteen-cent hamburgers and drank five-cent Cokes at the Canary Cottage, the cheapest good place in town, and from there went over to the Hotel Charlotte. We couldn't afford to do anything there but sit on the plush furniture in the massive, marbled lobby, watch people go by, and enjoy the curious breeze that constantly stirred the palms no matter the weather outside. We sat on facing sofas, sprawled our arms along the backs, and took up as much free space as we could.

"If anybody tries to run us off," I said, "tell them we answer only to J. Edgar Hoover."

After a while, I ran out of jokes and other things I felt comfortable saying, and so I just sat with my chin on my fist, listened to

Liza talk, and watched her finish a cup of cider that she had bought at a sidewalk stand down the street.

She jiggled the straw up and down in the ice. "Just what are you smiling about, Mr. Pleasants?"

"About a song, actually."

She laughed and looked at her cup. "Oh, I bet I know what it is." Then she sang the first few lines:

The prettiest girl
That ever I saw
Was sipping cider
Through a straw.

And just that snippet of a silly little ditty nearly filled that lobby, her voice was so clean and full and true. The whole place got a little quiet to make way for that voice, and heads turned and looked our way, through ferns and around fluted columns.

"Is there any song you can't make beautiful?" I asked. "We sang that song a thousand times, and yet I'd never heard it before now."

"Who's 'we'?" she asked.

I fidgeted and checked my nails. "Oh, a band I used to be in. Years ago. We toured around. That was our most requested song, believe it or not. Grove Keener—it was his band, Grove's band— he used to call it our 'signature tune,' can you believe it? Like we were Les Brown's big band at Duke. We'd do that song three times, some nights, before the audience would let us go."

"Tell me," Liza said. She curled her legs up beneath her on the sofa, her gray eyes for a second turning wide and somehow re-proachful, as if what I said hurt. Then her crooked, dimpled smile crept out again. "Tell me what it was like."

"Being in a band?"

"Yes."

"Okay." I took a deep breath, and then I told her.

Back before Roosevelt, but after the Crash, I worked at the Gasto-nia mill five days a week and spent the other two days on the road with the Carolina Cavaliers. Seems like they were the same two days, over and over and over again. Each Friday evening we piled into Ira Cannon's Model A, all six of us and our instruments, and jolted along a hundred miles of dirt roads and mud tracks to get to some crossroads in the middle of nowhere with a thrown-away school-house.

A couple of farm boys would carry the desks outside and stack them against the wall to clear a dance floor. The sun would sink behind the mountain long before showtime, so the boys also lighted kerosene lamps and situated them someplace in the school so that they wouldn't get knocked over and burn the place down like in To-baccoville in '29.

If the show was announced on the radio the week before, maybe some neighbor called the station and invited us to supper, but if not, we stopped on the way at a general store. The man at the store, because we were musicians, stared at each bill, front and back, and tugged at its corners before folding it into his cash drawer.

Later, outside the schoolhouse, we sat on the running board of the car and ate Nabs, sardines, sweet rolls, Co-Colas, whatever we'd bought. Usually I bought a few inches of baloney, say, and Ira bought some crackers, and so on, and then we portioned it out. We didn't look at each other or actually ask for anything, just nodded and said, "Much obliged."

Later we sat on the car or in the grass, smoked and listened to the crickets. With about twenty minutes till showtime and no customers in sight, we started making light of ourselves.

"Well, fellas, I wonder what tunes these cows would like to hear?"

"I just remembered, Greta Garbo's doing a fan dance tonight at the barbershop down in Valmead. No wonder we got no crowd. Bad timing, boys."

But with about five minutes to go, we saw lanterns flash like lightning bugs on the slopes all around, and heard faint talk and laughter in the pasture on one side and the woods on the other, and then a long string of cars hauled up the grade, and ten minutes after that, people packed that schoolhouse so thick, you'd think the attraction was indeed Garbo instead of a bunch of worn-out mill hands singing songs everyone knew already.

When it all ended, a couple of hours later, we divvied up the till. Fifty cents apiece on a good night, with maybe a dime extra for Grove 'cause it was his band and a dime extra for Ira 'cause it was his car. Then we all climbed into the Ford and rattled back to Charlotte, just in time to go on the air live on WBT's six A.M. farm show. That Saturday evening, if we were lucky and had the work, we were on the road again. Sometimes I put on my dress shoes Friday afternoon and didn't get the chance to take them off again until late Sunday night. Then back to the mill on Monday, of course.

In my dreams I'd try to play a tune on a spindle, feed into a loom a pearl-inlay guitar.

"Did you record?" Liza asked. She looked at her cider, now mostly water, and set the cup on the coffee table with strange deliberation, as if where she set it mattered.

"No," I said. "The band has, though, since I left 'em. In fact, they're scheduled to cut some sides tomorrow morning. In fact—" I gnawed my thumbnail.

"In fact, what?"

"In fact, I talked to the RCA Victor people just today. They had a cancellation in tomorrow's schedule, right after the Carolina Cavaliers. They said that based on my glowing recommendation, they would—"

"Oh," she said.

"—pencil you in, if I called them back by five. And then I wondered whether I should call Grove, to see if he and the boys could record a second session, as your backup band. And to lend you, you know, moral support."

We sat there and looked at each other.

"I appreciate your eventually getting around to telling me this," Liza said.

"You're welcome."

She took a deep breath. "Call them."

"I did," I said. "That's why I waited so long to tell you."

        ✾   ✾   ✾

The RCA Victor studio, at the Southern Radio Corporation offices on Tryon Street, was a big cleared-out storage room. Crates of Victrolas and radio sets were stacked along the walls of the nearest corridor. Liza and I sat on the floor in this narrowed passage, surrounded by dozens of men and women who talked, smoked, and tuned. They cradled guitars, fiddles, mandolins, banjos, washboards, jugs. A string-bass player stood with his arm around the waist of his ungainly instrument. They looked like an awkward couple waiting for a dance to start.

All the musicians wore their stage clothes: embroidered western shirts, white cowboy hats, neckerchiefs. The members of the Woodlawn String Band stood out in their stiff new overalls and bow ties. Everyone's outfits looked crisp and clean, except for a few mud-spattered pants cuffs. Not everyone could afford the streetcar.

"I don't know why we get so dressed up to record," a banjo player once told me. "No matter how good we sound, won't no one be able to see us. Maybe we dress up out of respect for the folks who sang the songs before we did."

Liza asked me, a little too loudly: "How come everyone looks like Gene Autry? I didn't know there were so many cowboys in North Carolina."

"There aren't any," I said, "but the new Gene Autry picture has a Charlotte band in it, and everybody here has seen it about a dozen times. To these folks, *Ride Ranger Ride* is not a Gene Autry picture but a Tennessee Ramblers picture that has Gene Autry in it. Now everybody tries to look like the Tennessee Ramblers."

Liza asked, "If they're a Charlotte band, how come they call themselves the Tennessee Ramblers? Are they from Tennessee?"

"No. Crazy Water Crystals brought them down from, uh, Rochester, New York, I believe."

"Well, where'd they get Tennessee from?"

I sighed. "I swear I don't know, Miss Candler. It's all show business, and I just don't have time to explain show business to you on this day and in this place."

Liza laughed. "Well, I'll be sure and quiz you later about all this Hollywood business, Mr. Laxative Man."

"I'll thank you not to call me Mr. Laxative Man. I'm a talent scout. I do not fool with laxatives. Besides, it's an all-purpose tonic. Ah, hell. I would like to know whether you pester the life out of your Aunt Kate like this. Is that why her face has closed up like a fist?"

"You can just hush about Aunt Kate, and what's wrong with you this morning anyway? You've been too sour to live." She squinted at me like the sun was in her eyes. "I swear I believe you're more nervous than I am."

"Yes, I'm nervous," I said. "You're about to step into that room and try to lay across a sheet of wax a voice that's the most beautiful sound in God's world. If these people like it, they'll roll it up like a sausage and run it through a press and stack copies of it in trucks like pulpwood and sell them for a few cents apiece, and you don't even know these people. To be honest with you, Miss Candler, I don't know whether they deserve to hang on to a voice like yours, or even to sully it with their fingers as it passes."

We looked at each other steadily.

"I believe I judge people pretty well, Mr. Pleasants," Liza whispered. "I don't think you need to worry at all."

I heard a pair of brogans scrape along, and Aunt Kate stood over us, blocking out the light, looking even more grim than usual. It is a thousand wonders she didn't empty that sanitarium.

"I just saw a streetcar run over a dog and keep on going," she said. "This place you live in is a bad place, Mr. Pleasants. This place you live in is the last place God made."

A bald man in a sweat-blotted shirt banged through a door a few yards down the hall. "Candler!" he read off his clipboard. "Liza Candler? We're ready for you, Miss Candler."

Liza didn't budge. She still looked at me. She didn't look scared, exactly; that would have been all right, that I would have understood. She looked at me as if I had forgotten the words in the middle of a duet.

"You'd best get up, ma'am," a fiddle player told her. "Get it over with."

I reached out a hand to help her up. She looked at it a moment, then grabbed it.

"Are you Miss Candler? I'm Frye Gooding, with RCA Victor. Pleased to meet you. Hello there, Alvin. Good to see you again."

"Yeah, nice to see, uh . . ." But Gooding already had swept her away, talking in her ear as if he were telling loud secrets: He had fallen behind schedule because some people kept blowing take after take, and he really wished more entertainers would learn at least the rudiments of the recording process, but now time was of the essence, he was sure she'd understand; and all the while he tap, tap, tapped her in the small of her back with his clipboard as he herded her toward the studio door. I followed them, waggling my fingers. Quite a grip that woman had. Thought for a second she wasn't going to let go.

I looked up just before I bumped into them. Aunt Kate had blocked all of us with a broomstick arm thrust across the doorway. Her eyes were shut and her face balled up like she smelled something awful.

"Dear Lord," she called, "smile upon Liza, your daughter, who pleases You so each Sunday with 'The Great Speckled Bird' and other hymns in Your name, and be with her as she sings for these strange New York men in their dark room full of machines. Amen."

"Amen," Liza muttered, and ducked beneath Aunt Kate's arm.

Bolts of black monk's cloth covered the walls and the ceiling. A lone microphone, the size and shape of a billy club, hung at eye level from the ceiling in the middle of the room. A technician cinched it up a bit on its cord, and when he let go, it swung slowly like a pendulum, not enough to stir the stifling air. The musicians stood around it, instruments at the ready: two fiddles, banjo, mandolin, guitar, upright bass. I stepped forward and shook the guitarist's slick, damp hand.

"Good to see you, Alvin," Grove Keener said.

I shook hands all around. "Morning, boys. How's everyone?"

"You shoulda brought your guitar, Alvin," Ira Cannon said. "A band can't never have too many guitars."

"I brought something better than that worn-out old guitar," I said. "Fellas, if you can't say anything else good about me when I'm gone, at least tell people that I'm the man who introduced you to Liza Candler."

After the introductions, Liza and Grove and the others huddled for a few minutes to run down the songs she had selected. As I expected, the Cavaliers knew all of them. I made myself scarce, perched on a stool behind the sound engineers' equipment, which looked like a dismantled tractor motor spread across a series of tables. Then Gooding gave the performers their final instructions. This was old hat to the Cavaliers, and they fidgeted and joked around, but Liza solemnly listened to every word.

"First you'll hear one buzz. Sid, let them try on that buzz for size. . . . Got that? Okay, then we'll have a wait—of a few seconds or a few years, depending on that damned equipment, ha ha, right Sid?—and then you'll hear two buzzes right together. Like this . . . After those buzzes, count to two—one Mississippi, two Mississippi— then go ahead, 'cause I'll be pointing at you, and we'll be recording by then. Any questions?"

"Mississippi's been sorta bad luck for us," Grove said.

"Yeah," Ira said. "The last time we played in Mississippi, the audience left in the middle of the show 'cause someone's cow had got out."

Grove asked, "Would you mind if we counted 'One Jimmie Rodgers, two Jimmie Rodgers' instead?"

"Hell, you can count 'One Liza Candler, two Liza Candler' if you want to. Just count to two before you sing. Okay? All set? Here we go. . . ."

The wait between buzzes was about a year and a half. I held my breath. Then the fiddlers, poised with their elbows up, drew their bows across their strings and pulled the rest of the band along. I watched the music, the way you can see it happen if you pay attention to the fingers and the strings and the flash of the picks, until Liza started singing, when the whole dark, close, choking box of a studio was replaced by other sights.

> Let us pause in life's pleasures
> And count her many tears
> Oh we all share in sorrow with the poor.

I saw Mr. Jennings braced for the worst at his rolltop desk, and I saw padlocked front doors all over Charlotte, at bank after bank— the Merchants and Farmers, the Independence National, even the

First National in its brand-new twenty-one-story skyscraper. Against its titanic brass doors, a small boy listlessly bounced a ball.

It's a song that'll linger
Forever in our ears
Oh hard times come again no more

I saw a tall but neat stack of furniture on a sidewalk. A man and a woman sat upright at opposite ends of the sofa, their children between them. All stared straight ahead at nothing. On the porch, a deputy nailed up a sign with a series of hammer blows.

It's a song this side of the weary
Hard times, hard times,
Come again no more

I saw hundreds of people in a slow single file around the Salvation Army building. Sawhorses funneled them into the side entrance, where women in uniforms handed them each a bowl and a spoon. Two blocks down the street, a newcomer with a valise hurried to get in on the end of the line. It was Cecil, measuring tape flapping around his neck.

Many days you have lingered
Too long around my door
Oh hard times come again no more

And it went on like that, for the rest of that song and for the next three songs, too. When the session ended I felt a hand clamp my shoulder. I jerked like a hare and suddenly rushed back into my body. My foot had fallen asleep, and my rear end hurt from the stool.

"Some people come in and do take after take, use up nearly all the wax," Gooding said. "But I never saw such a flawless session as this."

"It ain't natural," an engineer said, rapt in the roll of the wax cylinder.

"New York won't believe it," Gooding said. "This woman could

be bigger than the Carter Family. Where in the world did you find
her, Alvin?"

"A lot of people have asked me that," I said. Liza and the band
and the technicians talked excitedly and slapped each other on the
back and hugged each other. I do believe Ira cried, there beneath
that suspended microphone. I glanced around and saw Aunt Kate,
posted with folded arms beside the door. She looked like she wanted
to show pride but was too sad to do it, as if Liza had just sung a solo
at a funeral.

Charlotte wasn't a big town, then or now, and word got around. I
talked Liza up a bit myself. That Saturday night, a good half-hour
before the "Crazy Barn Dance" went on the air, the corridor outside the studio filled not only with the usual Monroe Brothers fans
but also with Grove Keener and his boys, a bunch of other musicians,
numerous members of the Kokenes family, and several of the reporters from the *Charlotte News*. The reporters, as a group, hailed
Mr. Tate when he arrived, fresh from the barbershop.

"Why so many damn newspapermen?" Ledford growled as he
stared through the control-room window. "Burke Davis, and Shipp,
and Cash—and there's Hargrove, too. What is this, a press con-
ference? Since when did any of those eggheads get interested in
hillbilly music?"

"What?" I said. "Oh. Well, I showed Liza around the *News* office yesterday, and they got more interested than usual. Especially
in the threat of a party afterward. What time's it?"

"Quit asking," Ledford said. "And sit down, willya? I see enough
marching in the newsreels."

I couldn't sit down. I roamed the control room, picked my way
over electrical cables and boxes of equipment, got into people's
way, bumbled and fumbled and tried not to stare at Liza. She sat
smiling in a folding chair across the studio, where she chatted with
the Monroes and with George Crutchfield, the guest announcer. I
was too anxious even to enjoy the news that Earl Gillespie had called
in sick at the last minute. "Probably burnt up with fever," Ledford
said. *"Please,* Alvin, sit down."

"Have a spoonful of Peruna," Aunt Kate said, her back to us. She stood in front of the window like a fence post in gingham, and said nothing else before the show began.

The red light flashed once, twice, then burned hellish and steady. The Monroe Brothers sang "What Would You Give in Exchange for Your Soul?" George Crutchfield talked about the wondrous virtues of Crazy Water Crystals. Then I had to sit down.

"This is a song for my Aunt Kate," Liza said, with a smile into the iron bloom of the microphone. She turned aside a little and coughed, so that I died for a second or two. Then she returned the smiles of Charlie Monroe on her left, Bill Monroe on her right. They nodded at each other over her head, and commenced the simple, familiar tune, Charlie on guitar and Bill on mandolin. Liza smiled at me, and at Aunt Kate, and at me again, through the plate glass and began to sing the hymn as no one on the airwaves had sung it before.

> *What a beautiful thought I am thinking*
> *Concerning a great speckled bird.*
> *Remember her name is recorded*
> *On the pages of God's holy word.*

When the song ended, I continued to listen to it. The Monroe Brothers swapped banter with Crutchfield. Liza stood to one side, tightened her guitar strings, and waited for her next song cue. I still listened to the song that had ended.

Ledford interrupted. "I mightily wish we had a clear-channel station," he said. "Fifty thousand watts blankets the Southeast, but some places still won't be able to tune in to Miss Candler tonight."

"Mr. Pleasants?" One of the technicians held out the earpiece of the wall phone. "Call for you, Mr. Pleasants."

"Huh? Me?"

"It's Mr. Gooding. From RCA Victor."

Aunt Kate turned to watch me as I made my way over. "Hello?" I cupped a hand over my other ear. "Hello, Frye?"'

No preamble, no pleasantries. "Alvin, I just got off the phone with New York. I sent 'em the rolls immediately, special courier."

"Oh, really? That was fast. So tell me, tell me, what did they think?"

His voice quavered. "They don't know what to think, Alvin. And frankly, I don't know what to think either."

"What's wrong? Didn't they like the record?"

"They liked it fine. What they could hear of it."

"I don't follow. Did something go wrong?"

"I'll say it went wrong. Not a word of Liza's singing got recorded. Not a word, Alvin! It's the damnedest thing—"

"Oh, for—Jesus, Frye, what the hell kind of operation are you running, anyway?" The others looked at me quizzically. "I mean, I expected better from Victor, for God's sake. This is awful. She will be so, so disappointed. Well, you'll just have to give her another chance on another date, with some equipment that actually works—"

"Alvin, you don't get me. Listen to what I'm saying. There was nothing wrong with the equipment. It picked up everything. Everything except the girl."

"You've lost me," I lied, much more quietly.

"It picked up every sound in that studio—the coughing and shifting around between numbers, the cues I gave the technicians, the buzzers, every note the Cavaliers played. Whenever they joined in at the choruses, that came through loud and clear, too. But there's no female voice on the record *anywhere*. I tell you, Alvin, it's as if she wasn't in the room."

"But of course she was in the room. I mean, we were there, we saw her. Frye, this is crazy."

"You think I don't know that, Alvin? You think I can't tell that for myself? I listened to her on the earphones the whole time the wax rolled. You should see me here, whiskey all down my tie because I can't hold my hand still long enough to take a shot. You should come over here and stumble around in the dark with the rest of us, among thousands of dollars of equipment dismantled and flung all over the floor of the studio, and no problems anywhere that we can see. You should see some of the top sound engineers in the country cross themselves and mumble about haints and witchcraft— witchcraft, Alvin! The evil eye! In the year of our Lord nineteen hundred and thirty-six!"

"Frye. Calm down."

He cut his voice to nearly a whisper. "I asked you before, and I'll ask you again—Where did you find that woman? But this time, Alvin, I don't want to know the answer."

Then he hung up.

In the studio, Crutchfield made another pitch for Crazy Water Crystals. I waved my hands wildly, like a controller at Douglas Field, until I got Liza's attention. Then I pointed toward the door to the corridor.

"Alvin. What's up?"

"Call Adelaide," I told Ledford as I headed out. "Call anybody with their radio on. Hell, call Earl. Ask 'em what they just heard broadcast. Ask 'em if it sounded all right."

"Alvin—"

"Boss, please, do it! Aunt Kate can explain." I vaulted the rail and landed beside the steps in the middle of the corridor, just as Liza shoved open the steel, red-lighted studio door.

"What in the world?" she said. "I have to be back in there in about two minutes—"

"RCA Victor called."

She froze.

"This happened five years ago, didn't it? This is why your session with Peer just 'didn't work out,' isn't it? Liza, what does this mean? *Why can't your voice be recorded?*"

"We don't know," Aunt Kate said. She stood in the control-room doorway and stared down at us.

"I can speak for myself!" Liza cried, then closed her eyes and took a deep breath and said, more calmly: "I have heard tell that in the old stories, the women and the men with powers wouldn't show up in mirrors, wouldn't be reflected if they looked into a pool. Maybe this is the same thing, only they didn't have all this fancy equipment back when those stories got told. . . . I don't know. . . ."

"An angel won't never show up in no photograph," Aunt Kate said.

"I'm not an angel!" Liza said. "And I'm not a witch either! I want to sing to people, Alvin. I want to perform, and record, and travel all around. *I want what you had, what you gave up.* For the past five years, I've been scared even to leave Yandro—knowing what I knew about myself—but when you came for me—I thought it might be—a sign—"

I nodded, eyes wide. "It was. That's exactly right. It was as much a sign as either of us ever will get in our lives. You did right to come."

Ledford poked his head out of the door, behind Aunt Kate's shoulder. "Alvin, Adelaide says it's coming through loud and clear, no problems at all. Now what in the world did you—Miss Candler, you best get back into that studio this very *instant!*"

She whirled and dashed for the studio door. When she reached it, she looked back around, her eyes like stars, her hair astream around her face, and she told me: "Yes. I was right to come." She slammed back through the door, and I stood in the corridor as those words whipsawed into me just the same as if she had sung them.

I don't remember how I got to the street, elevator or stairs or window or wings, but I remember the screech of tires and the horns and the shouts as I ran from one sidewalk to the other, back and forth, into diners and cigar stores and newsstands, and reached across people to wrench radio knobs until I heard what I needed so desperately, and so on all the way down the block, leaving a wake of shouts and jeers and laughter and a street filled with Liza's song.

I am proud to say that Liza sang in my presence just about every day for more than forty years of marriage, and in all those days I never heard her hit a note that wasn't true and good and fine. She did some radio, and she played a right many shows all around. I still get a few letters from people in the Carolinas and Virginia and Tennessee, folks who heard her in person years ago in Asheville or Greensboro or Union Grove or especially the Merle Watson Festival, that big mess of a crowd in North Wilkesboro she sang to in the last year of her life. Before she went on, she stood in the wings, in front of a big upright fan that made her hair float like a gray cloud, and I came back from the edge of the stage and reported at least one whole county out there on the hillside, and she smiled and said, "Well, Mr.

Laxative Man, I reckon I'll just do like always, and pretend I'm singing to you."

It's a hard job to write these people back and say that Liza's gone, but I take the opportunity to reassure them that she ever existed at all, that their memories have not played tricks on her voice, and that's what everybody really wants anyway.

Liza traveled with me all over the mountains after I quit Crazy Water Crystals and got on with the Smithsonian. We must have lugged my equipment into every hollow in the Appalachians, every schoolhouse dance and fiddlers' convention, trying to record and transcribe everything we could before it all vanished, before it all headed to Nashville and turned into Crazy Water and Martha White Flour and Purina Dog Chow and whatever else needs selling today. People that want to hear about all that would be just as well served to go to the fourth floor of Wilson Library in Chapel Hill. All my tapes are in their Southern Folklife Collection, along with thirty-seven thousand other recordings. Gospel choirs, washboard and Jew's-harp pickers, fiddlers, bluesmen, string bands, medicine-show pitchmen. So much music otherwise gone from the world.

I'm up there in the library about once a week myself. Takes me about near forever just to walk across Franklin Street these days, and I feel like a spectacle with my walking stick and my gray suit and hat, while skateboarders and tattooed women parade around me. But the young folks on the fourth floor know me and bring me whatever tapes I want to hear, and then they leave me alone as best they can. But I can tell they're nervous. They're afraid I'll just up and die with my headphones on, there in my favorite booth, the one with the framed receipt on the wall. I've got the numbers memorized: For song royalties in the last quarter of 1928, Pop Stoneman received $161.31, including $1.63 for 340 copies of "Prisoner's Lament." I wonder whether Pop Stoneman ever knew, even for a second, how lucky he was to make even a nickel off a lament.

I sit in that booth and listen to Mainer's Mountaineers and Fisher Hendley's Carolina Tar Heels and the Crazy Bucklebusters and Dorsey and Howard, the Dixon Brothers. I listen to "Wreck on the Highway" and "Let Me Be Your Salty Dog" and "Cocaine Blues" and "Let the Church Roll On" and "What Would You Give in Exchange for Your Soul?" So many others. I know them all by heart, but I need to hear them just the same.

And no matter what else I listen to beforehand, I always end up with one of the Liza tapes. I made dozens of them, with every new technology that came along, over the course of forty years. When I finally handed them over, all carefully dated and labeled just like the others, the librarians thought there was some mistake. They wondered why in the world I would record the zing of crickets, the bark of a distant hound, the scrape of a chair, and sometimes a cough.

That's all I heard on the tapes as well, to begin with. But as the years pass, my ears get better. Nowadays I hardly strain at all to hear "Hard Times" and "The Great Speckled Bird" and even

The prettiest girl
That ever I saw
Was sipping cider
Through a straw.

When I'm slumped in that booth, and the librarians creep past me thinking I've died or at least nodded off, I'm really just listening to a voice that never falters or fades, a voice that fills the library and the campus and the world and the mountain and the schoolhouse and yet finds room for me, calls me out of the dark and to the edge of the stage, to Liza in a kerosene glow.

JANE YOLEN

SISTER EMILY'S LIGHTSHIP

I DWELL IN POSSIBILITY. THE PEN SCRATCHED OVER THE PAGE, making graceful ellipses. She liked the look of the black on white as much as the words themselves. The words sang in her head far sweeter than they sang on the page. Once down, captured like a bird in a cage, the tunes seemed pedestrian, mere common rote. Still, it was as close as she would come to that Eternity, that Paradise that her mind and heart promised. *I dwell in Possibility.*

She stood and stretched, then touched her temples where the poem still throbbed. She could feel it sitting there, beating its wings against her head like that captive bird. Oh, to let the bird out to sing for a moment in the room before she caged it again in the black bars of the page.

Smoothing down the skirt of her white dress, she sat at the writing table once more, took up the pen, dipped it into the ink jar, and added a second line. *A fairer House than* . . . than what? Had she lost the word between standing and sitting? Words were not birds after all, but slippery as fish.

Then, suddenly, she felt it beating in her head. *Prose! A fairer*

House than Prose—She let the black ink stretch across the page with the long dash that lent the last word that wonderful fall of tone. She preferred punctuating with the dash to the hard point, as brutal as a bullet. *I dwell in Possibility.*

She blotted the lines carefully before reading them aloud, her mouth forming each syllable perfectly as she had been taught so many years before at Miss Lyon's Mount Holyoke Female Seminary.

Cocking her head to one side, she considered the lines. *They will do,* she thought, as much praise as she ever allowed her own work, though she was generous to others. Then, straightening the paper and cleaning the nib of her pen, she tore up the false starts and deposited them in the basket.

She could, of course, write any time during the day if the lines came to mind. There was little enough that she had to do in the house. But she preferred night for her truest composition and perhaps that was why she was struggling so. *Then those homey tasks will take me on,* she told herself: supervising the gardening, baking Father's daily bread. Her poetry must never be put in the same category.

Standing, she smoothed down the white skirt again and tidied her hair—"like a chestnut bur," she'd once written imprudently to a friend. It was ever so much more faded now.

But pushing that thought aside, Emily went quickly out of the room as if leaving considerations of vanity behind. Besides the hothouse flowers, besides the bread, there was a cake to be made for tea. After Professor Seelye's lecture there would be guests and her tea cakes were expected.

The tea had been orderly, the cake a success, but Emily headed back upstairs soon after, for her eyes—always sensitive to the light—had begun to tear up. She felt a sick headache starting. Rather than impose her ailments on her guests, she slipped away. They would understand.

Carlo padded up the stairs behind her, so quiet for such a large dog. But how slow he had become these last months. Emily knew that Death would stop for him soon enough. Newfoundlands were not a long-lived breed usually, and he had been her own shaggy ally for the past fifteen years.

Slowing her pace, despite the stabbing behind her eyes, Emily let the old dog catch up. He shoved his rough head under her hand and the touch salved them both.

He curled beside her bed and slept, as she did, in an afternoon made night and close by the window blinds.

It was night in truth when Emily awoke, her head now wonderfully clear. Even the dreadful sleet in her eyes was gone.

She rose and threw on a dressing gown. She owed Loo a letter, and Samuel and Mary Bowles. But still the night called to her. Others might hate the night, hate the cold of November, huddling around their stoves in overheated houses. But November seemed to her the very Norway of the year.

She threw open first the curtains, then the blinds, almost certain of a sight of actual fjords. But though the Gibraltar lights made the village look almost foreign, it was not—she decided—foreign enough.

"That I had the strength for travel," she said aloud. Carlo answered her with a quick drum roll of tail.

Taking that as the length of his sympathy, she nodded at him, lit the already ensconced candle, and sat once again at the writing table. She read over the morning's lines:

> *I dwell in Possibility—*
> *A fairer House than Prose—*

It no longer had the freshness she remembered, and she sighed.

At the sound, Carlo came over to her and laid his rough head in her lap, as if trying to lend comfort.

"No comfort to be had, old man," she said to him. "I can no longer tell if the trouble is my wretched eyes, sometimes easy and sometimes sad. Or the dis-order of my mind. Or the slant of light on the page. Or the words themselves. Or something else altogether. Oh, my dear dog . . ." She leaned over and buried her face in his fur but did not weep for she despised private grief that could not be turned into a poem. Still, the touch had a certain efficaciousness, and she stood and walked over to the window.

The Amherst night seemed to tremble in on itself. The street issued a false invitation, the maples standing sentinel between the house and the promise of road.

"Keeping me in?" she asked the dog, "or others out?" It was only her wretched eyes that forced her to stay at home so much and abed. Only her eyes, she was convinced. In fact she planned a trip into town at noon next when the very day would be laconic; if she could get some sleep and if the November light proved not too harsh.

She sat down again at the writing table and made a neat pile of the poems she was working on, then set them aside. Instead she would write a letter. To . . . to Elizabeth. "Dear Sister," she would start as always, even though their relationship was of the heart, not the blood. "I will tell her about the November light," she said to Carlo. "Though it is much the same in Springfield as here, I trust she will find my observations entertaining."

The pen scratched quickly across the page. *So much quicker,* she thought, *than when I am composing a poem.*

She was deep into the fourth paragraph, dashing "November always seemed to me the Norway . . ." when a sharp knock on the wall shattered her peace, and a strange insistent whine seemed to fill the room.

And the light. *Oh—the light!* Brighter even than day.

"Carlo!" she called the dog to her, and he came, crawling, trembling. So large a dog and such a larger fright. She fell on him as a drowning person falls on a life preserver. The light made her eyes weep pitchers. Her head began to ache. The house rocked.

And then—as quickly as it had come—it was gone: noise, light, all, all gone.

Carlo shook her off as easily as bath water, and she collapsed to the floor, unable to rise.

Lavinia found her there on the floor in the morning, her dressing gown disordered and her hands over her eyes.

"Emily, my dear, my dear . . ." Lavinia cried, lifting her sister entirely by herself back onto the bed. "Is it the terror again?"

It was much worse than the night terrors, those unrational fears which had afflicted her for years. But Emily had not the strength to contradict. She lay on the bed hardly moving the entire day while Mother bathed her face and hands with aromatic spirits and Vinnie read to her. But she could not concentrate on what Vinnie read; neither the poetry of Mrs. Browning nor the prose of George Eliot soothed her. She whimpered and trembled, recalling vividly the fierceness of that midnight light. She feared she was, at last, going mad.

"Do not leave, do not leave," she begged first Vinnie, then Mother, then Austin, who had been called to the house in the early hours. Father alone had been left to his sleep. But they did go, to whisper together in the hall. She could not hear what they said but she could guess that they were discussing places to send her away. For a rest. For a cure. For—Ever—

She slept, waked, slept again. Once she asked for her writing tablet, but all she managed to write on it was the word light ten times in a column like some mad ledger. They took the tablet from her and refused to give it back.

The doctor came at nine, tall and saturnine, a new man from Northampton. Vinnie said later he looked more like an undertaker than a physician. He scolded Emily for rising at midnight and she was too exhausted to tell him that for her it was usual. Mother and Vinnie and Austin did not tell him for they did not know. No one knew that midnight was her favorite time of the clock. That often she walked in the garden at midnight and could distinguish, just by the smell, which flowers bloomed and bloomed well. That often she sat in the garden seat and gazed up at the great eight-sided cupola Father had built onto the house. His one moment of monumental playfulness. Or she sat at the solitary hour inside the cupola contemplating night through each of the windows in turn, gazing round at all the world that was hers.

"Stay in bed, Miss Dickinson," warned the doctor, his chapped hands delicately on hers. "Till we have you quite well again. Finish the tonic I am leaving with your mother for you. And then you must eschew the night and its vapors."

Vinnie imitated him quite cruelly after he left. "Oh, the vay-pures, the vay-pures!" she cried, hand to her forehead. Unaccountably, Carlo howled along with her recitation.

Mother was—as usual—silently shocked at Vinnie's mimicry but made no remonstrances.

"He looks—and sounds—quite medieval," Austin commented laconically.

At that Emily began to laugh, a robust hilarity that brought tears to her poor eyes. Austin joined with her, a big stirring hurrah of a laugh.

"Oh, dear Emily," Vinnie cried. "Laugh on! It is what is best for you."

Best for what? Emily asked herself, but did not dare say it aloud. But she vowed she would never let the doctor touch her again.

Having slept all day meant that she was awake at midnight, still she did not venture out of the bed. She lay awake fearing to hear once more the horrid knock and feel the house shake and see the piercing white light. A line of poetry ran through her mind: *Me—come! My dazzled face.* But her mind was so befogged that she could not recall if it were her own line or if she had read it somewhere.

At the last nothing more happened and she must have fallen back to sleep some time after two. When she woke it was midmorning and there was a tray by her bed with tea and toast and some of her own strawberry preserves.

She knew she was well again when she realized Carlo was not in the room. He would never have left her side otherwise.

Getting out of the bed was simple. Standing without swaying was not. But she gathered up her dressing gown, made a swift toilette, then went downstairs carrying the tray. Some illnesses she knew, from her months with the eye doctors in Cambridgeport, are best treated like a bad boy at school. Quickly beaten, quicker trained.

If the family was surprised to see her, they knew better than to show it.

"Shall we have Susie and little Ned for tea?" she asked by way of greeting.

Sue came over promptly at four, as much to check up on Emily's progress as to have tea. Austin must have insisted. Heavily pregnant, she walked slowly while Ned, a rambunctious four-year-old, capered ahead.

"Dear critic," Emily said, answering the door herself. She kissed Sue on both cheeks and led her through into the hall. "And who is slower today, you with your royal front or me with my rambling mind."

"Nonsense!" Sue said. "You are indulging yourself in fancies. Neddie, stop jumping about. Your Aunt Emily is just out of a sickbed."

The boy stopped for a moment and then flung himself into Emily's skirts, crying, "Are you hurt? Where does it hurt? Shall I kiss it?"

Emily bent down and said, "Your *Uncle* Emily shall kiss you instead, for I am not hurt at all. We boys never cry at hurts." She kissed the top of his fair head, which sent him into paroxysms of laughter.

Sue made a *tch* sound with her tongue. "And once you said to me that if you saw a bullet hit a bird and he told you he wasn't shot, you might weep at his courtesy, but you would certainly doubt his word."

"Unfair! Unfair to quote me back at me!" Emily said, taking Sue's hands. "Am I not this moment the very pink of health?"

"That is not what Austin said, who saw you earlier today. And there is a white spot between your eyes as if you have lain with a pinched expression all night."

"And all morning, too. Come in here, Sue," Vinnie called from the sitting room. "And do not chastize her any more than I have already. It does no good you know."

They drank their tea and ate the crumbles of the cake from the day before, though it mortified Emily that they had to do so. But she had had no time to prepare more for their small feast. Neddie had three pieces anyway, two of his own and one Emily gave him from her own plate because suddenly the cake was too sweet, the light too bright, the talk too brittle, and Emily tired past bearing it all.

She rose abruptly. Smiling, she said, "I am going back to bed."

"We have overworn you," Sue said quickly.

"And I you," Emily answered.

"I am not tired, Auntie," Ned said.

"You never are," Vinnie said fondly.

"I am in the evening," Ned conceded. "And sometimes in . . ."

But Emily heard no more. The stairs effectively muffled the rest of the conversation as she sought the sanctuary of her room.

I dwell in Possibility—

She sat at the desk and read the wavering line again. But what possibilities did she, indeed, dwell in? This house, this room, the garden, the lawn between her house and Austin's stately "Evergreens." They were all the possibilities she had. Even the trips to Cambridgeport for eye treatments had held no great promise. All her traveling—and what small journeys they had proved—lay in the past. She was stuck, like a cork in an old bottle without promise of wine. Stuck here in the little town where she had been born.

She went over to the bed and flung herself down on her stomach and wept quietly into the pillow until the early November dark gathered around her.

It was an uncharacteristic and melodramatic scene, and when she sat up at last, her cheeks reddened and quite swollen, she forgave herself only a little.

"Possibly the doctor's tonic has a bite at the bottom," she whispered to Carlo, who looked up at her with such a long face that she had to laugh, her cheeks tight with the salty tears. "Yes, you are right. I have the vay-pures." She stood and, without lighting a lamp, found the wash basin and bathed her face.

She was not hungry, either for food or company, and so she sat in the gathering gloom thinking about her life. Despite her outburst, she quite liked the tidiness of her cocoon. She doubted she had the capacity for wings or the ability for flight.

When it was totally dark, she went back to her bed and lay down, not to sleep but to wait till the rest of the household slept.

The grandfather clock on the landing struck eleven. She waited another fifteen minutes before rising. Grabbing a woolen shawl from the foot of the bed, she rose ghostlike and slipped from the room.

The house breathed silent sleep around her. Mother, Father, Vinnie, Cook had all gone down the corridors of rest, leaving not a pebble behind for her to follow.

She climbed the stairs up to the cupola for she had not the will nor might to brave November's garden. Still, she had to get away from the close surround of family and the cupola was as far as she could go.

She knew which risers creaked alarmingly and, without thinking, avoided them. But behind her Carlo trod on every one. The passage was not loud enough to waken the sleepers who had heard it all before without stirring, yet Emily still held her breath till they reached the top unremarked.

Putting her hand on the dog's head for a moment, to steady them both, she climbed up into the dome of the house. In the summer there was always a fly or two buzzing about the windows and she quite liked them, her "speck pianos." But in November the house was barren of flies. She would have to make all the buzz herself.

Sitting on the bench, she stared out of the windows at the glittering stars beyond the familiar elms. How could she have abjured this peace for possibilities unknown?

"Oh, Carlo," she whispered to the dog, "we must be careful what we say. No bird resumes its egg."

He grunted a response and settled down at her feet for the long watch.

"Like an old suitor," she said, looking down fondly at him. "We are, you know, too long engaged, too short wed. Or some such." She laughed. "I think the prognosis is that my madness is quite advanced."

When she looked up again, there was a flash of light in the far-off sky, a star falling to earth.

"Make a wish, Carlo," she said gaily. "I know I shall."

And then the top of the cupola burst open, a great gush of sound enveloped them, and she was pulled up into the light.

Am I dead? she thought at first. Then, *Am I rising to Heaven?* Then, *Shall I have to answer to God?* That would be the prime embarrassment, for she had always held out against the blandishments of her redeemed family, saying that she was religious without that great Eclipse, God. She always told them that life was itself mystery and consecration enough. *Oh, do not let it be a jealous God,* she thought. *I would have too much to explain away.*

Peculiarly this light did not hurt her eyes, which only served to convince her that she was, indeed, dead. And then she wondered if there would be actual angels as well, further insult to her heresy. *Perhaps they will have butterfly wings,* she thought. *I would like that.* She was amused, briefly, in her dying by these wild fancies.

And then she was no longer going upward, and there was once more a steady ground beneath her feet where Carlo growled but did not otherwise move. Walls, smooth and anonymous, curved away from her like the walls of a cave. *A hallway,* she thought, *but one without signature.*

A figure came toward her, but if *that* were an angel, all of Amherst's Congregational Church would come over faint! It wore no gown of alabaster satin, had no feathery wings. Rather it was a long, sleek, gray man with enormous adamantine eyes and a bulbed head rather like a leek's.

A leek—I am surely mad! she thought. All poetry fled her mind.

Carlo was now whining and trembling beyond measure. She bent to comfort him; that he should share her madness was past understanding.

"Do not be afraid," the gray man said. *No—the bulbed thing—* for she now saw it was not a man at all, though like a man it had arms and legs and a head. But the limbs were too long, the body too thin, the head too round, the eyes too large. And though it wore no discernible clothing, it did not seem naked.

"Do not be afraid," it repeated, its English curiously accented.

It came down rather heavily on the word *be* for no reason that Emily could tell. Such accentuation did not change the message.

If not an angel, a demon—But this her unchurched mind credited even less.

She mustered her strength; she could when courage was called for. "Who—or what—are you?"

The bulb creature smiled. This did not improve its looks. "I am a traveler," it said.

"And where do you travel?" That she was frightened did not give her leave to forget all manners. And besides, curiosity had now succeeded fear.

"From a far . . ." The creature hesitated. She leaned into its answer. "From a far star."

There was a sudden rip in the fabric of her world.

"Can you show me?" It was not that she did not believe the stranger, but that she did. It was the very possibility that she had, all unknowing, hoped for, wept for.

"Show you?"

"The star."

"No."

The rip was repaired with clumsy hands. She would always see the darn.

"It is too far for sight."

"Oh."

"But I can show you your own star."

"And what do you want from me in exchange?" She knew enough of the world to know this.

For a moment the creature was silent. She feared she had embarrassed it. Or angered it. Then it gave again the grimace that was its smile. "Tell me what it is you do in this place."

She knew this was not an idle question. She chose her answer with care. "I tell the truth," she said. "But I tell it slant."

"Ah . . ." There was an odd light in the gray creature's eyes. "A poet."

She nodded. "I have some small talent."

"I, myself, make . . . poems. You will not have heard of me, but my name is . . ." And here it spoke a series of short, sharp syllables that to her ear were totally unrepeatable.

"Miss Emily Dickinson," she replied, holding out her hand.

The bulb creature took her hand in its and she did not flinch though its hand was far cooler than she expected. Not like something dead but rather like the back of a snake. There were but three long fingers on the hand.

The creature dropped her hand and gave a small bow, bending at its waist. "Tell me, Miss Emily Dickinson, one of your poems."

She folded her hands together and thought for a minute of the dozens of poems shoved into the drawer of her writing table, of the tens more in her bureau drawer. Which one should she recite—for she remembered them all? Which one would be appropriate payment for this gray starfarer?

And then she had it. Her voice—ever light—took on color as she said the poem:

> *Some things that fly there be—*
> *Birds—Hours—the Bumblebee—*
> *Of these no Elegy.*
>
> *Some things that stay there be—*
> *Grief—Hills—Eternity—*
> *Nor this behooveth me.*
>
> *There are that resting, rise.*
> *Can I expound the skies?*
> *How still the Riddle lies!*

When she was done, she did not drop her head modestly as Miss Lyons had taught, but rather stared straight into the starfarer's jeweled eyes.

It did not smile this time and she was glad of that. But it took forever to respond. Then at last it sighed. "I have no poem its equal. But Miss Emily Dickinson, I can expound the skies."

She did not know exactly what the creature meant.

"Give me your hand again."

And then she knew. "But I cannot leave my dog."

"I cannot vouchsafe the animal."

She misunderstood. "I can. He will not harm you."

"No. I mean more correctly, I do not know what such a trip will do to him."

"I cannot leave him behind."

The gray creature nodded its bulb head, and she unhesitatingly put her hand in its, following down the anonymous corridor and into an inner chamber that was something like a laboratory.

"Sit here," the starfarer said, and when she sat in the chair a webbing grew up out of the arms and bound her with filaments of surprising strength.

"Am I a prisoner?" She was not frightened, just curious.

"The lightship goes many miles quickly. The web is to keep you safe."

She thought how a horse starting too quickly to pull a carriage often knocks its passenger back against the seat, and understood. "And my dog?"

"Ah—now you see the problem."

"Can he sit here in the chair beside me?"

"The chair is not built for so much weight."

"Then he may be badly hurt. I cannot go."

The creature raised one of its long fingers. "I will put your dog in my sleeping chamber for as long as we travel." It took Carlo by the collar and led the unprotesting dog off to a side wall, which opened with the touch of a button, letting down a short bed that was tidily made. "Here," the creature commanded the dog and surprisingly Carlo—who ordinarily obeyed no one but Emily—leaped onto the bed. The starfarer pushed another button and the bed slid back into the wall, imprisoning the now-howling Carlo inside.

"I apologize for my shaggy ally," Emily said.

"There is no need." The gray creature bent over a panel of flashing lights, its six fingers flying between them. When it had finished, it leaned back into its own chair and the webbing held it fast.

"Now I will show you what your own planet looks like from the vantage of space. Do not be afraid, Miss Emily Dickinson:"

She smiled. "I am not afraid."

"I did not think *so*," the starfarer said in its peculiar English.

And then, with a great shaking, the lightship rose above Amherst, above Massachusetts, above the great masses of land and water and clouds and air and into the stars.

She lay on her bed remembering. Carlo, still moaning, had not seemed to recover quickly from the trip. But she had. All she could think about was the light, the dark, the stars. And the great green-blue globe—like one of Ned's marbles—that was her home.

What could she tell her family? That she had flown high above them all and seen how small they were within the universe? They would say she had had a dream. *If only I could have returned, like Mother from her ramblings, a burdock on her shawl to show where she had been,* she thought.

And then she laughed at herself. Her poems would be her burdocks, clinging stubbornly to the minds of her readers. She sat up in the dark.

The light. The marble of earth. She would never be able to capture it whole. Only in pieces. But it was always best to make a start of it. *Begin,* as Cook often said, *as you mean to go on.*

She lit a small candle which was but a memento of that other light. And then she went over to the writing table. Her mind was a jumble of words, images.

I do not need to travel further than across this room ever again, she thought. *Or further than the confines of my house.* She had already dwelt in that greatest of possibilities for an hour in a ship made of light. The universe was hers, no matter that she lived only in one tiny world. She would write letters to that world in the form of her poems, even if the world did not fully understand or ever write back. Dipping the pen into the ink jar, she began the first lines of a lifetime of poems:

> *I lost a World—the other day.*
> *Has Anybody found?*
> *You'll know it by the Row of Stars*
> *Around its forehead bound.*

GREGORY FEELEY

THE WEIGHING OF AYRE

HOOKEING LEVIATHAN, THE FISHERMAN DRAWS UP HIS LINE TO HOIST not the lantern-mouthed serpent but a glistening bulb with a tail like a whip. Thou art Homunculus, says Malcolm, with the dreamer's gift of perceiving things' true natures. From what sea have I pulled thee? He recalls with shame the warm rushing that sometimes terminates sleep, but this sea does not find its headwaters in him. The ocean lapping this levee contains all the souls of Christendom, each mote seething like *atomi* pressing upon a flask when water is brought to boyle.

The thrashing serpent (who but poorly resembles the homunculi of learned drawings) slips free the hoeck and falls to the sea, immediately to disappear. Malcolm regards his yieldless rod melancholicly and casts his leveen-hooke once more, and this time brings up a twining tapeworm, blind mouths probing the air. O parody of homunculus, you too dwell within man. Do all creatures that enter or quit the tubules of men bear the form of the original Worm? One peeps into the worlds beyond ken only to discover the generation of vipers.

Light is seeping into the sky, like dawn suffusing stained glass. Malcolm looks back to the worm, alert that moments of good illumination be exploited. Besides the suckers for drawing nourishment, the beast's head is ringed with tiny hooks, whereby it affixes itself to its host. Staring, Malcolm feels a pang of the purest melancholy. Hath every worm that crawls its hooks in me?

The sunlight brings him to consciousness, like a bubble rising through brightening waters to break upon the surface of day. The light is different here, a subtler quality than the strange smells or lowtide geography, yet it's the first sensation to impress upon him in the morning. Why should the sun's rays strike this low land aslant, what texture of the air so colors it?

Malcolm Weymouth crawled from his hired bed, bladder full of zuiden brew. The wind was up, as usual, and the squeal of windmills filled the air like birdsong. Voices in a half-familiar tongue rose through the floor-boards; spoken too fast for him to follow, Dutch became a music that snagged threads of memory he couldn't recall.

Vrouw Kluyver had filled the ewer, which she had carefully set with its chipped side facing away from him. Pouring, Malcolm noticed the design at basin's bottom, a Dutch dog—its breed unknown in England, but familiar on the barges he had seen here—pissing against what was plainly an orange tree. Allegory in the delftware, for the diner to find upon finishing his soup. Was the goodwife seeking to goad her English guest, a presumed supporter of his sovereign's ambitions to return William of Orange to the Dutch throne? Or had she even recognized his accent?

Malcolm pulled the pot from beneath the bed and inspected its interior before using it. Reading the evidence of rooms must also be a science, and need not remain the province of cutthroats like Monckton. Rising, he looked around the tiny chamber. The only trace of his English origin was the copy of Hooke's *Micrographia* on the table, and that only if the investigator look past the Latin title to the English text. Malcolm's accent was strong but he spoke fluently, and looked as Dutch as Vrouw Kluyver. If he met someone worldly enough to realize he wasn't Flemish, it would not be in this part of Delft.

He descended the stair slowly, savoring this last experience of the vertical. The steam of alien porridge rose to meet him, and voices resolving into comprehensibility like a specimen brought into focus. Slipping out the door—his arrangement with the innkeeper did not include meals, and he preferred not to converse with the travellers who ate there—Malcolm stepped into the tulip-scented Zuid-Holland morning, where wind vanes slowly turned like up-ended water-wheels and a salt breeze, uninterrupted by hillock or tumulus, blew ten miles from the sea.

How can one spy stars in so cloudy a sky? One reason for the peculiar quality of Dutch light was surely its shifting nature, for the immense sky had been at least partly obscured for all three of Malcolm's days here. A stacked mass of cloud, topped with asymmetrical turrets and domes like a fortress hewn from a knoll, was moving in from the west like Mahomet's mountain, drizzling a rainy smudge from its flattened bottom.

Holland inhabits the bottom of a basin, where the turbid air settles like precipitate in cloudy water. Malcolm knew nothing about the weather, but the analogy seemed sound. Live in the bilges of the *microcosme* and the splendors of the *macrocosme* must be diminished. Small wonder if the researchers of the Low Countries should turn their lenses from the heavens above to the muck beneath their feet.

But is it any greater wonder (he asked himself) that the telescopists, balked by the cataractous air above their heads, should turn rather to grinding mirrors, swing their instruments sidelong rather than upward like swivell'd cannons? Impressive enough their achievements—Huygens had erected a telescope 210 feet long, thus defeating the hobgoblin of chromatic aberration—in despite of their sodden weather; to what use would they put Newton's late contrivance of a telescope that worked by Reflection?

Malcolm fretted these matters as he walked the canal-path toward the center of Delft, so did not see his acquaintance until hailed. "Meister Veymout!" cried a voice, and Malcolm turned, startled, to see a hatted burgher looking up from what appeared to be a telescope. The figure straightened and waved, and Malcolm recognized the surveyor, who had yesterday spoken to him when the object of his inquiries took ill.

"Heer Spoors," said Malcolm, raising his hat. The object on the tripod was a theodolite, which was sighted along the frontage of a lot filled with workmen wielding barrows and picks, who seemed to be sinking piles for a foundation even as the remains of a previous structure were being cleared. "You are at your labors early this day."

"The daylight wanes, while work only multiplies. It is like that doctrine Antoni reviles, of nonlife erupting into life?"

"*Generatio spontanea,*" said Malcolm.

"Like maggots in meal!" The master craftsman laughed, and began to walk beside Malcolm. "You have lived in London, you say. How goes the pest there?"

Malcolm was anxious not to be taken for a spy, but saw no point in hiding his origin from Leeuwenhoeck's colleagues, since it was as a fellow of the Royal Society that he was presenting himself. "It lingers," he allowed. "Though certainly not like before the Fire."

Spoors pulled a long face. "Plagues light on cities, like sparks on dry tinder." Then, apparently moved by the theme of bodily infirmity, he asked, "You go today to see if Antoni is better? He had, you understand, an attack of diarrhoea."

Malcolm said that he had realized this. "I hope that Heer Leeuwenhoeck is able to receive me today. His letters to the Royal Society take long to reach us, and we are anxious to hear of his newest researches." It occurred to him that Spoors, who worked with far-seeing lenses, might be more valuable a source than Leeuwenhoeck.

Malcolm paused at a footbridge that arched across the canal, a sturdy wooden structure such as one might expect to find spanning a brook in an English deer park. The low arch blocked the waterway to all boats, even skiffs, and Malcolm stared at it, wondering whether it swung like a tollgate. Of course, he realized suddenly: this canal isn't for navigation, it merely drains some polder. The narrow channel was in fact a ruled gutter, engineered as carefully as an aqueduct.

Spoors, taking his surprise for uncertainty, pointed to the left. "The *comptoir* is this way," he offered, taking Malcolm's arm. "Allow me to conduct you; I would see that my friend is recovered before returning to work." And the surveyor led him into central Delft, past a street that stank of scorched hops and another crowded with pilgrims heading for the New Church ("The tomb of William the

Silent," Spoors explained) to the garment district where Malcolm, who had come to it yesterday from the opposite direction, recognized at last the clothier's shop of Antoni Leeuwenhoeck, who gazed through microscopes.

"You must pardon my yesterday's indisposition," said the draper as he led them to his small office in back. "I suffered, it seems, from a fluxion of *kleijne diertgens.*" Malcolm did not get a chance to ask what the Dutchman meant before they were standing about his crowded worktable, which was littered with drawings, bits of metal, and stoppered bottles and jars. No instruments were in view, and every visible object was small.

Malcolm began to murmur some expression of well-being, but Leeuwenhoeck was on to business. "What had I been showing you?" he asked, frowning at his lapse in recollection. He looked more the tradesman he plainly was than the microscopist his letters proclaimed. His wig and coat were in the fashion of the mercantile class, and his manners, like a new lens, were ground but unpolished.

"You had begun to demonstrate the 'globules' in a smear of human sperm," said Malcolm. "You said they bore tails and thrashed like tadpoles."

Leeuwenhoeck and the surveyor exchanged glances. "That was a trifle," Leeuwenhoeck said shortly. He gestured at a phial lying on the table. "Your Heer Oldenburgh asked that I examine the constituent parts of saliva, sweat, and other fluids of the body, but it is an investigation best left to anatomists."

Malcolm looked at the sample, which he had hoped to be shown through a microscope, and suddenly understood. "Of course," he said diplomatically. "Mr. Oldenburgh will see the sense of that." Indeed. He reminded himself that it was the microscope he was here to see, and wondered where Leeuwenhoeck's cabinet was.

"Show him the *diertgens,*" said Spoors.

Leeuwenhoeck brightened at the suggestion. "Good idea," he said. He picked up a bottle of cloudy liquid, which he unstoppered and began to decant into a fine glass pipe. Malcolm recognized, with a small thrill, the vessel Leeuwenhoeck had described in his letters for the viewing of aqueous substances.

"This water was taken from a stagnant pool upon which the sun had shone for two days," Leeuwenhoeck remarked. Stopping the pipe with a pinch of gum, he reached into his coat pocket and produced a metal plate about the size of a calling card. A bead of glass glinted in its center like a gem. The draper secured the pipe to a metal arm protruding from the plate, then held the plate up to the window and peered into the bead as 'twere a keyhole. "There they are," he said. Nodding with satisfaction, he handed the device to Malcolm and gestured that he look.

Wordlessly Malcolm took the scrap and peered into its tiny lens. He had to remove his spectacles and bring the lens so close to his eye that his lashes brushed the metal, but after a moment's adjustment the realm beyond jumped into view: the *kleijne diertgens*—which Malcolm had translated as *animalcula,* Latinizing the tradesman's homely Dutch—were swirling through a featureless medium like motes in a beam, and only those that slowed could be apprehended to have limbs. Legs there were, innumerable as a centipede's, and protuberances that might be heads. Malcolm stood rapt, staring at the swarming creatures until a perceptible dimming—the sun gone behind a Dutch pall—roused him to recollection of his surroundings. He lowered the microscope.

"They are quite as you describe them, Mijn Heer," said Malcolm. "No one in England has yet seen such wonders; Mr. Hooke has devoted his attentions to studying the minute parts of visible objects. But"—holding up the metal lozenge—"I am surprised by the simplicity of your device. It seems in design little more than a flea-glass, though greatly more powerful; but the microscopists of England use instruments that align paired lenses through a viewing tube."

"I have found," said Leeuwenhoeck, "that using lenses in train compounds not only their magnifying power, but their distortions as well. A single lens, well made, provides clearer results."

This was the opening Malcolm had been seeking. "Are the lenses ground to your own specifications?" he asked.

"I make my own lenses," Leeuwenhoeck answered. He seemed to notice Malcolm's surprise, for he added, "There is in this town no others who practice this art, and so the lens-makers decline to learn its mysteries."

"I see." Malcolm covered his confusion by looking back to the pipe mounted on the microscope. "These myriad creatures flourish where the sun shines on water?"

"Not only there." Leeuwenhoeck produced another pipe, containing a darker liquid. "The tiny creatures appear also to inhabit the interior of human bodies, as mites and fleas do the surface." He unclamped the first pipe from the microscope and affixed the second. "This is from a sample I took yesterday of my own diarrhoea," he said, handing it over.

Both men watched as Malcolm reluctantly raised the instrument to his face. "I see," he said again, wondering if he would be expected to clasp hands on taking leave of the draper.

Murky objects swam across the face of the lens, different (so far as Malcolm could tell) from the bright monsters of the infusoria. "Fascinating," Malcolm said gamely. "Have you catalogued the species of *diertgens* found in the human bowels?"

"No." Leeuwenhoeck picked a page off the desk and turned it facedown. "That again belongs to the realm of physicians. I had wondered whether the sites of illness—well, no matter."

Malcolm seemed to have stepped into another patch of boggy ground. "Indeed," he said, trying at levity, "it would be a serious matter should the physician find sperm globules in such a sample." The two Dutchmen stared at him. "But I have taken too much of your time," he added quickly. "I hope that I shall be able to call upon you when my business returns me to Delft." And the elaborate business of taking leave began, with Malcolm careful to show the draper the courtesy he would extend a British gentleman.

"A marvelous contrivance," said Spoors as they returned the way they had come. "As an ant may crawl upon a steeple, so creatures minute beyond ken may traverse a grain of sand. Bodies there are, which stand to us as we do to mountains; and we stride through life unsuspecting their existence."

The surveyor seemed disposed to talk, and Malcolm wished that the Dutch had coffeehouses. Instead they engage in furious commerce, relieved only in the evening by tobacco and drink. What Malcolm would lief bring round by degrees he would have to broach directly.

"It is indeed a marvelous device," he said casually. "I wonder not that Heer Leeuwenhoeck is reluctant to disclose the birthplace of such potent lenses."

"He makes them himself, as he said," replied Spoors. "I have dealt with grinders in Delft and beyond, and know that Antoni buys only unpolished blanks."

"Lenses and mirrors for your own work?" Malcolm said this carelessly.

"Indeed, for measurements must be exact." Spoors's voice held a trace of pride. This, thought Malcolm, might prove the entry-point he could pry wide to disclose the secret he sought.

"For the finest optical instruments one must go to the Hague," Spoors continued. "Telescopic devices must use twin lenses in train, and those who study the stars employ tubes of tremendous length." He chuckled. "Christiaan Huygens, who saw a ring around Saturn like a wedding band, constructed one three hundred feet long!"

"So I have heard," said Malcolm blandly. "Though my business follows the inquiries of the Royal Society, I would visit the Hague if I could. But I do misgive myself, for the state of war that exists between our countries counsels against my entry to that city."

Spoors made a scoffing sound. "Our countries share more qual-ities in common than does either with France," he said. "Your Charles recognized this when he made peace with us seven years ago in the face of a common enemy. Now, unable to forget how we burned his navy, he joins the French in attacking us. The beating we have given him this past year will soon convince him to forgo seeking by war what he cannot win in open trade."

This bluff effort at graciousness left Malcolm with feelings so stirred that he could not sort them to tell which lay paramount. Confusedly he asked without thinking: "What does a Surveyor of the Navy do?"

"Eh?" said Spoors. "You mean a surveyor of harbors and straits?"

"I beg your pardon; I mean one who surveys for a nation's navy." Malcolm reddened as he spoke: 'twas a foolish subject to touch upon. "I know one who works in His Majesty's naval office, and he does know that gentleman who bears this title."

Spoors grunted. "And what does he say of the Dutch?"

The question took Malcolm by surprise, though he might have

anticipated it. "I have never met Sir William Batten," he confessed. "But—" His countenance had deepened to the brick red of an oven, and felt as hot. "My friend hath spoken with him often, and remembered Sir William's dismay after the Dutch expedition sailed up the Thames and burned His Majesty's fleet."

"Ha! And what did he say?"

"Actually it was in July," Malcolm temporized, "when a second fleet appeared at Gravesend."

"And the English Surveyor of the Navy said . . . ?"

Malcolm's mouth, he thought miserably, would someday lead him to destruction. "He said, 'I think the Devil shits Dutchmen.'"

And the Delft surveyor threw back his head and roared, startling the street with a burst of Dutch laughter.

Malcolm knew Dutch laughter, though he had never heard so pure a specimen in his score and four of English life. His mother laughed like none of their neighbors, though not in latter years; and the pamphlets and broadsheets assailing the Dutch which he had surreptitiously read made much of the vile fun the lowlanders directed at their benefactors and superiors. The Dutch, young Malcolm gathered, were carefree and ungrateful children such as he could only dream of being, living across the ocean in a country where it did not hurt one to be Dutch.

Reading newer pamphlets, his last night in London, Malcolm found the same slurs he recalled from a dozen years earlier, probably the same sentences. "An Hollander is not an High-Lander, but a low-lander for he loves to be down in the dirt and wallow therein," said one, much taken by his own wit. Malcolm's unmet kinsmen were frugal yet frivolous; they kept Jews in their midst as a swineherd might live with pigs, they neglected proper distinctions between master and servant, and granted their women scandalous freedoms. "Escutcheons are as plentiful as Gentry is scarce, each man his own herald," observes the author of a nasty work entitled *A Brief Character of the Low Countries.* "They are generally so bred up to the Bible that each cobbler is a Dutch doctor of divinity," claimed another.

But most of the scurrilous pamphlets had the Dutchmen dev-
ilized by geography: such low and boggy country could give rise only
to such creatures as they. Holland is "the buttock of the world, full
of veins and blood but no bones in it." Another called it a "universal quagmire," while a poetaster characterized the industrious Dutch
as a

> *Degenerate Race! Sprung out of Mire and Slime*
> *And like a mushroom, ripen'd in small time.*

(The repeated allusions to the Republic's brief history bewildered
Malcolm. Had the English disdained their Commonwealth's short
pedigree?) "A Dutchman is a lusty, Fat, Two-Legged Cheese-
Worm." The author of *Observations Concerning the Present Affairs
of Holland*, pretending to impartiality, called the Dutch "usurpers
that deprive fish of their dwelling places," provoking in Malcolm a
bark of startled laughter. Most pamphlets, however, bore such forth-
right titles as *The Dutch-Mens Pedigree as a Relation, showing how
They Were first Bred and Descended from a Horse Turd which Was
Enclosed in a Butter-Box* or *The Obligations of the Dutch to England and their Continual Ingratitude*, and were crudely if vigorously
illustrated.

Yet these creatures of amphibious repugnancy, splashing in
mud and worse, were reviled particularly for their sense of mirth,
an odd quality to impute to vermin. Malcolm knew already that his
ancestral home was Europe's hotbed for the production of satirical
broadsides and engravings, which deeply affronted both England
and France; and that Holland's carefree production of gazettes—
the coffeehouse chatter of the Dutch, imprudently preserved on
paper—gave even deeper offense. One can understand an enemy's
hatred, but his laughter can only urge his destruction.

Malcolm tosses fitfully on a hard bed more like his pallet in Gre-
sham than the stuffed bolster of Vrouw Kluyver's hostelry. The scent
of stale tobacco lingers in its sheets along with more corporeal whiffs,
apprising the Englishman that the Dutch, with careless sybarism,
smoke after fucking. Loin-wrung and shallowly asleep, Malcolm
shifts a hip against the mean bedding just as a door slams in an ad-

jacent room. The jamb of sensations cracks memory like a nutshell, and the Englishman's pale Dutch face, smoothed by dissolution, frowns.

He had worked late, and so was yet asleep in the English dawn when the knocking boomed through his chamber, hardwood against his door like the knell of doomsday. Disoriented, Malcolm thrashed free of his sheets to find his door swung open and two men standing over him, foreshortened British faces gazing down as though he were an eel on a plate.

"Malcolm Weymouth," said the hawk-faced man, as though warning him not to deny it.

"Who are you?" Malcolm had sat up, but they were not granting him room to stand.

"Shut up," warned the shorter one in an ugly tone, but his superior gestured him silent.

"You are Malcolm Weymouth of Battersea," he said, "born of Richard Weymouth, mariner, and his wife Marte, a Dutchwoman."

"That I am." Malcolm wished he could reach for his hat.

"I am Silas Monckton, with warrant of the Council of State." Monckton straightened, carrying himself with the assurance of authority, and turned to survey the room. A batch of proof sheets lay upon his table, partially corrected. Monckton pointed at them with his stick. "Thou art a clerk for the Royal Society, and dost translate letters from French and Dutch correspondents."

"I am a junior fellow," Malcolm protested weakly. He had recognized the spymaster's name, and his entrails were gone weak with fear.

"Including," Monckton continued as though he had not heard, "letters from the Dutch Republic, with whom we are in deadly conflict."

"I do but translate observations of the natural world, for publication in *Philosophical Transactions*," said Malcolm in a constricted voice. Surely, he thought but could not say, this constitutes no treasonous communication with the enemy.

"I have read the letters." Monckton turned his head to study the sheets, then nodded. "The draper from Delft is no naturalist, but has simply extended the efforts of Robert Hooke."

"Indeed," said Malcolm, mind awhirl, "the man but carries forward studies initiated here." Copies of the first proofs had been circulated to several of the senior fellows for approval. He wondered how they could have reached His Majesty's agents.

"Yet the spyglass was invented in Holland," said Monckton. "Its application for military purpose was swiftly undertaken. And a Dutchman named Huygens, known to your Society, has lately devised a new method for grinding lenses that signally improves the power of the telescope."

"I did not know these things," replied Malcolm, mystified.

The spymaster settled into Malcolm's chair, not taking his eyes off the young man, and planted his stick between them like a banner. "The draper's microscope uses a single lens, knowest thou not that? yet is more powerful than any in England. Their lenses achieve greater power than ours, and avoid the distortions ours suffer. Canst thou not conceive, son of the nether lands, how these things might aid their prowess in war?"

"A stronger spyglass means farther vision," said Malcolm carefully, "yet the curvature of the Earth sets a firmer limit on their range. The greatest glass conceivable cannot see from Ipswich to the Hague."

Monckton looked at him carefully, like a vivisectionist wondering where to begin. "Hast thou seen schoolboys playing with a lens, such as cloth-merchants use to study the weave of a fabric? Hast seen them focus the sun's rays so to kindle a fire, or roast a nest of ants?"

"Aye, this I have." Dawning realization crossed Malcolm's features. "But none of these contrivances can be turned to warlike uses."

"No? Have none of the scientists of the Royal Society, formed by decree of His Majesty himself, thought to wonder whether it is possible for a magnifying glass to set fire to a ship, as Archimedes of Syracuse was said to have done?"

"Archimedes of Syracuse supposedly used a refracting mirror," said Malcolm. He remembered something about Dutchmen and mirrors, but could not order his thoughts. Sitting undoubleted on his low bed, his hair disordered and his bladder bursting, he spoke incautiously. "And His Majesty has expressed nothing but disdain for the science of microscopy."

"You shut your gob," cried the second man angrily. He raised a gnarled fist and took a step forward.

"Enough, Pitcairn," said Monckton. "Mister Weymouth may not mean to speak treason."

"I speak only facts." Frightened as he was, Malcolm found himself provoked by this avenue of intimidation. "I know nothing of your reports, nor anything of the Dutch war save what I hear in the coffeehouses." He stood, to dispel the detriment of being gazed down upon, and tried to think. "No lens could set a ship afire; it is simply not possible. The focal length is too short, and the angle between sun, lens, and target wrong. It is possible—" Professional caution urged him stay, but he felt he had better give something—"It is *possible,* under ideal circumstances, that a powerful mirror might perhaps burn a pinpoint hole in a sail."

"I see." Monckton leaned slightly back, and the imbalance was restored: Malcolm was standing abjectly before his seated interrogator.

Doggedly Malcolm continued: "The ship, however, would do better to arm itself with a cannon, which would still function in cloudy weather. It would also prove more durable, and easily aimed."

"I'm sure the Naval Office will be relieved by thy assurances." Though seemingly at ease, Monckton was regarding him with a curious intensity, which seemed not quite curiosity, nor amusement, nor disdain. With a start Malcolm recognized it as hatred. Largeskulled and horse-jawed, a former lieutenant (so the story went) to John Thurloe himself, Monckton brought the roundheads' fanatical rigor to the cause of the libertine Charles, as though the savage pursuit of a former enemy's interests conferred its own dour grace. The Dutch Republic in particular he seemed to hate with the virulence of any royalist, and Malcolm could feel the man's gaze lighting on those of his features thought to betray Dutch blood: the sensuous lips, the milk-fair features.

"The Naval Office has not asked my advice on any matter," said Malcolm, taking refuge in fact. "I do but work for the Royal Society, in matters mostly secretarial."

"The Royal Society would do well to examine more closely its hiring practices," said Monckton acidly. "This Dutchman writes accounts of lenses more powerful than any we know, and you look only to the descriptions of chaff and slime with which he busies himself. Other intelligences reach us of wonders emerging from the Dutch kilns, even as our navy falters in its war against the frogs. And when His Majesty's agents enquire as to why the members of the Royal Society have not brought matters in their knowledge to our attention, we discover that important letters have been entrusted to an equivocating *straddler*, a supposed Englishman neither truly English nor truly a man—"

Malcolm remembered making an angry exclamation, but whether he had taken a step forward or raised his hand he could never recall. He crashed backward, a stick against his throat and someone's foul breath in his face. Impact drove the wind from him, and before he was able to raise his hands he was struck between the legs with the force of a mallet. Gasping airlessly, Malcolm gaped upward to see, beyond Pitcairn's leering nearness, the austere gaze of Monckton standing over them.

"Let him up, Pitcairn. Our Royal Fellow may be as much Dutch as English, but he will do earnest labor, like a pilgrim marshaling his better half against his worse, in the service of virtue. It is our role, like figures of allegory, to persuade him of his duty."

No laughter at this, for laughter acknowledges to the world one's enjoyment, which Puritans will not acknowledge to themselves. Malcolm would not either, at least according to Grietje, who expressed hers freely. Having gotten behind her and set to work at loosening the strings belting her skirt, he heard her giggle. "Most men lift the hem," she observed with a glance over her shoulder. "Those who tug down the waistband are usually pretending they've got a sailor." And she galed into laughter to Malcolm's shriveling shock.

But even this did not deflate him for long. She threw her arms about him and thrust her beery tongue against his, uncorseted teats pressed against his chest. Grietje smelled of soap and sweat, and bent complaisantly to let Malcolm confirm, with clinical aplomb, that she was disease-free. Lying now drowsing, his leased love departed for other commerce, Malcolm feels peace in dissipation, as though, like a rock salmon, he has traveled up the estuary of his scarce-remembered homeland to convulse forth his seed.

Someone was knocking on the door. Malcolm came awake with a horrible start, although the knock was neither deferential nor peremptory. "Meynheer Weymouth!" called a young voice. The door swung open and an adolescent, grinning insolently, entered holding a steaming mug. "Meynheer Spoors' respects, sir," he said cheerfully, "and an invitation to come forth this night to observe the wonders of a new telescope."

Dumbly Malcolm accepted the cup, which hotly radiated the aroma of coffee. The first sip raced through his veins like the phantasmic pneuma and he felt his mind waken to join his body. Even the discovery that the voluptuous Dutch had put a dollop of cream in the coffee did nothing to still his dawning wonder.

The young man picked up Malcolm's breeches, turned them right-side-to, and slung them over the back of the chair. "It's a two-hour journey," he remarked, "so we must leave soon, I'm told to say, to catch the crescent Venus. I'll be without." And he closed the door behind him. He had not, Malcolm realized, said how he had known where to find Malcolm.

He drank more deeply of the coffee. An extraordinary experience, he reflected, having coffee in your room without having to go out to a coffeehouse for it. A second pleasure this day to which he could accustom himself.

The last time he had drunk coffee, he recalled as their carriage sped across a causeway separating two fields, was the afternoon before his departure. It was at Jonathan's, which the Secretary Member (he jestingly called himself that, though Malcolm did not dare) was wont to frequent. Malcolm had known the Secretary from his late visits to the Royal Society; but his appointment last year had elevated him beyond further acquaintance with Malcolm, who had no business in matters Naval or Parliamentary. Yet the Secretary (who heard everything) hailed Malcolm and came himself to his table—Malcolm standing with a start and a stammer—to demand whether it was true that "You go now to the court of Nicholas Frog?"

"To Delft, rather, sir," answered the junior fellow, blushing like a Dutchman. "To study late advances in the art of *Microscopy* for the Society." He wondered whether the Secretary knew better.

"Jesu, and should you profit from your expedition thence, you'll be the first." The Secretary's coffee was being delivered to his table, and he beckoned the waiter over. "The Dutch have sunk seven hundred of our ships in this God-forsaken war, while we have scarce touched theirs. They have flooded their own lands to stop the French advance, did you know that?"

Malcolm, who never listened to coffeehouse talk of the Dutch war, shook his head solemnly. The waiter's tray bore three gold-rimmed cups, the Secretary's and his two clerks', and Malcolm was served one of them. He sipped the steaming brew carefully, and discovered that the Secretary for the Affairs of the Admiralty was served a better bean than the common gentleman.

"Has the navy," he asked, "exacted a comparable toll against the Dutch?"

The Secretary scowled. "Their merchant ships hole up in harbor like rats, and scarce expose themselves. Such is the Dutchmen's wealth that they can stifle their trade thus, yet do not starve. Louis should have overrun them by now, but their terrible measures have stopped the French cold."

"You have visited Holland," Malcolm began.

"I have visited the Dutch, and the Dutch have visited *me.*" He said it grandly, like one who would tread the stage.

Malcolm knew what the Secretary signified, and though he had heard the tale before, he asked again now. "You heard their guns yourself?" he asked.

"All London heard them," the Secretary answered solemnly. "The sound of enemy fire as the Dutch burned our ships beat a tattoo I hear yet." He seemed to brood. "Yet their landing party did not kill our townspeople, nor plunder their houses. I spoke afterward to the folk of Medway, who told me that our own soldiers, who entered the country-towns after the Dutch withdrew, were far more terrible to the populace."

If the Secretary had wished to pull apart the knit loyalties of peaceable Malcolm like a digger prising a clam, he was going about it the right way. Malcolm smiled painfully, proud of his scrupulous Dutch forebears, ashamed of his ignoble English ones, and miserable that the Republican Dutch and the once-Republican English were not making common cause against the Popish Louis, who set ally against ally with the heft of his purse. Did the Secretary know how he was perturbing the fragile orrery of Malcolm's composure?

"So," continued the Secretary, as though proceeding from melancholy matters to others possibly less so, "you are to study the Dutchmen's facility with the flea-glass?"

"Mister Leeuwenhoeck's device, though it employs but a single lens, appears readily the equal of Hooke's," replied Malcolm cautiously. "I do not yet know whether the Holland gentility use them for amusements."

"I wish our gentility thought them more than amusements," said the Secretary morosely. "When His Majesty dismissed the study of *micro-phenomena* as 'the mere weighing of Ayre,' the apes of fashion took it as license to mock any investigation graver than gaping at a louse on a pin. I do fear that the sons of the gentry, from whom we look to recruit the naturalists of tomorrow, will think it no true calling."

And perhaps the Dutch thought it no true calling, reflected Malcolm in the carriage, if their best researches were conducted by a draper. The Dutch astronomers, on the other hand, were gentlemen of the finest education, their accomplishments recognized even in France. Huygens had contacts with the Dutch government through his father, who had introduced Leeuwenhoeck to the Royal Society. Uneasily Malcolm wondered how closely the Dutch government followed its citizens' optical researches.

"Here we are," announced the boy cheerfully from his perch behind Malcolm's seat. Malcolm peered into the twilight, and saw several men standing on the levee ahead of them like an assignation of smugglers. After a second's further scrutiny, he realized that they were bending over a large tube, like a band of gunners aiming a bombard. One straightened and came forward as Malcolm climbed down.

"You are Mister Weymouth, the English gentleman," he said in Dutch-accented Latin. "I am Cornelius van der Pluym, astronomer

of Leiden. With my *reflecting telescope,* based on the newest principles from Paris, I hope to discover that Venus, like Jupiter, Saturn, and our own Earth, possesses orbiting moons."

"I am honored that you have agreed to let me observe your
observations," replied Malcolm gravely in the same word-scant
tongue. He did not know whether the astronomer assumed he knew
no Dutch, or always conducted his discussions in the language of
science.

"Come this way, then, and see how the reflecting lens improves
upon the aerial design of Huygens," said van der Pluym, gesturing
that Malcolm precede him. "Keep him out of trouble," he added in
quiet Dutch to the servant.

Grinning in complicity, the servant led Malcolm around the
telescope, which stood on a brass and wood tripod as though meant
for a professor's study. The eyepiece, Malcolm noted with surprise,
emerged from the end of the tube rather than its side, as Newton's
model had. Peering into it, van der Pluym murmured something
which an assistant, shielding the light of a candle with his body, tran-
scribed into a notebook.

"Have you seen Meynheer Huygens' new telescope?" asked a
young man next to Malcolm, who introduced himself as Rudolf
Moete. Malcolm said he had not. "It comprises two distinct tubes,
separated by fifty feet or more. A train of mechanisms is required
to keep them aligned, for which Huygens must keep a crew ready.
Still, it is better than handling a single tube of such length, which
presents terrible difficulties."

"The reflecting model uses a convex mirror, does it not?" asked
Malcolm casually.

"Aye, and it must be perfectly formed, else the design be no im-
provement upon Huygens'. I do fear that van der Pluym's model
does not meet this standard."

Eventually Malcolm was given an opportunity to peer into the
eyepiece while the astronomer sketched his observations. A perfect
sickle, Venus showed nearly as large as the Moon but without flaw
or feature in its whiteness. Malcolm saw no pinpoint of light that
would signify a moon, but doubted his ability to resolve detail
through the impediment of his spectacles. He had not yet found an

ideal distance at which to set his eye when the astronomer tapped his shoulder, and he relinquished his place.

Moete stood a few yards off, smoking his pipe as he looked over the levee. Malcolm joined him, wondering how to raise the subject of mirror-making.

"The air is a lens," the young man said thoughtfully. "Have you ever seen waves of heat ripple above the ground on a hot day? So, faintly, does air refract light as it passes between warm and cool regions. It is my contention that twilight, with heat escaping from the earth, will ever be a poor time for viewing, and that the moons of Venus will be seen only on winter dawns."

"How interesting," murmured Malcolm. Those craftsmen who wrought mirrors must work closely with the lens grinders, he thought; the arts are too similar. He took a step forward, looking down as though to watch his footing, then stumbled on the sloping ground. Malcolm caught himself only as he fell to his knees, and his spectacles flew off his nose, to disappear with a splash into the water below.

"Oh, heavens," he cried as Moete helped him to his feet. "I have lost my eyeglasses in the polder. How could I get another pair made?"

Sunlight glittered off the Delft shop windows, still wet from a morning shower. Malcolm, back from the Hague and shaking rain from his hat, found everything made new, each glint bespeaking fresh-planed edges. He walked the streets with more familiarity now, without imaging that every face he met saw him for a foreigner. Was it myopia that made one suspicious of others' motives?

Leeuwenhoeck seemed pleased enough to see him. "My investigations continue," he said as he led the Englishman to his office. "An improved cutting blade has allowed me to refine my observations of the tubules within wood. I have also made studies of the sting of a bee."

Malcolm was more interested in the tiny animals, but knew Leeuwenhoeck's reticence on the subject. Looking about the office for a more friendly subject, he was startled to see a small canvas propped against the wall, an oil painting portraying (it appeared) the torments of Hell. Damned figures writhed and supplicated the empty sky as a variety of demons prodded them, tore their flesh, or consumed them whole.

"I did not know you favored paintings of a religious nature," said Malcolm uncertainly.

"It is by my friend Vermeer," said Leeuwenhoeck, glancing at it. "He seeks to allay his debt, so has accepted a commission from a pious widow to produce an allegory in the manner of Bosch. He consulted with me regarding plausible designs for his imps."

Malcolm looked closer and saw that one of the demons, its head a wheel of waving limbs, bore an unmistakable resemblance to the animalcules he had seen earlier. Another seemed to possess the magnified features of a louse.

As though reminded by the infernal landscape, Leeuwenhoeck said: "I have noticed that the *diertgens* which live in pond water seem to vary in number between summer and autumn, and may continue to do so throughout the year. And that while a cow's blood contains numerous globules, the *aqueous humour* of its eye contains none."

"I would be interested to hear whether the *diertgens* found in the human gut differ between men and women, or between sick men and healthful ones."

"Well, perhaps your British colleagues shall carry that investigation farther," the draper replied indifferently. "I cannot restrict my researches to a single subject, and find the variety of the natural world more appealing than the fluids of the human corpus."

Which was certainly disingenuous, Malcolm reflected as he returned to his inn. It was likelier that Leeuwenhoeck had misgivings about conducting investigations into the human body. Malcolm knew that the Dutchman could not fear ecclesiastical persecution, but he might fairly worry about trespassing upon the privileges of physicians, who doubtless enjoyed a monopoly on medical research.

"There's a young man to see you," said Vrouw Kluyver as Malcolm entered the inn. "A sailor, I think." Malcolm blushed, then looked to the tavern room. Thanking the goodwife, he straightened his hat and crossed the threshold, to find nothing but two idle workmen sitting over tankards. Puzzled, he looked toward the back rooms, where cards were played in evenings and private parties sometimes convened. Unlit by day, they seemed poor sites for an appointment. His heart pounding, Malcolm poked his head round a corner and peered uncertainly into the gloom.

"Look at you," an unfamiliar voice, English, said out of the darkness. Malcolm blinked, and the outline of a man behind a table slowly took form. "Gone bloody Dutch, like a tabby back in the wild, eh?"

"Who are you?" asked Malcolm, moving to block the light that disclosed himself. A coal glowed briefly, and Malcolm saw the face above the pipe: British features, expression insolent and knowing, beneath tousled black curls. "I've seen you before," said Malcolm, as the man sat back and smiled. He was wearing a seaman's jacket, and abruptly Malcolm recognized him. "You were on the ship that brought me over," he said wonderingly.

"Do you remember why you were brought over?" the man asked.

Malcolm looked at him carefully, then glanced back at the tavern room. "I am about my business," he said cautiously. "Have you a letter for me?"

The sailor looked Malcolm up and down. "Even wearing Dutch spectacles, I see. Hoping to interest young scholars? What would Master Monckton think of such dissipation?"

Malcolm caught his breath even as the blood surged to his face. "My English spectacles were broken, and by my own design, to get me entry to the Hague's finest lens-makers. If thou knowst what I am about, thou knowst well why."

"Your report I have." The man—Malcolm finally remembered his name was Skerrett—turned over several pages, which Malcolm recognized as not only the report he had sent to an Amsterdam address, but also a second one he had left unfinished in his room. "You were asked to learn more of Leeuwenhoeck's tiny animals, but relate nothing."

"I was asked only after submitting that report," Malcolm replied hotly. "Did that note come from you?" His only reply was the glow of the pipe. "I have come from Leeuwenhoeck directly," he said finally, "and he has grown close on the matter of *diertgens*. I will not get more from him this day."

The sailor looked at Malcolm searchingly. "The Crown is preparing to offer peace, do you know that?" He was tapping the contents of his pipe onto the papers. "The Dutch flooded their own lands, like a frog pissing itself, and stopped the French dead. Their navy ventures nothing, sailing forth only when certain of victory. They draw allies throughout Europe, and if they are not stopped this season we shall have to sue. Or did your sailor friends not tell you this?"

"You followed me in Amsterdam." Malcolm was at once sick and enraged. "You know enough to know me guiltless, yet seek the vilest advantage—"

Skerrett reached forward, faster than Malcolm could see, and grasped his wrist hard. "I seek advantage for England as vile as needs serve," he said softly, his calloused fingers tightening unto pain. "The Crown might e'en use such as thou, and throw it away afterward. Now hear me close: know'st thou the *interwaarden* between the stream feeding the brewery and its north embankment?"

"Yes," whispered Malcolm, trying to pull his hand free.

"Meet me there tomorrow sunset, and bring thy report." Skerrett abruptly released Malcolm's hand, causing him to stagger. "Continue thy inquiries in Leeuwenhoeck's work: they justify thy continued presence in Holland. And include them in the report, that it may look innocuous if seized."

He pushed back his chair and stood, glaring. "Englishmen die while thou dalliest," he said, pointing at Malcolm. Malcolm caught a glint of light and realized that the finger extending toward his nose was a knife tip. "Bring us results directly, or feel my present wrath." Something struck Malcolm's chest lightly, then fell with a clang to the floor: coins. Skerrett was out the door, his footfalls receding rapidly.

Malcolm stood long seconds in the dim light before he bent to retrieve the coins. Two half-guilders, sufficient for a few days' lodging. His papers were left derisively on the table, and Malcolm took them up, folding them prudently into a pocket before quitting the room.

Vrouw Kluyver was waiting for him in the tavern room. "You still want to go to Leiden?" she asked.

Malcolm had forgotten his earlier plans. "Is there a boat?" he asked. The prospect of leaving town seemed suddenly attractive.

"The *snipschuit* leaves twice an hour," she said. "But you have to change boats in the Hague, and from there passage to Leiden is only hourly."

So Malcolm took the canal boat, a narrow covered craft drawn by horses along a *trekvaart* that had been dug straight as an avenue for the sole purpose of boating passengers between towns. He paid for his ticket in a booth overlooking the canal, where the *snipschuit* had just entered the lock from the upper reach. Canalmen, swinging the balance beam's counterweight over the spectators' heads like an immense slow scythe, shut the mitre gates with a water-muffled thump. Malcolm watched as they bent to lift the sluice-gates, releasing a gush of water into the side-ponds. The boat, which filled the tiny lock like a loaf in a basket, slowly sank into the lock. By the time the lower gate was opened and the ship brought out like a toy from a box, Malcolm was queued up with the other passengers, burghers and prosperous tradesmen. He stepped into the canoo-shaped craft, which rocked gently as the passengers found their seats, and sat with a tentative smile next to a pipe-puffing gentleman leaning against the railing.

"Eighty minutes," the man remarked, taking his watch from his pocket and checking it.

"To the Hague?" Malcolm asked. "How can that be?" The two horses had tightened the towlines and were pulling the boat forward, at a pace at once too fast for them to sustain yet too slow to make such time.

"Watch," said the burgher. A pair of mounted canalmen were riding alongside the towhorses, both (Malcolm noticed) looking back over their shoulders. Together they slowly raised their free arms, then brought them down with a sudden shout. The horses leaped forward, and the boat seemed to lift and jerk forward at the same instant. A few men around them cheered.

"What was that?" asked Malcolm. They were now sailing much faster than before, while the horses were trotting easily.

The Dutchman chuckled. "We're riding the primary wave raised by the motion of the boat, which we caught as it overtook us. With the wave beneath us, the *snipschuit* can be hauled at less expenditure of energy than at faster or slower rates."

"That is astonishing." Malcolm stood and tried to look over the side, but the canal was so narrow that the clearance between boat and wall was no wider than a doorsill. "The primary wave propagates down the canal without dissipating, doesn't it?" He was trying to work out the physics.

The burgher sighed happily. "Sounds like a bird flying behind itself to shelter from the wind, doesn't it? Yet it works." His pleasure at the found economy was evident.

"Some say light is a wave," said Malcolm, thinking of it passing down a telescope tube. "That it spreads from the sun like ripples expanding from a pond."

"Nonsense," said the burgher comfortably. "Light streams like God's grace from heaven. Does God's grace waver?"

Leiden was a greater town than Delft, and its university (a long walk from the canal, which ran straight into the center of town like the Appian Way) seemed to contain as many foreigners as Dutchmen. Malcolm walked unremarked, a young Englishman among Germans, Frenchmen, and what sounded like Poles. Nobody knew the location of the observatory, so Malcolm presented himself at the university library, where he showed his letter of introduction to the Librarian, who seemed to find the matter highly irregular.

"This letter is signed by two physicians of the town of Delft," the venerable gentleman observed, glancing up from it reproachfully, "but you wish to speak to a Professor of Optics."

"Both the learned doctors are graduates of this university," Malcolm pointed out. "I might be able to get a letter from Meynheer van der Pluym, if that would help."

"It says," the Librarian continued, "that the physicians do not in fact know you, but are writing at the request of the Chamberlain of Sheriffs, Meynheer Leeuwenhoeck. The draper," he said, looking up.

"How did you know that?" asked Malcolm, startled.

"He was here last month, asking to see our books on *contagio*," the Librarian grumbled. "He had to have a student abstract the books' Latin that he might understand it."

"I can read my own Latin," Malcolm offered.

"Oh, you shall have your admission, as the draper had his." The Librarian scribbled something at the bottom of the letter and handed it crossly back. In the event, nobody asked to see the admission, and Malcolm wandered the library unchallenged.

The *Opticae Thesaurus* was there, and *Pantometria,* the earliest book to describe an optical instrument, and British, too. Two copies of *Micrographia,* as was just. No modern Dutch work, however; nothing to bespeak a *"Eureka!"* in optical design. Would the Dutchmen build a *speculum horribilis* and then not publish word of it? Perhaps they would, like an alchemist guarding the secret of the *aqua vitae.* Malcolm found it hard to believe, however.

The Dutch published no journal of philosophical research, but it occurred to Malcolm that a university boasting its own observatory might have shelves devoted to astronomy books. Following directions, he located the wall of astronomical works, where a student stood perusing a folio. At Malcolm's approach he looked up, and was Moete the telescopist. "The Englishman of the levee," he said, closing his volume. "You wear new spectacles, I see."

"Better than before," said Malcolm, touching his hat politely. "Your countrymen grind finer lenses than do mine, though it pains me to say't."

"Better at glass than mirrors, I fear." The young Dutchman pulled a long face. "The moons of Venus shall remain unobserved, unless our craftsmen learn to make a convex mirror of proper curvature."

"Perhaps the best craftsmen are otherwise occupied," suggested Malcolm, hoping not to flush his game.

Moete shook his head. "This is a small country, my friend, and the makers of sound lenses and mirrors are known to every astronomer by name. A good reflecting telescope requires a perfect parabola, else the light won't come to a point. Van der Pluym's model is the best they can do, and it is but indifferent good."

"Will you be pursuing astronomical observations tonight?" Malcolm asked.

Moete gave a brilliant smile. "Tonight it is going to rain. I shall enjoy a leisurely dinner, and be in bed before ten."

Malcolm wished him well, then returned to the main reading room. Was it possible that he was being elaborately gulled, shown inferior instruments and told of inadequate skills while artisans quietly crafted mirrors to set the British fleet ablaze? All Malcolm could do was report his findings, which his overseers must interpret as they would.

The Librarian eyed Malcolm suspiciously as he paged through the catalogue, which had been helpfully divided (in the French manner) into various classifications. Carefully Malcolm read down pages of book titles, looking for any that might suggest a treatise on optics or weaponry. Candidates he copied into his memorandum book. Most of the titles were in Latin, but some were in Mediterranean languages he scarcely knew. He stopped, frowning, at *Lo specchio ustorio ouero trattato delle settioni coniche.* "The Burning Glass"?

Malcolm left his post and sought out the book, which was shelved, unpromisingly, under Mathematics. Bonaventura Cavalieri's 1632 treatise seemed indeed to concern itself with conic sections, and Malcolm turned its pages bemusedly, wondering about the *specchio ustorio.* But when he saw Figura XXI and Figura XXII, he caught his breath: the drawings showed, unmistakably, designs for mirror arrangements that would set fires.

Malcolm read slowly through the accompanying text, which he copied down for more expert translation. The first design focused the sun's rays to ignite material in a cylinder, which then smoked at the top like a chimney, but the second arrangement sent a beam of concentrated sunlight across space like a bullet's path. A large concave parabolic mirror, its vertex removed like a tip snipped from the finger of a glove, gathered the light like a funnel, and a small convex parabolic secondary mirror cast it outward in a parallel beam. At the drawing's edge the beam terminated, meaningfully, in a curl of smoke.

So an Italian geometer had designed Archimedes' marvelous weapon, and forty years ago. Malcolm could see disadvantages to the design: the annular primary mirror lost most of the area it presented to the Sun to the opening in its center. Curious, he sketched a convex lens set like a jewel in the central space, which would bend the light passing through onto the same focus as the mirror. Would such a design—mirror and lens in conjunction—prove workable?

The craft of making mirrors was certainly not equal in 1632 to building such a weapon; and Malcolm doubted that it was today. After two hours' further search, however, he could confirm only that no other books existed on the subject.

Before leaving he sought out the medical section, curious what "books on *contagio*" Leeuwenhoeck might have read. The books were ordered by no scheme that Malcolm understood, but by reading all the titles he came to *De Contagione et Contagiosis Morbis,* published in 1546 in Venice by Hieronymus Fracastorius, a name that tugged at Malcolm's memory. The book's top was free of dust, unlike its companions to either side. What had Leeuwenhoeck sought here?

Malcolm took the volume to a table and began to turn its heavy pages, which some past owner had marginally annotated. Fracastorius, it proved, had made a study of epidemic diseases, which (he proposed) were infections spread by imperceptible particles. Each disease is caused by a different species of particle, which multiply rapidly and travel from afflicted sufferers to new victims by one of three means: by direct contact, through the air, and by transmission through soiled clothes and linen.

At the bottom of a page the annotator had noted in schoolboy Latin: *"Cf. Marcus Varro, who warned in the c. before Christ against miasmal swamps 'Because there are bred certain minute creatures which cannot be seen by the eyes, which float through the ayre and enter the body through the mouth and nose and there cause serious disease.' "*

Malcolm wondered at the significance of this. Did Antoni Leeuwenhoeck hope to discover Fracastorius' minute particles with his microscope? The answer suggested itself a second later: the draper was wondering whether his "little animals" were the causes of contagious disease.

The realization was faintly embarrassing. Malcolm hoped that Leeuwenhoeck hadn't confided this hope to his physician friends, who had (he knew) taken seriously the tradesman's researches when scholars and academicians had not. So startling were the *animalcula* on first sight—and can Varro, or any sage of the ancient world, ever actually have seen them?—that their discoverer could be forgiven a moment's wild surmise that he had uncovered the agent of all pestilence.

Abruptly Malcolm remembered something about the author, a mental poke from a direction he could not identify. He returned to Moete, who was sitting peaceably at a table. "Pardon me, but have you heard of a scholar named Fracastorius?"

"Girolamo Fracastoro?" The Dutchman seemed surprised at the question. "Of course, he was an Italian astronomer of the last century, colleague of Copernicus. Also a physician; wrote about plagues. I think we have some of his books."

Moete strode to the shelves, where he ran his hand along the ribbed spines before pausing and selecting one. "*Homocentria*," he pronounced, looking at the title page. "Fracastoro believed that the planets revolved in circular orbits round a fixed point, although he did not identify that as the Sun." A scrap of paper lay inside the cover, which Moete opened and read. "It says that Fracastoro also wrote a book about syphilis, in verse," he said.

"That's it," said Malcolm. "He gave syphilis its name, in a poem written in the classical manner. I had not known him for an authority on plagues as well." Nor on the heavens, for that matter.

Moete shrugged easily. "It was an age of great men," he said. "So long as you did not mind being harried by the Church of Rome."

Malcolm felt such a surge of friendliness that he was suddenly tempted to ask Rudolf to dinner. Only the knowledge that the last boat back to Delft left before eight prevented him. He bid the Dutchman a pleasant farewell, urged him to read *Philosophical Transactions,* and set out with directions for the observatory, where (he was told) junior students could be found at this hour cleaning the instruments.

Leiden University was sufficiently like Greenwich that Malcolm, after ten days in Delft or the Hague, felt at once comfortable and homesick. Some of the students he saw on the street were plainly British; they did not recognize him, Dutch-complected and

-attired, as a countryman. He saw one, English but not dressed like a student, come round a corner and realized with a horrible start that it was Skerrett.

The sailor turned to look Malcolm's way, and Malcolm spun to present his back. Red hair, Dutch jacket, he thought; and there is no reason for Skerrett to think me in Leiden. He took a few steps, then glanced sidelong over his shoulder. The sailor was continuing up the street, his pace unaltered.

Malcolm's heart was pounding against his ribs like an importunate fist. What in sweet heaven's name was Skerrett doing in Leiden? If the knavish sailor was engaged as a sergeant of spies, as seemed plain, he did no good to enter the field of battle himself. Or had he another spy in Leiden, whom he came now to see?

Malcolm faded into the back streets like a mouse into shadows, then took the most circuitous of routes back to the canal. The hours he would have spent studying the technology of Dutch astronomers were expended sitting in a carters' tavern, keeping his head down and waiting for the last canal boat to leave. Malcolm watched it depart through a window, then bought passage on a cargo ship. He spent the evening lying on sacks of corn—not even ground meal, he realized with dismay—and looking at the stars in the half-clouded sky.

When the first drops of rain spattered his face, he started awake, the dream enveloping him dispelled like a pond's reflection shattered by a stone. What was the dream? Malcolm knew that to chase would but drive it away, while returning to the position of sleep might coax it back. Positioning himself uncomfortably, he closed his eyes and sought to recapture the instant before waking. A splotch of cold rain struck his eyelid.

"It's coming down now," remarked the pilot, his voice carrying clearly over the still boat.

"Going to wet the young scholar," replied his companion with a snigger.

"He should be wet. He's spent few enough nights in the open, I'll warrant."

They didn't realize he was English, thought Malcolm with a stab of pleasure. And abruptly he had it: he had been dreaming of being

Girolamo Fracastoro, of all things. What currents had pulled the unmoored boats of his mind thither?

The second man climbed back and began dragging a tarpaulin over the sacks. Malcolm stood and helped, still wondering whether his drowsing mind had muttered wisdom or foolishness.

"Like the big sky?" the man asked, not unfriendly. Malcolm realized that he meant the perfect unobstructed half-dome of firmament evident between towns in this tabletop country. Dark clouds were scudding across it, visible only by the absence of stars.

Malcolm looked up, trying to imagine the heavens blown free of clouds and moonless. Such a sight would perhaps greet a sailor at sea, did he climb the topmost mast. "It's lovely," he said. "It makes me feel like a lens." There, what had he meant by that?

"*Eh?*" asked the man, thinking he had heard amiss.

"It makes me feel so small," Malcolm amended. "Like a mite beneath a great lens." But he knew he spoke truth the first time.

The man snorted and climbed back onto the seat, and the pilot returned him his pipe. But it's true, Malcolm thought as he crept under the canvas. It is by lenses that researchers discern the nature of the heavens, those same lenses that disclose the micro-world, which stands in relation to us as we do to the vastness above. Philosophers use the term *microcosme* to describe the world of human nature; but the true microcosme lies beneath the lens of the microscope: and we inhabit but an intermediate level between the great and small of the universe.

And I am a simple lens, to be turned upon either world at the instruction of those who would know. Is that what the dream about Fracastoro meant: that he looked to both stars and tiny creatures?

Malcolm fell asleep beneath the blanketing comfort of the tarpaulin, and woke only as they bumped against the bank to a stop. He peeked out and saw a loading dock and, beyond, the lights of a tavern: not Vrouw Kluyver's, but the one from which he had been rousted to visit the astronomers, a ruder establishment. Journey's end, evidently: Malcolm climbed out as the men began to unload the sacks.

A cup of ale seemed suddenly a needful thing, air for a smothering man. Malcolm spied through the windows to confirm that Skerrett did not sit within. His nerves wrung like laundry, he at last entered the tavern, each step a recitation of his back's aches and cricks. It was smokier than in the afternoons he had visited, and the clamor of voices was louder. Malcolm sat at the end of a bench and smiled at the carters who looked at him.

"What will you have, stranger?" asked the barmaid as she removed empty *flapkan* tankards from the table.

Malcolm might have been unknown to the evening crowd, but he wasn't an evening's transient. "Where is Grietje?" he asked, by way of establishing this.

The barmaid pulled a long face. "Taken ill," she said. "Like as not with the pox." She grinned as Malcolm paled, and flipped the lid of a *flapkan* in coarse parody. "Too many kisses, you know?"

Malcolm felt a pit open in his stomach, widening as its edges crumbled. "I am sorry to hear it," he said numbly. He did not know what his face betrayed, could not summon concern.

The barmaid, counting up orders from the rest of the table, asked Malcolm if he wanted one of the same. Nodding, he found his hands straying to his pockets, and set them on the table. The ale, when it came, proved to be cheap *kuyte* beer, harsher than the plum or honey brews he had sampled elsewhere. He drank without tasting it, and made his way through the tangle of drinkers like a sleepwalker. Outside the cold air sharpened his senses, and he noticed as he emptied his bladder that he was at least not afflicted by burning water.

And when might that come? Malcolm imagined himself consulting one of the physicians of Delft, and shuddered. He might have studied the progression of venerall maladies at Leiden today had he known. Dreaming of being Fracastoro indeed!

Gales of self-reproach gave way, on the walk home, to a moment of more temperate assessment. What did a tavern girl know of diagnostick? Poor Grietje might be suffering from any manner of ailment or pox: a word by which that spiteful goose might have meant anything. —But so, he told himself, might she have caught a fever or ague from her easy commerce with rogues, which she may have easily transmitted to Malcolm. If *coition* spread the clap or the pox, what other contagions could be contracted by the lesser embraces that accompany the act?

In the candlelight of his room, Malcolm shamefacedly examined himself for signs of infection. Nothing; which merely displaced his anxiety with a more definite mortification: the shame of the child who has stolen fruit uncaught. Tossing in bed, Malcolm dreams of fornication with a Dutchwoman who swells alarmingly. Feeling her distended abdomen, he wonders what he has engendered; but her waters break with a rush, drenching him in a mephitic flood that swarms with tiny creatures.

Pounding on the door, breaking the membrane of sleep. Authoritarian voices called his name, demanding admission. Malcolm kicked loose his blankets in a panic, then caught his breath and managed to shout, "One moment!" Straightening his clothing, he looked at his desk—clear of papers—then opened the door.

A swart Dutchman, rednosed, looked at him with mingled officiousness and curiosity. "I am bailiff for the Sheriffs of Delft," he said, raising slightly one shoulder, which was draped with a sash. "The sheriffs require your assistance on a matter of official business. You do understand Dutch?"

Assistance in official business? Was this some lowland euphemism for present arrest? Malcolm followed the man downstairs, past a curious Vrouw Kluyver and two brewery men carrying in the morning's barrel. The streets were nearly empty: it was still early, not yet breakfast-time. Wondering, Malcolm hurried after the bailiff, who strode off in the direction of the sheriffs' chambers.

The building was a fine one, but Malcolm was led round back, to a mean outhouse at the end of the yard. The bailiff bid Malcolm stand fast and returned with a sheriff, who glowered at Malcolm before unlocking the door with an iron key. A bad smell struck them as it swung open.

The room was small-windowed and dim, and Malcolm saw only a littered bench. "Be these an Englishman's shoes?" the sheriff asked, holding up a pair of low boots.

Bemused, Malcolm examined the pair, which smelled wet. "They appear so," he said, reluctant to touch them.

The sheriff grunted, then pointed behind Malcolm. "The body was found near an embankment at dawn. Though immersed, it appears not to have drowned."

Reluctantly Malcolm turned. Against the far wall stood a long table, a draped form atop it. Even in the poor light Malcolm could plainly recognize the human shape beneath.

The sheriff seized a pole and pushed open a skylight overhead, admitting a thin column of light into the room. Malcolm had not moved toward the table, and with an impatient sound the sheriff stepped forward and yanked back the sheet.

The body beneath—middle-aged, blanched blue like drained veal—seemed no Englishman that Malcolm could recognize, but rather a member of some strange race, a citizen of the republic of the dead. Though its eyes were closed, it resembled a sleeping man less than a statue would, although Malcolm could not say why. It was only as he stood over the supine figure (merely damp-haired now, but a trickle of water running from one ear) that he realized it was Pitcairn.

"The lungs are empty," said a new voice. Malcolm turned to see an older man enter the room. After a second he recognized him as one of Delft's physicians, an acquaintance of Leeuwenhoeck's. The doctor stepped up to the body and struck the chest with his fist. Malcolm jumped. "See?" asked the physician, nodding wisely. "Dead before he slid into the water."

"Do you recognize this body?" asked the sheriff.

"No," said Malcolm shakily. "Is he not from town?"

"Never saw him in my life," the sheriff answered. He returned to the bench and began poking among the effects.

The physician drew off the rest of the sheet, disclosing the body's nakedness. "No buboes," he remarked, lifting one knee to separate the legs. "Neither pocks nor lenticulae on the skin. Had the body not been in the water, one could prove dysentery by examining the breeches."

Malcolm recoiled. "How do you know it was not death by natural means?" he asked.

"Feel," said the physician, placing a hand under the lolling jaw.

"Enlargement of the lymphatic vessels denotes febrile illness." Malcolm made no move to copy him.

Malcolm's head was spinning. Why had they brought him here? Had Pitcairn—impossibly in Holland; in *Delft*—carried papers naming him? He looked sidelong at the sheriff, who was going through the pockets of a dripping waistcoat. Despite himself, Malcolm stared. Pitcairn had been traveling in the dress of a prosperous merchant.

The sheriff looked up, catching Malcolm's expression. Malcolm looked away, cursing himself: had the sheriff noted his surprise? But the Dutchman only said mildly, "Do English coats usually have so many pockets?"

Malcolm looked back. The waistcoat, held open, contained three slits on each inner side, into which the sheriff thrust his fingers one by one. "Empty," he said. "Now one, for money, I could understand."

Malcolm stepped closer. "I am not familiar with the cut of merchants' coats," he said. But would they hold three pairs of inner pockets, like serried gills? The sheriff matter-of-factly inverted the garment and pulled out the six puffs of lining, and Malcolm suddenly felt sick.

"Engorgement of the spleen," said the doctor, pressing down on Pitcairn's pallid belly. The cadaver farted in response, prompting a laugh from the sheriff.

"I am sorry I cannot help you," said Malcolm, wishing desperately to be gone. "If you worry about plague in England, I only know news of London, which is yet vexed with the dysentery. But men are not so quickly afflicted as to die of it while walking out."

"That is true," said the physician. "An autopsy would tell us more."

"I don't want to hear about it," the sheriff told him. He looked at Malcolm. "Thanks for your help. If you learn anything about missing countrymen, I want to know of it."

Malcolm left the building, shaken to his heels. He needed an ale, and didn't feel that he could walk all the way back to Vrouw Kluyver's before getting it. Standing in a tavern filled with breakfasting workmen, he drained a tankard of mead-flavored brew and found his wits softening like stewing beef while the bone of anxiety remained. He returned to the street, now filling with purposeful Dutch, and yearned for coffee.

What in God's name brought Pitcairn here? Malcolm worried the question like a beetle scrabbling to escape a pisspot, slipping back only to seek frantic purchase elsewhere. Grant that Skerrett was a sergeant of spies, where in this covert command stood Pitcairn? who could know neither science nor Dutch, nor possessed (Malcolm was certain) any quality save the willingness to carry out dirty jobs.

Work lay before him, for which enlightenment must wait. In the Kluyvers' back room Malcolm drew ink and coffee close, the backsides of old papers before him like a place-matt. Striving to focus his thoughts, he essayed a scheme for his report: a synopsis of Leeuwenhoeck's recent studies in microscopy, with the letter's true matter, of lenses and burning mirrors, concealed in a seeming aside. Methodically he commenced, but the repeated references to tiny organisms—in semen, pond water, man's very bowels—awoke in Malcolm something close to horror, he knew not why. Treat it in a sentence, he thought: devote the rest to lens-grinding and details of snowflakes.

He threw his notes in the fire, returned to his room and clean papers, and wrote his report in the form of a letter to Mr. Oldenburgh of the Royal Society, full of praise for the peace-loving Dutch and their hospitality to English naturalists. Writing about the *diertgens* troubled him, but a trip downstairs for a second ale dissolved at last the breakwater of his anxiety. Feeling better, Malcolm agreed to join Heer Kluyver in a pipe. If my compatriots tar me a Dutchman, he thought giddily, let me enjoy a Dutchman's pleasures.

The first lungful burned, and the second made him feel as though his head were adrift. "If it weren't for the beer and coffee, you'd be feeling a touch sick," said Kluyver judiciously. Inhaling carefully, Malcolm felt his senses sharpen, as though the world's soft moistness was drying. His anxieties, formless as spilling liquid, he caught within the confines of reason, a container any capable mind can wield.

At once relaxed and alert, he returned to his letter and *discoursed:* upon the possibility of tiny animals swarming through raindrops and dust motes even as their larger brethren fill seas and continents; of further animalcules lying beyond the resolving power of present lenses; of animalcules that may bite Man, as wolves and fleas do, though the victim never know it. Sportively he even proposed that the bite of some tiny creatures may prove venomous like an adder's, so their victims fall sick without comprehending the cause. Report on Leeuwenhoeck's studies? Let Skerrett, who wanted an innocuous-seeming report, rage.

"Commission accomplished," he declared, tucking the papers in a pocket. He strode out into full sunlight, wondering what face Skerrett would present to him when he handed the report over. Did the sailor know that Pitcairn was dead? Would he know that Malcolm knew? Perhaps he would not appear at all, his plans exploded with the death of his confederate, all plots in disarray.

Malcolm wondered what these plots were. He imagined that Pitcairn would be good at firing a lens-grinder's shop, or perhaps breaking a craftsman's fingers. Was Monckton insinuating a band of wreckers into Holland?

Without knowing it, his steps traced a path back toward the sheriff's hall, which he realized only when he looked up to see the bailiff, conversing before the gate with some burgher, pause to eye him curiously. Malcolm almost turned around, but then realized how odd this would look. Nodding slightly, he passed through the gate and went back to the yard, as though he had come with this intention. The door to the outbuilding was ajar, and he approached it cautiously. "Doctor?" he inquired.

"Come in," the physician called. Malcolm pushed the door open. A bad smell wafted out. The physician was standing over the far table, his back to the door. He turned, showing a hand red to the elbow. "Ah, the Englishman. I hoped you'd return. Come have a look at this."

"I don't think I should," said Malcolm quaveringly. The physician turned back to his work. He recognized now the smell: blood, as in a butcher's yard. The thought made his legs weak.

"The spleen," said the physician, "is a mass of disease, and filled with a foul matter, like the lees of oil." He continued to work, and Malcolm realized that he was expected to reply.

"Miasmal fever," he said. He had never worked with a medical specimen larger than a pea, but his book studies held good.

"Indeed," replied the physician. "An *intermittent* rather than a *continuous* fever, as your Sydenham classifies them. Rarely fatal by itself or quickly: and such splenetic ravage is the work of years. Your late countryman was weakened by the ague, but borne off by another illness. Come look at this."

With enormous reluctance, Malcolm took a step forward. The covering sheet was stained red, not the liquid splashes of fresh blood, but the turbid stains of paint. Pitcairn's face was untouched, but the underside of his jaw had been expertly dissected, and his chest opened down the middle like a gutted pig's. Beside the body lay three brownish nodes: each as small as a thumb joint and so dessicated that the ducts at their narrow ends were fraying in paper-thin layers, like an old hornet's nest. Malcolm stared at them in horror.

The physician noticed and dropped them in his pocket. "For my wife," he said. "She would rather plant new bulbs than get a bouquet of tulips." He twitched the sheet farther back. "Note the abscesses in the liver, also (I believe) the lungs. They argue dysentery, as perhaps I should. But these are chronic, not raging, ailments, and not what pushed this man down the embankment and into his grave. Had I to guess that, I would hazard what older physicians called the celestial influences, *influentia coeli.*"

"Influentia?" In England it was best known as the grippe, and killed only sometimes but spread like house-afire. Malcolm wondered what traces it might leave on a body.

"A great killer of those weakened already by other maladies," the physician remarked. "Your late countryman was a walking anthology of febrile illnesses, some—" he poked at the viscid spleen— "recently returned. Like a shed rotted through, it collapsed with one kick."

The physician pulled the sheet back over the opened body. "Is that fever not now epidemic in England?" he asked as he wiped his hands on a rag.

"Perhaps only in London," Malcolm answered weakly. The flap of the sheet had disturbed the air, and the stench of diseased innards blew over him. His last taste of Pitcairn.

The physician opened the door, and Malcolm followed him with relief into the yard. "What know you of Sydenham?" the Dutchman asked, as though all lettered Englishmen must know each other.

Malcolm was still seeking to recover the discrimination of his mental faculty, whelmed by the primacy of sight like an owl dazzled by a torch. "I read his book on fevers," he said vaguely. He had paged through it only to see whether the author had made use of a microscope in his researches. "His energies, if I recall, were devoted to treating the living, not inquiring into the mechanisms of pestilence."

"I must look back into it myself." They had reached the street, and the physician glanced at his watch, as though fain to be off, and scowled. "I do not like diseased foreigners dying in Delft and falling into our waters. My business is done, but I hope future visitors will be healthier."

And with a touch of his hat, he took his leave. Malcolm watched him disappear round a corner, feeling impugned by his shared nationality with Pitcairn. He wanted to rush after the physician and confide in him, explaining that the dead man was his persecutor, not countryman. *I am as much Dutch as English.* Spoken, he realized suddenly, with an undoubted English accent.

Malcolm felt unsettled in mind and stomach, as though he had had too much tobacco and needed more beer, or perhaps the reverse. As the sight of Pitcairn receded from the forecourts of his consciousness, the remaining mysteries returned, like vapors expanding to fill a void. Malcolm tried to recall what he knew of Sydenham, who practiced medicine in poorer London, despite the fact that his brother, as a founder of the Protectorate, had wielded tremendous power under Cromwell—

Realization fell on him like a roof collapsing, as though only a bulwark of refusal, holding back facts like a dike, had kept the truth at bay. A piece of it broke free and struck him, like wreckage swept by a flood, and Malcolm felt himself, awash in truth, go under.

What did Monckton know? He could ask Sydenham about febrile contagions, and doubtless had, but what did he *know?* That the grippe spread quickly, running through households and tenements like plague, while the miasmal fever afflicted only certain geographies. That smallpox ravaged the young, while dysentery proved mainly fatal among the elderly. That a man with plague could infect a city, but no one knew the particulars of contagion.

Malcolm walked out the town gates and along a canal path, unmindful of his surroundings. A nearby windmill squealed as a quickening breeze pushed its vanes, and ducks in the pond below quacked and thrashed their wings as though feeling the water being drained. Malcolm paused, then looked across the low wet ground that pooled at the foot of the windmill. The drier ground beyond had been divided by perpendicular ditches, as though order were being imposed on the vagaries of nature.

What did Monckton know? He knew what Leeuwenhoeck had written the Society, though not his every surmise. He had connections with scholars at Cambridge, so would know, if he inquired, that Fracastorius believed contagions to be spread by imperceptible particles, and that Marcus Varro believed that such particles were tiny creatures. Should he ask a professor of history, thought Malcolm with a numb shock, he would know the tale of how the plague reached Christendom when the Mongols besieging Caffa hurled the bodies of plague victims over the walls.

Pitcairn the factotum came to Holland, and died of a grippe while walking the waters outside Delft. What had he been doing there? Had he been carrying something strange, the sheriff would have asked Malcolm about it. Had he delivered papers to Skerrett? Was he come to collect Malcolm's?

Broken glass twinkled at the edge of the embankment, the first trash that Malcolm had seen in scrubbed Delft. The sight was faintly sickening, and he imagined Pitcairn's body floating in the water, to be seen by some early-rising workman. A carcass would spoil drinking water; he was glad that the town used the river.

Monckton, did he care to, knew enough. Sages had suggested since antiquity that the bad air and bad water that carried contagion might harbor minute particles as the actual agents; that certain fevers were spread by their victims did not contradict this. And with the advent of Hooke's micrographia and Leeuwenhoeck's improved instruments, these teachings could at last be tested.

The enormity of the realization crashed over Malcolm like a wave of nausea. Silas Monckton wanted to know whether the sources of contagion could be identified and marshaled, like weapons pressed into service. And Malcolm, of the Royal Society, had been cozened into assisting this project, on the grounds (less ignoble) of spying out Holland's researches in a different science.

So distracted was he that Malcolm was long minutes shifting his wonder from *What did Monckton know?* to *Is it true?* Do the *diertgens* thrive in the blood and humours like pond water, there to multiply and give affliction? That the venerall diseases were spread by the contact of genital mucosa, swarming with various living fluids (Malcolm winced at this), suggested as much. He wondered whether Pitcairn, drudge of the unspeakable, had been poking about the pestholes of England to contract the ague that had killed him.

To the north the *trekvaart* cut a straight line across the cultivated fields: Malcolm noticed it only when he saw a canal boat cruising statelily through a field of grain. A half mile away the canal crossed a stream, becoming an aqueduct notched with waste-weirs like a castle wall. Like animalcules carried through blood vessels, the boats slipped through the saturated tissues of Holland; and what they carried within them no one, at a distance, could say.

Malcolm returned to town and went to Leeuwenhoeck's office, where he knew the draper would be preparing sections from the lens of a cow's-eye he had lately acquired. Malcolm presented himself, but was turned away by a young medical student, who told him brusquely that Heer Leeuwenhoeck would not be able to receive him. A spyglass, which Malcolm had lent the draper as an example of British lenscraft, was thrust into his hands, and without ceremony he was bid good day.

And what, Malcolm thought, does this leave him? He did not care to wonder what Leeuwenhoeck knew or believed; the uncertainty of his own prospects was concern enough. He imagined being sent back to England to oversee researches into miasmic fevers on the Yorkshire moors, perhaps dying like Pitcairn in the process.

He turned the spyglass over in his hands, wishing he could make a present of it to young Moete. A triumph of English lensmakers, who labor to perfect the refraction of light while others strive to make it bounce. Would Moete appreciate the gesture? "I would rather *Reflect* than *prove Refractory*," he says in Malcolm's imagination. With the smile that, Malcolm now realized, he shall never see again.

He put the spyglass in his pocket, touching as he did so the folded letter. Harder to imagine Skerrett's response to Malcolm's offering. He wouldn't read it in the twilight, assuming he could read. Why meet in darkness and seclusion, when Malcolm could pass over the letter behind a privy? The arrangement seemed decidedly sinister.

Malcolm walked to the brewery, a white-washed structure built up against a stream, which carried for a hundred yards the smell of scorched mash. The brewers, unsurprisingly, made use of the city's sweetest and most fast-moving water; the ceramics manufacturies made do with the others. Malcolm followed the north side of the stream out of town, to an impoldered field so low that a river dike kept the stream in its banks. The *interwaarden* that lay between the water and the dike measured perhaps a hundred yards long, a fallow strip of land, probably submerged in winter, that even the enterprising Dutch could not put to use.

Malcolm sat and smoked a pipe as he watched a rain front roll in from the sea. The windmill turning a half mile away was, he realized after a moment, the same one he had seen earlier: the field it drained ran up to the dike. Below the windmill, an Archimedean screw reached down into the pond like a giant proboscis supping at a puddle.

A thin drizzle fell, and Malcolm hunched into his collar, willing himself not to grow soaked. Skerrett was (his vantage told him) not in the area; and Malcolm wanted to observe his arrival, so not to cede advantage to the rogue. Huddling in the open ground, he fell into a shallow doze, as midafternoon quickly deepened under the pall of cloud. The dreams that come take no coherent form: *diertgens* with snapping jaws; a conviction of nameless dread. Malcolm wakes in horror, neck-cricked and wet, and sees the sun settling onto the western horizon, flattening like a yolk about to break. He stands, looking around wildly for fear that Skerrett had already arrived.

No one is on the dike, but after a moment Malcolm saw motion in the field. A small boat, no larger than those wherrymen use to carry single passengers across the Thames, was making its way down a narrow ditch toward the dike. The seated figure—Malcolm instantly recognized Skerrett—was probably invisible to anyone at ground level, a drifting shadow on the darkening plain.

Malcolm also realized that Skerret had certainly seen *him*— standing against the sky like an archer's target. An awful pang cut through him: he had come early to anticipate the spy, but his strategy had misfired: first possession of the *interwaarden* betrayed one's presence to the latecomer, who sees you search for him.

The sun sank to a slice while Skerrett tied up his boat and climbed leisurely up the graded embankment. Even thus his gait bespoke insolence, and he did not trouble to look at Malcolm until he was ten feet away. "Early to the dance?" he asked sardonically.

Malcolm pulled the report from his pocket. "As commissioned," he said.

The sailor simply held out his hand. After a moment Malcolm, flushing, took the three steps forward to give it to him. Malcolm scarcely glanced at the sheets before tucking them away. "And so?" he said.

Malcolm faced him squarely. "The Dutch do not have the capacity to construct a burning mirror," he said solemnly.

"Pah," spat Skerrett. "You're not so stupid as that. Tell me you didn't inquire after Leeuwenhoeck's knowledge of plagues and I'll cut your throat right now."

Malcolm felt his belly tighten. "Your master wants to know whether Leeuwenhoeck's studies of *micro-phenomena* have disclosed the agents of contagion," he said, foolish with indignation. "Leeuwenhoeck won't say. He's a respectable man, and declined to speak much of experiments with human fluids. I also suspect he thought the knowledge dangerous. So you may tell Mr. Monckton that the Dutchman might share his surmise, but that *natural philosophers*, in England or Holland, will not turn their skills to warcraft."

Skerret laughed. "They don't, do they? While you've been gabbling with the close-mouthed Dutch, your betters in Cambridge have solved the problem. Your report will prove no more than an addendum to the true matter."

Malcolm gaped. Skerrett turned to go, then glanced back contemptuously, one foot already on the downward slope. "You light-benders can make far things look near, but you don't actually *do* anything, do you? Spectacle-makers! *Lens-wrights!* If Leeuwenhoeck keeps quiet, so much the better for us: Englishmen make use of what they know."

"And is that how Pitcairn came to die?" asked Malcolm. "Taking samples from pest-houses, that a tame microscopist might assay them for your armory?" Shame for his suborned colleagues fanned the coals of Malcolm's ire.

"*Die?*" The sailor stared.

"They found his body floating. He expired from a medley of contagions."

"Thomas dead!" Skerrett seemed genuinely shocked. He drew a breath and asked, "Did they find aught on his body?"

"Nothing at all," Malcolm said. He remembered the six empty inner pockets of Pitcairn's waistcoat.

"Then he died a hero. The arrows are over the wall! Whether they fire the roofs or no, more shall follow." Fierce jubilance entered his voice.

Malcolm stared at Skerrett. "You *what?*" he demanded. A second passed, as comprehension charged one like a sulphur globe and sparked comprehension in the other; then both men leaped.

Malcolm was the slower, but his better footing saved him. He saw the knife flash in the twilight, then turned and was running. Downhill in near darkness: madness, even with the Dutch builders' smooth inclines. He stumbled, plunged headlong and hit the ground fast, then was rolling and on his feet without pausing to look back.

The smell of asparagus rose about him as he tore through planted rows, then a slip on muddy ground sent him sprawling forward. He realized that he was falling into a ditch an instant before he struck water, and the cold shock cleared his mind as though the depths shone with sunlight. A man who stands up in a ditch is immediately overtaken, while one who swims underwater is invisible and soundless. Malcolm kicked, feeling his coat trail the surface for a second before he angled deeper, and brushed his hand against the shallow bottom. Ten strokes, his lungs burning, and he surfaced as quietly as he could. Angry thrashing noises reached him from some near distance, and he pushed his heels along the bottom, face up like an otter as he drifted slowly away.

What else floated in this water? Fevers bred in the miasma rising from stagnant waters; could such effluvia be introduced in a bottle, like holy water? Malcolm spat away the ditchwater on his lips.

The thought that the draining waters were infected brought horror, with an aftertaste of shame. *Englishmen* had done this, *naturalists?* Those who bent light had bent their neck to the yoke of Charles, who bent his in turn to the moneyed tyrant Louis.

The wind shifted, and the sound of the creaking windmill was suddenly louder. Shivering, Malcolm climbed from the water under the cover of noise and made for its source, invisible in the cloudy night. He did not hear pursuit, but neither stopped to listen.

Those who warp the light can shape the world. Malcolm hadn't believed it—what present use for those who count moons, or describe a louse's leg?—but he did now. The realm of other worlds is far away, but the micro-realm is all about us: we *are* it, as a foundry is its bricks. Who knows the strength of bricks shall be heeded by builders.

The ground grew wetter as he approached the windmill, and Malcolm found himself making shallow splashes with each step. Worried that these would betray him, he broke into a run. A wooden stairway hugged the bulwark, and Malcolm reached it in a spray of long strides. He had climbed three steps when he was hit from behind.

He crashed against the steps before him, losing his footing and kicking out (his nerves reacting faster than his mind) with one upended sole. The foot struck flesh, driving his shoulder against a step. Cold rain touched his back, and Malcolm realized that his coat had been slashed.

He kicked again, making glancing contact. Skerrett fell atop him, and Malcolm heard a soft *thunk* by his ear, the unmistakable sound of a knife biting wood. In a frenzy he kicked and scrambled upward. The middle of the staircase swayed beneath him.

A hand grabbed his foot, and Malcolm snatched at a bannister, which came loose as he pulled at it. In terror he swung it round, and it knocked against bone with a thrill. The hand let go, and Malcolm scrambled over the top.

The rain stung his spine, and Malcolm reached back to touch sticky warmth. How could he have been cut, and no pain? yet there seemed a lot of blood. Slipping in the mud, he stumbled toward the windmill, a great invisible rumbling overhead. The Archimedean screw emerged beneath the structure, disgorging into a channel that ran away from the windmill and across the plain like a highway. The water spilling from the screw was inaudible beneath the rain and the cavernous rumble of the gearing.

Feeling carefully along the canal wall, Malcolm found the edge of the sluice-gate with his fingertips. The screw was turning, and up-lifted water was pushing open the gate to flow through. He crawled forward several feet, until his hat brushed the cross-beam of the trestle. He was underneath the windmill, out of the rain but in total darkness.

Fumbling with his flint and touchwood, Malcolm got his pipe lit; then drawing hard on the tobacco (he had no paper on him), he produced enough of a light to see a few inches around. As beneath any mill, the ground under the trestle was scattered with sawdust and loose splints, some not yet wet. After a minute Malcolm got a small torch smoldering, and cast wavering shadows across the low space. And with the return of light Malcolm (to his surprise) could suddenly think.

What had Pitcairn done? Broken glass; spleen like cheese. Was Malcolm truly thinking, to think this?

Wooden-toothed but regular as crystal, the gearing of the shaft and bevel wheel turned as steadily as a wagon wheel meeting its re-flection in a puddle. Malcolm could only see the topmost flange of the screw, which revolved like the bore of a drill that dug out water instead of shavings. The yield seemed less than you could produce with a pump, yet it would in time drain a marsh.

Sawdust was sticking to his hands, which he noticed were black with blood. How badly was he hurt? He could not twist far enough to see.

The ground was littered with rubbish and broken bricks; Malcolm picked up the largest one and crawled over to the sluice. He lowered himself into the water—ah God, it was cold!—as the torch guttered out. The water was but three feet deep, yet the chill penetrated instantly to the bone.

Malcolm bent and wedged the brick between the sluice-gate and its stop, preventing it from swinging shut when the upflow of water ebbed. When the screw ceased turning, the water would run down it like a cascade.

But the screw was still turning, more rapidly than the vanes overhead: which seemed superior to the English models, so turned (if slowly) in even slight winds. Malcolm imagined the miller discovering the wedged sluice-gate in the morning, and wading in to remove the brick. He slid further into the water and felt for the pin. His fingers encountered only slippery smoothness, and he was suddenly weak. Immersion, he thought dizzily, would only open further his wound.

He climbed out with difficulty, then failed to get a second torch lit. Drenched and shaking fingers let the flint drop, and Malcolm could feel his sleeves drip on the touchwood. Very well, he thought: Some acts are fit only for darkness. He felt for another brick, feeling as though he were about to smash a fine watch.

He held the brick before him as he crept toward the gearing, thinking: *If I fumble, I'll lose my hand.* The brick brushed a moving surface, which knocked it almost from his grasp. Suppressing a scream, Malcolm leaned toward the source of the grinding roar, then gritted his teeth and thrust his hand into it.

Something seized the brick from his fingers, and he snatched his hand back. The gears screamed like a stabbed pig, and the shaft above groaned with dismay. Teeth splintered, and the gears slipped, snapping more teeth. With a shearing sound the vertical shaft was suddenly turning free, and the screw was still.

Malcolm was sobbing with fear, which rushed now into his heart just as the water in the tailrace was now flowing back into the field. It was only after a minute that he heard clumping overhead. Of course: the miller, resident in the mill itself, was coming forth to investigate.

He scrambled out from beneath the trestle, into wind and rain. How soon before the miller, investigating his broken gears, noticed the jammed gate and shut it? How fully could the field flood meanwhile?

Malcolm slipped and fell in mud, then crawled toward the sluice. It was raining harder now, and he could hear the miller's shouts, and see faint light from a window above. The sluice-gate had swung to as the upflow ceased, and was now open only by a brick's width. Malcolm saw a wooden bench a dozen feet away and toppled it into the sluice, wedging the gate wide open. The exertion and pain nearly caused him to fall in after it.

Had other ponds been polluted? Delft's drinking water came from the Schie, so seemed immune from infection. Had Pitcairn visited other cities on his way in from the Hague? Did his coat of foul pockets contain bottles of other plagues? Malcolm could not know.

A thump resounded through the trestle: not from above, where the miller was now throwing open the door, but below, in the stilled screw assembly. Unsocketed at the top like a disjointed chicken leg, the screw was being pushed out of place by the water flowing down it. A log nudged over a cataract, it tilted from its trough, and the rush of water was suddenly louder.

Jubilance filled Malcolm, jostling horror. The polder would be flooded before workmen stopped the sluice, its miasmal damps a shallow lake. Malcolm realized that he was looking at the sky, rain pelting his face. His back was very cold.

Was the air blowing in the storm being cleansed of infection by the rain? One could collect rainwater in a basin, examine it beneath the microscope for *animalcula*. But would the naturalists conduct such an experiment to identify and exterminate the creatures, or to breed them? Water in his eyes, Malcolm apprehended a world changed unforeseeably by the wresting of light, a watch-case prised open by naturalists yet unborn: men who knew that nature's secrets lay open to those who focus finely, children of the lens.

ROBERT REED

KILLING THE MORROW

You know, I've heard my share of disembodied voices. I'm accustomed to their fickle, sometimes bizarre demands. But tonight's voice is different, clear as gin and utterly compelling. I must listen. Sitting inside my old packing crate, my worldly possessions at arm's length, I am fed instructions that erase everything familiar and prosaic. Yet I cannot resist, can't offer even a token resistance, now crawling out of my little house and rising, my heart pounding as the last shreds of sanity are lost to me.

I've lived in this alleyway for eight months, yet I don't look back. I'm in poor physical condition and my shoes are worn through, but I walk several miles without rest, without complaint. And there are others, too: the streets are full of silent walkers. They exhibit a calmness, a liquid orderliness, that would disturb the healthy observer. Yet I barely notice the others. I want a specific street, which I find, turning right and following it for another mile. The tall buildings fall away into trim working-class houses. Another street beckons. I start to read the numbers on mailboxes. The house I want is on a corner, lit up and its front door left open. I step inside without ringing the bell, thinking that the place looks familiar . . . as if I've been here before, or maybe seen it in dreams. . . .

My new life begins.

More than most people, I have experience with radical change, with the vagaries of existence. Tonight's change is simply more sudden and more tightly orchestrated than those of the past. I'm here for a reason, no doubt about it. There's some grand cause that will be explained in due time. And meanwhile, there's pleasure: for the first time in years, existence has a palatable purpose, authority, and as astonishing as it seems, a genuine beauty.

An opened can of warming beer is set on the coffee table. I pick it up and sniff, then set it down again, which is uncharacteristic for me. An enormous television is in the corner, the all-sports channel still broadcasting, nothing to see but an empty court and arena. The game was canceled without fuss. Somehow I know that nobody will ever again play that particular sport, that it was rendered extinct in an instant. Yet any sense of loss is cushioned by the Voice. It makes me crumble onto a lumpy sofa, listening and nodding, eyes fixed on nothing.

Tools are in the garage, I'm told. I carry them into the living room, arranging them according to their use. Then armed with a short rusty crowbar I head upstairs, finding the bathroom and a big steel bathtub, and with the crowbar I start to batter the mildewed tile and plaster, startled cockroaches fleeing the light.

After a little while the front door opens, closes.

I go downstairs, part of me curious. A handsome woman is waiting for me, offering a thin smile. She's dressed in quality clothes, and she's my age but with much less mileage. That smile of hers is hopeful, even enthusiastic, but beneath it is a much-hidden sense of terror.

What's her name? I wonder. But I won't ask.

Nor does she ask about me.

With two backs available, we start to clear the living room of furniture and the dusty old carpeting. By now the television has gone blank. I unplug it, and together we carry it to the curb. Electronics are an important resource. Our neighbors—mismatched couples like ourselves—are doing the same job, stereos and microwave ovens and televisions stacked and covered carefully with plastic. Firearms make smaller, secondary piles. Then around midnight a large truck arrives. I'm dragging out the last of the carpeting, pausing long enough to watch a crew of burly men loading everything into the long trailer. One of them seems familiar. He was a police officer, wasn't he? I remember him. He bullied me on several occasions, for the fun of it. And now we are equals, animosity nothing but a luxury. I manage to wave at him. No response. Then I return to the house, never hurrying. Rain begins to fall, fat cold drops striking the back of my neck, and with them comes a fatigue, sudden and profound, that leaves my legs shaking and my breath coming in little wet gulps.

The Voice has already told us to sleep when it's needed. The woman and I move upstairs, climbing into the same bed without undressing. Nudity is permitted. Many things are permitted, we've been told. But I can't help thinking of the woman's terror as I lie beside her, looking as I do, unshaved and filthy, wearing sores and months of grime. It's better to do nothing, I decide. Just to sleep.

"Good night," I whisper.

She isn't crying, but when she says, "Sleep well," I hear her working not to cry, the words tight and slow. Was she married in her former life? She doens't wear any rings, yet she seems like a person who would enjoy, even demand marriage. She's awake for more than an hour, lying as motionless as possible, her ordinary old parts struggling to find some reason for the bizarre things that are happening now.

I feel pity.

Yet for the most part, I like these changes. The bed is soft, the sheets almost clean. I lie awake out of contentment, listening to the rain on the roof and thinking about my packing crate in the alleyway—feeling no fondness at all for that dead past.

I dream of grass, astonishing as that seems.

Of an apeman.

No, that's a lousy term. *Hominid* is more appropriate. The creature walks under a bright tropical sky, minding its own narrow business. A male, I realize. I'm sitting in the future, watching it from ground level and feeling waves of excitement. Here is an ancestor of the human species, naked and lovely, and it doesn't even notice me, strolling past and out of sight. I have seen through time, changing nothing. Aren't I a clever ape? I ask myself.

Not clever enough, a voice warns me.

A quiet, almost whispered voice.

We divide our jobs according to ability. Being somewhat stronger than the woman, I work to dislodge the bathtub from the wall, then lever it into the hallway and shove it down the splintering wooden stairs. And meanwhile the woman has cleaned the living room a dozen times, at least, the windows covered with foil and the air heavy with chlorine.

Vans and small trucks begin to deliver equipment. Thermostats and filters have been adapted from local stocks, I suppose. More sophisticated machinery arrives later. Jugs of thick clear fluid are stacked in the darkest corner. Perfect cleanliness isn't mandatory, yet the woman struggles to keep the room surgically clean, hoping that the Voice will applaud her efforts.

She's first to say, "The Voice comes from the future."

Obviously, yes.

"From the distant future," she adds.

I can't guess dates, but it seems likely.

"And this is a womb," she remarks, pointing at the old bathtub. "Here is where the future will be born."

The Voice speaks differently to different people, it seems. I assumed that the tub was an elaborate growth chamber, but how exactly does one grow the future?

Taking me by the waist, she says, "It'll be like our own child."

I make affirmative sounds, but something feels wrong.

"I love you," she assures me.

"I love you," I lie. Nothing is as vital to her as her illusions of the loving family.

Does the Voice know that?

In the night, between work and sleep, she invites me to her side of the bed. It's been a long time. My performance is less than sterling, but at least the experience is pleasant, building new bonds. Then afterward we cuddle under the sheets, whisper in secret tones, then drift off into a fine deep sleep, dreams coming from the darkness.

Rain falls in my dreams.

Motion, I learn, is matter shaped by the hand of Chaos. Tiny variations in wind and moisture will conspire to ignite or extinguish entire storms. And no conceivable machine or mind can know every fluctuation, every inspiration. It's not even possible to predict which minuscule event will produce the perfect day, leaving millions of lives changed, the fundamental shape of everything warped ever so slightly. . . .

Suppose you can reach back in time, says my dream voice. Suppose you're aware of the dangers in changing what was, but you have ego enough to accept the risks. Channeling vast energies, you create your windows entirely from local materials. It is thermally identical to the surrounding ground. You limit your study to a few useful moments. All you allow yourself is a camera and transmitter, intricate but indistinguishable from the local sand and grit. The hominid can stare at the window. He can stomp on it. He can fling it, eat it, or simply ignore it. But nothing, nothing, nothing he can do will make it behave as anything but the perfect grain of dirty quartz.

And yet, says the dream voice.

Despite your hard work and cleverness, there is some telling impact. Perhaps heat leaked from the mechanism, atoms jostled by their touch. Or perhaps its optical energies were imperfectly balanced, excess photons added to or taken away from the local environment. There would be no way to know what went wrong. But the consequences will spread, becoming apparent, growing from nothing until they encompass everything.

The universe, I'm learning, is incomprehensibly fragile.

How can any person, any intelligence, hope to put *everything* back where it belongs?

❖ ❖ ❖

A young man delivers foodstuffs and other general supplies, coming twice a week, and sometimes he lingers on the porch, telling me what he has seen around town. Factories and warehouses have been refurbished, he says. Old people and eerily patient children work and live inside them. Some of the factories make the machines that fill my living room/nursery. But the majority of the products are stranger. He grins, describing brilliant lights and tiny power plants, robots and more robots. Isn't it all amazing? Wondrous? And fun?

I nod. Astonishment does seem like the day's most abundant product.

The woman dislikes my chatting with the young man. She feels that he's a poor worker, obviously not paying ample attention to the Voice. For the first time, for just an instant, I wonder if the Voice doesn't touch people with equal force. For instance, the woman claims to hear it all of the time, her initial terror replaced with energy and commitment, or at least the nervous desire to please it. But for me there are long periods of silence, of relative peace. It's the woman who wakes first in the morning. It's the woman who loses track of time and hunger, scrubbing the floor until her hands bleed. And she's the one who snaps at the delivery boy, telling him:

"You're not helping us at all!"

To which he says, "Except I am." At once, without hesitation, he says, "Part of my job is to tell others what I see, to keep them aware of what's being done. How else can you know? You can't go anywhere. Your job is to stay put, and you're doing that perfectly."

The logic has its impact. She retreats with a growl, her anger helping her to polish the bathtub for the umpteenth time.

I wonder, in secret, if the delivery boy is telling the truth.

Or is he a clever liar?

And how can I wonder about such things? Just considering the possibility of subterfuge is a kind of subterfuge. Particularly when I find myself admiring the boy's courage.

In secret.

The past has been changed, I learn in my sleep.

Small events have evolved into mammoth ones.

Perhaps an excess heat caused an instability that altered the precise pattern of raindrops in a summer shower. Hominids made love in the rain. It's not that they wouldn't have had rain, but it's the delicate impact of thousands of raindrops that matter. Eggs and sperm are extraordinarily sensitive, I'm learning. Change any parameter—the instant of ejaculation; the angle of thrust; the simplest groan of thanks—and a different sperm will find its target. Even the drumming of raindrops will jostle the testicles enough, now and again, and produce different offspring. Which in turn means a different human evolution.

The species isn't altered appreciably. People remain people, good and not. Nor is the character of history changed. Humankind will master the same tools, then warfare and the intricacies of nation-states. What matters is that the specific faces will change, and the names, every historical figure erased along with every anonymous one, an enormous wavelike disruption racing out through time.

In order to kill myself, I don't have to kill my grandpa.

I just have to tickle his hairy balls.

They bring the embryo in, of all things, an old florist's van.

Each house on our street gets its own embryo, and the Voice fills everyone with a sense of honor and duty. We've sealed the bathtub's drain, then filled it with the heavy fluids. Tubes pump in oxygen. The workers connect the embryo to a plastic umbilical, then I help the woman check every dial and sensor, making certain that the tiny smear of living tissue is healthy.

It doubles in size, that day and every day, hands and feet showing before the end of the week. It's not growing like any human, but maybe that's a consequence of the fluids. Or synthetic genes. Or maybe all the generations of evolution between him and me.

The woman shivers, weeps. Holding herself, she announces, "At least one of us has to stay with it now. Always."

In case of some unlikely, unforeseen problem, yes. We can pick up the telephone, emergency services waiting to troubleshoot.

"Night and day," she says, with a thrill.

I'll give her the night shift, I decide.

"This is our child," she claims, repeating what the Voice tells her. Her own voice is stiff and dry. Unabashedly fanatical. "Don't you think he's lovely, darling?"

But he's not my child, or my grandchild, either. For an instant, I consider mentioning my dreams of Africa and the vagaries of time . . . but then I think again, some piece of me guessing that this woman has had no such dreams.

"Isn't he lovely?" she asks again.

I say, "Lovely," without feeling.

Yet the word itself is enough for her. She nods and smiles, her face lit up with the injected joy.

The past is a sea, I dream. A great flat mirror of a sea. Standing on the present, on a low shoreline, I carelessly throw a grain of sand over my shoulder. Its impact is tiny, too tiny to observe, but the resulting wave is growing, a small ripple becoming a mountainous wall rushing straight at me.

What can I do? Flee into the future? But with each step the future becomes the present, and I can never run so far that the wave won't catch me, utterly and forever dissolving my existence.

But there is one answer. Pack a bag, bend at the knees, and wait. Wait, then leap. With care and a certain desperate fearlessness, I can launch myself over the wave, evading it entirely. Then I'll fall again, tumbling onto the calm past, creating a second obliterating wave but my own life saved regardless.

Fuck the costs.

Our "child" is less childlike with each passing day.

Even the woman is having difficulty sounding like the proud parent.

Curled in a fetal position, this citizen from the future resembles a middle-aged man, comfortably plump and shockingly hairy, lost in sleep while his memories are placed inside his newly minted mind.

I can't help but notice, his brain is huge.

I sit alone with him in the morning and again in the early evening, nothing to do but watch his slumber as well as the humming and clicking machines. It's ironic that this creature, having his existence threatened by the most trivial event, is now employing the coarsest tomfoolery to save his ass. The entire Earth must be involved. Every human and every resource is being marshaled to meet some rigorous schedule. This is an invasion; and like any invasion, success hinges on the beachhead.

The future is attempting to leap over its extinction, very little room for error.

And I'm beginning to notice how the Voice, busy speaking to this superman's mind, speaks less and less to me.

The Voice has its limits, of course.

Yet at night my dreams persist, that different voice showing me wonders as fascinating as anything in my waking life.

The delivery boy begins to arrive at irregular intervals, but never as often as before.

"To save gas," he claims, always smiling. But that smile has a satirical bite to it. "And from now on, sorry. There's no more meat or eggs."

For health reasons, perhaps. Or the invaders could be vegetarians.

"Let me look at yours," says the boy, stepping indoors for the first time. He doesn't wait for approval, walking up to the bathtub and staring at the sleeping shape. "I wonder what he's like. When he's finished, I mean."

I have no idea. And that bothers me.

"Of course he'll be grateful for your help. I'm sure of that."

I'm nervous. It's against every rule to have visitors. What if the woman wakes early and finds the boy here? What if a neighbor reports me? Touching a shoulder, I try easing him toward the door, asking in a whisper, "What have you seen lately?"

He mentions giant machines that have rolled to the north. Bright lights show at night, and there's rumbling that might mean construction. A new city is being built, he hears. From others.

I ask about the people who built those rolling machines. Where have they gone?

"They've been reassigned, of course. There's always work to be done somewhere. Always, always."

He smiled at me, the message in his eyes.

Then we reach the door, and again he stands on the porch, telling me, "Once a week, and I don't know which day. No meat, no eggs. And that's a lovely boy you've got there. A real darling."

I wash myself daily, using a shower in the basement. Rationing my soap, I've managed to stay clean for six months in a row. My loose-fitting clothes come from the closets and drawers. When they're gone, I put the soiled ones in the sun, cleaning them with light and heat.

I wanted to seem more attractive to the woman, and for a little while she was responding.

But now she has doubts about sex, always distracted, needing to be in some position that leaves her able to monitor the dials. More and more she complains about being tired or disinterested. The man-child's presence makes her edgy. I wish she'd become pregnant, except of course a pregnancy would be a problem. A division of allegiances. But then I realize that if the Voice can speak to a mind, interfacing with its network of interlocking neurons, then shouldn't it be able to speak to glands as well? Couldn't it put all of our bothersome sperm and eggs to sleep?

One night, waking alone in bed, I feel a powerful desire to make love to a woman. I come downstairs and ask permission, and the woman's response is a sharp "Not here, no!" Which leads me to suggest that she abandon her post for a few minutes. I promise to hurry, and where's the harm?

She gasps, moans, and nearly collapses. "I can't do *that*."

We'll never couple again. I know it, and it both saddens and relieves me. Alone, I feel free. An old reflex lets me wonder where I could find someone else. A lady more amiable, someone that I've selected for myself.

Beginning tomorrow morning, the woman sleeps in the living

room, on sheets and pillows spread over the clean hard floor.

She won't leave me alone at my post.

She has a bucket next to the door where she pisses and shits. And when she looks at me, in those rare moments, nothing can hide her total scorn.

This is my last lucid dream.

I'm standing on the beach, sand without color and a wall of radiant ocean water roaring toward me. And a woman appears. Like the man in my bathtub, she has an elongated skull and a superior intellect, but her face is completely human, showing a mixture of fear and empathy, as well as a sturdy strength born of convictions.

"We think they are wrong," she begins. "Please remember this. Not all of us are like *them.*"

I nod, trying to describe my appreciation.

But she interrupts, telling me, "This is all we can do for you."

I can't recognize her language, yet I understand every word.

"Best wishes," she says.

Then she begins to cry.

I try to embrace her. I step forward and open my arms . . . but then the water is on me, the beach and her dissolving into atoms . . . and my hands struggle to reassemble her from memory, the task impossible for every good reason. . . .

A new delivery boy arrives.

Perhaps ten years old, he needs to make two trips from his station wagon, carrying the minimal groceries to the porch and no farther. I'm standing on my porch waiting for the second load. Fresh air feels pleasant. The lawn has grown shaggy and seedy, the old furniture and carpeting rotting without complaint amidst the greenness. A quick calculation tells me that this is late autumn, early winter. The trees should have changed and lost their leaves by now. Yet the world smells and tastes like spring, both climate and vegetation under some kind of powerful control.

The boy struggles with a numbered sack. Not only is he small, he looks malnourished. But he brings my food with a fanatical sense of purpose, and when I ask about the other boy, the older boy, he merely replies:

"He's done."

What does that mean?

"Done," he repeats, angry not to be understood.

Hearing our voices, the woman wakes and comes to the door. "Get back in here," she snaps. "I'm warning you!"

One last look at the improved world, then I retreat, taking both sacks with me. Meanwhile the boy fires up the station wagon, black smoke dispersing in all directions. He looks silly, that fierce little head peering through the steering wheel. He pulls into the next driveway, and I wonder who lives in that house. And what do they dream about?

The woman is complaining about my attitudes, my carelessness. Everything. I'm a safer subject than the lousy quality of today's barley and rice.

"Come here," she tells me.

Perhaps I will, perhaps I won't.

"Or I'll pick up the phone and complain," she threatens.

She won't. First of all, I terrify her. What if I extracted some kind of vengeance in response? And secondly, the thought of being entirely alone must disturb her. I know it whenever I stare at her, making her shrink away. As much as she hates me, without my presence she might forget that she's genuinely alive.

The future doomed itself.

Then it packed its bags, intending to save itself.

But like a weather system, the future is too large and chaotic to be of one mind, holding to a single outcome. Some of its citizens argued that they didn't have the right to intrude on the past. "Why should we supplant these primitive people?" they asked. "We screwed up, and if we were any sort of hominids, we would accept our fate and be done with it."

But most of their species felt otherwise. And by concentrating the energies of two earths, present and past, they felt there was a better than good chance of success.

Unaware of the secret movement in their midst.

Never guessing that there was a second surreptitious Voice.

Alarms wake me, and I rush downstairs just as the man-child is born. With a slow majesty, he sits up in the bathtub, the thick fluids sliding off his slick and hairy body. The beep-beep of the alarms quit, replaced with a scream from the woman. "Look at you," she says. "Oh, look at you!"

The man couldn't look more pissed, coughing until his lungs clear, then screwing up his face, saying something in that future language. A nearby machine activates itself, translating his words. "I want water. Cold water. Get me water."

"I'll get it," I say.

The woman is too busy grinning and applauding herself. "You're a darling lovely man, sir. And I took care of you. Almost entirely by myself, I did."

The man-child speaks again.

"I'm still thirsty," the machine reports, both voices impatient.

In the kitchen, propped next to the back door, is the same crowbar that I used on the bathtub. That's what I bring him. A useful sense of rage has been building, probably from the beginning; this stranger and his ilk have destroyed my world. It's only fair, only just, to take the steel bar in my hands and swing, striking him before he has the strength or coordination to fight me.

The woman wails and moans, too stunned to move.

That elongated skull is paper-thin, demolished with the first blow and its jellylike contents scattered around the room.

Too late, she grabs at me, trying to wrestle the crowbar from my hands. I throw her to the floor, considering a double homicide. But that wouldn't be right. Even when she picks up the phone and begs for help, I can't bring myself to kill her. Instead I demolish the wall above her head, startling her, and when she crawls away I lift the receiver, grinning as I calmly tell whoever is listening, "You're next, friend. Your time is just about done."

Outdoors is the smell of sweet chemicals and smoke. Strange robotic craft streak overhead, probably heading for crisis points. They ignore me. Maybe too much is happening; maybe their mechanisms were sabotaged at the factory. Either way, I'm left to move up the street, entering each house and killing the just-born invaders where I find them. It's messy, violent work, but in one living room I find the "parents" slain, presumably by their thankless "child." The ceiling creaks above their bodies. I climb the stairs on my toes, catching the murderer as she tries on spare clothes, pants around her knees and no chance for her to grab her bloody softball bat.

From then on I'm a demon, focused and confident and very nearly tireless.

Finishing my block, I start for the next one. Rounding the corner of a house, I come face to face with a stout woman wielding a fire axe. The two of us pause, then smile knowingly. Then we join forces. Toward dawn, taking a break from our gruesome work, I think to ask:

"What's your name?"

"Laverne," she replies, with a lifelong embarrassment. "And yours?"

"Harold," I confess, pleased that I can remember it after so long. "Good to meet you, and Laverne is a lovely name."

Later that day, she and I and twenty other new friends find the invaders barricaded inside a once-gorgeous mansion. Once it's burned to the ground, the city is liberated.

Where now?

Laverne suggests, "How about north? I once heard that they were building something in that direction."

I hug her, no words needed just now.

We name our daughter Unique.

The three of us are living in a city meant for the extinct future, in a shelter made from scraps and set between empty buildings. The buildings themselves are tall and clean, yet somehow very lonely edifices. They won't admit us, but they won't fight us either. And the climate remains ideal. Gardens thrive wherever the earth shows, and our neighbors are scarce and uniformly pleasant.

One night I speak to my infant daughter, telling her that perhaps someday she'll learn how to enter the buildings. Or better, tear them down and use their best parts.

She acts agreeable, babbling something in her baby language.

Laverne stretches out before me, naked and agreeable in a different sense. With a sly grin, she asks:

"Care to ride the chaos, darling?"

Always and gladly, thank you. And together, with every little motion, we change the universe in ways we happily cannot predict.

SUSANNA CLARKE

THE LADIES OF GRACE ADIEU

Above all remember this: that magic belongs as much to
the heart as to the head and everything which is done, should be
done from love or joy or righteous anger.

And if we honour this principle we shall discover that our magic
is much greater than all the sum of all the spells that were ever
taught. Then magic is to us as flight is to the birds, because then our
magic comes from the dark and dreaming heart, just as the flight of
a bird comes from the heart. And we will feel the same joy in performing that magic that the bird feels as it casts itself into the void
and we will know that magic is part of what a man is, just as flight is
part of what a bird is.

This understanding is a gift to us from the Raven King, the dear
king of all magicians, who stands between England and the Other
Lands, between all wild creatures and the world of men.

> —*From the Book of the Lady Catherine of Winchester*
> *(late fifteenth century),*
> *translated from the Latin by Jane Tobias (1775–1819)*

When Mrs Field died, her grieving widower looked around him and discovered that the world seemed quite as full of pretty, young women as it had been in his youth. It further occurred to him that he was just as rich as ever and that, though his home already contained one pretty, young woman (his niece and ward, Cassandra Parbringer), he did not believe that another would go amiss. He did not think that he was at all changed from what he had been and Cassandra was entirely of his opinion, for (she thought to herself) I am sure, sir, that you were every bit as tedious at twenty-one as you are at forty-nine. So Mr Field married again. The lady was pretty and clever and only a year older than Cassandra, but, in her defence, we may say that she had no money and must either marry Mr Field or go and be a teacher in a school. The second Mrs Field and Cassandra were very pleased with each other and soon became very fond of each other. Indeed the sad truth was that they were a great deal fonder of each other than either was of Mr Field. There was another lady who was their friend (her name was Miss Tobias) and the three were often seen walking together near the village where they lived— Grace Adieu in Gloucestershire.

Cassandra Parbringer at twenty was considered an ideal of a certain type of beauty to which some gentlemen are particularly partial. A white skin was agreeably tinged with pink. Light blue eyes harmonised very prettily with silvery-gold curls and the whole was a picture in which womanliness and childishness were sweetly combined. Mr Field, a gentleman not remarkable for his powers of observation, confidently supposed her to have a character childishly naive and full of pleasant, feminine submission in keeping with her face.

Her prospects seemed at this time rather better than Mrs Field's had been. The people of Grace Adieu had long since settled it amongst themselves that Cassandra should marry the Rector, Mr Henry Woodhope, and Mr Woodhope himself did not seem at all averse to the idea.

"Mr Woodhope likes you, Cassandra, I think," said Mrs Field. "Does he?"

Miss Tobias (who was also in the room) said, "Miss Parbringer is wise and keeps her opinion of Mr Woodhope to herself."

"Oh," cried Cassandra, "you may know it if you wish. Mr Wood-hope is Mr Field stretched out a little to become more thin and tall. He is younger and therefore more disposed to be agreeable and his wits are rather sharper. But when all is said and done he is only Mr Field come again."

"Why then do you give him encouragement?" asked Mrs Field.

"Because I suppose that I must marry someone and Mr Wood-hope has this to recommend him—that he lives in Grace Adieu and that in marrying him I need never be parted from my dear Mrs Field."

"It is a very poor ambition to wish to marry a Mr Field of any sort," sighed Mrs Field. "Have you nothing better to wish for?"

Cassandra considered. "I have always had a great desire to visit Yorkshire," she said. "I imagine it to be just like the novels of Mrs Radcliffe."

"It is exactly like everywhere else," said Miss Tobias.

"Oh, Miss Tobias," said Cassandra, "how can you say so? If magic does not linger in Yorkshire, where may we find it still? 'Upon the moors, beneath the stars, With the King's wild Company.' *That* is my idea of Yorkshire."

"But," said Miss Tobias, "a great deal of time has passed since the King's wild Company was last there and in the meantime York-shiremen have acquired tollgates and newspapers and stagecoaches and circulating libraries and everything most modern and com-monplace."

Cassandra sniffed. "You disappoint me," she said.

Miss Tobias was governess to two little girls at a great house in the village, called Winter's Realm. The parents of these children were dead and the people of Grace Adieu were fond of telling each other that it was no house for children, being too vast and gloomy and full of odd-shaped rooms and strange carvings. The younger child was indeed often fearful and often plagued with nightmares. She seemed, poor little thing, to believe herself haunted by owls. There was nothing in the world she feared so much as owls. No one else had ever seen the owls, but the house was old and full of cracks and holes to let them in and full of fat mice to tempt them so per-haps it were true. The governess was not much liked in the village:

she was too tall, too fond of books, too grave, and—a curious thing—
never smiled unless there was some thing to smile at. Yet Miss Ursula and Miss Flora were very prettily behaved children and seemed
greatly attached to Miss Tobias.

Despite their future greatness as heiresses, in the article of relations the children were as poor as churchmice. Their only guardian
was a cousin of their dead mother. In all the long years of their or-
phanhood this gentleman had only visited them twice and once had
written them a very short letter at Christmas. But, because Captain
Winbright wore a redcoat and was an officer in the _____ shires,
all his absences and silences were forgiven and Miss Ursula and Miss
Flora (though only eight and four years old) had begun to show all
the weakness of their sex by preferring him to all the rest of their
acquaintance.

It was said that the great-grandfather of these children had
studied magic and had left behind him a library. Miss Tobias was
often in the library and what she did there no one knew. Of late her
two friends, Mrs Field and Miss Parbringer, had also been at the
house a great deal. But it was generally supposed that they were visiting the children. For ladies (as every one knows) do not study
magic. Magicians themselves are another matter—ladies (as every
one knows) are wild to see magicians. (How else to explain the great
popularity of Mr Norrell in all the fashionable drawing rooms of
London? Mr Norrell is almost as famous for his insignificant face
and long silences as he is for his incomparable magicianship and Mr
Norrell's pupil, Mr Strange, with his almost handsome face and
lively conversation is welcome where ever he goes.) This then, we
will suppose, must explain a question which Cassandra Parbringer
put to Miss Tobias on a day in September, a very fine day on the
cusp of summer and autumn.

"And have you read Mr Strange's piece in *The Review*? What
is your opinion of it?"

"I thought Mr Strange expressed himself with his customary
clarity. Anyone, whether or not they understand any thing of the the-
ory and practice of magic, might understand him. He was witty and
sly, as he generally is. It was altogether an admirable piece of writing. He is a clever man, I think."

"You speak exactly like a governess."

"Is that so surprising?"

"But I did not wish to hear your opinion as a governess, I wished to hear your opinion as a . . . never mind. What did you think of the ideas?"

"I did not agree with any of them."

"Ah, *that* was what I wished to hear."

"Modern magicians," said Mrs Field, "seem to devote more of their energies to belittling magic than to doing any. We are constantly hearing how certain sorts of magic are too perilous for men to attempt (although they appear in all the old stories). Or they cannot be attempted any more because the prescription is lost. Or it never existed. And, as for the Otherlanders, Mr Norrell and Mr Strange do not seem to know if there are such persons in the world. Nor do they appear to care very much, for, even if they do exist, then it seems we have no business talking to them. And the Raven King, we learn, was only a dream of fevered medieval brains, addled with too much magic."

"Mr Strange and Mr Norrell mean to make magic as commonplace as their own dull persons," said Cassandra. "They deny the King for fear that comparison with his great magic would reveal the poverty of their own."

Mrs Field laughed. "Cassandra," she said, "does not know how to leave off abusing Mr Strange."

Then, from the particular sins of the great Mr Strange and the even greater Mr Norrell, they were led to talk of the viciousness of men in general and from there, by a natural progression, to a discussion of whether Cassandra should marry Mr Woodhope.

While the ladies of Grace Adieu were talking Mr Jonathan Strange (the magician and second phenomenon of the Age) was seated in the library of Mr Gilbert Norrell (the magician and first phenomenon of the Age). Mr Strange was informing Mr Norrell that he intended to be absent from London for some weeks. "I hope, sir, that it will cause you no inconvenience. The next article for the *Edinburgh Magazine* is done—unless, sir, you wish to make changes (which I think you may very well do without my assistance)."

Mr Norrell enquired with a frown where Mr Strange was going, for, as was well known in London, the elder magician—a quiet, dry little man—did not like to be without the younger for even so much as a day, or half a day. He did not even like to spare Mr Strange to speak to other people.

"I am going to Gloucestershire, sir. I have promised Mrs Strange that I will take her to visit her brother, who is Rector of a village there. You have heard me speak of Mr Henry Woodhope, I think?"

The next day was rainy in Grace Adieu and Miss Tobias was unable to leave Winter's Realm. She passed the day with the children, teaching them Latin ("which I see no occasion to omit simply on account of your sex. One day you may have a use for it,") and in telling them stories of Thomas of Dundale's captivity in the Other Lands and how he became the first human servant of the Raven King.

When the second day was fine and dry, Miss Tobias took the opportunity to slip away for half an hour to visit Mrs Field, leaving the children in the care of the nursery maid. It so happened that Mr Field had gone to Cheltenham (a rare occurence, for, as Mrs Field remarked, there never was a man so addicted to home. "I fear we make it far too comfortable for him," she said) and so Miss Tobias took advantage of his absence to make a visit of a rather longer duration than usual. (At the time there seemed no harm in it.)

On her way back to Winter's Realm she passed the top of Grace and Angels Lane, where the church stood and, next to it, the Rectory. A very smart barouche was just turning from the high road into the lane. This in itself was interesting enough for Miss Tobias did not recognise the carriage or its occupants, but what made it more extraordinary still was that it was driven with great confidence and spirit by a lady. At her side, upon the barouche box, a gentleman sat, hands in pockets, legs crossed, greatly at his ease. His air was rather striking. "He is not exactly handsome," thought Miss Tobias, "his nose is too long. Yet he has that arrogant air that handsome men have."

It seemed to be a day for visitors. In the yard of Winter's Realm was a gig and two high-spirited horses. Davey, the coachman and a stable boy were attending to them, watched by a thin, dark man—a very slovenly fellow (somebody's servant)—who was leaning against the wall of the kitchen garden to catch the sun and smoking a pipe. His shirt was undone at the front and as Miss Tobias passed, he slowly scratched his bare chest with a long, dark finger and smiled at her.

As long as Miss Tobias had known the house, the great hall had always been the same: full of nothing but silence and shadows and dustmotes turning in great slanting beams of daylight, but today there were echoes of loud voices and music and high, excited laughter. She opened the door to the dining parlour. The table was laid with the best glasses, the best silver and the best dinner service. A meal had been prepared and put upon the table, but then, apparently, forgotten. Travelling trunks and boxes had been brought in and clothes pulled out and then abandoned; men and women's clothing were tumbled together quite promiscuously over the floor. A man in an officer's redcoat was seated on a chair with Miss Ursula on his knee. He was holding a glass of wine, which he put to her lips and then, as she tried to drink, he took the glass away. He was laughing and the child was laughing. Indeed, from her flushed face and excited air Miss Tobias could not be entirely sure that she had not already drunk of the contents. In the middle of the room another man (a very handsome man), also in uniform, was standing among all the clothes and trinkets and laughing with them. The younger child, Miss Flora, stood on one side, watching them all with great, wondering eyes. Miss Tobias went immediately to her and took her hand. In the gloom at the back of the dining parlour a young woman was seated at the pianoforte, playing an Italian song very badly. Perhaps she knew that it was bad, for she seemed very reluctant to play at all. The song was full of long pauses; she sighed often and she did not look happy. Then, quite suddenly, she stopt.

The handsome man in the middle of the room turned to her instantly. "Go on, go on," he cried, "we are all attending, I promise you. It is," and here he turned back to the other man and winked at him, "delightful. We are going to teach country dances to my little cousins. Fred is the best dancing master in the world. So you must play, you know."

Wearily the young lady began again.

The seated man, whose name it seemed was Fred, happened at this moment to notice Miss Tobias. He smiled pleasantly at her and begged her pardon.

"Oh," cried the handsome man, "Miss Tobias will forgive us, Fred. Miss Tobias and I are old friends."

"Good afternoon, Captain Winbright," said Miss Tobias.

By now Mr and Mrs Strange were comfortably seated in Mr Woodhope's pleasant drawing room. Mrs Strange had been shown all over Mr Woodhope's Rectory and had spoken to the housekeeper and the cook and the dairymaid and the other maid and the stableman and the gardener and the gardener's boy. Mr Woodhope had seemed most anxious to have a woman's opinion on everything and would scarcely allow Mrs Strange leave to sit down or take food or drink until she had approved the house, the servants and all the housekeeping arrangements. So, like a good, kind sister, she had looked at it all and smiled upon all the servants and racked her brains for easy questions to ask them and then declared herself delighted.

"And I promise you, Henry," she said with a smile, "that Miss Parbringer will be equally pleased."

"He is blushing," said Jonathan Strange, raising his eyes from his newspaper. "We have come, Henry, with the sole purpose of seeing Miss Parbringer (of whom you write so much) and when we have seen her, we will go away again."

"Indeed? Well, I hope to invite Mrs Field and her niece to meet you at the earliest opportunity."

"Oh, there is no need to trouble yourself," said Strange, "for we have brought telescopes. We will stand at bedroom windows and spy her out, as she goes about the village."

Strange did indeed get up and go to the window as he spoke. "Henry," he said, "I like your church exceedingly. I like that little wall that goes around the building and the trees, and holds them all in tight. It makes the place look like a ship. If you ever get a good strong wind then church and trees will all sail off together to another place entirely."

"Strange," said Henry Woodhope, "you are quite as ridiculous as ever."

"Do not mind him, Henry," said Arabella Strange, "he has the mind of a magician. They are all a little mad."

"Except Norrell," said Strange.

"Strange, I would ask you, as a friend, to do no magic while you are here. We are a very quiet village."

"My dear Henry," said Strange, "I am not a street conjuror with a booth and a yellow curtain. I do not intend to set up in a corner of the churchyard to catch trade. These days Admirals and Rear Admirals and Vice Admirals and all His Majesty's Ministers send me respectful letters requesting my services and (what is much more) pay me well for them. I very much doubt if there is any one in Grace Adieu who could afford me."

"What room is this?" asked Captain Winbright.

"This was old Mr Enderwhild's bedroom, sir," said Miss Tobias.

"The magician?"

"The magician."

"And where did he keep all his hoard, Miss Tobias? You have been here long enough to winkle it out. There are sovereigns, I dare say, hidden away in all sorts of odd holes and corners."

"I never heard so, sir."

"Come, Miss Tobias, what do old men learn magic for, except to find each other's piles of gold? What else is magic good for?" A thought seemed to trouble him. "They show no sign of inheriting the family genius, do they? The children, I mean. No, of course. Who ever heard of women doing magic?"

"There have been two female magicians, sir. Both highly regarded. The Lady Catherine of Winchester, who taught Martin Pale, and Gregory Absalom's daughter, Maria, who was mistress of the Shadow House for more than a century."

He did not seem greatly interested. "Show me some other rooms," he said. They walked down another echoing corridor, which, like much of the great, dark house, had fallen into the possession of mice and spiders.

"Are my cousins healthy children?"

"Yes, sir."

He was silent and then he said, "Well, of course, it may not last. There are so many childish illnesses, Miss Tobias. I myself, when only six or seven, almost died of the red spot. Have these children had the red spot?"

"No, sir."

"Indeed? Our grandparents understood these things better, I think. They would not permit themselves to get overfond of children until they had got past all childhood's trials and maladies. It is a good rule. Do not get overfond of children."

He caught her eye and reddened. Then laughed. "Why, it is only a joke. How solemn you look. Ah, Miss Tobias, I see how it is. You have borne all the responsibility for this house and for my cousins, my rich little cousins, for far too long. Women should not have to bear such burdens alone. Their pretty white shoulders were not made for it. But, see, I am come to help you now. And Fred. Fred has a great mind to be a cousin too. Fred is very fond of children."

"And the lady, Captain Winbright? Will she stay and be another cousin with you and the other gentleman?"

He smiled confidingly at her. His eyes seemed such a bright, laughing blue and his smile so open and unaffected, that it took a woman of Miss Tobias's great composure not to smile with him.

"Between ourselves she has been a little ill-used by a brother officer in the _____ shires. But I am such a soft-hearted fellow— the sight of a woman's tears can move me to almost any thing."

So said Captain Winbright in the corridor, but when they entered the dining parlour again, the sight of a woman's tears (for the young lady was crying at that moment) moved him only to be rude to her. Upon her saying his name, gently and somewhat apprehensively, he turned upon her and cried, "Oh, why do you not go back to Brighton? You could you know, very easily. That would be the best thing for you."

"Reigate," she said gently.

He looked at her much irritated. "Aye, Reigate," he said.

She had a sweet, timorous face, great dark eyes and a little rosebud mouth, forever trembling on the brink of tears. But it was the kind of beauty that soon evaporates when anything at all in the nature of suffering comes near it and she had, poor thing, been very unhappy of late. She reminded Miss Tobias of a child's rag doll, pretty enough at the beginning, but very sad and pitiful once its rag stuffing was gone. She looked up at Miss Tobias. "I never thought . . ." she said and lapsed into tears.

Miss Tobias was silent a moment. "Well," she said at last, "perhaps you were not brought up to it."

That evening Mr Field fell asleep in the parlour again. This had happened to him rather often recently.

It happened like this. The servant came into the room with a note for Mrs Field and she began to read it. Then, as his wife read, Mr Field began to feel (as he expressed it to himself) 'all cobwebby' with sleep. After a moment or two it seemed to him that he woke up and the evening continued in its normal course, with Cassandra and Mrs Field sitting one on either side of the fire. Indeed Mr Field spent a very pleasant evening—the kind of evening he loved to spend, attended to by the two ladies. That it was only the dream of such an evening (for the poor, silly man was indeed asleep) did not in any way detract from his enjoyment of it.

While he slept, Mrs Field and Cassandra were hurrying along the lane to Winter's Realm.

In the Rectory Henry Woodhope and Mrs Strange had said their goodnights but Mr Strange proposed to continue reading a while. His book was a *Life of Martin Pale* by Thaddeus Hickman. He had reached Chapter 26 where Hickman discussed some theories, which he attributed to Martin Pale, that sometimes magicians, in times of great need, might find themselves capable of much greater acts of magic than they had ever learnt or even heard of before.

"Oh," said Strange with much irritation, "this is the most complete stuff and nonsense."

"Goodnight, Jonathan," said Arabella and kissed him, just above his frown.

"Yes, yes," he muttered, not raising his eyes from the book.

"And the young woman," whispered Mrs Field, "who is she?"

Miss Tobias raised an eyebrow and said, "She says that she is Mrs Winbright. But Captain Winbright says that she is not. I had not supposed it to be a point capable of so wide an interpretation."

"And if anything were to happen . . . to the children, I mean," whispered Mrs Field, "then Captain Winbright might benefit in some way?"

"Oh, he would certainly be a very rich man and whatever he has come here to escape—whether it be debts or scandal—would presumably hold no more fears for him."

The three ladies were in the children's bedroom. Miss Tobias sat somewhere in the dark, wrapped in a shawl. Two candles bloomed in the vast dark room, one near to the children's bed and the other upon a little ricketty table by the door, so that anyone entering the room would instantly be seen. Somewhere in the house, at the end of a great many long, dark corridors, could be heard the sound of a man singing and another laughing.

From the bed Miss Flora anxiously enquired if there were any owls in the room.

Miss Tobias assured her there were none.

"Yet I think they may still come," said Miss Flora in a fright, "if you do not stay."

Miss Tobias said that they would stay for a while. "Be quiet now," she said, "and Miss Parbringer will tell you a story, if you ask her."

"What story shall I tell you?" asked Cassandra.

"A story of the Raven King," said Miss Ursula.

"Very well," said Cassandra.

This then is the story which Cassandra told the children.

"Before the Raven King was a king at all, but only a Raven

Child, he lived in a very wonderful house with his uncle and his aunt. (These were not really his relations at all, but only a kind gentleman and lady who had taken him to live with them.) One day his uncle, who was reading books of magic in his great library, sent for the Raven Child and enquired politely how he did. The Raven Child replied that he did very well.

" 'Hmmph, well,' said Uncle Auberon, 'as I am your guardian and protector, little human child, I had better make sure of it. Show me the dreams you had last night.' So the Raven Child took out his dreams and Uncle Auberon made a space for them on the library table. There were a hundred odd things on that table; books on unnatural history; a map showing the relative positions of Masculine Duplicity and Feminine Integrity (and how to get from one to the other) and a set of beautiful brass instruments in a mahogany box, all very cunningly contrived to measure Ambition and Jealousy, Love and Self-sacrifice, Loyalty to the State and Dreams of Regicide and many other Vices and Virtues which it might be useful to know about. All these things Uncle Auberon put on the floor, for he was not a very tidy person and people were forever scolding him about it. Then Uncle Auberon spread the Raven Child's dreams out on the table and peered at them through little wire spectacles.

" 'Why,' cried Uncle Auberon, 'here is a dream of a tall black tower in a dark wood in the snow. The tower is all in ruins, like broken teeth. Black, ragged birds fly round and round and you are inside that tower and cannot get out. Little human child, when you had this terrible dream, was you not afraid?'

" 'No, Uncle,' said the Raven Child, 'last night I dreamt of the tower where I was born and of the ravens who brought me water to drink when I was too young even to crawl. Why should I be afraid?'

"So Uncle Auberon looked at the next dream and when he saw it he cried out loud. 'But here is a dream of cruel eyes a-glittering and wicked jaws a-slavering. Little human child, when you had this terrible dream, was you not afraid?'

" 'No, Uncle,' said the Raven Child, 'last night I dreamt of the wolves who suckled me and who lay down beside me and kept me warm when I was too young even to crawl. Why should I be afraid?'

"So Uncle Auberon looked at the next dream and when he saw

it he shivered and said, "But this is a dream of a dark lake in a sad and rainy twilight. The woods are monstrous silent and a ghostly boat sails upon the water. The boatman is as thin and twisted as a hedge root and his face is all in shadow. Little human child, when you had this terrible dream, was you not afraid?'

"Then the Raven Child banged his fist upon the table in his exasperation and stamped his foot upon the floor. 'Uncle Auberon!' he exclaimed, 'that is the fairy boat and the fairy boatman which you and Aunt Titania yourselves sent to fetch me and bring me to your house. Why should I be afraid?'

" 'Well!' said a third person, who had not spoken before, 'how the child boasts of his courage!' The person who spoke was Uncle Auberon's servant, who had been sitting high upon a shelf, disguised (until this moment) as a bust of Mr William Shakespeare. Uncle Auberon was quite startled by his sudden appearance, but the Raven Child had always known he was there.

"Uncle Auberon's servant peered down from his high shelf at the Raven Child and the Raven Child looked up at him. 'There are all sorts of things in heaven and earth,' said Uncle Auberon's servant, 'that yearn to do you harm. There is fire that wants to burn you. There are swords that long to pierce you through and through and ropes that mean to bind you hard. There are a thousand, thousand things that you have never yet dreamt of: creatures that can steal your sleep from you, year after year, until you scarcely know yourself, and men yet unborn who will curse you and scheme against you. Little human child, the time has come to be afraid.'

"But the Raven Child said, 'Robin Goodfellow, I knew all along that it was you that sent me those dreams. But I am a human child and therefore cleverer than you and when those wicked creatures come to do me harm I shall be cleverer than them. I am a human child and all the vast stony, rainy English earth belongs to me. I am an English child and all the wide grey English air, full of black wings beating and grey ghosts of rain sighing, belongs to me. This being so, Robin Goodfellow, tell me, why should I be afraid?' Then the Raven Child shook his head of raven hair and disappeared.

"Mr Goodfellow glanced a little nervously at Uncle Auberon to see if he were at all displeased that Mr Goodfellow had spoken out so boldly to the human foster child, but Uncle Auberon (who was quite an old gentleman) had stopped listening to them both a while ago and had wandered off to resume his search for a book. It contained a spell for turning Members of Parliament into useful members of society and now, just when Uncle Auberon thought he had a use for it, he could not find it (though he had had it in his hand not a hundred years before). So Mr Goodfellow said nothing but quietly turned himself back into William Shakespeare."

In the Rectory Mr Strange was still reading. He had reached Chapter 42 where Hickman relates how Maria Absalom defeated her enemies by showing them the true reflections of their souls in the mirrors of the Shadow House and how the ugly sights which they saw there (and knew in their hearts to be true) so dismayed them that they could oppose her no more.

There was, upon the back of Mr Strange's neck, a particularly tender spot and all his friends had heard him tell how, when ever there was any magic going on, it would begin to prickle and to itch. Without knowing that he did so, he now began to rub the place.

So many dark corridors, thought Cassandra, how lucky it is that I know my way about them, for many people I think would soon be lost. Poor souls, they would soon take fright because the way is so long, but I *know* that I am now very near to the great staircase and will soon be able to slip out of the house and into the garden.

It had been decided that Mrs Field should stay and watch the children for the remainder of the night and so Cassandra was making her way back to Mr Field's house quite alone.

Except (she thought) I do not believe that that tall, moonshiny window should be *there*. It would suit me much better if it were behind me. Or perhaps on my left. For I am sure it was not there when I came in. Oh, I am lost! How very . . . And now the voices of those two wretches of men come echoing down this dark passageway and they are most manifestly drunk and do not know me. And I am here where I have no right to be. (Cassandra pulled her shawl closer round her.) "And yet," she murmured, "why should I be afraid?"

"Damn this house!" cried Winbright. "It is nothing but horrid black corridors. What do you see, Fred?"

"Only an owl. A pretty white owl. What the devil is it doing inside the house?"

"Fred," cried Winbright, slumping against the wall and sliding down a little, "fetch me my pistol, like a good fellow."

"At once, Captain!" cried Fred. He saluted Captain Winbright and then promptly forgot all about it.

Captain Winbright smiled. "And here," he said, "is Miss Tobias, running to meet us."

"Sir," said Miss Tobias, appearing suddenly out of the darkness, "what are you doing?"

"There is a damned owl in the house. We are going to shoot it."

Miss Tobias looked round at the owl, shifting in the shadows, and then said hurriedly, "Well, you are very free from superstition, I must say. You might both set up as the publishers of an atheist encyclopedia tomorrow. I applaud your boldness, but I do not share it."

The two gentlemen looked at her.

"Did you never hear that owls are the possessions of the Raven King?" she asked.

"Do not frighten me, Miss Tobias," said Captain Winbright, "you will make me think I see tall crowns of raven feathers in the dark. This is certainly the house for it. Damn her, Fred. She behaves as if she were my governess as well."

"Is she at all like your governess?" asked Fred.

"I cannot tell. I had so many. They all left me. You would not have left me, would you, Miss Tobias?"

"I do not know, sir."

"Fred," said Captain Winbright, "now there are two owls. Two pretty little owls. You are like Minerva, Miss Tobias, so tall and wise, and disapproving of a fellow. Minerva with two owls. Your name is Jane, is it not?"

"My name, sir, is Miss Tobias."

Winbright stared into the darkness and shivered. "What is the game they play in Yorkshire, Fred? When they send children alone into the dark to summon the Raven King. What are those words they say?"

Fred sighed and shook his head. "It has to do with hearts being eaten," he said, "that is all I recall."

"How they stare at us, Fred," said Winbright. "They are very impertinent owls. I had always thought they were such shy little creatures."

"They do not like us," said Fred sadly.

"They like you better, Jane. Why, one is upon your shoulder now. Are you not afraid?"

"No, sir."

"Those feathers," said Fred, "those soft feathers between the wing and the body dance like flames when they swoop. If I were a mouse I would think the flames of Hell had come to swallow me up."

"Indeed," murmured Winbright, and both men watched the owls glide in and out of the gloom. Then suddenly one of the owls cried out—a hideous screech to freeze the blood.

Miss Tobias looked down and crossed her hands—the very picture of a modest governess. "They do that, you know," she said, "to petrify their prey with fear; to turn it, as it were, to stone. That is the cruel, wild magic of owls."

But no one answered her, for there was no one in the corridor but herself and the owls (each with something in its beak). "How hungry you are, dearest," said Miss Tobias approvingly. "One, two, three swallows and the dish goes down."

☙   ☙   ☙

About midnight Mr Strange's book appeared to him so dull and the night so sweet that he left the house and went out into the apple orchard. There was no wall to this orchard but only a grassy bank. Mr Strange lay down beneath a pear tree and, though he had intended to think about magic, he very soon fell asleep.

A little later he heard (or dreamt that he heard) the sound of laughter and of feminine voices. Looking up, he saw three ladies in pale gowns walking (almost dancing) upon the bank above him. The stars surrounded them; the night-wind took their gowns and blew them about. They held out their arms to the wind (they seemed indeed to be dancing). Mr Strange stretched himself and sighed with pleasure. He assumed (not unreasonably) that he was still dreaming.

But the ladies stopt and stared down into the grass.

"What is it?" asked Miss Tobias.

Cassandra peered into the darkness. "It is a man," she said with great authority.

"Gracious heaven," said Mrs Field, "what kind of man?"

"The usual kind, I should say," said Cassandra.

"I meant, Cassandra," said the other, "what degree, what station of man?"

Jonathan Strange got to his feet, perplexed, brushing straw from his clothes. "Ladies," he said, "forgive me. I thought that I had woken in the Raven King's Other Lands. I thought that you were Titania's ladies come to meet me."

The ladies were silent. And then: "Well!" said Mrs Field, "What a speech!"

"I beg your pardon, madam. I meant only that it is a beautiful night (as I am sure you will agree) and I have been thinking for some time that it is (in the most critical and technical sense) a magical night and I thought perhaps that you were the magic that was meant to happen."

"Oh," cried Cassandra, "they are all full of nonsense. Do not listen to him, my dear Mrs Field. Miss Tobias, let us walk on." But she looked at him curiously and said, "You? What do *you* know of magic?"

"A little, madam."

"Well, sir," she said, "I will give you a piece of good advice. You will never grow proficient in the art as long as you continue with your outmoded notions of Raven Kings and Otherlanders. Have you not heard? They have all been done away with by Mr Strange and Mr Norrell."

Mr Strange thanked her for the advice.

"There is much more that we could teach you . . . ," she said.

"So it would seem," said Strange, crossing his arms.

". . . only that we have neither the time nor the inclination."

"That is a pity," said Strange. "Are you sure, madam, that you will not reconsider? My last master found me to be a most apt pupil, very quick to grasp the principles of any subject."

"What was the name of your last master?" asked Miss Tobias.

"Norrell," said Strange softly.

Another short silence ensued.

"You are the London magician," said Cassandra.

"No, indeed," cried Strange, stung. "I am the Shropshire magician and Mr Norrell is the Yorkshire magician. We neither of us own London as our home. We are countrymen both. We have that, at least, in common."

"You seem, sir, to be of a somewhat inconsistent, somewhat contradictory character," said Miss Tobias.

"Indeed, madam, other people have remarked upon it. And now, ladies, since we are sure to meet again—and that quite soon— I will wish you all a goodnight. Miss Parbringer, I will give you a piece of advice in return for yours (for I am certain that it was given in good faith). Magic, madam, is like wine and, if you are not used to it, it will make you drunk. A successful spell is as potent a loosener of tongues as a bottle of good claret and you will find the morning after that you have said things you now regret."

With that he bowed and walked back through the orchard into the house.

"A magician in Grace Adieu," said Miss Tobias thoughtfully, "and at such a time. Well, let us not be disconcerted. We will see what tomorrow brings."

✿   ✿   ✿

What tomorrow brought was a courteous note from Mr Woodhope, expressing his hopes that the ladies of Grace Adieu would do his sister the honour of meeting her at the Rectory that afternoon. On this occasion the invitation included Miss Tobias, although, in general, she did not visit in the village (and was no great favourite with Mr Woodhope).

Despite the misgivings which all the ladies felt (and which Mrs Field had several times spoken out loud), Mr Strange met them with great good manners and a bow for each and he gave no hint to any one that this was not the first time he had seen them.

The talk was at first of the commonest sort and, to the ladies of Grace Adieu who did not know him, Mr Strange seemed of an easy and sociable character, so it was a trifle unsettling to hear Arabella Strange ask him why he was so silent today. Mr Strange replied that he was a little tired.

"Oh," said Mrs Strange to Mrs Field, "he has been up all night reading books of magical history. It is a bad habit that all magicians get into and it is that, as much as anything, which weakens their wits in the end." She smiled at her husband as if expecting him to say some clever or impertinent thing in return. But he only continued to look at the three ladies of Grace Adieu.

Halfway through their visit Mr Woodhope rose and, speaking his great regret and looking at Miss Parbringer, begged that they would excuse him—he had parish business to attend. He was very anxious that Mr Strange should go with him, so much so that Strange had no alternative but to oblige him. This left the ladies alone.

The conversation turned to the articles Mr Strange had published in the quarterly reviews and, in particular, those passages where he proved that there could never have been such a person as the Raven King.

"Mrs Strange," said Cassandra, "you must agree with me—those are most extraordinary opinions for a magician, when even our common historians write the King's dates in their history books—four or five times the span of a common life."

Arabella frowned. "Mr Strange cannot always write exactly

what he pleases. Much of it, you know, comes from Mr Norrell. Mr Norrell has studied magic for many years more than any other gentleman in England, and certainly with much greater profit. His opinion must carry great weight with anyone who cares about English magic."

"I see," said Cassandra, "you mean that Mr Strange writes things which he does not entirely believe, because Mr Norrell tells him to. If I were a man (and, what is much more, a magician) I should not do any thing, write any thing, if I did not like it."

"Miss Parbringer," murmured Miss Tobias, reprovingly.

"Oh, Mrs Strange knows I mean no offence," cried Cassandra, "but I must say what I think and upon this topic of all things."

Arabella Strange smiled. "The situation," she said, "is not exactly as you suppose. Mr Strange has studied for a number of years with Mr Norrell in London and Mr Norrell swore at the beginning that he would not take a pupil and so it was considered a great honour when he consented to take Jonathan. And then, you know, there are only two true magicians in England and England is at war. If those two magicians quarrel, what follows? What greater comfort could we offer the French than this?"

The ladies took their tea together and the only slight incident to disturb the remainder of the visit was a fit of coughing which seized first Cassandra, and then Mrs Field. For several moments Mrs Strange was quite concerned about them.

When Henry Woodhope and Strange returned the ladies were gone. The maid and Mrs Strange were standing in the passageway. Each was holding a little white linen cloath. The maid was exclaiming loudly about something or other and it was a moment before Jonathan Strange could make himself heard.

"What is it?" he asked.

"We have found some bones," said his wife, with a puzzled air. "Small, white bones, it would seem, of some delicate little creatures, and two little grey skins like empty pods. Come, sir, you are the magician, explain it to us."

"They are mouse bones. And mouse skins too. It is owls that do that. See," said Strange, "the skins are turned quite inside out. Curious, is it not?"

Mrs Strange was not greatly impressed with this as an explanation. "So I dare say," she said. "But what seems to me far more miraculous is that we found these bones in the cloaths which Miss Parbringer and Mrs Field had to wipe their fingers and their mouths. Jonathan, I hope you are not suggesting that these ladies have been eating mice?"

The weather continued very fine. Mr Woodhope drove his sister, Mr and Mrs Field and their niece to _____ Hill to see the views and to drink and eat by a pretty, hanging wood. Mr Strange rode behind. Once again he watched all the party carefully and once again Mrs Strange told him that he was in a grave, odd mood and not at all like himself.

On other days Mr Strange rode out by himself and talked to farmers and innkeepers on the highways all around. Mr Woodhope explained this behaviour by saying that Strange had always been very eccentric and that now he had become so great and full of London importance, Mr Woodhope supposed he had grown even more so.

One day (it was the last day of Mr and Mrs Strange's visit to their brother) Mrs Field, Miss Tobias and Cassandra were out walking on the high, empty hills above Grace Adieu. A sunlit wind bent all the long grasses. Light and shade followed each other so swiftly that it was as if great doors were opening and closing in the sky. Cassandra was swinging her bonnet (which had long since left her head) by its blue ribbons, when she saw a gentleman on a black mare, come riding to meet them.

When he arrived, Mr Strange smiled and spoke of the view and of the weather and, in the space of five minutes, was altogether more communicative than he had been in the entire past fortnight. None of the ladies had much to say to him, but Mr Strange was not the sort of gentleman who, once he has decided to talk, is to be put off by a lack of encouragement on the part of his listeners.

He spoke of a remarkable dream he had had.

"I was told once by some country people that a magician should never tell his dreams because the telling will make them come true. But I say that that is great nonsense. Miss Tobias, you have studied the subject, what is your opinion?"

But Miss Tobias was silent.

Strange went on. "I had this dream, Mrs Field, under rather curious circumstances. Last night I took some little bones to bed with me—I happened upon them quite recently. I put them under my pillow and there they stayed all night while I slept. Mrs Strange would have had a great deal to say to me upon the subject, had she known of it. But then, wives and husbands do not always tell each other every thing, do they, Mrs Field?"

But Mrs Field said nothing.

"My dream was this," said Strange. "I was talking to a gentleman (a very handsome man). His features were very distinct in my dream, yet I am quite certain that I never saw him before in all my life. When we came to shake hands, he was very reluctant—which I did not understand. He seemed embarrassed and not a little ashamed. But when, at last, he put out his hand, it was not a hand at all, but a little grey-furred claw. Miss Parbringer, I hear that you tell wonderful stories to all the village children. Perhaps you will tell me a story to explain my dream?"

But Miss Parbringer was silent.

"On the day that my wife and I arrived here, some other people came to Grace Adieu. Where are they now? Where is the thin dark figure—whether boy or young woman I do not know, for no one saw very clearly—who sat in the gig?"

Miss Tobias spoke. "Miss Pye was taken back to Reigate in our carriage. Davey, our coachman, conveyed her to the house of her mother and her aunt—good people who truly love her and who had wondered for a long, long time if they would ever see her again."

"And Jack Hogg, the Captain's servant?"

Miss Tobias smiled. "Oh, he took himself off with remarkable speed, once it was made plain to him that staying would do no good at all."

"And where is Arthur Winbright? And where is Frederick Littleworth?"

They were silent.

"Oh, ladies, what have you done?"

After a while Miss Tobias spoke again. "That night," she said, "after Captain Winbright and Mr Littleworth had . . . left us, I saw someone. At the other end of the passageway I saw, very dimly, someone tall and slender, with the wings of birds beating all around their shoulders. Mr Strange, *I* am tall and the wings of birds were, at that moment, beating around my shoulders . . ."

"And so, it was your reflection."

"Reflection? By what means?" asked Miss Tobias. "There is no glass in that part of the house."

"So, what did you do?" asked Strange a little uncertainly.

"I said aloud the words of the Yorkshire Game. Even you, Mr Strange, must know the words of the Yorkshire Game." Miss Tobias smiled a little sarcastically. "Mr Norrell is, after all, the Yorkshire magician, is he not?"

"I greet thee, Lord, and bid thee welcome to my heart," said Strange.

Miss Tobias inclined her head.

Now it was Cassandra's turn. "Poor man, you cannot even reconcile what you believe in your heart to be true and what you are obliged to write in the quarterly reviews. Can you go back to London and tell this odd tale? For I think you will find that it is full of all kinds of nonsense that Mr Norrell will not like—Raven Kings and the magic of wild creatures and the magic of women. You are no match for us, for we three are quite united, while you, sir, for all your cleverness, are at war, even with yourself. If ever a time comes, when your heart and your head declare a truce, then I suggest you come back to Grace Adieu and then you may tell us what magic we may or may not do."

It was Strange's turn to be silent. The three ladies of Grace Adieu wished him a good morning and walked on. Mrs Field alone favoured him with a smile (of a rather pitying sort).

A month after Mr and Mrs Strange's return to London, Mr Woodhope was surprised to receive a letter from Sir Walter Pole, the politician. Mr Woodhope had never met the gentleman, but now Sir

Walter suddenly wrote to offer Mr Woodhope the rich living of Great Hitherden, in Northamptonshire. Mr Woodhope could only imagine that it was Strange's doing—Strange and Sir Walter were known to be friends. Mr Woodhope was sorry to leave Grace Adieu and sorry to leave Miss Parbringer, but he comforted himself with the thought that there were bound to be ladies, almost as pretty in Northamptonshire and if there were not, well, he would be a richer clergyman there than he was in Grace Adieu and so better able to bear the loneliness.

Miss Cassandra Parbringer only smiled when she heard he was going and that same afternoon, went out walking on the high hills, in a fine autumn wind, with Mrs Field and Miss Tobias—as free, said Miss Parbringer, as any women in the kingdom.

SUSAN PALWICK

GI JESUS

I DON'T KNOW IF IT WAS A MIRACLE OR NOT, WHAT HAPPENED AT THE hospital. I can't make up my mind about that. I always thought those headlines about "Instant Miracle Cures" in the trashy supermarket newspapers were a crock. You know the ones: THALIDOMIDE BOY GROWS ARMS TO PROTECT MOM FROM RAPIST! "I had to save her, and it was the only way!" BARNEY PERFORMS CPR ON SEARS SANTA CLAUS! "I was walking through the TV department and all of a sudden I couldn't breathe, and this little purple guy jumps straight out of the set and starts pounding on my chest!" SIAMESE TWINS SEPARATE WHEN THE MEN THEY LOVE MOVE TO OPPOSITE COASTS! "The doctors said it could never be done because we shared a brain, but love conquers all!"

I never believed any of that stuff, but what happened at the hospital would sound just like that, if I let it. So I don't know anymore. Maybe my story's a crock too, or maybe those trashy ones are truer than anybody ever thought. One thing I can tell you, though: if there are miracles, they don't happen in an instant. Whatever a miracle is, it takes its own sweet time growing. When I see those newspapers now, I wonder what stories those people would tell if they had more than two square inches of the *Weekly World News* to do it in. Because if anything real happened to them they do have stories, trust me on that, and probably long ones, too.

Mine started months ago, the day I went to church with Mandy. I'm not religious, never have been—nobody in my family ever has been, so far as I know—but Mandy's been my best friend for thirty years, and when your best friend calls you up crying and asks you to go to church with her, you do it, even if you've never been too sure you even believe in God, even if you're very sure that you don't believe in anything the priest in that church has to say. The last time I'd been in that church was when Mandy and Bill got married. I was their maid of honor, and I shouldn't have been. Cindy should have been. So I guess the story really started back then, twenty years ago, because when Mandy asked me to be maid of honor I said, "Now wait a minute, how come you aren't asking your sister that? That's a sister's job."

We were sitting in Sam's Soda Shop, where we always went to have important conversations. Mandy had called me and told me to meet her there, and I figured she needed to tell me about some fight she'd had with Bill, or fret about how his mother still didn't like her. We'd ordered what we always did, a root beer float for me and a vanilla shake for her, and then she came out with the maid of honor thing and I choked and started spurting root beer out my nose. There are certain ways of doing things, in a little town like this. I don't know how it works other places, but if you get married in Innocence, Indiana, and you don't ask your sister to hold the bouquet, that has to mean you don't love her. What's worse, it means you want everybody to know you don't love her, because even sisters who can't stand each other do what's right at weddings. And I knew Mandy loved Cindy. She was the only person in her family who did. "You have to ask Cindy," I said. "She's your *sister.*"

Mandy hadn't touched her shake. She hadn't even taken the paper wrapper off the straw. "I can't ask her. My parents would kill me."

"Your parents?" I'd never liked Mandy's parents, and I wasn't very good at hiding it. I knew they must be mad at Cindy about something, but they were always mad at Cindy about something: smoking or drinking or having too many boyfriends or having the wrong boyfriends or having boyfriends at all. Plenty of other girls in town did all the same things Cindy did, but they lied about it and Cindy never would. Mr. and Mrs. Mincing were ashamed of her: not because of what she did, but because everybody knew about it. They cared about their reputation more than they cared about Cindy, and Mandy knew that as well as I did, and she hated it too. So I shook my head at her and said, "Mandy, your parents are *already* married, aren't they? What business is it of theirs? Whose wedding is this, anyway?"

"They're paying for it," Mandy said, in this tiny voice she gets when she's really upset, and then, all in a rush, "She's pregnant. She's starting to show: that's how we found out. And she won't say who the father is and she won't say she's sorry and I'm not supposed to tell anybody, Cece, not even you, so you have to *promise* to keep it a secret."

"Oh," I said, thinking a lot of things even I knew better than to say, like if she's showing already it's not going to be a secret for long, like if your mother's so happy about the lovely grandchildren you and Bill are going to give her, why can't she love this grandchild too? But I saw right away that Mandy's parents would never let Cindy be in the wedding, and I knew Mandy would do whatever they wanted, because she always did. She never could talk back to them. That's why she was the favorite daughter.

Mandy was my best friend, but sometimes I got just plain disgusted with her. She never stuck up for herself at all, and somehow she got everything she wanted. Here she was marrying Bill and planning this big wedding while Hank Heywood, who made me dizzier than anybody I'd ever met, hadn't even kissed me yet. And if I ever did get married my dad couldn't afford to pay for a fancy wedding, and my mother had died when I was a baby, so there wouldn't even be anybody to fuss over the dress and stand there crying during the ceremony. It wasn't fair.

I wanted to say something really mean to Mandy, right then, but I knew I was just feeling sorry for myself when I should have been feeling sorry for Cindy. So I took a swig of root beer float to calm myself down and tried to say something useful instead. "What does Bill say about this?"

"Bill's staying out of it."

Bill stayed out of a lot of things, mainly debt and drugs and trouble, which was why Mandy's parents liked him so much. A fine upstanding young man, they said. I could have told them a few things about what he got into and what stood up when he did it. I'd had a scare myself, about a year before Mandy and Bill started going together, but nobody knew about that except Bill and I wasn't about to tell a soul, and neither was he. I'll say this much for Bill: he knew how to keep a secret. He knew how to keep promises too, mostly. Turned out I was just late, but we had a few nervous weeks there, and the whole time he said, "Now don't you worry about anything, Cece. I'll get the money for a good doctor if that's what has to happen, I promise." He'd have done it, too. Funny, I never doubted that, even though I knew full well I didn't love him and he didn't love me. I don't doubt it now. He was a better man when he was seventeen and scared than when he was thirty-five and broke his big promise, the one he'd made to Mandy at the altar, in front of the priest and all those people and God, if you believe in God.

But I'm getting way ahead of myself. So I said to Mandy, "Well now, look, if I'm not your maid of honor who will be?" Because I still didn't like the idea, not one bit. A bridesmaid, fine, but maid of honor? Standing at the altar next to Mandy and Bill, knowing that Cindy should have been the one up there and that I wasn't any better than her, just luckier? Knowing that Bill knew all this too, and that Mandy didn't know any of it and now I'd never be able to tell her? Even back then I watched enough soap operas to know that once you get into a tangle like that, you don't get out. You're in it for life. Your kids are in it, probably, and their kids too. It doesn't end.

"I guess I'd have to ask my cousin Sandra," Mandy said, looking at me like I'd just drowned the last puppy in the world. She still hadn't touched her shake, and I gave up. First of all, Sandra was the snootiest bitch in the county; I didn't know anybody who liked her, not even Mandy, and Mandy liked everybody. Secondly, there was the cousin thing. If you don't ask your sister to be your maid of honor and ask your best friend instead, maybe you can get away with it. "We're so close." "We're just like sisters." Something like that. But not to ask your own sister, and then to ask *another* relative, some cousin you don't even like? That's ten times more of an insult all around, and there's no way of hiding it.

"Okay," I said. "I'll do it." I guess I didn't sound very honored, but I've never been good at lying about things like that. Mandy smiled at me and let out a big sigh of relief, and finally reached for her shake.

So I was the maid of honor, and Sandra and our friends Christy and Diane were the bridesmaids. We carried pink sweetheart roses and white carnations, and wore pink satin dresses with big bunches of tulle at the shoulders. I still have that dress hanging in my closet, not that I'll ever be able to fit into it again, not that I've been able to for years now. I always thought I'd give it to my daughter, when I had one. That's never going to happen now, I guess, even if I ever do get married. You hear stories on the news about women having babies after forty, but that always smacks of Instant Miracle Cure to me. And going through the Change is enough work, without having to chase a toddler around while you're doing it. I guess I could give the dress to one of Mandy's girls, but what would I say? "This is the dress I wore when your mother married the man who ran off with his secretary fifteen years later"? The girls are real bitter about Bill. The oldest was only thirteen when it happened, and when you're that age everything's easy: black and white, right and wrong. And the other three believed whatever their big sister told them.

So no one will ever get to wear that dress again, which is too bad, really. It's still the fanciest dress I've ever owned, and I was excited about wearing it in the wedding, even if it should have been Cindy's dress. I squared my conscience about that by promising myself that if I had to be maid of honor I was going to do it my way: I was going to be real nice to Cindy, so that maybe Mandy would be brave enough to be nice to her too, and then when Mr. and Mrs. Mincing saw the two of us being nice their hearts would soften and they'd take Cindy back into the family. I was going to fix everything, oh yes I was. I had it all planned out.

That's the kind of plan you can only come up with when you're nineteen and don't know how anything works yet. I'd never been in a wedding before: I didn't know how scared I'd be, in front of all those people. I didn't know that Cindy would sneak into the church late and sit in the very back pew, rows and rows behind the rest of the family, cowering there trying to hide. Cindy'd always been so bold about everything that I thought she'd be bold about the wedding too—especially since by then everybody in town knew she was expecting, it wasn't like it was a secret at all—but maybe the church made her lose her nerve. Who could blame her? The priest had been saying something boring but pretty nice, and then all of a sudden he gets going on how we're there to bless the joining of two souls, to make a marriage that will last until death, longer than youth and longer than beauty, longer than the sinful desires of the body. He wasn't looking at Mandy and Bill anymore by the time he said that; he was glaring over their heads, practically yelling at the back of the church. And then all three of us knew what must have happened, even though we hadn't seen Cindy come in. You could feel everybody else in the church fighting not to turn around and stare at that back pew. Some of them did, mostly kids, before their parents yanked them back around again. I couldn't see that from where I was, of course, but Hank told me about it after the ceremony. That was only about a week before he got shipped out to Vietnam: he was one of the last ones to get sent over. He never did kiss me before he left—he was so shy, Hank—but he wrote me letters until he disappeared. He just vanished into the jungle; nobody ever found out what happened to him. I wore one of those silver POW/MIA bracelets for a while, you know, back when everybody was wearing them. After a while it stopped being the thing to do; people would give you funny looks when they saw it, ask what it was. Some people thought it was a Medic Alert bracelet, thought I was diabetic or something. And it was ugly, to tell you the truth, so finally I took it off. But I've never stopped wondering what happened to Hank. A lot of my nightmares are about jungles, even now.

So. Anyway. I'm standing up there at Mandy's wedding, I can't see anything but the altar and the priest—he was young then, hand-some, like that guy in *The Exorcist*—and he's thundering along about the transience of youth and beauty and the body like we're not at a wedding at all, more like we're at a funeral, and Mandy's making little choking noises and Bill's clutching her hand and all three of us are glaring at that guy. Shut up, shut up, *shut up*. Well, he didn't. Never so much as looked down at us. I should have said something. Maybe I would, now, but I was too scared then, espe-cially since it wasn't my church and who was I to challenge some-body else's priest? I tried to catch his eye, I did, I'll say that much for myself, but he wouldn't look at me, so I was left staring at the statue on the wall behind him, the one of Jesus nailed to the cross. If you want to feel lousy about having a body, all you have to do is look at that thing. Ouch. Every nail. Every drop of blood, I swear, and that poor man in so much pain he must have been out of his mind with it, just praying to die soon so it would be over. You can tell all that, from that statue. I guess that makes it good art. I tried to talk to Mandy about it once, but Mrs. Mincing was there and she gave me a lecture about how Jesus wasn't suffering on the cross, he was at peace, he was happy to be doing the Lord's will, and if I'd been a godly person I would have known that. Well, religious or not, you'd never know it from looking at that statue. Even now, when-ever I think about what might have happened to Hank in the jun-gle, I wonder if he wound up looking like that. It's what my father looked like, when he was dying of cancer.

So I'm standing there looking at that statue, figuring that's what Cindy feels like too—like she's nailed to a piece of wood with every-body staring at her and nobody doing a thing to help—and I'm thinking, well, I'll talk to her at the reception, I *will*, even if the whole town cuts me dead for it. I'll go up to her and say something friendly. Better yet, I'll go up and give her a big hug. Except that I never got my chance, because Cindy didn't go to the reception. Of course she didn't: I should have known she wouldn't. She walked out of that church and she disappeared. For years. Like Hank.

Well, it ate at Mandy like you wouldn't believe. She thought it was her fault, because if she'd included Cindy in the wedding maybe everything would have happened differently. "You were right," she

kept saying. "You were right all along. I should have asked her."
Which made me feel like dirt, of course. I kept telling her I hadn't
been right, I'd just been self-righteous, and that's not the same
thing. Her parents paid for that wedding and it was their show all
along, not hers and Bill's, and they sure didn't want any spotlights
on Cindy. Mandy couldn't have done anything.

"Blame the priest," I kept telling her. "Blame your parents, if
you have to blame somebody." Mr. and Mrs. Mincing didn't even
look for Cindy: just said good riddance, as if you can wash a daughter off your hands as easily as a speck of dust. Mandy and Bill looked,
got the police to put out a missing-person report, checked with bus
stations and lying-in homes and hospitals, everyplace they could
think of. They printed up fliers with Cindy's picture, and every year
on Cindy's birthday they put ads in papers all over the country:
"Happy Birthday Cindy, We Love and Miss You, Please Call Your
Sister Mandy Collect." They did all that stuff for six or seven years,
I don't even remember how long it went on, and they couldn't find
a clue. It wasn't cheap, either, taking out all those ads. Bill was a
prince about it, he really was, and it can't have been easy on him. I
used to wonder if maybe he was the father of Cindy's baby, especially after what had happened to me, but I decided that no, he
couldn't be, because Cindy had to have gotten pregnant while Bill
and Mandy were a steady couple—practically engaged already—and
I just couldn't believe that Bill would do such a thing. I still can't,
even with what he did later. And there were plenty of other guys
who could have been the father. So I think he was so good about
the search because he was a decent man, not because he felt guilty.

But finally, after years of not finding anything, Bill told Cindy
that their marriage was haunted and that she had to choose between
looking for Cindy and living with him. She and I had a long talk at
Sam's Sodas over that one, believe me. She didn't touch her vanilla
shake at all that time, and we talked and talked and finally I told her
I thought Bill was right. "You've done everything you can," I told
her. "You'd have found her by now if she wanted to be found. Wherever she is she wants you to be happy, Mandy." I don't know if I believed that even while I was saying it, but Mandy did, and she said
it made her feel better, and she prayed for Cindy every night and

settled down to loving Bill and her kids the rest of the time.

You can't forget a lost sister, though. Mandy and I still talked about Cindy, how she'd probably gone to some big city—Chicago, Houston—and gotten a good office job, because Cindy could type like nobody's business. We decided Cindy was happy. We knew it. We had her life all planned out for her. Except that we didn't know anything, of course, and we knew *that*, even though we never admitted it. We told each other that she'd probably had her baby and then gotten married to some nice young lawyer or doctor who wanted kids, in a church with a *nice* priest this time. Mandy always insisted on that, that this new priest would be kind, he'd forgive Cindy her past the way her husband forgave her her past, the way priests are supposed to forgive, because that's what Christ did. That's what Mandy said; I didn't know, not being religious. The only priest I'd ever met was the one who married Mandy and Bill, and I'd heard so many different things about Christ from so many different people that I didn't know what to think. Seems to me you can make anything you want to out of Christ; he's like a politician that way.

After Mandy and Bill stopped looking for Cindy they seemed happy for a long time. Bill was going great guns with his CPA business—even in a little town like Innocence, everybody needs their taxes done—and Mandy kept busy taking care of the kids, which would have been a full-time job for anybody. They looked like the perfect family, and I was jealous again. Thinking back on it, I guess I should have known better. There was plenty of tension there, like the way Bill always talked about how his girls were going to go to college, not just get married right out of high school and have babies like all the other women in town. The girls were smart enough to know that every time he talked that way he was putting down their mother, and they didn't like it. Mandy didn't mind that so much— she wished she'd been able to go to college too—but whenever Bill talked about teenagers having babies she remembered Cindy, and the old wound opened all over again. So really, that family was in an awful mess even before Bill fell for his secretary.

That was the first time Mandy ever called me crying, when she found out about Bill and Genevieve. That was the girl's name, a movie-star kind of a name, the sort of name most wives around here wouldn't trust even if she hadn't been twenty-two and blond, with the kind of figure you usually only see on swimsuit calendars. She said the whole thing, too, Genn-eh-vee-ehve, didn't shorten it to Jean or Jenny, so everybody thought she gave herself airs. God only knows what she thought she was doing in a little town like this, aside from making trouble. Somebody said she came here after college— of *course* Bill would fall for a college girl, even if she only majored in phys-ed—to work and save enough money to go to California and be an actress. Seems to me like if she'd really wanted to be an actress she wouldn't have settled down in Muncie with Bill after the divorce, but what do I know? Maybe she really loved him. He was handsome, Bill was, even then. He'd kept himself fit all those years when Mandy and I were getting bigger and bigger, Mandy from having four kids and me from sitting around Yodel's Yarns, eating candy bars and dreaming about the day when Hank would come home from 'Nam and walk through the door and ask me to help him pick out a nice wool blend for a cable sweater because it's cold back here, away from the jungle, and what are you doing tonight, Cece? Want to help me stay warm?

I'd been dreaming about Hank all those years, and Mandy had been dreaming about Cindy, and Bill, it turned out, had been dreaming about platinum-blond secretaries with 38C cups and twenty-four-inch waists who took *Penthouse* letters in the nude at the hot sheets hotel on the highway. The kid who worked the front desk told his girlfriend, who told her cousin, whose hairdresser gave Mandy's godmother her monthly perm. It made it a lot harder on Mandy, that all those people had known before she did, and of course she was beside herself. Who wouldn't be? But when she called me crying and started ranting about Genevieve, calling her a slut and a bitch and a little whore, I still thought, *This isn't the Mandy I know.* Because she never used words like that, and they were the kinds of words her parents had used about Cindy, the words that priest would have used if he hadn't been in a church. "I hope she rots and dies," Mandy hissed at me. "I hope she gets hit by a truck. I hope she burns in hell."

Mandy wanted me to be angry too, to keep her company, and of course I felt sick about the whole thing. But mostly I was sad, lis-

tening to her, because I felt like everyone I knew had died somehow, changed into other people when I wasn't looking, people I
didn't like very much. The Mandy who'd cared about people even
when they got into trouble had turned into her mean mother and
into that horrible priest both, and the Bill who made promises turned
into the Bill who broke them, and the Cece who was smart and pretty
and deadset on marrying Hank turned into—well, what I am now.
Not pretty, except maybe in the face, and not married, and not
much of anything, really, except somebody who runs on at the mouth
and runs a yarn store, helping people who still know how to knit pick
out patterns for baby blankets. I'd turned into Aunt Cece—that's
what Mandy's four girls always called me—just like I really was
Mandy's sister, just like Cindy really had never existed.

I couldn't spend a lot of time being sad, though, because there
was too much else to do. First of all, I was mad myself, mainly at
Bill. Mandy wanted Genevieve to rot and die and I wanted Bill to
rot and die—or part of him, anyway, the upstanding part. And I knew
I had to stop hating Bill and concentrate on loving Mandy and the
girls instead, because that's what they needed now. That's what Bill
had taken away from them: knowing that they were loved, the way
you know the sun will always come up, the way you know there will
always be air to breathe whether you've done anything to deserve it
or not. And right then, I had to keep Mandy from doing anything
that would make her hate herself later on. So I said, "Mandy, honey,
I know you want that woman to die right now, but when you calm
down you won't feel so good about saying so, I know you won't, and
you have to think about that. You have to be careful now, because
you're so upset. You have enough to feel bad about, without adding
anything that doesn't have to be there. I don't care a fig about that
woman, or Bill either. All I care about is you and the kids. You just
sit tight, Mandy. I'll be there in ten minutes."

So I went over and stayed there, shut down Yodel's Yarns for a
solid week and did what Mandy needed me to do: cooked, did laundry, answered the phone and the door. News got around fast, the
way it always does about something like that. I kept the people
Mandy didn't want to see away from her and made coffee for the
ones who were welcome. I looked after the kids and tried to help

them make some kind of sense out of what had happened. I helped Mandy find a lawyer and went with her to talk to him, because I knew I'd hear more of what he was saying than she could. I did the same kinds of things that Mandy had done for me when my father died. But that makes sense, because when a marriage dies it's pretty much like a person has, anyway.

Mandy's parents had moved to Albuquerque for their arthritis years before that—and good riddance, if you ask me—so I was really the only person around who could do all those things for her. I did whatever I could to help, but the whole time I felt like I didn't know Mandy at all anymore, like there was this new person where my best friend had been and I just had to keep pretending she was the person she was supposed to be, because otherwise what would I do? There I was, in this house I knew as well as I knew my own, better maybe—it was the house where Mandy'd grown up; she and Bill had taken it when her folks left—doing all the things I'd known how to do my whole life, like making sandwiches and telling the kids stories, and I felt completely lost.

So now maybe you can understand a little bit how I felt the second time Mandy called me crying. That was four months ago, about five years after Bill left, and I'd gotten used to the new Mandy by then but sometimes I still missed the old one, the one who loved everybody and never cursed anybody out, even the people who'd hurt her. The new one was a lot tougher, I've got to give her credit for that, but she was colder too, more selfish, less able to be nice to people just for the sake of being nice. I guess she had to be that way. Maybe she missed that earlier part of herself too. People who didn't like Mandy, before Bill left, always said that she'd never grown up, that she was just a little girl inside, and that's what they meant, I guess: that she was so sweet to everybody, that she always tried to think the best of people. Mandy grew up fast, after Bill and Genevieve, and the people who hadn't liked her before started to like her better. They said she'd finally found her backbone. Seemed to me she'd lost her heart, or thrown it away because it hurt her too much, and I wasn't sure she'd made such a good trade.

So I was almost glad, when she called me crying again, because it meant she'd gotten her heart back, whatever else had happened.

Oh, I was scared too, and guilty about that first flash of gladness. All three of those feelings went through my head in the minute between the time when I picked up the phone and the time when I could understand what she was saying. Because she was crying so hard I couldn't, at first. I thought something must have happened to one of the kids, or Bill had come back—I didn't know what. It was 9:45 on a Sunday morning, and I'd just started a donut and my first cup of coffee. I was standing in the kitchen in my robe, holding the phone in one hand and my coffee mug in the other, saying, "Mandy, what's wrong? Mandy, you have to slow down, I can't understand you, what happened?"

"Cindy's come home," she said finally, in a great gasp, and my knees went weak and the coffee mug shattered on the floor—my favorite mug, too, it was the one my father always used, all the way from Hawaii. It had bright fish and flowers all over it. I don't know where Dad got it; he'd never been to Hawaii. I always meant to ask him, and a few months after he died I was drinking coffee out of that mug and I realized that I never had asked, that I'd forgotten to ask, and that now I never could. And I started bawling like a baby, just like I was bawling now, with the mug in a zillion pieces on the floor and hot coffee everywhere.

"Oh, Mandy," I said. "Oh Mandy. I'll be right there. Just let me get dressed. Is she—is she—"

Is she happy, I wanted to know, does she have the life we made up for her? But Mandy said, "No, no, don't come here, meet me at the church."

"What?" I said. Mandy hadn't been in that church since her wedding, because of the priest. She said she never could believe that Father Anselm knew any more about God than the tomatoes in her garden did, probably less. She said she'd go back when the church got a new priest, but the last I'd heard Father Antsy was still there, even though Catholics usually rotate priests every five years. Bill always made it into a joke and said the Church had forgotten about Innocence, but Mandy thought we were stuck with Antsy because the bishop couldn't find anybody else who wanted him. So it seemed to me that church was the last place she'd want to go.

"There?" I said. "Why? I don't—"

"Ten o'clock Mass," Mandy said, still crying. "Hurry."
Then she hung up. I looked at the clock; it was 9:50. "Oh, Lord,"
I said, and ran to get ready.

Well, you can imagine how fast I drove to get there. If I was ever
going to get a speeding ticket in my life, it would have been then,
and I don't know what I would have said if I'd been stopped. "I'm
late for church, Officer." But nobody stopped me, even though I was
zooming along at about seventy miles an hour. I thought Cindy
would be at the church too. I kept wondering what she'd look like,
after all this time.

I got there after the service started, of course, and had to sneak
in those big doors, feeling like some kind of thief, thinking about
Cindy sneaking into the wedding so long ago. It was dark inside, except for the stained glass and the candles. I didn't think it was pretty,
today. The place stank of incense and the organ howled and rum-
bled and wheezed like something out of some old movie, probably
one with Vincent Price. There weren't many people there: two or
three families, some old ladies, and Mandy. I saw her right away,
sitting in the third pew.

By herself. I hustled up and slid in beside her. "Mandy!
Where—"

"Shhhh," she said, and reached out and grabbed my hand and
squeezed, hard. "She wants us to pray for her."

"Us?" I said. "Who, us?" Mandy knows I'm not religious.
"Where *is* she?"

People were glaring at us, by then. "Home," Mandy whispered.
In the candlelight I could see that she was crying again. "Hush, Cece.
Just pray. Pray for her to be well."

Which meant she wasn't, which meant, as far as I was concerned, that we had no business sitting there in that stink, that we
should have been with Cindy, taking care of her or taking her to a
doctor or doing something that would do some good. I couldn't see
how this was going to do any good, sitting in this cave listening to
Father Antsy droning about the temptations of television. When he
got going on Teenage Mutant Ninja Turtles as the four reptiles of

the Apocalypse I whispered to Mandy, "Look, I can't stand this, I'm leaving, I'll go to your house—"

"No," she whispered back, and grabbed my hand again. "She asked for you to be here. Because I told her—how we used to talk. How we used to tell ourselves she was happy. It meant a lot to her, that you did that. She wants you here, Cece. She asked us to come to Mass because she couldn't. Please."

Well, I didn't feel I could leave, after that, but I sure couldn't pray, either. I just sat there, fuming, wondering what was wrong with Cindy, trying not to listen to Antsy—he'd started in on soap operas—staring at that horrible cross up front, with that Jesus looking like he was going to open his mouth and scream in agony any second. Which was pretty much how I felt, just then. I heard Antsy saying something about body and blood and thought, *Well, now he's talking about TV movies,* and then everybody stood up and filed out into the aisle and I did too, I just followed Mandy, I was so distracted I couldn't think straight, and I took the stale biscuit and the sip of wine and then I remembered, when we sat back down again, that I wasn't supposed to do that, that at Mandy's wedding she'd said you were only supposed to take the communion if you were Catholic. I couldn't see that it mattered. Father Antsy wouldn't know the difference—I hadn't been in that church for twenty years and he wasn't exactly a big yarn buyer, so for all he knew I was a Catholic cousin visiting from another state—and anyhow I hadn't had much breakfast, not that a tiny little stale biscuit helped much. Mandy had said the wine and biscuit were supposed to be Christ's body and blood, I remembered that now, and the whole thing made me a little sick to my stomach, and even angrier. This priest lectures about the sinfulness of the body and then he makes people eat stale biscuits that are supposed to be pieces of a body—what kind of sense does that make? It's no better than those mountain climbers who eat each other when they run out of food, in my opinion. I don't see how anybody can believe that about Jesus' body anyway. The biscuit's just a cracker; it's not even meat. If they fed you hamburger, well, maybe that would be different, but they don't, and thank goodness too.

So anyway, finally the Mass was over and we drove back to Mandy's house, with me shooting questions at her the whole way.

Cindy'd shown up at five in the morning, just knocked on the door and there she was, standing on the porch, said she'd taken Greyhound from New York, said she didn't know where her baby was, it had been a boy and she'd left it in a train station where somebody would be sure to find it, said she'd done a bunch of things since then, in New York and Florida, wouldn't say what they'd been, but from the sound of it they hadn't been anything good. She hadn't been doing anything like what we'd imagined for her, that much was sure. "She's very thin," Mandy said, trying not to cry, "and she looks very tired, and she has a terrible cough. She wanted to know if I thought I could still love her. I told her, of *course*, Cindy, do you have any idea how much time I spent looking for you? And she said, but you didn't know I'd look like this, and then she asked me if I thought God could still love her."

God's too busy watching television, I thought, but I didn't say that. Antsy was the one watching television, and if there was a God, he probably didn't like Antsy any better than I did. So I just said, "She's home. She's home now. She's come home to get better. It's going to be all right, Mandy."

But when I saw her—lying in bed upstairs, with Mandy's oldest girl feeding her soup and the younger ones standing there looking scared—I knew it wasn't going to be all right, and that getting better wasn't what Cindy had come home for. She looked like the Christ hanging in that church, the same way I always pictured Hank looking in the jungle, the way way my father had looked at the end: like somebody who's dying by inches and can't even think of what to hope for anymore, except for the pain to be over.

That was the beginning of the darkest time I've ever known. Mandy kept saying that Cindy was going to get better, she was, of course she was, she had to, and even when Cindy got worse instead Mandy wouldn't take her to a doctor. I think she knew the truth, deep down, and was afraid to hear it from someone else. I was over there as much as I could, helping to take care of Cindy, but most of the time I'm not sure she knew where she was or who we were, or who she was herself. And finally even Mandy had to see that, and she took

Cindy to the doctor and the doctor said Cindy should go into the hospital right away, right now, and Mandy said nonsense and took Cindy home again. And she screamed at me when I said the doctor was right. And in the meantime the girls had gotten more and more sullen and angry and confused, and the oldest one's boyfriend had gotten killed on his motorcycle, and the youngest one had started staying out way too late and getting bad grades in school. And it seemed to me like Mandy'd gotten her heart back only to have it broken again, for good this time, and maybe her mind too. I was afraid for her.

I was afraid for myself. A few days after Cindy came back I'd started having belly pains and the runs, and I told myself it was just the excitement, just worry and stress, it would get better in a little while. It didn't, though. It got a little worse each day, and each day I got a little more scared, because intestinal cancer was what had killed my father, and this was how it had started. I was afraid to go to the doctor and I was afraid not to go to the doctor, and I was too embarrassed to talk to anybody except Mandy about it. Too many times when I've been sick, even with a cold, people have blamed me for it, because I'm overweight. I don't know if those extra fifty pounds are my fault or not, but being sick isn't. Mandy knows that.

But I couldn't talk to Mandy, because she had too many problems of her own, and I knew she was counting on having me there, and how could I tell her I was afraid I might be going away too? Half the time she was so distracted she couldn't understand what you were saying even if it was about something simple, like buying milk. How could I tell her I was afraid I had cancer?

I couldn't. And if I couldn't talk to her I couldn't talk to anybody, and that hurt almost as much as my belly did. I lay awake for hours at night, worrying, and I looked worse and worse all the time, more and more exhausted, and nobody at Mandy's house even noticed. All of them were looking more and more exhausted too, and I guess it was silly of me to feel like they didn't care about me anymore, but that's how I felt anyway.

The morning after Mandy refused to put Cindy in the hospital, I woke up and thought, I'd better go to the doctor today. Don't ask me why I decided to do it then: because Mandy's pig-headedness made me see my own, maybe, or because the pain had woken me up in the middle of the night—that had never happened before—or because there was so little hope left that what did it matter? I'd already decided I had cancer. What could the doctor say that would be any worse than that? He'd just be telling me what I already knew.

So I called the doctor's office and told them what was going on and made an emergency appointment—they were mad at me for making them find a space that day, you could tell—and I closed the store for a few hours and went over there. It was Dr. Gallingway, the same one who'd treated my father. I'd never much liked him, but he was the best doctor around for that kind of thing. The nurse came and asked me a bunch of questions and took a bunch of blood and had me get undressed and get into one of those ridiculous paper gowns, and then Dr. G. came in.

"You've let yourself go," he said, looking at me. "You used to be an attractive woman, Cece."

You see what I mean? No hello, Cece, how are you, what are you doing these days? Just an insult, and then he starts lecturing me on how I have to watch my diet, I'm ruining my health the way I live—as if he has any idea how I live when he hasn't even seen me for ten years—and I'm already at risk for cancer because of my family history. As if I didn't know that.

I just sat there and looked at him. Later I thought of lots of things I should have said—"You've let yourself go, Dr. Gallingway. You used to have manners. You used to have hair"—but of course none of that occurred to me when it would have been useful. I just sat there feeling ashamed, and when he finally wound down I said, "Well, I guess the question's whether you want to make any money off my unhealthy lifestyle or not. Because if you don't stop talking to me that way I'm walking out of here."

Dr. Gallingway shut up, goggling at me like his stethoscope had just demanded a raise, and I swallowed hard and told him why I was there. When I was done he shook his head and said, "You shouldn't have waited so long to come in. First thing tomorrow morning I want you to go over to the hospital for an upper GI."

"Sounds like a soldier," I said. It was supposed to be a joke, even though when I said it I thought of Hank, dying in the jungle somewhere.

He didn't laugh. He looked at me and said, "It stands for *gastrointestinal*," a little more slowly than he'd been talking before.

"I know," I told him. You pronounce that very well, Dr. Gallingway. How many years of medical school did it take for you to learn such a long word? I thought about saying that, I swear, but I'm glad I didn't. It was like Mandy's saying she wanted Genevieve to die: one of those mean things you'll probably regret later, when it's too late.

I remembered when my father had his upper GI. He'd called it Upper Guts, Inner, because he couldn't remember all those syllables. I teased him about it, on the way to the test. I think that was the last time Dad and I laughed about anything, because when they did the test they saw something growing in there and they told me they had to keep him in the hospital and then they told me they had to operate and then they told me it was cancer. I drove home from Dr. Gallingway's office wishing I could just die in my sleep.

The upper GI was at eight in the morning in a room that looked like the inside of a rocketship, all metal and huge machines. I'm not a morning person, especially when I'm not allowed to have my coffee and donut, especially when I haven't gotten any sleep because I spent all night crying, and I never much liked science fiction movies. The last one I saw was *Alien*, and I didn't exactly want to think about that right now, with my own gut feeling just like something was about to come busting out of my belly. I sat there in another smock—cotton, this time, and at least they'd let me keep my underwear on—hoping the doctor who did the test wouldn't have too many tentacles and wouldn't look at me like he thought I did. At least I'd never met him before, so he couldn't tell me I used to be an attractive woman.

When he came in I saw that he was real young and handsome, and wearing, I swear, a collar that made him look just like a priest. Later he told me that it was a lead shield to protect his neck from radiation, but when I first saw him it didn't incline me to be friendly.

I hadn't been too impressed with doctors and priests lately, and here was somebody who looked like both.

He smiled at me and held out his hand and said, "Good morning, Ms. Yodel. I'm Dr. Stephenson," and I thought, well, at least he has manners. He asked me how I was feeling and I told him, and I told him about Dad, and I thought, well, here comes the lecture.

He didn't lecture me, though. He just looked serious and said, "I'm sorry. You must be very frightened," which made me feel better right away, because I hadn't been able to tell anybody about being scared, not even Mandy, and you'd think Dr. Gallingway could have said something nice like that, with all the money I was paying him, but of course he didn't. Then Dr. Stephenson said, "Your symptoms could be caused by a lot of other things, you know."

Well, I didn't know that. Dr. Gallingway sure hadn't bothered to say anything like that. So I decided I liked Dr. Stephenson, even if he did look like a priest. He knew his job was to make people feel better, not worse. You'd think every doctor would know that—and every priest, for that matter—but as far as I could tell not too many of them had figured it out. It made the entire world seem a little bit friendlier, meeting someone like that. The way I felt then, it was almost worth having to have the upper GI.

"So what we're going to do," he said, "is have you drink a glass of this barium"—he held up this big paper cup of white stuff, looked like one of Mandy's vanilla milk shakes, with a big plastic straw in it—"and I'm going to watch it on the fluoroscope, this screen over here, as it travels down your esophagus into your stomach and your small intestines. The barium tastes chalky, kind of like Mylanta, and the test doesn't hurt. It's boring, more than anything, because it takes a long time. Sometimes I'll have you roll over onto your sides and onto your stomach, so I can see things more clearly on the screen, and during part of the test I'll have to press on your abdomen with that balloon paddle over there." He pointed at this weird plastic and rubber thing hanging on the wall, looked like a plastic tennis racket with a rubber middle, had a bulb dangling from it, like one of the ones they use to inflate blood pressure cuffs. "That's to make the barium move around to the places I want to look at. Do you have any questions, before we start?"

"Yes," I said. "Barium's radioactive, right? How do I get it out of me?" I was worried that even if the barium didn't find any cancer, it could cause cancer if it stayed in there.

He nodded and said, "It comes out the way anything else you eat comes out, and the barium's not all that radioactive, actually. After you leave here, make sure to drink a lot of fluids for the rest of the day, to flush the barium out of your system. Prune juice is good; it moves things along."

"How about coffee?" I said.

He laughed. "That's fine. That moves things along too."

The test wasn't bad, really. It was interesting even at the beginning, because I could look at the screen, so I could watch the barium traveling down my throat and into my stomach. It looked just like those pictures of the inside of the body you see in books, only in black and white. The barium was white in the cup, but on the screen the barium was black and my innards were white, like a negative.

Dr. Stephenson said my throat looked fine and my stomach looked fine, and we'd have to wait awhile for the barium to move through the small intestine. I should move around, he said. I'd have wanted to move around anyway, because it was cold in there. So he went away for a while and I walked around and read the labels on the machines and wondered how my father had felt, pacing in a little room like this, in the last minutes when he didn't know yet that something was growing in his gut.

So, of course, I'd gotten myself pretty scared again by the time Dr. Stephenson came back, especially since the pain was acting up. He took the balloon paddle off the wall and had me lie down again, and I craned my head back so I could see the screen, and he turned on the machine. And the face of Jesus stared out at me from the fluoroscope, just the same way he looked on that cross in Mandy's church, like *he* was in so much pain he could hardly stand it.

"Oh my God," I said. "Look at that!"

"What's wrong?" said Dr. Stephenson. He didn't act like he'd noticed anything, and I thought maybe I was crazy. When I looked at the screen again I could see that Jesus' face was made up of all the curls and folds of my gut, but it still looked like Jesus' face, with

the thorny crown and everything. It was just like one of those pictures you see on the cover of the *National Enquirer:* Jesus in somebody's fingerprints, the Devil in somebody's cornflakes, Elvis everyplace. I always thought all that stuff was nonsense, even worse than
Instant Miracle Cures, and here it was happening to me.

"Doesn't that," I said, "doesn't it look to you like, well, like a
face?" I didn't want to say whose face. Dr. Stephenson would think
I was a religious fanatic.

He cocked his head sideways and squinted at it and said, "Why,
so it does. I see what you mean. Isn't that interesting. I'm going to
press on your stomach with the balloon now, Ms. Yodel." And he
did, and I watched Jesus' face kind of roll around on the screen. He
must have been seasick in there. He looked about as green as I felt.
And Dr. Stephenson worked away with his balloon and told me
about how fluoroscope images are like Rorschach blots—you can see
anything in them if you look hard enough. Once he did an upper GI
on a little boy who swore he saw Big Bird.

The place where Dr. Stephenson was pressing now made Jesus'
mouth open and close, like he was trying to say something. "Get me
out of here," probably. And I wondered how he'd gotten in there to
begin with and then I realized, of course: it was that stupid biscuit,
the one I'd eaten by mistake when I went to church with Mandy.
The pain had started right after that, come to think of it. So there
must have been something to its being Christ's body, although if that
was true I didn't see how Catholics walked around without belly-
aches all the time. Maybe it didn't hurt, if you were Catholic. Maybe
that's why you weren't supposed to eat the biscuit unless you were.
I mean, you'd think they'd *tell* people something like that, honestly,
there should be a Surgeon General's warning. Here I was, I'd been
in pain for months, I'd thought I was dying, I was paying all this
money for this upper GI—which wasn't cheap, believe me—and the
whole time the problem was nothing but a piece of stale biscuit.

Well, I got pretty mad when I started thinking like that, let me
tell you. I was fuming, by the time the test was over. Dr. Stephenson squeezed my hand and grinned at me and said, "I have good
news for you, Ms. Yodel, I see no evidence of a Mass," and I just
looked at him like he'd lost his mind.

"A mass," he said gently after a minute, "a lump, that means I don't see anything that could be cancer."

You're damn right there's no cancer, I thought, furious, and then I thought I'd had to drink this stuff that could cause cancer, maybe, to find out I didn't have any, and I got even madder. But none of that was Dr. Stephenson's fault and he'd been real nice to me, so I had to try to be polite. "Thank you," I said, "I'm very glad to hear that." And then I realized that must sound very cold to him, so I said, "You're a very nice man. Most doctors don't explain things as well as you did. Thank you," and that made him look happy and I felt a little better, about him, anyhow.

Not that I felt better about anything else. How was I going to get Jesus out of there? With prune juice? He'd been in there for months and plenty of other things had come out, but he hadn't. Who do you talk to about something like that? Any doctor would think I was crazy, and I couldn't see myself going to Father Antsy. He'd just tell me everyone should have Jesus inside them, and that's fine if you're a believer, but I didn't feel much more religious than I had before I ate the biscuit. Jesus hurt, and that's the truth, and I wanted my intestines back to myself. If it had been the Devil inside me, maybe a priest would have been some help. I wondered if Jesus could make your head turn all the way around, like Linda Blair's.

I thought about all of this when I was getting dressed, and I walked through the hospital lobby still thinking about it, so mad I wasn't even looking where I was going, and I practically walked straight into Mandy.

"Cece!" she said, and grabbed me and started crying. She didn't even ask me what I was doing there, which shows you how upset she was. "Cece, I finally decided the doctor was right, Cindy's upstairs now, I brought her here two hours ago and went home to get her toothbrush because I'd forgotten it and I was just heading out the door again when they called me to say she's dying, she'll only last another few hours, and she knows it, too. She's asked for Father Anselm."

"She asked for *him?*" I said. We were already heading for the elevators. "Why in the world would she do that? He's the one who drove her away from here in the first place!"

"She wants last rites," Mandy said. "He's the only Catholic priest in town. It has to be him. Last rites are a formula: how badly can he do? She's dying and she wants forgiveness, Cece."

"She won't get it from him," I said. A wedding's a formula too, and we both knew what Antsy had done with that. "That man wouldn't forgive his own grandmother if she took too long crossing the street. He'd blame it on her sinful body." It's a good thing Mr. and Mrs. Mincing were in New Mexico, baking their joints, or Cindy probably would have wanted them there too. All three of those people should have been asking Cindy's forgiveness, as far as I was concerned, but I guess Cindy was too sick to see it that way. Or maybe if she'd been able to see it that way she wouldn't have wound up where she was in the first place.

It seemed like that elevator took forever to come, and when we finally got upstairs we found Cindy pretty much looking like a corpse already, lying there just barely able to blink with about five tubes in each arm, and old Antsy standing next to her bed, holding his Bible and yammering away. I don't know if he'd done the rites yet or not; he was halfway into a rip-roaring sermon, from what I could tell. "Cynthia Marie, let us pray that the Lord will see fit to wash clean your heinous sins," that kind of thing, as if the Lord might think about it and decide not to after all, with that poor woman dying and wanting just this one thing before she went. It made me crazy, and I guess the Jesus in my belly must have felt the same way, because my stomach started hurting something awful. I could just picture the little guy squirming around down there, just wishing he could set this idiot straight, and I decided I'd help him out.

"Oh, *shut up,*" I said—exactly what I'd been wanting to say to that man for twenty years now, ever since the wedding—and Mandy actually giggled and Father Antsy glared at me like I'd just committed a really world-class sin. But my belly quieted down, so I figured Jesus approved. "You want to talk about heinous sins?" I asked Antsy. "Before you start in on Cindy's, why don't you think about your own?" He glared even harder when I said that, but I kept talking anyway. The Jesus in my belly must have given me confidence, or maybe I was a little loopy with being so tired. "Listen to yourself," I said. "When's the last time you said anything nice to anybody?

I know all the things you hate, Father Anselm. You hate bodies and
you hate TV and you hate people who make mistakes. Why don't
you talk about what you love, for a change? Isn't that part of your
job?"

"I love God," he said, looking down his long skinny nose at me,
and my belly panged and I thought, *GI Jesus doesn't think so.*

"If you love God," I said—as if I was some kind of authority on
God, what a joke!—"it seems to me you've got to love people too,
since God's supposed to love them. I don't think you've gotten that
part down yet. Why don't you practice? Tell Cindy something you
love about her. Go on."

He looked down at her, down at the bed, and wrinkled that nose
like Cindy was some piece of meat that had fallen behind the re-
frigerator and stayed there way too long, and he said in the coldest
voice I've ever heard, a voice that would turn antifreeze into icicles,
a voice that would give the Grinch nightmares, "God loves you, my
daughter."

"And you don't?" Mandy said. She was shaking. "No, of course
you don't. How could you? Get out of this room, Father Anselm."

Antsy got, in a hurry, and I gaped like an idiot. I'd never heard
Mandy talk that way to anybody. Even when she wanted Genevieve
to die, she never sounded like that. She practically had sparks coming out of her ears, she was so mad. At first I couldn't believe it and
then I thought, well, why not? Here's the old Mandy who cares about
people joining forces with the new Mandy, the one who sticks up
for herself, and they make a pretty good pair after all, don't they?
"Good for you," I said softly. I'd never been so proud of her.

She didn't answer, just went over to the bed and took one of
Cindy's hands in hers and started rubbing it, and I went over too.
Cindy just stared up at the ceiling. There was no way to tell if she'd
even heard anything that had just happened, or if she'd hear anything we said now, but I knew I had to say something to her, because I'd never have another chance. And it occurred to me that I'd
said a lot of things to Cindy, all those months she'd been at Mandy's
house, but they'd always been about the present, not the past. "How
are you feeling today, Cindy? Can I get you some water? Do you
want another blanket?" I'd never said anything about how we'd all

gotten to where we were, and I'd never told her anything about how I felt.

"I'm so sad you're so sick," I told her, and then, all in a rush, "It isn't fair, you know, it isn't, not one little bit. I know you think you're being punished for something, but what happened to you could have happened to just about any girl in this town, Cindy. It could have happened to me. I had a pregnancy scare when I was seventeen years old, I never even told Mandy that, and when she and Bill got married and I was standing up in front of the altar I felt just awful, because I wasn't any better than you were and by rights you should have been the one up there, if your mother and daddy hadn't been so mean about what had happened to you. I know Mandy thought so too, she did. I wanted to tell you all of that, but you left before I could. I don't blame you for leaving; I'd have done the same thing in your place. And whatever else you did, after you left, well, I'm not in any position to judge. All I can say is I wish you hadn't suffered so much, Cindy." We still didn't know much about what had happened to her, or where, but we'd seen things when we were taking care of her. Scars, from needles it looked like—and from other things too, things I didn't want to think about. It looked like people had hurt her, and not by accident either, and it looked like she'd tried to hurt herself. "You were just a little girl, Cindy, no worse than anybody else, and more than I wish anything I wish you hadn't had to go through your life thinking you were bad."

It was the truth, that's all. She hadn't so much as twitched the whole time I was talking, and I still couldn't tell if she'd heard a word I'd said. I bent and I kissed her forehead and I said, "God bless you, Cindy," because I knew she believed in God, even if I wasn't sure I did, and I knew she'd wanted some kind of blessing from Father Antsy and she hadn't gotten one. Mine probably wouldn't do her much good, but at least I'd tried. And when I straightened up from kissing her I realized that the pain in my belly was gone, completely gone, for the first time in months, and I thought, well, GI Jesus must have liked it, whether Cindy did or not.

Mandy hadn't said anything. She just stood there, holding Cindy's hand and looking at me, and I could see she was about to start crying again and I didn't think I could take it. "I'm going home

now," I said, "so you can say your goodbyes in private. Call me—
later. All right?"

She nodded, and I left. It wasn't even that I wanted to give her
privacy, because I knew Mandy wouldn't have minded if I stayed,
but it was just too sad in that room. Whenever I looked at Cindy I
thought about my father, and Hank in the jungle, and that poor
wooden Christ on his cross, and I just couldn't stand it, not after a
sleepless night and no breakfast. I wouldn't have been any good to
Mandy if I'd stayed, and I had things I had to do for myself. On my
way home I bought a gallon of prune juice, and as soon as I got
home I started drinking it. I didn't like the idea of that barium
spending one more second sloshing around my insides than it absolutely had to.

I drank prune juice for the next two hours, and then I drank water
for two hours after that, and nothing was happening except that I
had to pee every two seconds. All that liquid was coming out, but
the barium wasn't. I was starting to get pretty worried about it when
the phone rang, and I thought, Oh, Lord, that'll be Mandy, crying
her head off, and it was and she was. I kept saying over and over,
"I'm so sorry, Mandy," and finally I realized that she was trying to
say something herself.

"Cece, listen to me, it's not what you think, she's not dead, she's
better."

"She can't be better," I said, as gently as I could, and I thought,
well, it's over. Cindy's dead and Mandy's gone clean out of her
mind, and now I'm going to have to bring up those four girls all by
myself. And then I remembered that Mandy was religious, and I
thought, maybe this is just church talk. Maybe she's trying to comfort herself. "You mean—she's in heaven now, Mandy?" It felt weird
even saying the word, but if it helped her that was what counted.
"With the—angels?" Like I said, I was really tired.

"*Angels?*" Mandy said. "I don't believe in angels any more than
you do, Cece Yodel! I mean she's better, right here in the hospital,
every bit as alive as I am!"

I nearly groaned. If Cindy was still alive that meant they'd put her on some kind of machine, and people could keep breathing for years on those things, sucking money into the hospital faster than a drowning man gulps seawater. "Mandy, I really truly don't think she'll ever be better—"

"But she *is*," Mandy said, babbling. "It's a miracle, that's all, that's the only word for it, she's so much better the doctors can't believe it, *they* say it's a miracle even, her fever's gone and she knows who I am and they did some blood tests and they're *normal* now, Cece, they were all haywire before and they've just gone back to plumb normal, Cece, I swear to God I'm not crazy and I'm not making this up—"

"I know you aren't," I said. All of a sudden I knew what had happened. "Mandy, honey, I can't tell you how happy I am and I'll be there just as soon as I can but I have to go now, all right?"

I did, too. The prune juice was finally working. I rushed into the bathroom and got there just in time, and sat there, just being happy, while the prune juice did what it was supposed to do. So there, Father Antsy. Even Jesus needs a body to work miracles with, and he picked mine, how do you like that? I know religious people think pride is a sin and most of the time I agree with them, but this time I felt like I hadn't had anything to feel proud of in so long that maybe I deserved it, and anyway I was mainly happy for Mandy and Cindy. And I sat there thinking about miracles, and I thought, Well, GI Jesus, how about one more miracle, how about letting us know where Hank is? How about bringing him home, happy and healthy?

I figured Jesus wouldn't have enough time for that, though, because he was probably on his way out of my body, now that Cindy was better. I wondered what he'd look like when he left, if maybe he'd look happy too, finally. When the juice had finished its work I looked down wondering if I'd see a tiny cross in there, or a little guy in a beard and loincloth, or what.

Well, that was just silliness, of course. What came out was white, whiter even than the barium had been when I drank it, white as freshly bleached sheets or new snow or any of the other things people talk about when they're trying to describe whiteness—so white it looked almost like it glowed, but maybe that's because it was radioactive, I don't know. It didn't look like anything to do with Jesus, though. It looked like a big fish, and then when I flushed and it was whirling around it changed shape and looked like a bird, and then it was gone. Which just goes to show you that Dr. Stephenson was right: if you look at a shape that isn't much like anything in particular, you can see anything you want.

So I had to laugh at myself, the way I'd given myself all those airs about pulling off a miracle. Oh, Cindy's been getting a little stronger every day since then: the next day she drank some Sprite and the day after that she sat up in bed and then she started going to the bathroom by herself and watching game shows and asking for cheeseburgers. She's coming home from the hospital tomorrow. So it sure looks like an Instant Miracle Cure, but even if it is, it probably has nothing to do with me or my intestines. Cindy just decided she wasn't ready to die, that's all—you hear stories about that all the time—or the blood tests were all wrong to begin with. You hear stories about that, too. So I'm still not going to say I'm religious. But I have been putting in a few prayers for Hank, just in case there's a God after all.

MARTHA SOUKUP

WAKING BEAUTY

SHE SOUGHT HIM OUT IN A DREAM. IT ISN'T HARD, IF YOU KNOW HOW.
Amy didn't know how but she wanted it, she worked it out.

He worked down the hall. His name was Edward; he only had
a cubicle. Amy had a small office to herself, where she did nothing
interesting, but she did it very well. Great stacks of paper came into
her office every day, and small tidy reports, printed and bound by
her assistant Cindy (who didn't even have a cubicle), often with com-
puter disks full of spreadsheets and animated graphs attached, left
her office every day for the office of one of several men three flights
up and with much bigger offices than hers. She rarely saw those men.
She wrote their last names and floor number on a line on an envelope with holes in it, and a string to tie it together, after she crossed
her own name off the envelope.

Every day, the next-to-last thing she did was to cross out her own
name.

There was nothing interesting at all about taking the stacks of
reports and information sent to her by people she never saw and
turning them into something simple and neat for other people she

never saw. People she never saw made decisions about thousands and millions of dollars, fortunes she never saw, based on her reports. It was a large, but uncomplicated, puzzle, a nest of questions that resolved into one simple conundrum, falling naturally into simple patterns and simple answers.

Approached right, it was as natural and meditative as solving a crossword, one that took six hours and four cups of coffee instead of one cup and twenty minutes to work. And it earned Amy her office with its door that shut (though the door was made of glass and anyone could look in and see her with her papers) and a paycheck every two weeks, like an award certificate for excellence in puzzle-solving.

This man Edward down the hall in his cubicle had not won a prize like that, but he would, she thought, or he would leave the company for brighter chances. Beautiful confident men didn't stay in cubicles, for women and men both to stop and linger and chat every time they went by his desk. Those men and women always looked, especially the women, more pleased than people in office buildings had any right to, as though Edward were having the best time and had been nice enough to share it with them. Everyone liked Edward.

That alone meant he wouldn't stay in a cubicle in the middle of an office floor. It didn't take a talent for patterns to see that one. He wouldn't always be shared, he would be snatched up. It might not be so long before he had an office on another floor, maybe even a big office three flights up.

And that meant she didn't have much time to try.

On Thursdays the puzzle often had fewer pieces in it. The men and women who sent reports to her were tired, but they weren't in the mad rush to finish late projects at week's end that they would be in on Friday, and they weren't as clogged with weekend business as they were on Monday. This Thursday Amy finished putting all the pieces in place very early, a little after one. She didn't tell Cindy. She called Cindy into her office, pushing a button on her phone instead of walking the few steps outside her glass door.

"I'd like copies of all these," she said to her assistant, who had graduated last year with honors in cultural anthropology and English, and now made photocopies and processed words all day. Amy had no illusions about people earning what they got. Patterns were not about fairness. She handed Cindy a thick stack of papers and odd receipts that would not feed through an automatic feeder. "I'd like everything sized to fill a full sheet of paper."

"Okay," said Cindy. She never complained or questioned. Amy assumed her real life was entirely out of the office, her workdays a kind of unmurmuring sleepwalk until she could be where her life came fully awake.

"After that you can take your lunch." Cindy had told her she took late lunches so the last part of the day would go the fastest. Everyone looked for the patterns they were the most comfortable in.

Now, without her assistant at the desk outside her office, without someone with Cindy's unthinking grasp of Amy's regular patterns and routines to watch her, Amy could break her patterns. Soon. One was left she didn't want to break.

At one-thirty Edward walked by on his way to lunch. He paused at her glass door and smiled a little smile, more hesitant than the well-met smile she saw him give everyone else. Amy smiled back at him, looked down at her desk, and smiled up again. Edward gave her a little half-wave, with his left hand that had the ring on it, and went on to the elevators.

This was the pattern between them that had made her decide to try. She saw another woman hastily neaten a stack of papers and grab her purse, not looking at all as though lunch were a thought that had randomly occurred to her. This sort of thing always went on, despite Edward's ring. The patterns of office gossip did not make it clear to Amy whether Edward engaged in office affairs or only in office flirtations: either way, she had no interest in something that empty, not like the woman chasing after Edward for lunch. Amy just smiled when he paused by her office.

She turned back to her desk to look for the pattern that could break through the patterns.

It was simply another puzzle. People naturally fit into their patterns, sleepwalking. Cindy sleepwalked. Everyone did. More often than not, Amy knew perfectly well, she sleepwalked too. Edward too, though he seemed more awake than everyone else; it was what made her notice him.

The next three hours Amy spent poring over her notes on her officemates' patterns, the routines she'd charted for weeks, looking for a key. She was working on hope and dreams and faith, instead of her usual mundane reliance on business forms and patterns: but she was falling into her routine of puzzle-solving, that natural thing. When Edward came back from lunch, the woman who had grabbed her purse to dash out with him chattering at his side, he glanced through her glass door and saw charts full of lines and curves all over her desk. He raised an eyebrow just a bit: it wouldn't look at all like the usual form of work that occupied her. By the time Cindy got back from her late lunch, the papers and charts were hidden away, the day's final reports retrieved from Amy's desk drawer for copying.

Cindy returned with the bound reports, and Amy slid them into envelopes and crossed out her name. She was satisfied. She felt the puzzle was solved.

Before she left, she went back for a cup of coffee, past Edward's cubicle. She stopped at his cubicle as she returned, and stood a moment. Edward was putting his own papers away, but he looked up at her, looked her in the eye, steady. She smiled and walked on, sipping cold coffee.

At home she had a different life. Some cats and some plants and a boyfriend who expected to marry her. It was a life hard to remember in the office. He stayed over that night and she moved absently in bed with him, thinking about her other life. When she fell asleep she dreamed of it.

She took no more time to think about her plans. All her charts suggested Friday was the best day for it; Friday everyone was near-asleep in an end-of-week daze. There would never be a better time.

She wore her black lace bra, under a simple blue dress that buttoned down the front. She wore a touch of the expensive perfume from the back of the bathroom cabinet. Aside from that she dressed no differently than any other day.

She went into work and she went into her office and she closed the glass door. She took out the charts and the puzzle patterns and spread them on her desk, and she did the easy part that was hard, the thing she didn't quite understand that was simple.

A half-twist of the way things were.

The barest touch on the pattern at all.

She took well-worn patterns and encouraged them to be just enough stronger. She gently nudged the people in the building to move in a dream of their daily routines.

Yet she had only imagined she could do this. It was a way of moving patterns no one had seen but her, and though the solution was so clear, that clarity might have fooled her. She might only be imagining she could reach out in this way and nudge this pattern thusward, reach down another way and strengthen a braid of reflexes into compulsions.

This hallucinatory clarity: it was of stepping outside her own patterns, doing, for the first time, what she wanted and decided, alone.

With care and deliberation, she worked the solution to the puzzle she had set, using nothing more than the dreamlike ritual of a building full of people with no reason to wake. It was only the dream of a workday a little more for everyone else, so that they would sleepwalk a little more, and she could sleepwalk a little less. Only the same dream they always dreamed. Just once, just this once. There was something she needed to find out.

She finished, and she waited.

There was a long quiet moment.

The building felt as it always did on a Friday afternoon: only, she thought, a little more so.

Finally, she could only go see for herself.

She opened her glass door and went out among the cubicles. She stood and looked at her assistant. Cindy was typing exactly as she usually typed. Amy quietly took the paper from the top of the stack and replaced it with a blank sheet. Cindy kept typing. Sometimes a word could be read among the garble of letters on her screen: "Gentlemen" and "trends" and "profit" and "quit" and "facilitate." After a bit, she picked up the phone, which hadn't rung, said "Cindy Washington," and kept on talking, pausing now and then to listen. Amy could faintly hear the dial tone.

"Make ten copies of this for me," she said to her assistant, passing her the blank paper. Cindy glanced at it and nodded. It fit her dream.

Amy removed her right shoe and put it on Cindy's desk. Cindy ignored it. The shoe didn't fit her dream. Amy left it there and slipped off her other shoe, curling her toes in the carpet. No one would notice.

People walked up and down the office halls. Snippets of their conversation made sense. Snippets did not.

"I'm saying he can't keep batting .300 through the end of the month, he's been playing over his head," one man said to another as they passed, and the other man replied, "Okay, but you'll have to file it in triplicate." They smiled knowingly at each other and moved on.

By the coffee machine a woman carefully measured dry creamer into a mug of cool water, stirred it, blew on it, and drank it.

A young man was punching the copy button on the copy machine, over and over. There was no paper in the hopper. Two women stood in line behind him. One was talking about a soap opera, or possibly gossiping about her friends (if her friends were very busy and dramatic), and the other answered with advice about how she had rid her apartment of ants. The light flashed steadily under the copy tray, and no copies came out of the machine. Another man came to stand in the line, and the first man left, carrying a large stack of no paper, carefully, in his hands.

Amy walked to Edward's cubicle. His phone was ringing. She watched him answer, say "What? Who is this?", listen, and hang up baffled. He glanced up and saw her. She smiled.

"What's with everyone today?" he said. "Someone called my extension to order chow mein. Or are you going to ignore me, too?" She smiled again and shook her head.

Then she was overcome with shyness. She realized she had nothing to say. Somehow she'd skipped this part in her plans. She stood another moment blushing, and turned and hurried away. Around the next wall was the reception area (the receptionist with every line on hold, talking into a busy signal), and a couch, big, white and overstuffed, which was empty. She fell into it breathless.

Now she knew for certain this wasn't her dream, no hallucination. If she had been the dreamer, she could have dared anything. In a dream, why not, when it isn't real?

She had wanted something more real than an office flirtation, though, much more real than that, so she had taken everyone else away into a dream. Left, herself, in real life, but not alone, not by one other person. With one other. She had not expected this exposed and vulnerable feeling.

It was not too late to go back into her office and end these things.

And he sat down next to her.

At first she thought it was one of the others. "Go away," she said, not expecting the sleepwalker would register it. There was no answer, and a sort of pressure in the air made her turn her head around to look to see what it was.

Edward looked back at her. His weight on the couch curved the seat to pull her toward him.

He may be dreaming, too, after all, she thought. She wasn't sure how well she'd worked the patterns she'd tried to bind and bend.

"You," he said.

She watched him. She memorized his face and hair. She memorized the curiosity in his eyes. She had no idea what to say. She memorized his throat.

"Did this," he said. He sounded less shocked than interested.

"How else could I get you alone?" she said, a sudden balloon of laughter trying to fly up her throat.

"You might have pulled the emergency stop button in the elevator," he said.

She did laugh.

"Of course, I'd have to say to everyone else, 'Excuse me, this elevator's taken,' and kick them off," she said.

"You get one of those signs from a restaurant," he said. " 'Reserved for Party.' "

"Or from an airplane for saving your seat. *'Occupado.'* " She liked him just enormously. This was the longest conversation they had had.

"Sure, that's no problem. Everyone else could walk. Get their own *Occupado* sign if they don't like it."

While they were talking the receptionist was sharpening pencils at her desk. She sharpened one and then another, and the first one again, until they were small. She shook her head at them, threw them out, and opened another box of pencils. She stuck them in eraser-end first, producing a painful squeal of outraged metal that did not change her bored expression. Edward paid no attention to the noise, and neither did Amy, as he looked at her seriously; and the receptionist paid no attention to them sitting together on her reception-area couch.

"What do you do in that office all day?" Edward asked. "You're all glassed away from us out here, and I keep meaning to ask you, to meet you, but you always look so busy and terribly important. I'd hate to bother you."

"Oh, just reports for people who don't have time to figure things out for themselves," she said, knowing he was flattering her and flattered that he would. "It's not glamorous or anything. You wouldn't be interested."

"In what you do all day? Sure I would," he said, and he was a little bit closer on the couch. So she told him. And she asked him about what he did, and he explained a little and it seemed to her a lot more interesting than she would have thought someone else's form of paper-pushing would, but mostly he brought his questions back to her, and seemed very interested, and his knee was barely against her thigh, and later it was warm and firm there and she thought she could sit like that for the rest of her life, really, it felt so nice, though he didn't seem to notice they were touching and kept asking questions. She even answered the ones about her home and her family, though that all seemed impossibly far away. Their faces were so close she thought she felt his breath. Their officemates walked up and down the hall talking nonsense seriously as she and Edward talked with each other.

She didn't ask about his wedding ring, and he didn't say anything about it. He didn't ask if she had a boyfriend, and she didn't say anything about it. It felt as if they were in a time more real than life, with only the barest thread of a connection to it. None.

A messenger came out of the elevator and fell into the dream, not even glancing at the couple he had to walk around to get to the desk.

"I wondered what would happen when someone came from outside," Edward said.

"Oh," she said, "yeah. You noticed."

"I don't think I could have missed it," he said. "You did this all? And just so we could talk?"

Amy looked at him, his face open and curious and calm, and felt she must be blushing, and said, "Yes."

"You're incredible," he said to her then. "And I'm honored." It was simple and clear and burst the last piece of tension she'd held wide open.

So then she couldn't help it. She slid all the rest of the way against him and kissed him.

"Are you very afraid of me?" she whispered.

"No," he said. He drew his thumb around the curl of hair on her cheek. He wove his fingers into her hair and pulled her as close as she could be pulled.

The messenger talked with the receptionist, his gaze passing through Amy as Edward slowly, slowly unbuttoned her dress. He asked the receptionist to initial his crossword magazine as Edward kissed Amy between the lacy cups of her black bra. And by the time he thanked her and went back to the elevator to descend out of the office dream, Amy had put her hands up into the warmth under Edward's shirt. The receptionist was initialing her Post-It pad, one slip at a time, with an abbreviated sharpened-down pencil, sliding them forward across her desk and complaining to the departed messenger that there shouldn't be that much to sign.

Men and women dreamed in and out of the room, while Amy and Edward lay each other back on the broad soft sofa, and an hour passed and two and three.

She leaned back on his chest, a suction of perspiration between them. "It's four," she said.

"Mmm."

"I have to undo all this so that everyone can get home." Patterns, patterns.

"Don't get up," he said, touching her somewhere he knew now she liked.

Amy closed her eyes and felt every bit of her body. Rolled around and leaned over him, her elbows on the couch. "It's time," she said. He hadn't stopped touching her, so she took his wrist. "But we could talk."

"Talk," he said.

"You don't want to."

"If we have to," he said.

"I can't do this again," she said. "It's not the kind of pattern that can be repeated. When you do this once, you change things enough that no one will fall into this same pattern again."

"You can only be innocent once," he said.

"I've heard that," she said.

"So."

"Do you love me?" she said.

He made an unreadable gesture with his hands and shoulders. The ring was still on his left hand. "Yes. In a way. —I love you here, now. I love what you feel for me. You honor me."

"Do you love me tomorrow?" she said.

"In memory," he said. "I will in memory." He kissed her wrist.

"Yes," she said.

"Do you love me?" he said.

"In a way," she said, not knowing how she meant it except that it was different from how he had.

He kissed her. She said, "You have a wife."

"In the real world," Edward said, "yes." He took her hand. "That's my real world, and I hadn't thought to leave it today, but we did. And I never want you to think I've regretted the trip."

"Then tomorrow," she said.

"Is tomorrow," he said.

"You have your life," she said, and she thought of hers, which she had never once mentioned to Edward. It seemed far away, a haze of a pattern never as real as this long moment already slipping away.

"And a beautiful dream," said Edward, "for the rest of it."

She turned away, put on her bra, put on her dress. She made sure to turn the sofa cushions over before they left the reception area. The receptionist was buzzing other workers at random on the intercom. Amy kissed Edward once more, his arms strong and sweet around her, before she went back to pull the patterns loose to settle where they belonged. The feel of his arms and lips stayed on her as she pulled the strands of the dream loose, and the people outside her glass door shook themselves and looked at the clock and grabbed their coats and jackets. Monday would be a nightmarish day of an office trying to catch up from a wasted Friday.

At the elevator he smiled at her, and she smiled back. "Sweet dreams," he said softly, as they parted in the lobby in a swirl of a hundred office workers.

But it wasn't a dream.

So she never troubled Edward about what had happened, and she gave her notice the next week, and she found a job culling patterns somewhere else. And perhaps she married her boyfriend, and perhaps she didn't; and the rest of her life passed in a sort of a dream and a sleepwalk.

And the memory of one waking day.

CARTER SCHOLZ

MENGELE'S JEW

At a Party function, Dr. Josef Mengele corners Werner Heisenberg, the physicist. Isolated as he is at Auschwitz, that *anus mundi,* Mengele must take every opportunity to keep up with the most recent scientific developments. He prides himself that his knowledge extends even to atomic physics, while other medical men are content to remain glorified pharmacists.

—Suppose you have a cat in a box, says Heisenberg with a tight smile. —This little paradox, by the way, comes from my friend Erwin Schrödinger.

—Ah, Schrödinger. What a loss to German science, says Mengele.

—In the box is a mechanism. It holds a radioactive nucleus that may or may not decay according to the laws of quantum probability after, say, one minute. A Geiger counter detects any such decay, and triggers a hammer, which breaks a capsule of poison gas. After a minute, there is a fifty percent chance that the nucleus has decayed. The question is, after that minute, is the cat alive or dead?

Mengele thinks. The question must be subtler than it seems, yet he cannot imagine what Heisenberg is driving at. He regards the physicist's fine Aryan features, the reddish hair combed straight back, the intense eyes twinkling under heavy brows.

—But surely, there is a fifty percent chance . . . ?

—So one would think. But in the sealed box, the cat is neither alive nor dead. The cat is in a mixed state, composed of overlapping probability waves.

—That is because we cannot see inside the box . . .

—No, no, it is not a matter of incomplete knowledge. It is *the way things are.*

—This is stupendous! Mengele is thunderstruck. He literally falls back a pace. At once an objection forms in his sharp mind. —But when one opens the box . . .

—At that moment, the two waves converge, and the cat lives or dies.

—Merely by the act of observation!

—That's one interpretation.

—And if one never opens the box?

—Then I suppose, the cat remains in limbo, though Einstein rejects this interpretation. He finds it too idealist.

—Einstein, says Mengele pointedly, —is a jew.

Heisenberg regards him for a moment, then turns away.

Across the room Himmler is speaking. —It's easy enough to say, The jewish race is being exterminated, this is our program and we're doing it. But most of you know firsthand what it means when a hundred corpses are lying side by side, or five hundred, or a thousand. Not so easy. To have stuck it out and at the same time to have remained decent fellows, this is a page of glory in our history that will never be written.

Mengele is bored by the speech, though his handsome features remain alert. The graceful hand at his side flickers right, left, like an electron restless between energy levels, or as though he is conducting a Wagner aria.

In São Paulo, in the Estrada da Alvaranga, Mengele lies wearily on a bed in a tiny room. His hair is white, his breathing labored. His frail legs can barely support his weight, so he spends most of each day recumbent. In the evenings he takes a light meal that Elsa prepares for him. Sometimes he listens to the radio. Last night he found a station from the south, the announcer's voice deep in static, *a nona sinfônia de Beethoven regeda por Wilhelm Furtwängler.* It took him back to 1943 Berlin: the chorus of blond straightbacked youths like feverish angels following Furtwängler's frantic beat through Schiller's verse, *alle Menschen werden Brüder,* rushing as if to some divine consummation, *seid umschlungen Millionen,* gilt eagles glinting in the hall's dim light, and the tears came, for the beauty of the music, but also for the loss of that bright, pure Aryan world.

Daylight falls through the dusty window. Grime and paint have sealed it shut. The air is close and warm. The narrow room is just large enough for a cot and a night table. Mengele keeps the door shut and locked from inside. Weatherstripping across the sill presents a barrier to insects, though some inevitably get in. Even now a fly crawls across the day's *Estado da São Paulo,* resting atop Speer's memoirs, books by Hannah Arendt and Martin Buber, and Mengele's own notebook.

Near the books is a curious device. He has been forced to make changes from Schrödinger's description, but Mengele is not without ingenuity. The mechanics of the hammer and the vial of poison gas proved unworkable. Instead, he has used a simple rodent trap with a springloaded steel arm. The trap cradles a pressurized canister of hydrocyanic acid under its cocked arm so that the arm, when tripped, will snap down and break the valve, releasing the gas. So powerful is the spring, it takes all Mengele's strength to draw it back and lock it.

The only problem with cyanide gas, with Zyklon B, is that it goes bad. Fortunately his apparatus needs little, but every few months he must send an agent to buy fresh from a fumigator. The family chemical and farm equipment business in Buenos Aires still supports him with money, but it is too far away to be a reliable source of cyanide. He suddenly wonders if his current canister is fresh enough. It is behind the *Estado.* He lifts his head, and the fly springs into the air, buzzing. In the jaws of the trap, the canister's expiration date faces him. The date is yet to come. He shuts his eyes, his head falls back onto the pillow.

The sealed box into which this device will go is still imaginary, but an outline has begun to form. First Mengele noticed the ladder at the foot of the bed, more a suggestion than a presence. From day to day it grew more definite, like the onset of some disease, the vague malaise that precedes true symptoms until at last he could no longer pass it off as imagination. The ladder is of hewn wood lashed with hemp rope. It leans against the wall, so vivid that it attracts one's touch which, however, meets only air. Mengele has complained to Elsa of cobwebs in that corner, and she has swept and dusted around and through the ladder, but she has seen nothing. So, the doctor concludes, it is a matter of his superior perceptions.

Once the ladder became visible, he could see the trapdoor in the ceiling. Though tightly closed, the trapdoor somehow affords a view into the cell above. And the cell, Mengele has realized, is no more or less than the observation tower of his old Serra Negra house—the same six-foot cube from which he so often surveyed that dismal neighborhood. The tower has somehow been transported from Serra Negra to São Paulo.

Last of all to become visible was the jew, sitting slumped in a chair above Mengele's head. It worries Mengele that he is able to see the jew inside the cell, but so far it seems all right, for the jew is quite immobile: impossible to tell if he's alive or dead.

The problem of introducing his real device into this imaginary cell remains to be solved. The question of the trigger is also unanswered—he has no radioactive material, nor a Geiger counter—but that is of little concern, for it is not the outcome that matters. Quite the opposite. Mengele is interested only in the mixed state that obtains before the cell is opened, the mixed state during which quantum possibility is infinite and undecided.

The jew's outline is vague and shifting, as though the doctor is peering into a mist: it is a nondescript figure that variously takes the form of a young woman, a toothless old man, twin children. This multiplicity baffled him at first, but reflection made all clear. Schrödinger's experiment of the cat is purposely simplified, so that only two outcomes are possible. In the general case, however, there is an infinity of outcomes. At every moment, quantum transitions in every corner of the universe split the world into countless divergent replicas of itself. If reality consists of so many mixed states, is it not possible to reclaim, by correct observation, not the Reich that was but the thousand-year Reich that might have been?

A trigger more complex and subtle than Schrödinger's would not trip the cyanide, but would engage further conditions. As soon as Schrödinger's box is sealed, there are two cats: one alive, one dead. But as soon as a more complex device is armed, two, four, eight, countless intermediate states come into being. Armies, races of ghosts multiply and march forth to await some final determination.

As he considers the device, its poised steel arm like a gate under which the infinite possibilities of the cosmos pass, the room above his head seems to fill with jew upon jew, neither alive nor dead, until they are packed as tightly as cordwood. With a device of sufficient intricacy, judgment could be put off indefinitely.

In Berlin, Himmler has finished speaking. Heisenberg, expressionless, applauds with the rest. Mengele leans to address him.

—But surely the cat knows. Is not the cat's consciousness sufficient to resolve the uncertainty?

—Hm? Well, who knows, maybe not.

—But if you put a man in the box.

Heisenberg appears interested. —Wigner raised the same point.

Mengele racks his memory. Ah yes: Eugene Wigner, another physicist. Hungarian. Probably a jew, probably in America. It is astounding that Heisenberg, with his questionable friends, holds the high position he does. But, of course, Heisenberg's mother is friends with Himmler's mother. The applause fades, the band stumbles into a Strauss waltz.

—And what does Wigner say?

—To him it's a matter of consciousness. Only when the *meaning* of an observation enters the consciousness of an observer do the probability waves collapse to reality. This places a rather grave responsibility on living things with consciousness. Perhaps Wigner wished to spare cats this responsibility.

Mengele quips, —So men are conscious, though cats are not. What about jews?

Heisenberg's smile is pained. —Excuse me.

Mengele thinks, if two observers are involved in the same system, each has the power to collapse it to reality. The occupant of the box observes the mechanism before the experimenter does. That's a problem. But suppose the occupant is ignorant of the purpose, the *meaning* of the experiment. Then even as the gas floods the box, his perceptions are not *scientific* observations.

The afternoon is dim, chill, cloudy. On the wind comes a heavy, black, sweetish smoke. From the camp's observation tower, Mengele sorts the new arrivals. Below him, guards split the line in two. Those fit to work, or those specimens holding some interest for his researches, he directs to the right with a minute flick of his gloved hand. The remainder, to the left. The guards usher them along, this way, don't worry, we're going to disinfect you with a nice hot shower. *Reinheit macht frei.* A Strauss waltz plays on the loudspeakers. Mengele's pointing finger, right, left, keeps a kind of time.

Camp rules insist that a doctor certify the results of the disinfection. Not so easy, as Himmler observed, to remain a decent fellow after that. He has seen it so many times, through the peephole: hundreds of jews packed so tightly that they remain standing even after the gas has been evacuated, their naked bodies fouled with excreta, their faces still gripped by expression from which life has fled. Viewed through the lens, it is a remote and obscure surrealist tableau. Impossible to assign meaning. More than once Mengele has wanted to clap his hands at this moment, and command them, like Lazarus, to come forth. And more than once, yes, he would swear it, the multitude has trembled, swayed, sighed, quivered on the brink of responding to his thought.

To sign the report, is this to observe? Is this the moment when the mixed state of life and death collapses to its final reality? Excuse me, Mengele doubts it. To be sure, he would not claim that these corpses can be brought back. But if the quantum universe truly divides at every subatomic transaction, then in other universes death, defeat, and exile can be not reversed but negated. Not only is the future a welter of possibility, but the past itself is provisional, a mixed state awaiting its proper observer. In such a cosmos of eternal possibility, there are no judges. There is no guilt. There is only the flicker of quanta, eternally dancing like Siva at the root of all becoming, deferring all judgment and consequence, yes, to the will of that determined observer who assigns the highest meaning to the experiment.

So although Mengele signs the papers he is not, to his way of thinking, the observer in this situation. The final, intimate task of moving bodies to the crematoria is left to the Sonderkommandos, selected from the prisoners' own ranks. A privileged position: one earns extra food, favors, status. It seems to Mengele that the Sonderkommandos are the true observers, entering the chambers after the gas has dispersed, embracing the befouled corpses to separate them one from another, hauling them out, searching body cavities for hidden valuables. Mengele has often watched one particular Sonderkommando leader as he delivers his fellows to the furnace, moving like Shadrach unscathed amidst the flames and smoke, surrounded by a black aura of determination more intense than Mengele's own: one of the secret just ones on whom the earth rests. Such a one is the true observer, the true creator of this final reality.

In Serra Negra, a journalist comes to see him under carefully negotiated conditions. Mengele does not admit or deny his identity. The journalist does not press the question. The entire interview has a remote, hypothetical tone, as if Mengele were performing the thought experiment of being Mengele. Do you feel guilt? the journalist asks. To have condemned so many, tortured so many. The question baffles and annoys him. Guilt? You have no conception of the world we could have brought into being. What you call history, what the victors have written, was a mere preliminary. In the ruins of our collapse you see atrocity, and I agree! I agree. But, excuse me, it might have been very different.

After a pause the journalist says,—I am Jewish. I am here to try to understand. But you cannot deny or erase the suffering. Had you won the war, there would have been even more suffering. What you did was an enormous crime, but the crime you meant to accomplish was incomparably greater.

Mengele says,—Suffering to no purpose is indeed atrocious. The suffering, say, of old age, which helps no one. But suffering to a purpose is meaningful, even if it is another's purpose. You do not know, says Mengele, thinking of the Sonderkommando. Even in Auschwitz there was a sense of shared purpose.

The journalist cuts him off.—Shared? Do you truly suggest that this is the meaning of our suffering? Jews sharing the Nazi purpose?

—What I say is subtle, Mengele begins.

—What you say is abominable, the man says.—I will hear no more. You, you who have judged so many, have you no fear of being judged?

—Have you a wallet? Mengele asks.—Show me it.

The journalist looks blank, then shifts a thin haunch and pulls from a rear pocket a worn leather billfold stuffed with papers and cards.

—That is the flayed skin of a horse, says Mengele.—The jew Isaac Bashevis Singer writes, To animals, all men are Nazis.

Mengele never saw what the journalist wrote. Yet the man must have broken his pledge of confidentiality—you could not trust them, ever!—for Mengele heard thereafter of inquiries to Bonn, and so he built the observation tower, and so ultimately he fled Serra Negra for São Paulo.

Mengele lies atop the bedsheets, a thin acrid sweat on his white emaciated limbs. The fly buzzes steadily around the room, turning and turning on random paths.

If we are merely collections of unresolved possibilities, under the eye of some final determiner, how can we know if our very consciousness is true or false? How can we know, even, that we live? Perhaps, though we think ourselves alive, we are dead, and unaware of it. If so, when did our consciousness start to deceive us? If we exist in a mixed state, the only certainty is nonexistence before and after; all else is illusion. Birth itself is a deception, death the corrective.

And if consciousness deceives, then death, the liberation, can be conferred only by an observer. This was the revelation that he, *schöne Josef,* had brought like an angel to call the jews who had waited so long for their messiah! He, not the Sonderkommando, is one of the secret just ones, who after all this time has realized the true and highest meaning, that no matter how long or cleverly deferred, the final outcome of the atrocious experiment of life never varies.

The fly bounces against the ceiling. Above it the jew in his cell is getting to his feet and looking around, as though able for the first time to see outside. The jew turns to observe Mengele. Never in his life has Mengele quailed from the eyes of another person, not even the Sonderkommando, but he quails now. The jew is sharply defined, more real than the room, the tired afternoon sunlight, the grime on the window, and Mengele is unable to look away from his burning eyes. They are the eyes of Martin Buber, of Hannah Arendt, of the journalist, of the Sonderkommando, of a gypsy child. They are seven million lives passing and lost. Not suspended, not mixed, not reclaimable by some jesuitical parsing of the atom, but lost beyond recall.

—Stop it! cries Mengele.—You are finished, all of you! I have sentenced the entire jewish race to death! You live only in my mind! It is I who assign meaning! I! His raises his arm to sweep the vision aside, and knocks the volume of Martin Buber onto the trap. The steel arm slams down, and the canister flies across the room, valve broken, to bang against the locked door. Gas erupts into the room. Mengele struggles out of bed, but his legs will not hold him, and as he staggers and falls he hears a rush of music, *alle Menschen werden Brüder,* as the final determination descends upon him and ushers him into the universal fraternity of death.

JOHN M. FORD

ERASE/RECORD/PLAY
A DRAMA FOR PRINT

[THE CURTAIN IS UP AS THE AUDIENCE ENTERS. THERE IS A SMALL *table upstage right; on it is a large reel-to-reel tape recorder, the reels facing the audience. Behind the table is a stool, high enough so that the person on it will be clearly visible, and a stand microphone at the appropriate height for that person. A lectern faces stage left.*

Aside from this, the stage is completely empty; there is no back-drop, so that the rear wall is visible, and some of the equipment over-head dangles slightly in view.

As the audience finishes finding their seats, DR. GORDON enters. He is in his late forties. He wears casual trousers and jacket, no tie. His shirt has French cuffs with cuff links. He sits on the stool and adjusts the microphone. As the house lights go down, a spotlight il-luminates him. The recorder clicks loudly without being touched, and the reels of tape begin to turn.]

DR. GORDON
(*FACING THE AUDIENCE DIRECTLY*)
Is that working now? The power's been much more reliable the last couple of months, but . . .

INTERVIEWER
(a disembodied voice from somewhere above the audience)
Fine, thank you, Dr. Gordon. I have a battery-operated recorder, but—

DR. GORDON
—but you can't get batteries at all here. Yes. Shall we go on, then?

INTERVIEWER
Your actors—

DR. GORDON
Players. We don't call them actors, or myself a director.
(a beat)
It's a way of defusing criticism, if you like.

INTERVIEWER
What do you prefer to be called?

DR. GORDON
Doc.
(getting no response)
I have an M.D. in psychiatry. I'm a licensed therapist. In fact, twice licensed. I had to be recertified, afterward.

INTERVIEWER
The players were all in the same camp, correct?

DR. GORDON
(looking at the audience)
That's right. Camp Eighteen.

INTERVIEWER
Everyone knows where they were?

DR. GORDON
We know where everyone was released from. There were some movements between camps. . . . *(he shrugs)* So yes, everyone knows who wishes to know.

INTERVIEWER
Some don't wish to know?

DR. GORDON
Oh, some, always. But most consider it . . . a kind of family name. You may have noticed people wearing their numbers on their clothing.

INTERVIEWER
Yes. I'd seen that.

DR. GORDON
There were twenty-five camps. It's been decided that each of the first twenty-five days of Liberation Month will be the corresponding number's day to celebrate.

INTERVIEWER
Do you expect them to celebrate?

DR. GORDON
I expect them to celebrate as though they had never before in their lives had cause for celebration. *I* certainly intend to. I'm a Nine, by the way.

INTERVIEWER
So they see their status as . . . inmates as a matter of . . .

(a pause)

DR. GORDON
(humorously)
Lose your script?

INTERVIEWER
Can you fill in the blank?

DR. GORDON
(coldly serious)
That's a dangerous thing to ask around here.

(light again)
You said "matter of," so you probably meant to say "a matter of pride." But I don't believe it's that. A matter of fact, certainly. A matter of history, it is to be hoped. A matter of identity . . . such as it is.

[WALTER, MARK, PARIS, ADELINE, VIRGINIA, and HOWARD, the six *PLAYERS*, enter downstage left. They are all around thirty.

WALTER is handsome, and carries himself with confidence. MARK is a large man, who moves carefully though not awkwardly. PARIS is a slight woman, attractive, with a dancer's grace. ADELINE is angular of face and body, and occasionally shows a little stiffness in movement. HOWARD is rather short and self-conscious. VIRGINIA is strong-looking, precise, a bit wary.

They carry seriously thumbed playtexts, and are dressed in re-

hearsal clothes: jeans, sweatshirts, sneakers. All wear long sleeves.
WALTER *wears a football jersey showing the number 18, but no player or team name.*

    They glance briefly at the backstage hardware. MARK *stumbles, does not fall, clutches his script to himself; the others look at him, without hostility. They sit down, apparently at random, facing* DR. GORDON.

    DR. GORDON *turns ninety degrees on his stool to face them over the lectern; as he does, the light on the tape recorder fades, leaving its meters glowing in darkness.* DR. GORDON *takes a script, as well-worn as the others', from his pocket.]*

"There are only two immutable rules of play," Dr. Gordon said. "One: Inviolability of Text. You may neither omit lines, nor add your own verbal material. You may speak the lines with any tempo or inflection you think right, pause as you choose, but no cuts, no ad-libs. You may *do* anything you feel is right while speaking, except as defined by Rule Two.

    "Rule Two: The Cut Rule. Physical contact is allowed, up to and including *simulated* acts of violence. You all did very well in Fake Fisticuffs 101, by the way." The players grinned and nodded; Paris laughed softly. "But anyone involved in a contact situation who doesn't like the way it's going can stop it at once by yelling 'Cut!' "

    Adeline said, "Are we chicken if we Cut?" The tightness of her voice concealed any meaning.

    "Damned if I know," said Dr. Gordon. "The other thing is that only a player who's actually been touched in the scene can Cut it. That includes me." He smiled, riffled through his copy of the text. "Okay, I know you're all anxious to perform, so let's start."

    The players stood up, opening their scripts.

    Dr. Gordon said, "Act One, Scene One: A Wood near Athens. Enter Theseus and Hippolyta, with Attendants. That's Walt and Ginny; the rest of you, strike poses in the rear."

    "Attentive poses?" Mark said.

    "How about classically Greek?" said Paris.

    Dr. Gordon said, "Statuary, that's good. Want to illustrate, Paris?"

Virginia said, "Shall I have a bow? Like Diana?"

"Why not?" Dr. Gordon said, and Virginia slung an imaginary longbow and quiver while Paris demonstrated positions of marble ballet.

Walter held his textbook loosely at his side, and looked straight at Virginia. "Now, fair Hippolyta," he said, "our nuptial hour draws on apace; four happy days bring in another moon: but O, methinks . . ." He paused, but he did not look as if he had forgotten the line. He said, low and slow, ". . . how slow the old moon wanes." He took a step toward his bride-to-be. "It lingers my desires, like to a step-dame or a dowager, *long, withering* out a young man's revenue."

"Four days will quickly steep themselves in night," Virginia said, quite crisply. "Four nights will quickly dream away the time. And— *then*—the moon, like to a silver bow new-bent in heaven"—she unslung her own invisible weapon, reached for an arrow—"shall behold the night of our solemnities." She concluded with an arrow nocked, casually aimed at what definitely was not Theseus' heart.

Theseus shrugged with both hands in the air, turned to Dr. Gordon. "Go, Philostrate," he said, cocking a look at the book in his hand. "Stir up the Athenian youth to merriments. . . ."

[DR. GORDON *nods and turns back to the audience; the light on the* PLAYERS *dims and they freeze into tableau as the tape begins to roll.*]

INTERVIEWER

Your players don't memorize the script?

DR. GORDON

They memorize as much as they please. They're not going to face an audience who are programmed to think that scripts break the illusion; they're each other's audience, and the illusion they create is their own.

INTERVIEWER

So they're not going to perform before an audience—

DR. GORDON

Is that what I said? *(without pausing)* Memorization is a great mumping boogeyman that hangs around the theater, scaring people away. It's necessary to meet it face-on, go a few back-alley rounds with it. I can do all of *Hamlet* and *Lear*, all the male parts in *Guys and Dolls* and *A Funny Thing Happened on the Way to the Forum*, including the songs—(*he hums a bit of "Comedy Tonight," then abruptly leans forward and speaks in a quiet but almost threatening tone*) And I have no more idea of what I've been doing for the last five years than any of *those* people do.

[He turns back to the players and the action resumes as before.]

"Hippolyta." Walter extended a finger; he delicately turned the point of Virginia's arrow aside, took a step closer. "I woo'd thee with my sword . . ." He put the finger on her shoulder. She tilted her head to look at it resting there. ". . . and won thy love . . . doing thee injuries."

Among the attendant statuary, Adeline turned her head, took a silent step.

Walter said quietly, "But I will wed thee in another key, with pomp, with triumph, and with revelling."

Virginia let her bow fall, raised a hand as if to brush Walter's hand away like an insect; but she just put her fingers on his.

Adeline took two long steps, said sharply, "Happy be Theseus, our renowned duke!"

"Thanks, good Egeus. What's the news with thee?"

INTERVIEWER

Egeus is a man?

DR. GORDON

Apparently. A parent, anyway. (*He pauses, as if waiting for a laugh that does not come.*)

Egeus has a daughter, Hermia. Hermia is supposed to marry Demetrius, a nice young Athenian manly fellow of a lad, but Hermia's fallen in love with Lysander, another nice young etcetera, who's so equal in virtue to Demetrius that for four hundred years nobody's been able to tell them apart without a program. But it *does* matter to Hermia, and Athens has this serious parental consent law—Shakespeare didn't make this up, by the way.

"I beg the ancient privilege of Athens," Adeline said, her voice rising to a cackle, her hands in claws, "as she is mine, I may dispose of her: which shall be either to this gentleman . . ." Egeus spread wings over Mark. "Or . . . to her *death,* according to our law, *immediately* provided in that case." She took a step toward Paris as Hermia; Paris spun to face Duke Theseus and dropped to her knees.

Walter/Theseus reminded Paris/Hermia coolly and impassively that the law of Athens was, after all, the law, and parents were to be obeyed. He looked into space, not at the quietly pleading Hermia: but he didn't miss Hippolyta's recovering her bow and selecting another arrow. In what might have been a conciliatory voice, he offered Hermia an alternative to Demetrius or Death: a convent and a vow of chastity. Hippolyta shot the arrow squarely between his feet.

INTERVIEWER

How long does it take to teach them to play like this?

DR. GORDON

It isn't necessary to teach people to play. It's with time and society that they learn play is foolish, a distraction from the goals of wealth and empire. It's necessary to *un*teach that.

But to answer your question, we spend three weeks on improvisation games and independent reading before running through the play together.

INTERVIEWER

Before a full rehearsal.

DR. GORDON

Before we read together at all. I *do* mean what I say. "Rehearsal" implies that it doesn't really count, and for our purposes *everything* counts. As for "full," no, we don't do little bits here and there. If you ate a bean yesterday, a carrot today, and a little piece of beef tomorrow, would you say you'd had stew three days running?

The two male suitors, Mark as Demetrius and Howard as Lysander, had stepped forward to flank Hermia. Mark said, "Relent, sweet

Hermia, and Lysander, yield thy crazed title to my certain right."
There was nothing very certain in his voice, and something a little
crazed. Howard paused with his mouth open, looking up at the
other suitor, a full head taller than him: he swallowed and said, "You
have her father's love, Demetrius. Let me have Hermia's—do *you*
marry him."

Demetrius scratched his head and looked at Egeus, as if seriously considering the offer. Egeus fluttered and squawked. Theseus
reiterated that the law was the law and Hermia was up against it;
then he departed with the court, Egeus, and Demetrius, who followed his future father-in-law rather like a large bumbling puppy.
He paused to throw a big smooch at Hermia, who wiped it off her
cheek and scraped it from her delicate fingers like a stranger's snot.

Hermia and Lysander dithered in romantic silence for a minute
or so, looking at each other, and here, and there.

Dr. Gordon said very quietly, "You may use the books."

Howard said, "For aught that I could ever read . . ." He froze for
just an instant, then went on: "Could ever hear by tale or history . . ."
He looked up from the book, straight into Paris's eyes, and there was
a sudden light in his face. "The course of true love never did run
smooth." He looked down again, and then, perhaps too fast, said, "But
either it was different in blood—"

"O cross!" Paris said, "Too high to be enthralled to low."

Howard was still half-paralyzed. "Or else misgraffèd in respect
of years—"

"O spite!" Paris's voice was sharp but not raised, a quiet ache.
"Too old to be engaged to young."

"Or else it stood upon the choice of friends—"

"O . . . hell to choose . . . *love* . . . by another's eyes."

They went on for two dozen more lines, but there was nothing
more to compare with that first shock. No one else moved at all.

Then Adeline stumbled forward. Howard said, "Look, here
comes Helena," and she plunged between the two of them as if she
saw neither.

Helena was in love with Demetrius, of course—how else should
it be a romantic comedy?—and her distraction was not much re-
duced on hearing of Hermia and Lysander's plan to elope on the

following night. Left alone on stage, Helena decided, "I will go tell him of fair Hermia's flight," to prove to Demetrius Hermia's lack of affection for him. In her closing lines, "Herein mean I to enrich my pain, to have his sight thither and back again," there was a distinct touch of Egeus's vulture cackle.

INTERVIEWER
It must be confusing to have each act—*player* perform so many parts.

DR. GORDON
Sometimes it is hard to tell who is who, yes.

"Is all our company here?" Paris stood in the center of the stage, book in both hands, while the others shuffled in from all around her.

Howard came in with long, Rudy Valentino steps; he struck a profile and sat down hard. "You were best to call 'em gen'rally, man by man, accordin' to the scrip."

Paris gave Howard a doubtful look. "Here is the scroll of every man's name which is thought fit through all Athens to play in our interlude before the duke and the duchess, on his wedding-day at night."

"Fir-r-r-st," Howard said, "good Peter Quince, say what the play treats on, then read the names of the actors, and so grow to a *point.*"

"Marry, our play is"—she squinted through imaginary eye-glasses—*"The Most Lamentable Comedy"*—another squint—*"and Most Cruel Death of Pyramus and Thisbe."*

"A very good piece of work, I assure you," Howard said, "and a merry."

The other players gaped at him.

"Now, good Peter Quince, call forth your actors by the scroll. Masters, spread yourselves." Howard stretched out his arms, bowling Virginia over; his left fist landed on massive Mark, who looked at it as if it had fallen from the sky.

Paris/Quince said, "Answer as I call you. Nick Bottom, the weaver."

"Ready!" Howard sprang up. "Name what part I am for, and proceed."

"You, Nick Bottom, are set down for Pyramus."

"What is Pyramus? A lover or a tyrant?"

"A lover," Paris said, "that kills himself most gallant for love."

Howard mused. "That will ask some tears in the true performing of it."

INTERVIEWER

How many died?

DR. GORDON

One in four.

INTERVIEWER

In absolute numbers—

DR. GORDON

In absolute numbers *what?* Would ten thousand adequately horrify? A hundred thousand? Or do we only count graves in millions now?

Suppose you had a mother and father. A brother and sister. One dies. Does that matter?

INTERVIEWER

But the figures—

DR. GORDON

They were never meant as death camps. There was a sincerity— a kind of sincerity, at least—in the word "Re-education." Re-education through good will, firm ideology, and the drug LX, of course.

We believe that no one died in the first six months. We have a few paper records from that period, and because we do not trust them, we have opened the graves. As I say, if any prisoners died in the first six months, the bodies are well hidden.

Mark, as Snug the carpenter, said, "Have you the lion's part written? Pray you, if it be, give it me, for I am . . . slow of study." He put a finger to his mouth.

"You may do it extempore," Quince said kindly, "for it is nothing but roaring."

"Let me play the lion too," Bottom shouted. "I will roar, that I will do any man's heart good to hear me. I will roar, that I will make the Duke say, 'Let him roar again, let him roar again!'"

Walter, who was currently Snout the tinker, gave his head a tilt of ducal disapproval.

"And you should do it too terribly," Quince lectured Bottom, "you would fright the Duchess and the ladies"—Virginia showed a bit of surprise that a mere lion should worry Hippolyta—"that they would shriek; and that were enough to hang us all."

"That would hang us," the players chorused, nodding among themselves, "every mother's son."

INTERVIEWER
Have people been hanged for bad acting?
DR. GORDON
(offhand)
Some have certainly 'scaped the noose by good acting. And those who own the rope and the scaffold have certainly hanged those who have frightened them.
INTERVIEWER
There were tribunals, after the liberation. Executions.
DR. GORDON
Hangings, necks broken, drawers soiled, slow writhing strangulations, bodies mutely protesting the deaths of their brains . . .

There were one hundred forty-seven public executions. Forty had refused to take LX, and freely confessed their actions. Another eighty had not taken the drug, but tried to pretend they had; a grave mistake. Four were cleared of having been in the camps at all, though a bit late. The rest were LX subjects, convicted on circumstantial evidence. It was a while before we understood the real difficulty of telling Group A from Group B.
INTERVIEWER
A and B?
DR. GORDON
We could say Guards and Prisoners, but some did more than guard. Torturers and Victims, but not all tortured and some fought

back. Tyrants and Lovers . . . sometimes, perhaps. There are no
words to mean what we want to say; so we say Group A, Group B.

                    INTERVIEWER
        Non-judgmental.
                    DR. GORDON
        Judicious.
                    INTERVIEWER
        And the difference . . . ?
                    DR. GORDON

Oh, Group B is the majority party. The ones who own the rope
now.

The Athenian workmen sorted out the rest of their roles, and agreed
to meet in the wood the following night for rehearsal. They went out
by their several exits.

"End of Act One," Dr. Gordon called out. "Coffee break."

Virginia had brought in her milk ration ("Go ahead, I never
drink the stuff") and Mark a box of vanilla wafers, so they sat around
the stage sipping and nibbling in great content.

Howard said, "The fairies come on next, right?"

Dr. Gordon said, "That's right. Walter is Oberon and Paris is
Titania. And Virginia's playing Puck. The rest of you will fill in as
Titania's fairy court." He nodded slightly at Howard. "When you're
not otherwise engaged."

Mark said, "Should we have something, for the fairy parts?
Some kind of costumes or something?"

Dr. Gordon said, "Do you want them?"

Adeline said, "Not whole costumes."

Howard said, "No. But you mean, say, hats when we're the
fairies?"

Mark took the empty cookie box and put it on his head. Walter
laughed out loud.

Dr. Gordon said, "It's a lovely improv, Mark, but I don't think
it's very elfin." He leaned on the lectern. "Let's think about this. How
do you see fairies?"

"In my mind's eye," Walter said, with a small silly grin.

"Small. Tiny," Virginia said.

Mark said, "That leaves me out," and they all laughed.

"Fairies," Paris said, in a barely audible grumble. "Sugar-plum . . ."

Virginia said, "They *are* supposed to be little. The play talks about them hiding in acorns."

Walter said, "The characters talk about a lot of things that actors can't really do."

Adeline said, "We *could* play small," and stood on tiptoe, her hands arched at shoulder level, peeping over something.

Virginia said, "More than that. They can be invisible. They're light, and graceful. They can *fly*."

They were all silent; and then they were all looking at Paris.

She looked back, turning her head rapidly from one to another. Then, furiously, she tore the laces of her sneakers loose, kicked them across the floor, and sprang up to stand on one foot. "Is this what you had in mind?" She whirled, leapt to the other foot. "Is this elfin enough for you?"

Walter looked at his own shoes for a long moment, then pulled them off, stood up, flexed his feet. "Yeah. That's good."

Paris stopped, nearly stumbled. Hands were raised to catch her, but she did not fall. Her left foot came down with a bump. "And suppose . . ." she said hesitantly, "the workmen, the players, wear work shoes. Heavy ones."

Adeline said, "Clogs, maybe, so we can just kick them off to change."

Dr. Gordon said, "And the Athenian nobles?"

"Sandals, right?" Mark said. "The Athenians wore sandals."

Dr. Gordon said, "There is a property room down that hall, the heavy door on the right. I would you would make free with it."

Paris hung back as the others went down the hall. She turned to Dr. Gordon, opened her mouth.

"Sssh," Dr. Gordon said. "When you're sure of what you want to say, tell them. That's the whole idea."

INTERVIEWER

Tell me about the drug.

DR. GORDON

Lethe Experimental. LX. Sometimes called Compound Sixty. Administered by intravenous injection, it produces brief nausea, and drowsiness and disorientation lasting between one and three hours. By intramuscular injection, the effects are subdued but prolonged. LX readily crosses the blood-brain barrier.

INTERVIEWER

And its main effect?

DR. GORDON

I assumed that was the part you already knew. Lethe Experimental causes a loss of long-term memory. It seems to act as a kind of phage, attacking memory RNA.

INTERVIEWER

How far back does the memory loss go?

DR. GORDON

All psychoactives have drastically different effects on different people. LX is certainly no exception. Further, the doses—and circumstances of doses—were different in almost every case.

Think of raindrops on a train window . . . how they find their own, unpredictable paths; some split off early, some cross the entire pane. That is Compound Sixty in the human brain.

INTERVIEWER

Then—

DR. GORDON

I'm answering your question; it's not a simple answer. You *know* we've lost the camps, and they were in operation for five years. Some people have had their internal time completely reset to sometime in the past; others know the correct date but have no useful recollections since adolescence. Most who were college students remember nothing of college—you can read what you like into that. I had to take a recertification test for my medical license, and I'll swear I did *better* on it than I would have before, though I'd spent several years in practice.

We have only a very few cases of people forgetting their names—we think those may be, you'll pardon the expression, natural amnesia rather than drug effects. But most people have lost the memory of parents, siblings, a spouse, children—rarely a whole family, but almost always one or two people.

INTERVIEWER

Could some of that reflect wishful thinking? The desire to forget someone?

DR. GORDON

(He considers his response for a long time. When he finally speaks, it is with a distance that approaches contempt.)

The data do not support that hypothesis.

Virginia adjusted the rolled cuffs of her jeans, loosened her shoulders, and glided barefoot into center stage, where Adeline, shoeless as well, was busily miming what looked like mail sorting. Beside her stood a tall hat-rack that the players had seized from the prop room, to stand in for the fairy forest.

"How now, spirit!" Puck said, in a voice that really did not seem to be Virginia's; too high, too careless. "Whither wander you?"

"Over hill, over dale," Adeline chanted, "Thorough bush, thorough briar, over park, over pale, thorough flood, thorough fire," and explained in verse her fairy duties before Titania Queen of Spirits should arrive. "I must go seek some dew-drops here, and hang a pearl in every cowslip's ear." She unslung an apparently massive burden of dew from the bare tree, shouldered it.

"The King doth keep his revels here tonight," Puck said, "take heed the Queen come not within his sight: for Oberon is passing fell and wrath, because that she as her attendant hath a lovely boy, stol'n from an Indian king—"

"*Cut!*" Paris said, a fully contained shriek.

"You can't," Dr. Gordon said, smoothly, firmly. "You're not in contact. Puck, go on."

"She never had so sweet a changeling," Virginia coolly went on, explaining that Oberon wanted the child, but Titania would not give him up; and there was Trouble in Fairyland. "But room, fairy! Here comes Oberon!"

"And here my mistress," Adeline said, her voice all there's-a-fire-in-the-woodpile-*now*, "would that he were gone!"

Adeline's fairy ducked and doubled back behind Paris as Titania. Paris seemed composed now, standing straight. Walter, as Oberon, strode in from the opposite direction. Dead center, Puck cocked an elbow and leaned nonchalantly against the hatrack.

"Ill met by moonlight, proud Titania."

"What, jealous Oberon? Fairies, skip hence; I have forsworn his bed and company."

Puck looked from one fairy monarch to the other, shuddered, and held up the playbook to hide her face.

It got worse. Oberon and Titania's quarrel, to hear them describe it, was turning the whole natural world sidewise and shaking it: fogs, fevers, rotten corn, early winter. "And this same progeny of evils comes," Titania said, "from our debate—from *our* dissension: we are their parents and original."

Puck turned her head, like a spectator following a tennis ball in play.

"Do you amend it then," Oberon said, with a bad imitation of indifference. Then he said, "Why should Titania cross her Oberon?" with an even worse imitation of sweetness. "I do but beg a little changeling boy. . . ."

Paris spat back at him, speaking of the child's mother, a priestess, and a friend, of Titania's—"But she, being mortal, of that boy did die," she said, all cold metal. *"And for her sake do I rear up her boy. And for her sake I will not part with him."*

Oberon took a moment to absorb this. "How long within this wood . . . intend you stay?"

"Perchance till after Theseus' wedding day," she said idly; then, almost offhand, "If you will patiently dance in our round, and see our moonlight revels . . . go with us. If not, shun me, and I will spare your haunts."

"Give me that boy, and I will go with thee."

"Not for thy fairy kingdom. Fairies, away!" She turned to go, then turned back and smiled thinly at Oberon. "We shall chide downright if I longer stay."

Titania's court departed. "Well, go thy way," Oberon muttered. "Thou shalt not from this grove till I torment thee for this injury."

Puck turned, still holding the book in front of her face, and began to slink after Titania's train.

"My gentle Puck," Oberon said crisply. Puck froze. "Come hither." She did.

The Fairy King told Puck of a flower whose nectar had the power to make a sleeper fall in love with the first thing seen on awaking. He ordered Puck to bring a flower to him.

"I'll put a girdle round about the earth in forty minutes," Virginia said, and was gone, with a *whoosh* of takeoff.

Oberon explained his plan to twist Titania's mind. "But who comes here? I am invisible—" He took a step back and put his own script in front of his face.

Mark, now wearing Demetrius' sandals, shuffled in, apparently alone. He turned, revealing Adeline as Helena clutching the tail of his shirt, dragging after him on her knees.

"I love thee not," Demetrius said, "therefore pursue me not." He turned this way and that, Helena remaining firmly attached. "Hence, get thee gone, and follow me no more!"

"You draw me, you hard-hearted adamant," she said, and jumped up to hang on his shoulders.

Oberon lowered his book long enough to display a broad, malicious grin; then he hastily raised it again.

"Do I entice you?" Demetrius said. "Do I speak you fair? Or do I rather not in plainest truth tell you I do not, nor I cannot, love you?" He twisted his shoulders, trying to shake Helena off—but instead he threw her off; she landed hard on her shoulder and hip, with a groan.

The players stared. Dr. Gordon held out a hand, and they did not move.

Adeline threw her arms around Mark's legs and hugged. Mark went down on first backside then back. He waggled his head.

Adeline crawled on top of him. "And even for that do I love you the more," Helena said. She grabbed him by the shoulders and shook him furiously, bouncing his head on the stage. "Spurn me!" *bonk* "Strike me!" *kabump* "Neglect me!" *wham* "Lose me!" She fell on him, exhausted. "Only give me leave, unworthy as I am, to follow you." She slithered off.

Dazed, Demetrius sat up. "Tempt not too much," he said dizzily, "th' hatred of my spirit . . ." He stood uncertainly, then said with gathering speed, "for I am sick when I do look on thee." He turned his back, bent over, made a dreadful noise.

The other players were folded double with silent laughter.

The mismatched lovers went on for a while longer, until Demetrius fled, and Helena resumed the chase.

INTERVIEWER

You insist that they make no changes at all in the dialogue. But cutting and altering plays—particularly Shakespeare—is very common.

DR. GORDON

Aye, it is common.

(a beat)

Tampering with someone else's construction is a liberty many take, but to me it is a privilege one has to earn. You have to know what you're doing, at least well enough to argue the point.

My people aren't theater people—at least, not before the suffered sea-change of Compound Sixty. So the rule is that they read all of the words. Even if most of them roll off their tongues and are lost in the air, a few will bounce. Resonate. Explode in the mind. And they can't, *I* can't, tell *which* words, before the moment.

INTERVIEWER

You see play therapy as a kind of discovery process?

DR. GORDON

Learning is a big enough word for it. Someone once said, "joy is the light that shines into unsuspected chambers of the heart."

INTERVIEWER

So learning the truth makes people happy, you would say.

DR. GORDON

What *I would say* is that denying people the truth makes them frustrated: and frustrated, ignorant people are not happy.

(a pause)

I apologize for my brusqueness. We are all grateful for your country's contribution to the liberation, and we hope that your soldiers' withdrawal goes smoothly.

❁   ❁   ❁

Puck returned from her travels bearing the flower of enforced love. Virginia's hand was arched, two fingers above, the thumb below: unmistakably gripping a hypodermic syringe. She placed it on her script held as a tray, handed it to Oberon, then made as if stripping off rubber gloves.

Oberon picked up an invisible syringe, examined it with narrowed eyes and a flat, clinical smile. He then passed back the tray, and told Puck to administer the flower juice to the young Athenian fellow she would find elsewhere in the wood.

"Fear not, my lord," Puck said, "your servant shall do so." She snapped the script under one arm, saluted, turned smartly, and marched off.

Still examining the hypodermic, humming faintly to himself, Oberon departed as well.

Titania and her fairy court—all the players except Walter as lurking Oberon—entered. After a long yawn, Paris/Titania ordered her host to sing, dance a turn, and then go hunting the creatures of the night. "Sing me now asleep; then to your offices, and let me rest." She curled up on the floor at the rear of the stage, and the others sang her to sleep.

"Hence, away!" Adeline said just above a whisper. "Now all is well: one aloof stand sentinel." She waved the rest away, then crouched, hands folded on one knee, at the edge of the stage.

Hands swept in from the darkness beyond. One sealed the fairy's mouth; others, disembodied in the dim light, pulled her out of sight.

Oberon came in, daintily wiping his hands, scraping a foot clean on the ground. He knelt by sleeping Titania, drew out the syringe. He spoke softly, kindly, even lovingly. "What thou seest when thou dost wake, do it for thy true love take; love, and languish, for his sake. . . . Be it ounce, or cat, or bear, pard, or boar with bristled hair, in thy eye that shall appear when thou wak'st—it is thy dear. *Wake*"— he enclosed her face and neck with his arm, stabbed into her throat; she kicked once and was still—"when some vile thing is near."

Oberon stood, backed away, watching to left and right, and disappeared into the night. A moment later, Titania too faded from sight.

INTERVIEWER

You said the camps were not intended as death camps. How did they get that way?

DR. GORDON

One life at a time.

INTERVIEWER

You said no one died for the first few months.

DR. GORDON

As far as we know. *(smiles)* Whatever that means.

(a beat)

Do you want me to guess?

INTERVIEWER

I'd like your opinions. Your theories.

DR. GORDON

Hypotheses. There's a difference.

All right. First, I think re-education didn't work. LX doesn't turn people into blank slates; it's unreliable, as close to random as doesn't matter. I think someone got frustrated, and took out that frustration on someone else. Then, in the calm after the storm, whoever did it wished it hadn't been done.

Compound Sixty can do that. Can make it didn't happen. And once that was realized, well then, why stop? How many wishes would the genie in the bottle grant?

INTERVIEWER

More than three.

DR. GORDON

It wasn't really three, in the original story, you know. Aladdin had as many wishes as he wanted.

He did, however, eventually have enough, and set his slave free.

INTERVIEWER

And lived happily ever after?

DR. GORDON

No. Not in the original. Muslim stories always end, "they lived happily, until Death came for them."

(he sighs)

Then there's Hypothesis B. No time of innocence. Just the knowledge, just the will, just the act. A reckoning piling up in memory: a dagger of the mind, that marshaled . . . *them* . . . the way that they were going.

Lysander and Hermia entered, hand in hand. "Fair love," Howard said sweetly, "you faint with wandering in the wood, and to speak troth . . . I have forgot our way."

Hermia stopped and stared at him.

Howard shrugged, spread his hands. "We'll . . . rest us, Hermia," he said, squeezing the words out like toothpaste, "if you-u-u think it guh-guh-good? And, uh . . . tarry. For the, uh, comfort. Of the day."

Paris tapped her foot. "Be it so, Lysander." She sat down. "Find you out a bed; for I upon this bank will rest my head."

Lysander dropped quickly to his knees, began brushing the ground to receive Hermia's head. "One turf shall serve as pillow for us both," he said.

Hermia sat straight up.

Howard said, "One heart, one, uh, bed, two, er, bosoms, and one troth—" He was stopped by Paris's forefinger pressed hard against his forehead.

"Nay, good Lysander; for my sake, my dear . . . lie further off." She pointed with her other hand. "Do not lie so near."

"O take the sense, sweet, of my innocence!" He raised his hands, palm up—and flopped forward, his head landing in Hermia's lap. Somewhat muffled, he went on: "Lff tks th' mnng'f lff's cnf'renth."

She stuck her fingers in his ears, lifted his head and shook it.

They finally agreed on an acceptable distance between bunks, and slept.

INTERVIEWER

There is, of course, some corollary evidence.

DR. GORDON

You mean the Castillo Diary.

INTERVIEWER

Yes.

DR. GORDON

Twenty little pieces of paper torn from an examining-table roll, written on with shoe-polish ink and a split fingernail for a pen, crumpled and stained from their hiding places. It names sixteen persons guilty of rape, torture, murder . . . and so forth, and so on.

INTERVIEWER

Do you believe it's a fake, as some claim?

DR. GORDON

I believe it is absolutely genuine, and that everyone it names is guilty. Do you know why?

INTERVIEWER

Tell me.

DR. GORDON

Suppose you were creating a false diary. A blanket claim of innocence will never stand, and might hang you even higher. You must create what a court would call "reasonable doubt." You name persons, and say they are guilty of crimes. And indeed, most of them are. But here and there, perhaps whenever lucky seven hits *(he pretends to roll dice),* you name an innocent: a victim in a marked grave, someone who had nothing to do with the camps at all. So when your lies are found out, they will discredit your truth by association. Isn't that a lovely paradox?

INTERVIEWER

But I'd heard that the Castillo names—

DR. GORDON

Castillo gives us names and crimes. You've read the diary; will you ever forget the acts of James Edward Sloan? But, *true or false,* the diarist thinks the names will mean something very specific in terms of guilt and innocence—and they do not mean that. The diarist, true or false, does not imagine that a man named James Edward Sloan will himself read your account to a tribunal and say, "If I did these things, I wish to be hanged," and mean exactly what he says, to an audience that knows there are two other James Edward Sloans on the voting rolls. And if you hang a name, a man's neck breaks.

The diary is real because it is useless: Castillo did not realize what it would have to prove.

INTERVIEWER

Yet three of the names were tried and executed. And five more committed suicide.

DR. GORDON

What's in a name?

Puck appeared, pacing, hands behind her back. "Through the forest have I gone, but Athenian found I none on whose eyes I might approve this flower's force in stirring love. Night and silence—" She nearly tripped over Lysander. "Who is there?" She examined the body, picked up one of Howard's feet by its sandal strap. "Weeds of Athens he doth wear." She wiped her forehead with a *whew!* gesture. "This is he my master said despiséd the Athenian maid—and here the maiden, sleeping sound, on the dank and dirty ground."

She raised Lysander's wrist, took his pulse, gave the injection without any fuss but for one comic twitch of Lysander's legs. "I must now to Oberon," Puck said, and ran off.

Demetrius came on, breathing hard, looking back over his shoulder. He turned—and saw Helena in front of him, in the pose of a football tackle.

"Stay," she said, "though thou kill me, sweet Demetrius!"

They exchanged a few brisk words, and then Demetrius executed the downfield run, with a quick feint to the hatrack and a dodge past the defense.

Helena jumped in frustration, slamming both feet on the ground. She paced back and forth, limping a little as she bemoaned her state, and sat down on something soft. "But who is here? Lysander, on the ground?" He snored, loud as a diesel horn. "Dead, or asleep? I see no blood, no wound—Lysander, if you live, good sir, awake!"

His eyes sprang open. He sighed from the soul. "And run through fire I will, for thy sweet sake."

Helena looked around, alarmed.

"Transparent Helena!" Howard said.

Adeline looked down at herself, patted her ribs, held her hands up to the light.

Lysander professed his love for her. She decided that he was mocking her, over her crummy luck in pursuing Demetrius. He pressed on, in terms that might make anyone doubtful, until she fled. Lysander paused long enough to deliver a nasty farewell to his still-sleeping former beloved, and skipped lightly offstage in pursuit of his new steady girl.

Hermia woke up. "Help me, Lysander, help me! Do thy best to pluck this crawling serpent from my breast . . . !" She looked around, rapped her knuckles on the tree, sighed. "Ay me, for pity! What a dream was here—" Her face contorted. "A *dream,*" Paris said, not in Hermia's voice, nor Titania's, nor Quince's. "A child . . . in a play, not a dream—" which was not in the script.

Dr. Gordon looked straight at her, his hands and face tight.

Adeline came in, put her large hands on Paris's shoulders. Paris twisted and cried out. Adeline said "We're in *contact,* okay, Doc? *Cut,* already."

Dr. Gordon nodded. The others came in and circled Paris. Most sat; Walter stayed standing, rocking in the wooden-soled clogs he had put on for the next scene, knotting his fingers together. Something haunted his handsome face. Virginia knelt a little distance away, spoke in a flat, unstrung voice. "Something came back, didn't it. Was it your name? Your name wasn't Paris, was it. Not really."

"No," she said. "But no . . . no, I knew my name and I wanted to change—I took it, but I didn't take it *from* anyone—"

"It's all right," Adeline said, and hugged her again. "Not your name, then. What was it? Take your time. We've all got plenty of time."

"There was a child," Paris said miserably.

"Whose child?" Virginia said, with a coolness more cruel than cruelty; she twitched her head away.

"Mine, I think—I think she was mine. Or he, I don't—at a play, a child, mine—"

"She's hyperventilating," Dr. Gordon said. "Have her breathe slowly and evenly."

Slowly, his face a statuary mask, Howard put out a hand, touched Paris on the breastbone. "E-e-easy," he said. "Breathe with me, now. One . . . two."

Adeline said, "In a play, you said. Do you mean, at a play?"

"Yes. At a play. With fairies. Sugar—sugarplum fairies. I called her Sugarplum. That was it. A girl called Sugarplum, but her *name,* her name . . ."

"One . . . *two*. One . . ."

"I know that play," Mark said. *"The Nutcracker*. Do you remember that name, Paris?"

"No. . . ."

"One . . . *two*."

Virginia, her face turned from the others, was silently mouthing *I'm sorry. I'm sorry.*

Mark said, "Do you remember anyone else at the play? A husband? A friend? A friend's child?"

Walter looked at Mark. "Were you in the theater?"

"People went to the *Nutcracker* show in groups," Mark said, slowly, tightly, "families, or mothers with all their children. Every Christmas." He stopped, gnawed his lip, but the words seemed to struggle up on their own: "I was a train conductor. Every Christmas, I saw people going to and from the city, to see that show. I never saw it. People always took their children. I never had any children."

INTERVIEWER

What effects, precisely, do you hope the play will produce?
(DR. GORDON *turns his head, frowns, then turns back to the players without speaking.*)

INTERVIEWER

How do you know when the therapy is successful?

DR. GORDON

A smile is a serious symptom, laughter a dangerous one. The critical signs are difficult to discuss in polite company.

INTERVIEWER

Could you be . . . a little more specific?

DR. GORDON

We are haunted.

Wait for the epilogue.

"We can stop for a while," Dr. Gordon said.

"No," Paris said, "I'll finish." The rest of the company drew back. She blew her nose, shut her eyes, and spoke: "Lysander, look how I do quake with fear . . . methought a serpent ate my heart away, and you sat smiling at his cruel prey. Lysander! What, removed?

Lysander, lord!" She looked around. "What, out of hearing? Gone? No sound, no word? Alack—*where are you?* Speak an if you hear, speak, of all loves!" She clutched the tree, pulled herself slowly upright. "I swoon almost with fear. . . . No?"

Silence.

She put her fists on her hips. "Then I well perceive you are not nigh," she said, tapping a foot in annoyance. "Either death, or you, I'll find—immediately."

Applause.

The workmen assembled for their rehearsal, thumping in their wooden shoes.

"Are we all met?" Bottom the weaver said.

"Pat, pat," Peter Quince said, "and here's a marvellous convenient place for our rehearsal." Quince moved from place to place, pointing out the green plot to be used for stage, the hawthorn hedge for dressing room. Each time Paris crossed the stage, she carefully ducked under the tree in the middle.

Bottom intoned, *"Pee*-tah Quince . . ." from somewhere in the backwoods of Richard Burton territory.

"What sayest thou, bully Bottom?" Quince said, in the voice of patience tried.

"There are things in this comedy of"—he dodged a look at his script—"Pyramus and Thisbe that will never please. First, Pyramus must draw a sword to kill himself, which the ladies cannot abide. How answer you that?"

"By'r lakin," said Walter as Snout the tinker, "a parlous fear." He was looking directly at Virginia, who as Starveling the tailor said, "I believe we must leave the killing out, when all is done."

INTERVIEWER

When was the idea of . . . that Group A would . . .

DR. GORDON

Even people with whole memories find it hard to date the birth of ideas. Some believe that the idea was there, in seed at least, all along—that, as the purpose of the camps was re-education, eventually everyone would be re-educated.

The idea, in what became its actual form, was certainly there by the third year. Documents were being destroyed as a matter of course by then. And everyone in Group B was receiving LX at least once a month.

By the beginning of the fourth year there was a complete plan. We have copies; there was no attempt to destroy them. There are sections covering change of clothing, destruction of personal evidence, creating marks of . . . physical abuse—and finally the administration of LX, in diminishing circles of givers and recipients. *(distantly)* Mathematicians call that a Josephus problem: as the moving point stabs, who is counted out, who is counted in.

By that time, of course, there was no longer even the pretense of re-education. The camps were about two things only: the systematic degradation of human beings and the systematic destruction of the evidence thereof. Burying Group A within Group B, shuffling the deck so that the kings and queens of Lesser Hell, the knaves and the jokers, would be lost among the faceless numbers.

INTERVIEWER

How many . . . Group As were there?

DR. GORDON

Of those who came out . . . of us . . . one in eight. This is a Diophantine problem, however: from A subtract one hundred twenty hanged, from B four the same. Include blank variables for those lost to the hunger of the mob, suicide, the wasted labor of the rope merchants.

Hark in thine ear: change places, and which is the justice, which is the thief?

Quince ruffled furiously through the script, presumably looking for killing to cut.

Bottom stood up. "Not a whit! I have a device to make all well." He raised a hand, put the other in his shirt. "Write me a *proh*-logue, and let the prologue seem to say we will do no harm with our swords, and that Pyramus is not killed indeed."

Quince peered over her spectacles.

"And for the more better assurance," Bottom went on, "tell them that I, *Peeh*-ramus, am *not* Pyramus, but"—he mimed a drum roll—"Bottom the weaver! This will put them out of fear."

"Well . . ." Quince said, then gave up. "We will have such a prologue."

They worried about the Lion frightening the court ladies, and getting moonlight into the chamber where the play would go on, and the difficulties of showing a wall onstage. "You can never bring in a wall," Snout said, and leaned against the hatrack tree.

As they finally settled down to rehearsal, Virginia slipped out of her wooden shoes, circled the tree and came up behind the nervously directing Peter Quince.

"What hempen homespuns have we swaggering here," Puck said, "so near the cradle of the Fairy Queen? What, a play toward? I'll be auditor . . . an actor too, perhaps, if I see cause."

She raised her book and was invisible.

Quince said, "Speak, Pyramus. Thisbe, stand forth."

Howard spread his feet, flexed his knees, raised both his hands above his head. Adeline, playing Flute playing Thisbe, leaned forward curiously.

"Thizzzbeee . . ." Howard said, then coughed and dropped his voice an octave. "Thisbe, the flowers of odious savors sweet—"

"Odorous, *odorous*," Quince said through clenched teeth.

Bottom paused, checked his script, nodded gravely. "Odorous savors sweet; so hath thy breath, my dearest Thisbe dear. But hark, a voice! Stay thou but here awhile, and by and by I will to thee appear." He turned, sweeping an imaginary cape for several feet in all directions, and strode offstage.

"A stranger Pyramus than e'er played here," Puck said, and skipped lightly after him.

As the play went on alongside them, Bottom leaned forward to study his lines, while Puck peered over his shoulder. Suddenly alight with inspiration, she took a pair of socks out of her pocket and arranged one over each of Bottom's ears. Then she picked up a length of rope, took a step back, coiled her arm and pinned the tail on the donkey. Bottom's eyes popped.

"Pyramus, enter," Peter Quince was saying, "your cue is past; it is 'never tire.'"

Flute swallowed, flipped back a page in the script, and repeated, "As true as truest horse that yet would never tire."

Sock ears drooping, rope tail tucked into his waistband, Bottom clumped back on stage. The other players goggled at him.

Bottom looked at them, smiled with delight at his reception, adjusted the collar of his shirt, and announced, "If I were fair, Thisbe, I were only thine."

"O monstrous!" Quince cried, "O strange! We are haunted! Pray, masters! Fly, masters! *Hellllp!*"

The players ran every which way, while Puck chased them, shaking with laughter. Bottom, sure he was being made fun of, wandered past the tree. Beyond, the huddling Peter Quince rolled over and stretched, kicking off her shoes, and was again the sleeping Titania.

Bottom sang, in a quavery voice, whistling in the graveyard: "The o-o-ousel cock, so black of hue, with orange-tawny bil-l-l, the throstle with his note so true, the wren with little quil-l-l . . ."

Titania stirred, smiled, stretched her arms in welcome. "What angel wakes me from my flowery bed?"

INTERVIEWER

What about long-term effects of the drug?

DR. GORDON

We haven't discovered any. So far as we know, LX does not affect the ability to form new memories, nor to learn, even when administered continuously over a long period of time.

INTERVIEWER

Was that done?

DR. GORDON

We believe that some people were given LX on almost a daily basis.

INTERVIEWER

Why?

DR. GORDON

Experimentally. To see what would happen. That's obvious enough. I can think of another reason.

(a beat)

I imagine you'd like to hear what it is?

INTERVIEWER

Yes.

DR. GORDON

To go back to the same victim over and over, and have that person not know it: to begin the humiliation new on a daily basis. To have this . . . experiment in pain be the first on a mind with no tolerance, a body with no conditioned responses. Do you know the Eastern story, of the renewable houris of Paradise?

"I pray thee, gentle mortal," Titania breathed, "sing again: mine ear is much enamor'd of thy note . . . so is mine eye enthrallèd to thy shape; and thy fair virtue's force perforce doth move me—on the first view!—to swear I love thee."

Bottom shivered, making his ears and tail flop about. "Methinks, mistress, you should have little reason for that. And yet, to say the truth, reason and love keep little company together nowadays. . . . The more the pity that some honest neighbors will not make them friends."

Titania, infatuated with the puzzled but delighted Bottom, summoned her fairy court to bring him his desires; Peaseblossom, Mote, Cobweb, and Mustardseed hastened to comply. As the idyll faded from view, Oberon reappeared, wondering with elfin malice what Titania had seen on awakening. Puck tripped in, and reported on events, briskness overcome by glee at the disorder in the wood that night.

Then Paris and Mark came to the tree, sandaled as Hermia and Demetrius.

"Stand close," Oberon said, "this is the same Athenian." He went invisible behind his script. Puck began to do likewise, then stopped; holding the book just below her eyes, crept over to Demetrius and peered up at him from several angles. "This is the woman," Puck said, "but *not* this the man."

Hermia was demanding to know why Demetrius had murdered Lysander, and insisting that he kill her as well. Demetrius, who had no recollection of killing anybody, was trying to explain this to Hermia, pointing out that as far as he, Demetrius, knew, Lysander was alive and well—not, of course, that he would lose much sleep if someone *had* done for the guy. Finally Hermia stormed off: "See me no more, if he be dead or no." And Demetrius, exhausted in more ways than one, went to sleep on the ground.

Puck had crept halfway across the stage when Oberon snapped, "What hast thou done?" As Puck slunk back, holding an extremely forced grin, Oberon chewed her out for having love-potioned the wrong lover. Puck pointed out that it was hardly *her* fault that one person out of a million actually *meant* all that true-to-thee-alone stuff, but accepted instructions to begin setting things right again, beginning with bringing Helena in to make up with Demetrius. "I go! I go! See how I go, faster than arrow from the Tartar's bow—"

Oberon crouched by Demetrius. "Flower of this purple dye, hit with Cupid's archery, sink in apple of his eye: when his love he doth espy, let her shine as gloriously as the Venus of the sky. . . ." He shoved the needle in.

> DR. GORDON
> (*distantly*)
> No, no, go not to Lethe, neither twist
> Wolf's-bane, tight-rooted, for its poisonous wine.
>> INTERVIEWER
> That isn't Shakespeare, is it?
>> DR. GORDON

John Keats. The "Ode on Melancholy." He's telling the sad heart not to give up—not just suicide, but abandoning thought and memory, the mind's life. Lethe.

I remember quoting that to a patient, in my office, in my old practice. I remember saying it more clearly than I see your face.

But who did I say it to? And what did he or she do with the advice?

Puck backed onstage, beckoning with a curled finger. Along came Helena and Lysander, walking lightly, in some sort of trance. Puck gestured elaborately and snapped her fingers. Instantly the couple set to, Lysander furiously plighting troth and Helena insisting she was having none of his sick jokes, that she knew perfectly well he loved Hermia.

"*Demetrius* loves her," Lysander insisted, "and he loves not *you*—"

Oberon gave the snoozing Demetrius a swift kick. He sat up straight. "O Helen! Goddess, nymph, perfect, divine!"

Lysander and Helena turned and stared.

Demetrius plighted some troth of his own to Helena, who took it with no better grace than she had Lysander's.

Oberon and Puck watched this scene with the uttermost fairy bewilderment. Then, silently, Oberon counted heads, one, two, three, and gestured to Puck, who nodded and departed, to return in a moment leading Hermia.

Now it was a chorus for four voices. Everybody was in love, nobody believed anybody else's protestations, everybody got to make a short joke about Hermia. Oberon began banging his hand against the side of his head. Puck sat down comfortably in the middle of the squabble, an expression of sheer delight on her face. Finally the boys decided to have it out like men, at swords' point, and marched off in step. The girls picked their own directions.

Oberon clasped his hands behind his back, strolled left, right. Puck smiled at him; he smiled back, crooked a finger. Puck got up and skipped toward him.

"*This* is *thy* negligence," Oberon yelled, driving Puck back halfway across the stage. "*Still* thou mistak'st—or else commit'st thy knaveries wilfully."

"Believe me, king of shadows, I mistook. . . ." Puck began, and dissembled on for a bit before shrugging and admitting, "And so far am I glad it so did sort, as this their jangling I esteem a sport."

INTERVIEWER

Is there some kind of profile of those more likely to have been in Group A?

DR. GORDON

(*apparently not hearing*)

Have I said how much we appreciate your soldiers' standing aside, and letting us solve our own problems?

INTERVIEWER

Surely there must be *some* patterns, some psychological type—

Dr. Gordon

Of course. We've lost our memories, but we haven't lost all human history. We know from it that people of middle authority, people who were already part of a system, used to passing orders along, were prime choices.

As far as evidence is concerned, there were certain types of offices where records were destroyed wholesale during the final stages. The police, naturally, and the army. The railroads. Hospitals and group medical practices. Universities. There are plenty of patterns to find, profiles to cast, if you wish. Or you can say that the search-and-burn units went where there were masses of material for them to find and destroy.

Of those who we are most sure were Group A—because they refused LX, and confessed it openly, the ones who *believed* even unto the end of the world—six were writers, four were poets. *(barely controlling himself)* A professor of classical literature told the court with the utmost pride that he had shot fifteen children cleanly through the head because they could not understand that value was an absolute.

They had faith . . . in a way that the train conductors did not.

Howard/Lysander came on stage, jabbing and slashing with an invisible sword. A step behind him came Virginia/Puck, carrying a box.

Lysander took up a fencer's stance, called out, "Where art thou, proud Demetrius? Speak thou now!"

Puck put the box on the floor, stood on it, cleared her throat, and said in a fair imitation of Mark's Demetrius, "Here, villain, drawn and ready. Where art thou?"

"I will be with thee straight," Lysander said, and charged offstage, right past the unseen fairy.

Mark/Demetrius entered from the opposite direction. From his pose, he was carrying something more than a sword—a two-handed battle-axe, perhaps, or a machine gun. "Lysander, speak again," he said.

Puck got down from the box, plodded across the stage until she was behind Demetrius, and arched herself in the best style of Errol Flynn swordplay. "Follow my voice; we'll try no manhood here."

Demetrius turned, growled, shouldered arms, and stamped off.
A few more tricks with voices in the dark, and the heroes both
collapsed, still muttering challenges at each other, and slept. Before
long Helena came by, weary and confused, and went to sleep as
well—and of course Hermia arrived at last to make it a foursome.

"On the ground," Puck said, "sleep sound; I'll apply to your eye,
gentle lover, remedy." She readied the syringe, plunged it into
Lysander's throat. "When thou wak'st, thou tak'st true delight in the
sight of thy former lady's eye; and the country proverb known, that
every man should take his own, in your waking shall be shown." She
stood, stretched, sighed. "Jack shall have Jill, nought shall go ill; the
man shall have his mare again, and all shall be well."

Puck departed, leaving all four sleeping together.

INTERVIEWER
One in four died, one in eight of the survivors—

DR. GORDON
So that among any group of six there are eleven chances in
twenty that at least one was Group A, and for their lives one and a
half others are dead. Add a seventh player, and it's six in ten there's
a villain among them, and another quarter-mortal past the hour of
caring.

But can one be six-tenths a murderer, or three-quarters buried
in the limepits?

(*He removes one of his cuff links, pulls down the cuff, shows his
bare wrist to the light.*)

No shackle scar here. What odds would you lay on the other
hand?

INTERVIEWER
I'm not certain I follow you, Doctor.

DR. GORDON
There is a wonderful passage in the plan documents, section
four, paragraph eight. "Because the subjects have no memory of
events, some of them can usefully be employed to confuse the evidence, particularly body evidence."

(*He holds up his hands.*)

Isn't that amazing? It's *iambic pentameter,* and it even—

(*reciting*)
Because the subjects have no memory
Of èvents, some of them can usefully—
INTERVIEWER
You mean that some of the prisoners—tortured their guards?
DR. GORDON
(*He stops still, waits a moment to see if his point will be grasped.*
It isn't, and he continues, flatly and wearily:)
Supply the tools, give the order with authority, and the job will
be done. We've known that for a very, very long time.
INTERVIEWER
But surely no guilt can attach—
DR. GORDON
We can take no pride even in our wounds and scars. To what
shall we attach guilt?

Titania was still wooing the jackasserized Bottom with all the charms
of the fairy kingdom—though Bottom kept surprising even himself
with a desire for hay and dried peas. Oberon hung on the tree,
watching the scene, his smile now soft and unvengeful.

As Titania and Bottom fell asleep, nestled together, the lark and
the spiny echidna, Puck came in, looking exhausted.

"Welcome, good Robin," Oberon said, "see'st thou this sweet
sight? Her dotage now I do begin to pity. . . ." He had the changeling
child now, and was ready to release his Queen. He closed in, sat
down behind her, slid the needle in most gently. "Be as thou wast
wont to be, see as thou wast wont to see. . . ."

She gasped and awoke. "My Oberon! What visions I have seen!
Methought I was enamored of an ass."

"There lies your love."

"How came these things to pass?" They all stopped, and quite
a long moment went by before Paris continued, "Oh, how mine eyes
do loathe his visage now. . . ."

Puck tugged off the sock ears and the rope tail. As Oberon and
Titania danced, Virginia took off Howard's workingman's clogs and
buckled on the sandals of Athens. Paris concluded the dance, slipped
on her own sandals and sank into sleep as Hermia; Walter and Vir-

ginia departed as Oberon and Puck and returned as Theseus and Hippolyta.

"But soft, what nymphs are these?" said the Duke of Athens, regarding all the lovers cluttering his forest.

Adeline stirred without waking, and from Helena's slumber Egeus's cracked voice said, "My lord, this is my daughter here asleep, and this Lysander; this Demetrius is, this Helena. . . ."

A blast of horns voiced by Walter and Virginia woke the four, who tried without much success to explain what they were all doing under the same tree. Egeus displayed an unhealthy desire to have his daughter immediately either married or hanged, which Demetrius interrupted with the admission that he really did love Helena after all.

"Egeus, I will overbear your will," Theseus said, and it took little imagination to hear the ". . . or we'll see who gets his neck stretched" underneath it. The Duke then decreed "a feast in all solemnity"—the unspoken counterpart being "triple bachelor party"—and the Athenians departed, the lovers agreeing to discuss their night's dream . . . but probably not in too much detail.

Bottom wandered on stage, carrying his shoes. He looked down at his bare feet, danced a little jig-step, and sat down under the tree. "I have had a most rare vision," he said. "I have had a dream . . . past the wit of man to say what dream it was." He pulled the clogs on, clip-clopped his feet on the floor. "Man is but an ass if he go about to expound this dream. Methought I was—there is no man can tell what. Methought I was—and methought I had—" He slashed his hands through the air, stood up. "But man is but a patched fool if he will offer to say what methought I had!" He looked up at the tree, squinting through its branches at the rising sun. "The eye of man hath not heard, the ear of man hath not seen, man's hand is not able to taste, his tongue to conceive, nor his heart to report, what my dream was. I will get Peter Quince to write a ballad of this dream; it shall be called 'Bottom's Dream' . . . because it hath no bottom!" He chuckled, sighed. "And I will sing it in the latter end of a play, before the Duke. Peradventure, to make it the more gracious, I shall sing it at . . . her . . . death."

He wheezed, took hold of the hatrack, and walked off, dragging the tree behind him.

INTERVIEWER
Do you see the action in the wood as a metaphor for justice coming out of injustice?
DR. GORDON
Have you ever been in psychotherapy?
INTERVIEWER
Surely you don't hold that a faith in justice is a form of insanity.
DR. GORDON
Not the faith in its value. But the belief that it's the natural order of things, I'd call that a delusional structure, yes. Truth won't always out, the wages of sin are bankable, and those who live by the sword perish mostly of syphilis.

As I've said, we don't exist in a vacuum, on a bare stage. We remember what happened long ago. There were camps before ours, liberations before ours, tribunals before ours. Group A knew all that and planned accordingly.

When they saw the end coming, they in a sense abolished the camps themselves. But they did so in a way that also abolished justice. Once, before LX, before us, the victims knew the torturers' faces—and the torturers knew themselves; if they hid, they felt guilt that would punish and betray them, and if they felt no guilt, they could not truly hide.

But all we know is that some of us did what was done. And so we are all in hiding, and we are all guilty.

The Athenian court discussed the strange events of the night before—Duke Theseus playing the amused skeptic at all this fairy business. The Duke was interested in tonight's amusements—who was up for a party, and what had his master of ceremonies arranged? "Call Philostrate."

"Here, mighty Theseus," Dr. Gordon said. The major-domo provided the Duke with a list of proposed entertainments, which Theseus dismissed one after another—"We'll none of that . . . that is an old device . . . that is some satire, keen and critical, not sorting with a nuptial ceremony." Then he came to *Pyramus and Thisbe.* . . .

Philostrate did his best to argue against the play. It was ridiculous; it was being staged by a bunch of working stiffs; it was only good for a few laughs at the players' expense.

Theseus insisted. He explained to Hippolyta that he had already seen any number of spectacles put on by bored professionals; sincerity, however clumsy, was to be preferred to expert indifference: "Love, therefore, and tongue-tied simplicity, in least speak most, to my capacity."

The workmen were sitting on boxes, changing their clogs for ballet slippers as they changed themselves into actors. Howard as Bottom had a yardstick thrust through a belt loop, Pyramus's sword; Adeline as Flute wore a sheet over head and shoulders, Thisbe's cloak; Walter as Snout carried a foam-rubber brick balanced on one shoulder to illustrate Wall. Virginia as Starveling the tailor was kitted out with a candle and a ball of twine, for Moon's lantern and thornbush, and a long leather strap dangled from her wrist, leashing an invisible dog. Mark as Snug the carpenter, who would be Lion, sat contentedly admiring his new buskins and pawing the air until, with a desperate gesture, Paris/Quince dropped a mophead on his scalp.

Dr. Gordon, as Philostrate the master of ceremonies, rapped on the lectern, cleared his throat, and said unctuously, "So please your grace, the, hrrrm, Prologue is addressed."

Momentarily lifting his brick, Walter as Theseus said, "Let him approach."

Quince took little steps forward. "If we offend, it is with our good will," he said, and took a little bow. Philostrate tilted his head, and Theseus made a that's-nice gesture.

"That you should think, we come not to offend but with good will to show our simple skill," Quince said. "That is the true beginning of our end." His voice sped up. "Consider then, we come but in despite. We do not come, as minding to content you, our true intent is." He started to spread his hands, but they were too tightly clutched on his script. "All for your delight, we are not here!" He got a hand loose, gestured at the players. "That you should here repent you, the actors are at hand . . . and by their show, you shall know all that you are like to know."

"This fellow doth not stand upon points," Theseus said; Paris/Quince looked down at her ballet shoes, and that was exactly what she was doing. She stepped lightly off.

"Who is next?" the Duke said, and the whole company stood, paraded once around the stage, and took up poses. Quince introduced them, Pyramus, Thisbe, Wall, Moon, and Lion, and then crouched in front of Philostrate's lectern.

Walter hoisted his brick again, and Theseus said, "I wonder if the Lion be to speak?"

Mark doffed his mop, said as Demetrius, "No wonder, my lord—one lion may, when many asses do." He replaced his mane; Walter did likewise with his brick, and as Snout explained how he was a Wall, that divided the lovers Pyramus and Thisbe.

He removed the brick again. The Duke turned his head, held the brick alongside his mouth, and said aside, "Would you desire lime and hair to speak better?"

Demetrius said from behind Lion's mane, "It is the wittiest partition that ever I heard discourse, my lord."

"Pyramus draws near the wall: silence!"

Pyramus appeared, walking as though he expected the earth to open beneath him at any moment. "O grim-look'd night! O night with hue so black! O night, which ever art when day is not! O night . . . O night . . ."

Quince ruffled through the script, leaned his head on his forearm in woe. Pyramus shouted "Alack!" Quince raised three fingers. Pyramus nodded. "Alack, alack!"

"Thou wall," Pyramus told the wall, "O wall, O sweet and lovely wall, show me thy chink, to blink through with mine eyne." He inclined his head, Wall swung his brick into place.

"Tha'ggs, Waw," Pyramus said, rubbing his nose, "Jove shield thee well for this. But what see I? No Thisbe do I see. O wicked wall, through whom I see no bliss, curs'd be thy stones for thus deceiving me!"

Wall adjusted the brick, turned his head for the Duke to say, "The wall, methinks, being sensible, should curse again."

Pyramus raised the brick, leaned under it, and said very earnestly, "No, in truth, sir, he should not. 'Deceiving me' is Thisbe's cue. She is to enter now, and I am to spy her through the wall. You shall see it will fall pat as I told you: yonder she comes." He turned, gestured, and bashed his head against the brick.

Howard and Adeline extruded woo through the hole in Wall, sounding if anything more sincere than Lysander and Helena the night before. They arranged a rendezvous somewhere without bricks in the way, and departed.

"Thus have I, Wall, my part dischargéd so, and being done, thus Wall away doth go." Wall bowed, tucked the brick under his arm, and sat down next to Virginia. She turned, and as Hippolyta said, "This is the silliest stuff that ever I heard!"

Walter looked into space for a quarter-minute or so, then smiled kindly at her, said very gently, "The best in this kind are but shadows . . . and the worst are no worse, if imagination mend them."

"It must be your imagination, then, and not theirs," she said, but her voice was more doubtful than sarcastic.

"If we imagine no worse of them than they of themselves . . ." Walter stopped, raised his eyes to the darkness above the stage, the shadowed metal and the dangling flyropes. ". . . they may pass for— *excellent* men."

> INTERVIEWER
> They do . . . wonderfully with very little.
> DR. GORDON
> Theater is participatory. Given the least assistance in maintaining the illusion, the audience will do wonders. Just as your audience does.
> INTERVIEWER
> My audience—
> DR. GORDON
> Of course. Anyone listening to us now would believe we're in a theater.
> INTERVIEWER
> We *are* in a theater.

DR. GORDON
(hastily)

Oh, yes, of course.

INTERVIEWER
(slightly uneasy)

I should probably make clear—

DR. GORDON
(breaking in)

One moment, please! We can hear—yes, we definitely can hear the Martian war machines just outside the studio now! A heat ray is passing very close to the window—*(he rubs his sleeve across the microphone, making a hissing sound)* We may be cut off the air at any moment, ladies and gentlemen, so please—

[The recorder comes to a loud halt. The PLAYERS *stop still.]*

DR. GORDON
(mildly)

Do your soldiers always have first chance to buy batteries, even before correspondents?

INTERVIEWER
(bewildered and angry)

What on earth are you doing, Doctor?

DR. GORDON

Getting you to play the game.

INTERVIEWER

What game?

DR. GORDON

Audience Participation, of course. You can see that no elaborate staging is necessary.

Every time the game turns mean or rough or ugly, people with the very best of thoughts and intentions ask why everyone didn't just refuse to play in the first place.

(wry)

Now a few people will always believe that this theater doesn't exist. And that Martians attacked it.

(a beat)

Or you could do some careful editing.

[The recorder starts again. The action resumes.]

Duke Theseus pointed offstage. "Here come two noble beasts in, a man and a lion."

Mark came in, clawing air and mouthing growls. Then he stood up straight, removed his mane and held the mop over his heart. He explained carefully that he was Snug the joiner, not a lion, and he certainly did not intend to eat anyone present at the performance. Then he replaced the mop and folded himself into a sphinx.

Virginia stood and took center stage, dragging the empty leash, and held up the candle to declaim Moon. The Athenians didn't seem to believe it was the Moon. She hid the candle for a moment, as Hippolyta wished the Moon to change.

By Moon's light, Thisbe appeared. "This is old Ninny's tomb. Where is my love?"

Lion stood up, crept behind her, cleared his throat delicately. "Growl?"

Thisbe shrieked and dashed offstage. Lion got on all fours, looked around perplexed for Thisbe's mantle to maul. Adeline snuck back, dropped it in front of him, bowed and ran off again.

Mark nuzzled the sheet for a moment, then slipped off his mop and said as Demetrius, "Well roared, Lion!"

Walter called, "Well run, Thisbe!"

Virginia hid her candle. "Well shone, Moon! Truly, the moon shines with a good grace."

Walter tossed Mark a prop bottle marked KETCHUP. The Lion shook it over Thisbe's sheet, crawled off. The Duke said, "Well moused, Lion."

Pyramus returned. "Sweet Moon, I thank thee for thy sunny beams. . . ." He hunted for Thisbe, but found only the discarded cloak: he picked it up with two fingers, held it at arm's length. He threw an arm across his eyes. He howled at the Moon, who stuck fingers in her ears. He fell on the floor and pounded it, then stood up again, brushed himself off with the sheet, and embraced it. "But stay, o spite! But mark, poor knight, what dreadful dole is here? Eyes, do you see? How can it be? O dainty duck, O dear!" He heaved a sob, blew his nose on the sheet. "Thy mantle good, what! Stained with blood? Approach, ye Furies fell! O fates, come, come! Cut thread and thrum, quail, crush, conclude, and quell!"

Theseus had buried his face in his arms. He raised his head, shook it gravely, and said, "This passion, and the death of a dear friend, would go near to make a man look sad."

Pyramus, meanwhile, had drawn his yardstick and was sharpening it on his thigh. "Come tears, confound! Out sword, and wound the pap of Pyramus. Ay, that . . ." He examined his chest. "*Left* pap, where heart doth hop." He thrust, clamping the stick under his arm. "Thus die I, thus, thus, thus! Now am I dead, now am I fled; my soul is in the sky." He raised his arms in the direction of his soul; the sword hit the stage. He picked it up, put it firmly in place again. "Tongue, lose thy light; Moon, take thy flight. . . ." He waited patiently for Moon to notice his cue and leave.

"Now die! Die! Die! Die . . ." He stiffened, toppled to the floor. "Diiiiiiiie. . . ."

Thisbe entered. She was much put out by what she found. She catalogued Pyramus' manly virtues, while making a valiant try at cardio-pulmonary resuscitation. "Tongue, not a word: come, trusty sword. . . ." She couldn't find it. Pyramus reached under himself and handed it up. "Come, blade, my breast imbrue! And farewell, friends, thus Thisbe ends: adieu, adieu—" She counted hastily on her fingers. "Adieu."

The court kept silence for a while. The lovers stayed resolutely dead.

The Duke consulted his script. "Moonshine and Lion are left to bury the dead."

Demetrius said, "Ay, and Wall too."

Bottom sat up, tumbling Thisbe into the wings. "No, I assure you; the wall is down that parted their fathers. Will it please you to see the epilogue, or to hear a Bergomask dance between two of our company?"

"No epilogue, I pray you," the Duke said, with a wild wave of his hands, "for your play needs no excuse. Never . . ." He bit his lip, inhaled. ". . . excuse, for when the players are all . . . dead . . ." Walter struggled; the others did not move. ". . . there need none to be blamed." He shrugged, smiled again. "Marry, if he that writ it had played Pyramus, and hanged himself in Thisbe's garter, it would have been a fine tragedy—and so it is, truly, and very notably discharged. But come, your Bergomask; let your epilogue alone."

The players formed a circle, all standing; Paris and Howard stepped into the center, began to move in a stately step around one another, carrying themselves precisely, one hand lifted, almost but not quite touching.

INTERVIEWER

What exactly is a Bergomask dance?

DR. GORDON

The word comes from Bergamo, a town in Italy. Today we would say *Bergamesque*. In Shakespeare's day the people there were proverbial rustics.

INTERVIEWER

What is it like?

[DR. GORDON says nothing; he continues to watch the dance. MARK and VIRGINIA join the circle, and then WALTER and ADELINE. From a circle dance it becomes linear, a courtly dance in the Regency fashion, with much bowing and waving of fans.

Abruptly, HOWARD puts his hand on PARIS's shoulder, and the dancers freeze; then PARIS puts her arm around HOWARD's neck, and they begin a close dance, a tango. The others follow.

Partners are changed, hold each other closer. Then all at once all form disappears, and the six players are in a shifting, balletic, erotic knot; hands slip over throats and under shirts, lips touch, bodies collide.

DR. GORDON begins to rise from his chair, but sits back, folds his arms firmly upon the lectern.

WALTER pushes back the cuffs of VIRGINIA's sweatshirt, showing bandages wrapping her wrists; he closes his hands over them and they dance to his direction.]

INTERVIEWER

Were there orgies in the camps?

[DR. GORDON still does not turn to speak. Slowly his head falls forward into his folded arms on the lectern, and he shudders: his face is out of sight, but he must be weeping.

WALTER releases VIRGINIA and steps aside. She rejoins the group.

WALTER pulls off his dancing shoes and dons Theseus's sandals again; he claps his hands and all stop. They are breathing hard; they rearrange their clothing.
DR. GORDON raises his head, brushes his hair into place. There are no tears on his face.]

"The iron tongue of midnight hath told twelve," Theseus said. "Lovers, to bed: 'tis almost fairy time." The couples held hands. "Sweet friends, to bed; a fortnight hold we this solemnity in nightly revels and new jollity."

All went out but Virginia, who held her arms crossed, sleeves pulled down again to half-cover her hands, then knelt to remove her slippers. Puck stood, stretched. "Now the hungry lion roars," she said, softly, softly, "and the wolf behowls the moon; whilst the heavy plowman snores, all with weary task fordone." She danced lightly from compass point to point, calling up the spirits of the night: "Every one lets forth his sprite in the church-way paths to glide; and we fairies that do run, by the triple Hecate's team, from the presence of the sun . . . following darkness . . ." She paused, said not singing, "like a dream. . . . Now are frolic; not a mouse shall disturb this hallowed house. *I* am sent, with broom before, to sweep the dust behind the door."

Oberon and Titania entered, with all fairies after, and they danced again—but this time all lightly, politely, humming ring-around-the-rosy like a children's game until ashes, ashes, they all fell down.

Oberon laid his blessing on the house and all in it, and all the children to come of the love within. He turned to look at Dr. Gordon, who sat very straight. "And the owner of it blest," the Fairy King said, "ever shall in safety rest; trip away, make no stay, meet me all by break of day."

The fairies flitted away, leaving only Puck again. "If we shadows have offended, think but this, and all is mended: that you have but slumbered here while these visions did appear . . . and this weak and idle theme, no more yielding than a dream, gentles, do not reprehend—if you pardon, we will mend." She paused, and when she began again, her voice was cool and earnest; good evening, this is the news: "And as I am an honest Puck, if we have unearnéd luck, now to 'scape the serpent's tongue . . . we *will* make amends ere long; else the Puck a liar call. So. Goodnight unto you all."

[She bows and runs off. A full minute goes by, but none of the players return. Slowly, the lights of the playing space fade out.]

INTERVIEWER

Was that the Epilogue?

DR. GORDON

No. There's no Epilogue; the law of Athens suppressed it, re-member?

But just think: you've survived the whole play.

(a pause)

INTERVIEWER

Last question.

DR. GORDON

Yes?

INTERVIEWER

Why?

(DR. GORDON just smiles.)

INTERVIEWER

What I mean is—

DR. GORDON

I know what you mean. Why this, and not something else? Why this, and not an answer to the question that we keep asking, and may have to keep asking for the rest of our lives?

I do not know what I did. That was taken from me. I do not know what will happen next. That is not given to me. But I know, here, now, what I am doing. And I can live with it.

[He stands up and walks offstage. The tape reels continue to turn. Then, with a mechanical click, they stop, and begin to spin back-ward at high speed, with a high-pitched squealing. The machine stops. The stage goes dark.]

CURTAIN

MARK KREIGHBAUM

I REMEMBER ANGELS

Your ad said you were looking for "human stories?" Stories of the "first time?" What sort of . . . oh, yeah, I see the list now.
Do you mind if I ask why—
Oh, I get it. You're kind of like our human scientists who visit your worlds and study things? It seems weird that you'd want to talk to just regular people like me, though.
Yeah. Yeah, I would.
"True stories?" Yeah, I understand.

I remember my first real love.

Erin and me were at this dinner party on a houseboat in Sausalito. I got to sit next to her and we talked about cartoons while we ate food with names I couldn't pronounce. She wore this elegant pink dress, and we argued about basketball.

She smiled unself-consciously, a thing I've always liked in women, and she laughed at most of my jokes.

Before the dessert, I knew we were in love.

A lie? No! No.

Well . . . yeah. How did you know?

Her name wasn't Erin. There was no houseboat. We never spoke.

Let me try again. Please?

I remember my first kiss.

Her name was Cathy and she had an overbite. She used to beat me at checkers and she taught me how to whistle. I taught her how to play basketball. She got a lot of scrapes and cuts while she was learning, but never complained and never cried. I've always admired courage in a woman.

We were in the treehouse her father had built for her. I remember the smell of the oak and wood shavings, like old fire. We were sitting on a musty pink blanket eating white bread right out of the wrapper and reading comic books. Whenever I see a comic book now, I think of her.

Somehow, we got onto the subject of kissing—maybe Sue Storm kissed Mr. Fantastic or something, I don't know—and we tried it ourselves. Our lips met, this brief perfect touch, and then we both giggled and went back to reading.

Cathy died in a fire later that year. Her father had fallen asleep in his bedroom with a cigarette.

What?

No, I . . .

Yeah. Lies.

Cathy moved away over the summer without telling anyone in our class. We never kissed.

I'm sorry.

I can try again? Thank you.

Yes, I promise. No more lies.

I remember . . . *no.*

Wait. Wait. Please. Give me another chance. I'll do a better one, one you've never heard. And all true. Every word. I promise.

Really? Thank you. I appreciate it. I . . . you've been real patient. Thank you.

I remember angels.

Growing up during the year of the Riots was strange. Have you ever read accounts of those English kids during World War II who were sent to live out in the country because of the fear of German bombing raids? A lot of those kids had the best times of their lives out there. I'm sure you've heard veterans reminisce about their time in the war, too, no matter how horrible it really was.

Well, anyway, I was ten years old and the streets were on fire. It was exciting. Every day you could see something you'd never seen before. I never thought much about all the people who were killed. Just never thought about it.

I didn't have any friends. No mother. No brothers or sisters. I've never really had any close friends. So, anyway, I spent most of my time alone, reading, and watching the streets. Watching the stories on the streets.

I saw a rape one afternoon, and angels after.

You got used to the smoke from the fires pretty quick. You just had to make sure you stayed away from the waste plants and factories— the smoke from them could tear up your throat. There was this one kid at school who'd had that happen to him, and he had to talk through a box after. We all thought it was cool.

Anyway, my usual spot on the roof of our apartment building wasn't any good because the wind was bringing toxic smoke there. So, I went to Reagan Park instead, but I kept kind of out of sight on the roof of a maintenance shed, because a lot of crackers used the park to buy drugs and stuff. They didn't usually bother us kids, and sometimes they'd give us candy. But the dealers didn't like being watched.

I brought along a couple of comic books a looter gave me, and I watched the people who came to the park.

Some kids came to play basketball and they swore a lot because of all the holes in the court and the backboard was all shot up. But they played for a couple hours anyway, and I was just hypnotized by how graceful and quick they were. They yelled at each other and got into fights that I knew instinctively weren't for real, though sometimes it sounded like they wanted it to be, if you know what I mean. I watched them play. Even now, you know, I follow all the basketball teams and I guess I keep wondering if I'll see one of those kids playing two guard or something. They were that good. I know I'll recognize them if I see them.

After they left, there were just some winos sleeping under the trees and drinking from paper bags, so I started reading my comic books.

Then it was noon, because I heard the big whistle go off at the Guard headquarters and I saw all the jeeps going down McAllister.

A couple guys came into the park and hung out by the rest room, dealing, though they only got one or two customers in what seemed like hours. They didn't seem to care, just standing by the rest room, smoking and talking. Later, this woman came.

She was real tall, and she didn't dress like a hooker, though you could tell she was one, because those were the only women you ever saw in Reagan Park, and besides she moved with this extra wiggle that I'd never seen anyone but hookers use. She wore a loose, billowing, pink dress that went down to her ankles. The day was cold and windy and her dress whipped around her legs like curtains in a storm. She kept holding it down. She wore black nylons. Her black hair was tied into a ponytail that she wore over one shoulder. She had on a pair of these white gloves that went all the way up to her elbows. I remember looking at those gloves and being confused by them. They seemed like such a strange thing for her to wear, and I remember thinking that she must have had to wash them a lot. Even to this day, if I see a woman wearing gloves like that, it makes me feel strange.

The woman came up to the two men and talked with them. One of them gave her a cigarette and she laughed at whatever he said. Her laugh was loud, like she didn't care who heard it.

They stood there and talked for a while, then they all went into the rest room. I don't remember if I knew what they were doing in there, but I do remember losing interest and going back to my comic books.

Some time later, I heard the sound of metal jangling and looked up to see a squad of four Guards come across the park. They were in full battle dress with their automatic rifles slung over their shoulders. I could read the insignia on their helmets, and recognized the unit, my father's unit.

They were laughing and shoving each other, a lot like the kids who'd been playing basketball, though they were all much older. As they were walking across the park, the woman and the two men came out of the rest room.

The Guards saw them and aimed their rifles at them. The two guys put up their hands right away, and so did the woman, after a second.

Then they made the woman and the dealers turn around and put their hands on the wall of the rest room. The woman's pink dress kept whipping up in the wind, but she couldn't take her hands off the wall to do anything about it. I saw that she wasn't wearing any underwear.

The Guards handcuffed the woman and the two men and took away everything in their pockets, including their cigarettes. I thought they might beat them up. I'd seen that happen a few times. But instead, they just talked with the men and the dealers nodded and snuck glances at the woman. One of the Guards kept playing with the woman's ponytail.

Finally, they took the handcuffs off the men, gave them back their cigarettes, though they kept everything else they'd taken, and the dealers left the park.

Then, they raped the woman right there, though I can't remember whether I really understood what was happening at first— I didn't know much of anything about sex; though, when they made her get down on her knees like that, I knew. I knew.

They didn't even take her inside the rest room. I watched them hit her a lot of times, though she didn't scream, or fight back. I remember one of them used a big knife to cut off her ponytail and put it in his pack.

When they'd all finished with her, she scrunched up into a ball with her arms around her knees, her pink dress down. I saw . . . I saw specks of red on her white gloves.

The men left.

She was still just lying there, scrunched up, when these three people came. I wondered where they'd come from, because they were at the rest room so fast without my seeing them.

All three of them wore the same thing, long white gowns that you could almost see everything through. And they were bald, very tall. I couldn't tell if they were men or women.

They all sat down with the woman, not touching her, but just crouched around her, heads bowed like they were praying.

After a while, they all stood up. Very slowly, she took off her dress, lifting it over her head and dropping it to the ground. She took off all her clothes like that, slowly, and then dropped them down on the ground.

The last things she took off were her gloves. And after she removed them, she looked up and I swear she seemed to look right into my eyes. She wasn't mad at all that I was seeing her naked, or that I'd watched her being raped, or anything. She just looked at me and gave the most beautiful, unself-conscious smile I'd ever seen. Like she knew me, was glad to see me. No one had ever looked at me like that. Nobody. It was like she was my sister and she loved me.

The other people all hugged her and then they were gone.

I don't know. I might have closed my eyes. I might have. I was crying, saying I'm sorry, I'm sorry, thinking about the Guards and the insignia, and I might have closed my eyes. I can't swear I didn't.

Anyway, one second she was there, smiling, and the next she was gone.

The angels took her home.

I went back to Reagan Park a hundred times, even during the worst of the Riots when the Guards were shooting anybody out after dark. I went back a hundred times and waited. Took off all my clothes and waited.

But the angels never came back.

My father? He was killed during the Riots.

No, I don't remember how.

Next week? Well, yeah, I suppose I can come back then. If you really want me to.

Thank you for listening.

MAUREEN F. McHUGH

THE COST TO
BE WISE

i

THE SUN WAS UP ON THE SNOW AND EVERYTHING WAS BRIGHT TO LOOK at when the skimmer landed. It landed on the long patch of land behind the schoolhouse, dropping down into the snow like some big bug. I was supposed to be down at the distillery helping my mam but we needed water and I had to get an ice ax so I was outside when the offworlders came.

The skimmer was from Barok. Barok was a city. It was so far away that no one I knew in Sckarline had ever been there (except for the teachers, of course) but for the offworlders the trip was only a few hours. The skimmer came a couple of times a year to bring packages for the teachers.

The skimmer sat there for a moment—long time waiting while nothing happened except people started coming to watch—and then the hatch opened out and an offworlder stepped gingerly out on the snow. The offworlder wasn't a skimmer pilot though, it was a tall, thin boy. I shaded my eyes and watched. My hands were cold but I wanted to see.

The offworlder wore strange colors for the snow. Offworlders always wore unnatural colors. This boy wore purples and oranges and black, all shining as if they were wet and none of them thick enough to keep anyone warm. He stood with his knees stiff and his body rigid because the snow was packed to flat, slick ice by the skimmer and he wasn't sure of his balance. But he was tall and I figured he was as old as I am so it looked odd that he still didn't know how to walk on snow. He was beardless, like a boy. Darker than any of us.

Someone inside the skimmer handed him a bag. It was deep red and shined as if it were hard and wrinkled as if it were felt. My father crossed to the skimmer and took the bag from the boy because it was clear that the boy might fall with it and it made a person uncomfortable to watch him try to balance and carry something.

The dogs were barking, and more Sckarline people were coming because they'd heard the skimmer.

I wanted to see what the bags were made of so I went to the hatch of the skimmer to take something. We didn't get many things from the offworlders because they weren't appropriate, but I liked offworlder things. I couldn't see much inside the skimmer because it was dark and I had been out in the sun, but standing beside the seat where the pilot was sitting there was an old white-haired man, all straight-legged and tall. As tall as Ayudesh the teacher, which is to say taller than anyone else I knew. He handed the boy a box, though, not a bag, a bright blue box with a thick white lid. A plastic box. An offworlder box. The boy handed it to me.

"Thanks," the boy said in English. Up close I could see that the boy was really a girl. Offworlders dress the same both ways, and they are so tall it's hard to tell sometimes, but this was a girl with short black hair and skin as dark as wood.

My father put the bag in the big visitors' house and I put the box there, too. It was midday at winterdark, so the sun was a red glow on the horizon. The bag looked black except where it fell into the red square of sunlight from the doorway. It shone like metal. So very fine. Like nothing we had. I touched the bag. It was plastic, too. I liked the feeling of plastic. I liked the sound of the word in lingua. If someday I had a daughter, maybe I'd name her Plastic. It would be a rich name, an exotic name. The teachers wouldn't like it, but it was a name I wished I had.

Ayudesh was walking across the snow to the skimmer when I went back outside. The girl (I hadn't shaken free from thinking of her as a boy) stuck out her hand to him. Should I have shaken her hand? No, she'd had the box, I couldn't have shaken her hand. So I had done it right. Wanji, the other teacher, was coming, too.

I got wood from the pile for the boxstove in the guest house, digging it from under the top wood because the top wood would be damp. It would take a long time to heat up the guest house, so the sooner I got started the sooner the offworlders would be comfortable.

There was a window in the visitor's house, fat-yellow above the purple-white snow.

Inside everyone was sitting around on the floor, talking. None of the teachers were there, were they with the old man? I smelled whisak but I didn't see any, which meant that the men were drinking it outside. I sat down at the edge of the group, where it was dark, next to Dirtha. Dirtha was watching the offworld girl who was shaking her head at Harup to try to tell him she didn't understand what he was asking. Harup pointed at her blue box again. "Can I see it?" he asked. Harup was my father's age so he didn't speak any English.

It was warming up in here, although when the offworlder girl leaned forward and breathed out, her mouth in an O, her breath smoked the air for an instant.

It was too frustrating to watch Harup try to talk to the girl. "What's your kinship?" he asked. "I'm Harup Sckarline." He thumped his chest with his finger. "What's your kinship?" When she shook her head, not understanding all these words, he looked around and grinned. Harup wouldn't stop until he was bored, and that would take a long time.

"I'm sorry," the girl said, "I don't speak your language." She looked unhappy.

Ayudesh would be furious with us if he found out that none of us would try and use our English.

I had to think about how to ask. Then I cleared my throat, so people would know I was going to talk from the back of the group. "He asks what is your name," I said.

The girl's chin came up like a startled animal. "What?" she said.

Maybe I said it wrong? Or my accent was so bad she couldn't understand? I looked at my boots; the stitches around the toes were fraying. They had been my mother's. "Your name," I said to the boots.

The toes twitched a little, sympathetic. Maybe I should have kept quiet.

"My name is Veronique," she said.

"What is she saying?" asked Harup.

"She says her kinship is Veronique," I said.

"That's not a kinship," said Little Shemus. Little Shemus wasn't old enough to have a beard, but he was old enough to be critical of everything.

"Offworlders don't have kinship like we do," I said. "She gave her front name."

"Ask her her kinship name," Little Shemus said.

"She just told you," Ardha said, taking the end of her braid out of her mouth. Ardha was a year younger than me. "They don't have kinship names. Ayudesh doesn't have a kinship name. Wanji doesn't."

"Sure they do," Shemus said. "Their kinship name is Sckar-lineclan."

"We give them that name," said Ardha and pursed her round lips. Ardha was always bossy.

"What are they saying?" asked the girl.

"They say, err, they ask, what is your," your what? How would I even ask what her kinship name was in English? There was a word for it, but I couldn't think of it. "Your other name."

She frowned. Her eyebrows were quite black. "You mean my last name? It's Veronique Twombly."

What was so hard about 'last name'? I remembered it as soon as she said it. "Tawomby," I said. "Her kinship is Veronique Tawomby."

"Tawomby," Harup said. "Amazing. It doesn't sound like a word. It sounds made-up, like children do. What's in her box?"

"I know what's in her box," said Erip. Everybody laughed except for Ardha and me. Even Little Sherep laughed and he didn't really understand.

The girl was looking at me to explain.

"He asks inside, the box is." I had gotten tangled up. Questions were hard.

"Is the box inside?" she asked.

I nodded.

"It's inside," she said.

I didn't understand her answer, so I waited for her to explain.

"I don't know what you mean," she said. "Did someone bring the box inside?"

I nodded, because I wasn't sure exactly what she'd said, but she didn't reach for the box or open it or anything. I tried to think of how to say it.

"Inside," Ardha said, tentative. "What is?"

"The box," she said. "Oh wait, you want to know what's in the box?"

Ardha looked at the door so she wouldn't have to look at the off-worlder. I wasn't sure so I nodded.

She pulled the box over and opened it up. Something glimmered hard and green and there were red and yellow boxes covered in lingua and she said, "Presents for Ayudesh and Wanji." Everybody stood up to see inside, so I couldn't see, but I heard her say things. The words didn't mean anything. Tea, that I knew. Wanji talked about tea. "These are sweets," I heard her say. "You know, candy." I knew the word 'sweet,' but I didn't know what else she meant. It was so much harder to speak English to her than it was to do it in class with Ayudesh.

Nobody was paying any attention to what she said but me. They didn't care as long as they could see. I wished I could see.

Nobody was even thinking about me, or that if I hadn't been there she never would have opened the box. But that was the way it always was. If I only lived somewhere else, my life would be different. But Sckarline was neither earth nor sky, and I was living my life in-between. People looked and fingered, but she wouldn't let them take things out, not even Harup, who was as tall as she was and a lot stronger. The younger people got bored and sat down and finally I could see Harup poking something with his finger, and the outland girl watching. The she looked at me.

"What's your name?" she asked.

"Me?" I said. "Umm, Janna."

She said my name. "What's your last name, Janna?"

"Sckarline," I said.

"Oh," she said, "like the settlement."

I just nodded.

"What is his name?" She pointed.

"Harup," I said. He looked up and grinned.

"What's your name?" she asked him and I told him what she had said.

"Harup," he said. Then she went around the room, saying everybody's names. It made everyone pleased to be noticed. She was smart that way. And it was easy. Then she tried to remember all their names, which had everyone laughing and correcting her so I didn't have to talk at all.

Ayudesh came in, taller than anyone, and I noticed, for the first time in my life, that he was really an offworlder. Ayudesh had been there all my life, and I knew he was an offworlder, but to me he had always been just Ayudesh.

Then they were talking about me and Ayudesh was just Ayudesh again. "Janna?" he said. "Very good. I'll tell you what, you take care of Veronique, here. You're her translator, all right?"

I was scared, because I really couldn't understand when she talked, but I guessed I was better than anybody else.

Veronique unpacked, which was interesting, but then she just started putting things here and there and everybody else drifted off until it was just her and me.

Veronique did a lot of odd things. She used a lot of water. The first thing I did for her was get water. She followed me out and watched me chip the ice for water and fill the bucket. She fingered the wooden bucket and the rope handle.

She said something I didn't understand because it had 'do' in it and a lot of pronouns and I have trouble following sentences like that. I smiled at her but I think she realized I didn't understand. Her boots were purple. I had never seen purple boots before.

"They look strange," she said. I didn't know what looked strange. "I like your boots," she said, slowly and clearly. I did understand, but then I didn't know what to do, did she want me to give her my boots? They were my mother's old boots and I wouldn't have minded giving them to her except I didn't have anything to take their place.

"It is really cold," she said.

Which seemed very odd to say, except I remembered that offworlders talk about the weather, Ayudesh had made us practice talking about the weather. He said it was something strangers talked about. "It is," I said. "But it will not snow tonight." That was good, it made her happy.

"And it gets dark so early," she said. "It isn't even afternoon and it's like night."

"Where you live, it is cold as this, umm," I hadn't made a question right.

But she understood. "Oh no," she said, "where I live is warm. It is hot, I mean. There is snow only on the mountains."

She wanted to heat the water so I put it on the stove, and then she showed me pictures of her mother and father and her brother at her house. It was summer and they were wearing only little bits of clothes.

Then she showed me a picture of herself and a man with a beard. "That's my boyfriend," she said. "We're getting married."

He looked old. Grown up. In the picture Veronique looked older, too. I looked at her again, not sure how old she was. Maybe older than me? Wanji said offworlders got married when they were older, not like the clans.

"I have boyfriend," I said.

"You do?" She smiled at me. "What's his name?"

"Tuuvin," I said.

"Was he here before?"

I shook my head.

Then she let me see her bag. The dark red one. I loved the color. I stroked it, as slick as leather and shining. "Plastic?" I said.

She nodded.

"I like plastic," I said.

She smiled a little, like I'd said something wrong. But it was so perfect, so even in color.

"Do you want it?" she asked. Which made me think of my boots and whether she had wanted them. I shook my head.

"You can have it," she said. "I can get another one."

"No," I said. "It isn't appropriate."

She laughed, a startled laugh. I didn't understand what I'd done and the feeling that I was foolish sat in my stomach, but I didn't know what was so foolish.

She said something I didn't understand, which made me feel worse. "What did you say?" she said. " 'Appropriate'?"

I nodded. "It's not appropriate," I said.

"I don't understand," she said.

Our lessons in appropriate development used lots of English words because it was hard to say these things any other way, so I found the words to tell her came easily. "Plastic," I said, "it's not appropriate. Appropriate technologies are based on the needs and capacities of people, they must be sustainable without outside support. Like the distillery is. Plastic isn't appropriate to Sckarline's economy because we can't create it and it replaces things we can produce, like skin bags." I stroked the bag again. "But I like plastic. It's beautiful."

"Wow," Veronique said. She was looking at me sharp, all alert like a stabros smelling a dog for the first time. Not afraid, but not sure what to think. "To me," she said slowly, "your skin bags are beautiful. The wooden houses," she touched the black slick wood wall, "they are beautiful."

Ayudesh and Wanji were always telling us that offworlders thought our goods were wonderful, but how could anyone look at a skin bag and then look at plastic and not see how brilliant the colors were in plastic? Dye a skin bag red and it still looked like a skin bag, like it came from dirt.

"How long you, um, you do stay?" I asked.

"Fourteen days," she said. "I'm a student, I came with my teacher."

I nodded. "Ayudesh, he is a teacher."

"My teacher, he's a friend of Ayudesh. From years ago," she said. "Have you always lived here? Were you born here?"

"Yes," I said. "I am born here. My mother and father are born in Tentas clan, but they come here."

"Tentas clan is another settlement?" she asked.

I shook my head. "No," I said. "No. Sckarline only is a settlement."

"Then, what is Tentas clan?"

"It is people." I didn't know how to explain clans to her at all. "They have kinship, and they have stabros, and they are together—"

"Stabros, those are animals," she said.

I nodded. "Sckarline, uh . . . is an appropriate technology mission."

"Right, that Ayudesh and Wanji started. Tentas clan is a clan, right?"

I nodded. I was worn out from talking to her.

After that she drank tea and then I took her around to show her Sckarline. It was already almost dark. I showed her the generator where we cooked stabros manure to make electricity. I got a lantern there.

I showed her the stabros pens and the dogs, even though it wasn't really very interesting. Tuuvin was there, and Gerdor, my little uncle, leaning and watching the stabros who were doing nothing but rooting at the mud in the pen and hoping someone would throw them something to eat. The stabros shook their heads and dug with their long front toes.

"This is Tuuvin?" Veronique said.

I was embarrassed. One of the stabros, a gelding with long feathery ears, craned his head toward me. I reached out and pulled on the long guard hairs at the tips of his ears and he lipped at my hand. He had a long purple tongue. He breathed out steam. Their breath always reminded me of the smell of whisak mash.

"Do you ride them?" Veronique asked.

"What?" I asked.

"Do you, um, get on their backs?" She made a person with her fingers walking through the air, then the fingers jumped on the other hand.

"A stabros?" I asked. Tuuvin and Gerdor laughed. "No," I said. "They have no like that. Stabros angry, very much." I pretended to kick. "They have milk, sometimes. And sleds," I said triumphantly, remembering the word.

She leaned on the fence. "They are pretty," she said. "They have pretty eyes. They look so sad with their long drooping ears."

"What?" Tuuvin asked. "What's pretty?"

"She says they have pretty eyes," I said.

Gerdor laughed but Tuuvin and I gave him a sharp look.

The dogs were leaping and barking and clawing at the gate. She stopped and reached a hand out to touch them. "Dogs are from Earth," she said.

"Dogs are *aufwurld*," I said. "Like us. Stabros are *util*."

"What's that mean?" she asked.

"Stabros can eat food that is *aunwurld*," I said. "We can't, dogs can't. But we can eat stabros so they are between."

"Are stabros from Earth?" Veronique asked.

I didn't know, but Tuuvin did, which surprised me. "Stabros are from here," he said. "Ayudesh explained where it all came from, remember? *Util* animals and plants were here but we could use them. *Aunwurld* animals and plants make us sick."

"I know they make us sick," I snapped. But I translated as best I could.

Veronique was looking at the dogs. "Do they bite?" she asked. Bite? "You mean," I clicked my teeth, "like eat? Sometimes. Mostly if they're fighting."

She took her hand back.

"I'll get a puppy," Tuuvin said, and swung a leg over the side of the pen and waded through the dogs. Tuuvin took care of the dogs a lot so he wasn't afraid of them. I didn't like them much. I liked stabros better.

"There's a winter litter?" I said.

"Yeah," he said. "but it hasn't been too cold, they might be okay. If it gets cold we can always eat 'em."

The puppy looked like a little sausage with short arms and legs and a pink nose. Veronique cooed and took it from Tuuvin and cradled it in her arms. She talked to it, but she talked in a funny way, like baby talk, and I couldn't understand anything she said. "What's its name?" she asked.

"Its name?" I said.

"Do you name them?" she asked.

I looked at Tuuvin. Even Tuuvin should have been able to understand that, the first thing anybody learned in lingua was 'What's your name?' But he wasn't paying any attention. I asked him if any of the dogs had names.

He nodded. "Some of them do. The dark male, he's a lead dog, he's called Bigman. And that one is Yellow Dog. The puppies don't have names, though."

"I think this one should have a name," Veronique said, when I told her. "I think he'll be a mighty hunter, so call him Hunter."

I didn't understand what hunting had to do with dogs, and I thought it was a bitch puppy anyway, but I didn't want to embarrass her, so I told Tuuvin. I was afraid he would laugh but he didn't.

"How do you say that in English?" he asked. "Hunter? Okay, I'll remember." He smiled at Veronique and touched the puppy's nose. "Hunter," he said. The puppy licked him with a tiny pink tongue.

Veronique smiled back. And I didn't like it.

Veronique went to find her teacher. I went down to the distillery to tell Mam why I wasn't there helping. Tuuvin followed me down the hill. The distillery stank so it was down below Sckarline in the trees, just above the fields.

He caught me by the waist and I hung there so he could brush his lips across my hair.

"It's too cold out here," I said and broke out of his arms.

"Let's go in the back," he said.

"I've got to tell Mam," I said.

"Once you tell your mam, there'll be all these things to do and we won't get any time together," he said.

"I can't," I said, but I let him make up my mind for me.

We went around the side, tracking through the dry snow where no one much walked, through the lacey wintertrees to the door to the storage in the back. It was as cold in the back as it was outside, and it was dark. It smelled like mash and whisak and the faint charcoal smell of the charred insides of the kegs. Brass whisak, Sckarline whisak.

He boosted me on a stack of kegs and kissed me.

It wasn't that I really cared so much about kissing. It was nice, but Tuuvin would have kissed and kissed for hours if I would let him and if we would ever find a place where we could be alone for hours. Tuuvin would kiss long after my face felt overused and bruised from kissing. But I just wanted to be with Tuuvin so much. I wanted to talk with him, and have him walk with me. I would let him kiss me if I could whisper to him. I liked the way he pressed against me now, he was warm and I was cold.

He kissed me with little kisses; kiss, kiss, kiss. I liked the little kisses. It was almost like he was talking to me in kisses. Then he kissed me hard, and searched around with his tongue. I never knew what to do with my tongue when he put his in my mouth, so I just kept mine still. I could feel the rough edge of the keg beneath my legs, and if I shifted my weight it rocked on the one below it. I turned my face sideways to get my nose out of the way and opened my eyes to look past Tuuvin. In the dark I could barely make out Uukraith's eye burned on all the kegs, to keep them from going bad. Uukraith was the door witch. Uukraith's sister Ina took souls from their mother and put them in seeds, put the seed in women to make babies. The kegs were all turned different directions, eyes looking everywhere. I closed mine again. Uukraith was also a virgin.

"Ohhhh, Heth! Eeeuuuu!"

I jumped, but Tuuvin didn't, he just let go of my waist and stepped back and crossed his arms the way he did when he was uncomfortable. The air felt cold where he had just been warm.

My little sister, Bet, shook her butt at us. "Kissy, kissy, kissy," she said. "MAM, JANNA'S BACK IN THE KEGS WITH TUUVIN!"

"Shut up, Bet," I said. Not that she would stop.

"Slobber, slobber," she said, like we were stabros trading cud.

She danced around, still shaking her butt. She puckered up her lips and made wet, smacking noises.

"Fucking little bitch," I said.

Tuuvin frowned at me. He liked Bet. She wasn't his little sister.

"MAM," Bet hollered, "JANNA SAID 'FUCKING'!"

"Janna," my mother called, "come here."

I tried to think of what to do to Bet. I'd have liked to slap her silly. But she'd go crying to Mam and I'd really be in trouble. It was just that she thought she was so smart and she was really being so stupid.

Mam was on her high stool, tallying. My mam wore trousers most often, and she was tall and man-faced. Still and all, men liked her. I took after her so I was secretly glad that men watched her walk by, even if she never much noticed.

"Leave your little sister alone," she said.

"Leave her alone!" I said. "She came and found me."

"Don't swear at her. You talk like an old man." Mam was acting like a headman, her voice even and cool.

"If she hadn't come looking—"

"If you had been working as you're supposed to, she'd have had no one to look for, would she."

"I went out to see the visitors," I said. "There are two. An old man and a girl. I helped Da carry their things to the visitors' house."

"So that means it is okay to swear at your sister."

It was the same words we always traded. The same arguments, all worn smooth and shining like the wood of a yoke. The brand for the kegs was heating in the fire and I could smell the tang of hot iron in the dung.

"You treat me like a child," I said.

She didn't even answer, but I knew what she would say, that I acted like a child. As if what Tuuvin and I were doing had anything to do with being a child.

I was so tired of it I thought I would burst.

"Go back to work," Mam said, turning on her stool. Saying, 'this talk is done' with her shoulders and her eyes.

"It's wrong to live this way," I said.

She looked back at me.

"If we lived with the clans, Tuuvin and I could be together."

That made her angry. "This is a better life than the clans," she said. "You don't know what you're talking about. Go back to work."

I didn't say anything. I just hated her. She didn't understand anything. She and my Da hadn't waited until they were old. They hadn't waited for anything, and they'd left their clan to come to Sckarline when it was new. I stood in front of her, making her feel me standing there, all hot and silent.

"Janna," she said, "I'll not put up with your sullenness—" It made her furious when I didn't talk.

So she slapped me, and then I ran out, crying, past Bet who was delighted, and past Tuuvin, who had his mouth open and a stupid look on his face. And I wished they would all disappear.

Veronique sat with Tuuvin and me at dinner in the guesthouse. The guesthouse was full of smoke. We all sat down on the floor with felt and blankets. I looked to see what Veronique would be sitting on and it was wonderful. It was dark, dark blue and clean on the outside, and inside it was red and black squares. I touched it. It had a long metal fastener, a cunning thing that locked teeth together, that Veronique had unfastened so she could sit on the soft red and black inside. Dark on the outside, red on the inside; it was as if it represented some strange offworld beast. My felt blanket was red but it was old and the edges were gray with dirt. Offworlders were so clean, as if they were always new.

Ayudesh was with the old man who had come with Veronique. Wanji was there, but she was being quiet and by herself, the way Wanji did.

Tuuvin had brought the puppy into the guesthouse. "She asked me to," he said when I asked him what he was doing.

"She did not," I said. "People are watching a dog in this house. Besides, you don't understand her when she talks."

"I do, too," he said. "I was in school, too."

I rolled my eyes. He was when he was little but he left as soon as he was old enough to hunt. Men always left as soon as they were old enough to hunt. And he hated it anyway.

Veronique squealed when she saw the puppy and took it from Tuuvin as if it were a baby. Everyone watched out of the corner of their eyes. Ayudesh thought it was funny. We were all supposed to be equal in Sckarline, but Ayudesh was really like a headman.

She put the puppy on her offworld blanket and it rolled over on its back, showing her its tan belly. It would probably pee on her blanket.

My da leaned over. "I hope it isn't dinner." My da hated dog.

"No," I said. "She just likes it."

My dad said to her, "Hie." Then to me he said, "What is she called?"

"Veronique," I said.

"Veronique," he said. Then he pointed to himself. "Guwk."

"Hello Guwk," Veronique said.

"Hello Veronique," said my da, which surprised me because I had never heard him say anything in English before. "Ask her for her cup," he said to me.

She had one; bright yellow and smooth. But my da handled it matter-of-factly, as if he handled beautiful things every day. He had a skin and he poured whisak into her cup. "My wife," he waved at mam, "she makes whisak for Sckarline."

I tried to translate but I didn't know what 'whisak' was in English.

Veronique took the cup. My da held his hand up for her to wait and poured himself a cup. He tossed it back. Then he nodded at her for her to try.

She took a big swallow. She hadn't expected the burn, you could see. She choked and her face got red. Tuuvin patted her on the back while she coughed. "Oh my God," she said. "That's strong!" I didn't think I needed to translate that.

ii

The sound of the guns is like the cracking of whips. Like the snapping of bones. The outrunners for the Scathalos High-on came into Sckarline with a great deal of racket; brass clattering, the men singing and firing their guns into the air. It started the dogs barking and scared our stabros and brought everyone outside.

Scathalos dyed the toes and ridgeline manes of their stabros kracken yellow. They hung brass clappers in the harnesses of their caravan animals and bits of milky blue glass from the harnesses of their dogs. On this sunny day everything winked. Only their milking does were plain, and that's only because even the will of a hunter can't make a doe stabros tractable.

Veronique came out with me. "Who are they?" she asked.

Even after just three days I could understand Veronique a lot better. "They are from a great clan, Scathalos," I said. "They come to buy whisak." We hoped they would buy it. Sometimes, when Scathalos outrunners came, they just took it.

"They're another clan?" she asked. "Where are the women?"

"They're outrunners," I said. "They go out and hunt and trade. Outrunners are not-married men."

"They have a lot of guns," she said.

They had more guns than I had ever seen. Usually when outrunners came they had one or two guns. Guns are hard to get. But it looked as if almost every outrunner had a gun.

"Does Sckarline have guns?" Veronique asked.

"No," I said.

"They're not appropriate, right?"

A lot of people said we should have guns, whether Ayudesh and Wanji thought they were appropriate or not. They had to buy the clips that go with them. Ayudesh said that the offworlders used the need of the clips to control the clans. He said that it wasn't appropriate because we couldn't maintain it ourselves.

My da said that maybe some things we should buy. We bought things from other clans, that was trade. Maybe guns were trade, too.

The dogs nipped at the doe stabros, turning them, making them stop until outrunners could slip hobbles on them. The stabros looked pretty good. They were mostly dun, and the males were heavy in the shoulders, with heads set low and forward on their necks. Better than most of our animals. The long hairs on their ears were braided with red and yellow threads. Handlers unhooked the sleds from the pack stabros.

Two of them found the skimmer tracks beyond the schoolhouse. They stopped and looked around. They saw Veronique. Then another stared at her, measuring her.

"Come with me," I said.

Our dogs barked and their dogs barked. The outrunner men talked loudly. Sckarline people stood at the doors of their houses and didn't talk at all.

"What's wrong?" Veronique asked.

"Come help my mam and me." She would be under the gaze of them in the distillery, too, but I suspected she would be under their gaze anywhere. And this way Mam would be there.

"Scathalos come here for whisak," I said to my mam, even though she could see for herself. Mam was at the door, shading her eyes and watching them settle in. Someone should have been telling them we had people in the guesthouse and offering to put their animals up, but no one was moving.

"Tuuvin is in back," Mam said, pointing with her chin. "Go back and help him."

Tuuvin was hiding the oldest whisak, what was left of the three-year-old brass whisak. Scathalos had come for whisak two years ago and taken what they wanted and left us almost nothing but lame stabros. They said it was because we had favored Toolie Clan in trade. The only reason we had any three-year-old whisak left was because they couldn't tell what was what.

So my da and some of the men had dug a cellar in the distillery. Tuuvin was standing in the cellar, taking kegs he had stacked at the edge and pulling them down. It wasn't very deep, not much over his chest, but the kegs were heavy. I started stacking more for him to hide.

I wondered what the outrunners would do if they caught us at our work. I wondered if Tuuvin was thinking the same thing. We'd hidden some down there in the spring before the stabros went up to summer grazing but then we'd taken some of the oldest kegs to drink when the stabros came back down in the fall.

"Hurry," Tuuvin said softly.

My hands were slick. Veronique started taking kegs, too. She couldn't lift them, so she rolled them on their edge. Her hands were soft and pretty, not used to rough kegs. It seemed like it took a long time. Tuuvin's hands were rough and red. I'd never thought about how hard his hands were. Mine were like his, all red. My hands were ugly compared to Veronique's. Surely he was noticing that, too, since every time Veronique rolled a keg over her hands were right there.

And then the last keg was on the edge. Uukraith's eye looked at me, strangely unaffected. Or maybe amused. Or maybe angry. Da said that spirits do not feel the way we feel. The teachers never said anything at all about spirits, which was how we knew that they didn't listen to them. There was not much space in the cellar, just enough for Tuuvin to stand and maybe a little more.

Tuuvin put his hands on the edge and boosted himself out of the cellar. In front of the store we heard the crack of the door on its hinges and we all three jumped.

Tuuvin slid the wooden cover over the hole in the floor. "Move those," he said, pointing at empty kegs.

I didn't hear voices.

"Are you done yet?" Mam said, startling us again.

"Are they here?" I asked.

"No," she said. "Not yet." She didn't seem afraid. I had seen my mam afraid, but not very often. "What is she doing here?" Mam asked, looking at Veronique.

"I thought she should be here, I mean, I was afraid to leave her by herself."

"She's not a child," Mam said. But she said it mildly, so I knew she didn't really mind. Then Mam helped us stack kegs. We all tried to be quiet but they thumped like hollow drums. They filled the space around us with noise. It seemed to me that the outrunners could hear us thumping away from outside. I kept looking at Mam, who was stacking kegs as if we hid whisak all the time. Tuuvin was nervous, too. His shoulders were tense. I almost said to him, 'you're up around the ears, boy,' the way the hunters did, but right now I didn't think it would make him smile.

Mam scuffed the dirt around the kegs.

"Will they find them?" I asked.

Mam shrugged. "We'll see."

✿   ✿   ✿

There was a lot to do to get ready for the outrunners besides hiding the best whisak. Mam had us count the kegs, even Veronique. Then when we all three finally agreed on a number she wrote it in her tally book. "So we know how much we sell," she said.

We were just finishing counting when outrunners came with Ayudesh. They came into the front. First the wind like a wild dog sliding around the door and making the fires all sway. Then Ayudesh and then the outrunners. The outrunners looked short compared to Ayudesh. And they looked even harder than we did. Their cheeks were winter red. Their felts were all dark with dirt, like they'd been out for a long time.

"Hie," said one of the men, seeing my mother. They all grinned. People always seemed surprised that they were going to trade with my mam. The outrunners already smelled of whisak so people had finally made them welcome. Or maybe someone had the sense to realize that if they gave them drink we'd have time to get things ready. Maybe my da.

My mam stood as she always did, with her arms crossed, tall as any of them. Waiting them out.

"What's this," said the man, looking around. "Eh? What's this? It stinks in here." The distillery always stank.

They walked around, looked at the kegs, poked at the copper tubing and the still. One stuck his finger under the drip and tasted the raw stuff and grimaced. Ayudesh looked uncomfortable, but the teachers always said that the distillery was ours and they didn't interfere with how we ran it. Mam was in charge here.

Mam just stood and let them walk all around her. She didn't turn her head to watch them.

They picked up the brand. "What's this?" the man said again.

"We mark all our kegs with the eye of Uukraith," Mam said.

"Woman's work," he said.

He stopped and looked at Veronique. He studied her for a moment, then frowned. "You're no boy," he said.

Veronique looked at me, the whites of her eyes bright even in the dimness, but she didn't say anything.

He grinned and laughed. The other two outrunners crowded

close to her and fingered the slick fabric of her sleeve, touched her hair. Veronique pulled away.

The first outrunner got bored and walked around the room some more.

He tapped a keg. Not like Mam thumped them, listening, but just as if everything here were his. He had dirty brown hair on the backs of his hands. Everywhere I looked I was seeing people's hands. I didn't like the way he put his hands on things.

Then he pointed to a keg, not the one he was tapping on but a different one, and one of the other men picked it up. "Is it good?" he asked.

My mam shrugged.

He didn't like that. He took two steps forward and hit her across the face. I looked at the black packed dirt floor.

Ayudesh made a noise.

"It's good," my mam said. I looked up and she had a red mark on the side of her face. Ayudesh looked as if he would speak but he didn't.

The outrunner grabbed her braid—she flinched as he reached past her face—and yanked her head. "It's good, woman?" he asked.

"Yes," she said, her voice coming almost airless, like she could not breathe.

He yanked her down to her knees. Then he let go and they all went out with the keg.

Ayudesh said, "Are you all right?" Mam stood back up again and touched her braid, then flipped it back over her neck. She didn't look at any of us.

People were in the schoolhouse. Ayudesh sat on the table at the front and people were sitting on the floor talking as if it were a meeting. Veronique's teacher was sitting next to Ayudesh and Veronique started as if she was going to go sit with him. Then she looked around and sat down with Mam and Tuuvin and me.

"So we should just let them take whatever they want?" Harup said. He wasn't clowning now, but talking as a senior hunter. He sat on his heels, the way hunters do when they're waiting.

Ayudesh said, "Even if we could get guns, they're used to fighting and we aren't. What do you think would happen?"

Veronique was very quiet. She sat down between Tuuvin and me.

"If we don't stand up for ourselves, what will happen?" Harup said.

"If you provoke them they'll destroy us," Ayudesh said.

"Teacher," Harup said, spreading his hands as if he was telling a story. "Stabros are not hunting animals, eh. They are not sharp toothed like haunds or dogs. Haunds are hunters, packs of hunters, who do nothing but hunt stabros. There are more stabros than all the haunds could eat, eh. So how do they choose? They don't kill the buck stabros with their hard toes and heads, they take the young, the old, the sick, the helpless. We do not want to be haunds, teacher. We just want the haunds to go elsewhere for easy prey."

Wanji came in behind us, and the fire in the boxstove ducked and jumped in the draft. Wanji didn't sit down on the table, but as was her custom, lowered herself to the floor. "Old hips," she muttered as if everyone in the room wasn't watching her. "Old women have old hips."

When I thought of Kalky, the old woman who makes the souls of everything, I thought of her as looking like Wanji. Wanji had a little face and a big nose and deep lines down from her nose to her chin. "What happened to you, daughter?" she asked my mam.

"The outrunners came to the distillery to take a keg," Mam said.

I noticed that now the meeting had turned around, away from Ayudesh on the table towards us in the back. Wanji always said that Ayudesh was vain and liked to sit high. Sometimes she called him 'High-on.' "And so," Wanji said.

My mother's face was still red from the blow, but it hadn't yet purpled. "I don't think the outrunners like to do business with me," Mam said.

"One of them hit her," I said, because Mam wasn't going to. Mam never talked about it when my da hit her, either. Although he didn't do it as much as he used to when I was Bet's age.

Mam looked at me, but I couldn't tell if she was angry with me or not.

Harup spread his hands to say, 'See?'

Wanji clucked.

"We got the three-year-old whisak in the cellar," Mam said.

I was looking but I didn't see my da.

"What are they saying," Veronique asked.

"They are talking," I said, and had to think how to say it, "about what we do, but they, eh, not, do not know? Do not know what is right. Harup want guns. Wants guns. Ayudesh says guns are bad."

"Wanji," Tuuvin whispered, "Wanji, she ask—eh," and then in our own tongue, "tell her she was asking your mam what happened."

"Wanji ask my mother what is the matter," I said.

Veronique looked at Tuuvin and then at me.

"Guns are bad," Veronique said.

Tuuvin scowled. "She doesn't understand," he said.

"What?" Veronique said, but I just shook my head rather than tell her what Tuuvin had said.

Some of the men were talking about guns. Wanji was listening without saying anything, resting her chin on her head. Sometimes it seemed like Wanji didn't even blink, that she just turned into stone and you didn't know what she was thinking.

Some of the other men were talking to Ayudesh about the whisak. Yet, Harup's wife, got up and put water on the boxstove for the men to drink and Big Sherep went out the men's door in the back of the schoolhouse, which meant he was going to get whisak or beer.

"Nothing will get done now," Tuuvin said, disgusted. "Let's go."

He stood up and Veronique looked up at him, then scrambled to her feet.

"Now they talk, talk, talk," I said in English. "Nothing to say, just talk, you know?"

Outside there were outrunners. It seemed as if they were everywhere, even though there were really not that many of them. They watched Veronique.

Tuuvin scowled at them and I looked at their guns. Long black guns slung over their backs. I had never seen a gun close. And there

was my da, standing with three outrunners, holding a gun in his
hands as if it were a fishing spear, admiring it. He was nodding and
grinning, the way he did when someone told a good hunting story.
Of course, he didn't know that one of these people had hit Mam.

Still, it made me mad that he was being friendly.

"We should go somewhere," Tuuvin said.

"The distillery?" I asked.

"No," he said, "they'll go back there." And he looked at
Veronique. Having Veronique around was like having Bet, you always had to be thinking about her. "Take her to your house."

"And do what?" I asked. A little angry at him because now he
had decided he wasn't going back with us.

"I don't know, teach her to sew or something," he said. He
turned and walked across to where my dad was standing.

The outrunners took two more kegs of whisak and got loud. They
stuck torches in the snow, so the dog's harnesses were all glittering
and winking, and we gave them a stabros to slaughter and they
roasted that. Some of the Sckarline men like my da—and even
Harup—sat with them and drank and talked and sang. I didn't understand why Harup was there, but there he was, laughing and
telling stories about the time my da got dumped out of the boat fishing.

Ayudesh was there, just listening. Veronique's grandfather was
out there, too, even though he couldn't understand what they were
saying.

"When will they go?" Veronique asked.

I shrugged.

She asked something I didn't understand.

"When you trade," she said, "trade?"

"Trade," I said, "trade whisak, yes?"

"Yes," she said. "When you trade whisak, men come? Are you
afraid when you trade whisak?"

"Afraid?" I asked. "When Scathalos come, yes."

"When other people come, are you afraid?" she asked.

"No," I said. "Just Scathalos."

She sat on my furs. My mam was on the bed and Bet had gone to sleep. Mam watched us talk, sitting cross-legged and mending Bet's boots. She didn't understand any English. It felt wrong to talk when Mam didn't understand, but Veronique couldn't understand when I talked to Mam, either.

"I have to go back to my hut," Veronique said. "Ian will come back and he'll worry about me."

Outside the air was so cold and dry that the inside of our noses felt it.

"Don't you get tired of being cold?" Veronique asked.

The cold made people tired, I thought, yes. That was why people slept so much during winterdark. I didn't always know what to say when Veronique talked about the weather.

"We tell your teacher, you sleep in our house, yes?" I offered.

"Who?" she said. "You mean Ian? He isn't really my teacher like you mean it. He's my professor."

I tried to think of what a professor might be, maybe the person who took you when your father died? It always seemed English didn't have enough words for different relatives, but now here was one I didn't know.

The outrunners and the Sckarline hunters were singing about Fhidrhin the hunter and I looked up to see if I could make out the stars that formed him, but the sky had drifting clouds and I couldn't find the stars.

I couldn't see well enough, the light from the bonfire made everyone else just shadows. I took Veronique's hand and started around the outside of the circle of singers, looking for Ayudesh and Veronique's teacher or whatever he was. Faces glanced up, spirit faces in the firelight. The smoke blew our way and then shifted, and I smelled the sweat smell that came from the men's clothes as they warmed by the fire. And whisak, of course. The stabros was mostly bones.

"Janna," said my da. His face was strange, too, not human, like a mask. His eyes looked unnaturally light. "Go on back to your mother."

"Veronique needs to tell the offworlder that she's staying with us."

"Go on back to the house," he said again. I could smell whisak on him, too. Whisak sometimes made him mean. My da used to drink a lot of whisak when I was young, but since Bet was born he didn't drink it very often at all. He said the mornings were too hard when you got old.

I didn't know what to do. If I kept looking for Veronique's grandfather and he got angry he would probably hit me. I nodded and backed away, pulling Veronique with me, then when he stopped watching me, I started around the fire the other way.

One of the outrunners stumbled up and into us before we could get out of the way. "Eh—?"

I pulled Veronique away but he gripped her arm. "Boy?"

His breath in her face made her close her eyes and turn her head.

"No boy," he said. He was drunk, probably going to relieve himself. "No boy, outsider girl, pretty as a boy," he said. "Outsider, they like that? Eh?"

Veronique gripped my hand. "Let go," she said in English.

He didn't have to speak English to see she was afraid of him.

"I'm not pretty enough for you?" he said. "Eh? Not pretty enough?" He wasn't pretty, he was wiry and had teeth missing on one side of his mouth. "Not Sckarline? With their pretty houses like offworlders? Not pretty, eh?"

Veronique drew a breath like a sob.

"Let go of her, please," I said, "we have to find her teacher."

"Look at the color of her," he said, "does that wash off? Eh?"

"Do you know where her teacher is?" I asked.

"Shut up, girl," he said to me. He licked his thumb and reached towards her face. Veronique raised her hand and drew back, and he twisted her arm. "Stand still." He rubbed her cheek with his thumb and peered closely at her.

"Damn," he said, pleased. "How come the old man isn't dark?"

"Maybe they are different clans," I said.

He stared at her as if weighing what I'd said. As if thinking. Although he actually looked too drunk to do much thinking. Then he leaned forward and tried to kiss her.

Veronique pushed him away with her free arm. He staggered and fell, pulling her down, too.

"Let go!" she shrieked.

Shut up, I thought, shut up, shut up! Give in, he's too drunk to do much. I tried to pull his arm off, but his grip was too strong.

"What's this?" another outrunner was saying.

"Fohlder's found some girl."

"It would be fucking Fohlder!"

Veronique slapped at him and struggled, trying to get away.

"Hey now," Ayudesh was saying, "hey now, she's a guest, an off-worlder." But nobody was paying attention. Everybody was watching the outrunner wrestle with her. He pinned her with her arms over her head and kissed her.

Veronique was crying and slapping. Stop it, I kept thinking, just stop it, or he won't let you alone.

Her grandfather tried to pull the outrunner off. I hadn't even seen him come up. "No no no no no," he was saying as if scolding someone. "No no no no no—"

"Get off him," another outrunner hauled him away.

Ayudesh said, "Stop! She is our guest!"

"She's yours, eh?" someone said.

"No," Ayudesh said, "she should be left alone. She's a guest."

"Your guest, right. Not interested in the likes of us."

Someone else grunted and laughed.

"She likes Sckarline better, eh?"

"That's because she doesn't know better."

"Fohlder'll show her."

You all stink like drunks, I wanted to scream at them, because they did.

"Think she's dark inside like she is outside?"

"Have to wait until morning to see."

Oh, my da would be so mad at me, the stupid bitch, why didn't she stop, he was drunk, he was drunk, why had she slapped at him, stupider than Bet, she was as stupid as Bet my little sister, I was sup-

posed to be taking care of her, I was supposed to be watching out
for her, my da would be so mad—

There was the bone crack of gunfire and everybody stopped.

Harup was standing next to the fire with an outrunner gun
pointed up, as if he were shooting at Fhidrhin up there in the stars.
His expression was mild and he was studying the gun as if he hadn't
even noticed what was going on.

"Hey," an outrunner said, "put that down!"

Harup looked around at the outrunners, at us. He looked slowly.
He didn't look like he usually did, he didn't look funny or angry, he
looked as if he were out on a boat in the ice. Calm, far away. Cold
as the stars. He could kill someone.

The outrunners felt it too. They didn't move. If he shot one of
them, the others would kill him, but the one he shot would still be
dead. No one wanted to be the one that might be dead.

"It's a nice piece," Harup said, "but if you used it for hunting
you'd soon be so deaf you couldn't hear anything moving." Then he
grinned.

Someone laughed.

Everybody laughed.

"Janna," Harup said, "take your friend and get us more whisak."

"Fohlder, you old walking dick, get up from that girl." One of
them reached down and pulled him off. He looked mad.

"What," he said, "what."

"Go take a piss," the outrunner said.

Everyone laughed.

iii

Veronique stayed with me that night, lying next to me in my blankets and furs. She didn't sleep. I don't think. I was listening to her
breath. I felt as if I should help her sleep. I lay there and tried to
think if I should put my arm around her, but I didn't know. Maybe
she didn't want to be touched.

And she had been a stupid girl, anyway.

She lay tense in the dark. "Are you going to be a teacher?" I
asked.

She laughed. "If I get out of here."

I waited for her to say more, but she didn't. 'Get out of here' meant to make someone leave. Maybe she meant if she made herself.

"You come here from Earth?" I asked. To get her to talk, although I was tired of lingua and I didn't really want to think about anything.

"My family came here from Earth," she said.

"Why?"

"My father, he's an anthropologist," she said. "Do you know anthropologist?"

"No," I said.

"He is a person who studies the way people live. And he is a teacher."

All the offworlders I had ever met were teachers. I wondered who did all the work on Earth.

"Because Earth lost touch with your world, the people here are very interesting to my father," she said. Her voice was listless in the dark and she was even harder to understand when I couldn't see her properly. I didn't understand so I didn't say anything. I was sorry I'd started her talking.

"History, do you know the word 'history'?" she asked.

Of course I knew the word 'history.' "I study history in school," I said. Anneal and Kumar taught it.

"Do you know the history of this world?"

It took my tired head a long time to sort that out. "Yes," I said. "We are a colony. People from Earth come here to live. Then there is a big problem on Earth, and the people of Earth forget we are here. We forget we are from Earth. Then Earth finds us again."

"Some people have stories about coming from the Earth," Veronique said. "My father is collecting those stories from different peoples. I'm a graduate student."

The clans didn't have any stories about coming from Earth. We said the first people came out of the sun. This somehow seemed embarrassing. I didn't understand what kind of student she was.

"Are you here for stories?" I asked.

"No," she said. "Ian is old friends with your teacher, from back when they were both with the survey. We just came to visit."

I didn't understand what she'd said except that they were visiting.

We were quiet after that. I pretended to sleep. Sometimes there was gunfire outside and we jumped, even Mam on the bed. Everyone but Bet. Once Bet was asleep it was impossible to wake her up.

I fell asleep thinking about how I wished that the Scathalos outrunners were gone. I dreamed that I was at the offworlders' home, where it was summer but no one was taking care of the stabros, and I said I could take care of the stabros, and they were all glad, and so I was a hero—and I was startled awake by gunfire.

Just more drinking and shooting.

I wished my da would come home. It didn't seem fair that we should lie there and be afraid while the men were getting drunk and singing.

The outrunners stayed the next day, taking three more kegs of whisak but not talking about trade. The following day they sent out hunters but didn't find their own meat and so took another stabros, the gelding I'd shown to Veronique. And more whisak.

I went down to the distillery after they took more whisak. It was already getting dark. The dark comes so early at this time of year. The door was left open and the fire was out. Mam wasn't coming anymore. There was no work being done. Kegs had been taken down and some had been opened and left open. Some had been spilled. They had started on the green stuff, not knowing what was what and had thrown most of it in the snow, probably thinking it was bad. Branded eyes on the kegs looked everywhere.

I thought maybe they wouldn't leave until all the whisak was gone. For one wild moment I thought about taking an ax to the kegs. Give them no reason to stay.

Instead I listened to them singing, their voices far away. I didn't want to walk back towards the voices, but I didn't want to be outside in the dark, either. I walked until I could see the big fire they had going, and smell the stabros roasting. Then I stood for a while, because I didn't want to cross the light more than I wanted to go home. Maybe someone was holding me back, maybe my spirit knew something.

I looked for my father. I saw Harup on the other side of the fire. His face was in the light. He wasn't singing, he was just watching. I saw Gerdor, my little uncle, my father's half brother. I did not see my father anywhere.

Then I saw him. His back was to me. He was just a black outline against the fire. He had his hands open wide, as if he was explaining. He had his empty hands open. Harup was watching my father explaining something to some of the outrunners and something was wrong.

One of the outrunners turned his head and spat.

My father, I couldn't hear his voice, but I could see his body, his shoulders moving as he explained. His shoulders working, working hard as if he were swimming. Such hard work, this talking with his hands open, talking, talking.

The outrunner took two steps, bent down and pulled his rifle into the light. It was a dark thing there, a long thing against the light of the fire. My father took a step back and his hands came up, pushing something back.

And then the outrunner shot my father.

All the singing stopped. The fire cracked and the sparks rose like stars while my father struggled in the snow. He struggled hard, fighting and scraping back through the snow. Elbow-walking backwards. The outrunner was looking down the long barrel of the rifle.

Get up, I thought. Get up. For a long time it seemed I thought, Get up, get up. Da, get up! But no sound came out of my mouth and there was black on the snow in the trampled trail my father left.

The outrunner shot again.

My father flopped into the snow and I could see the light on his face as he looked up. Then he stopped.

Harup watched. No one moved except the outrunner who put his rifle away.

I could feel the red meat, the hammering muscle in my chest. I could feel it squeezing, squeezing. Heat flowed in my face. In my hands.

Outrunners shouted at outrunners. "You shit," one shouted at the one who shot my father. "You drunken, stupid shit!" The one who shot my father shrugged at first, as if he didn't care, and then he became angry, too, shouting.

My breath was in my chest, so full. If I breathed out loud the outrunners would hear me out here. I tried to take small breaths, could not get enough air. I did not remember when I had been holding my breath.

Harup and the hunters of Sckarline sat, like prey, hiding in their stillness. The arguing went on and on, until it wasn't about my father at all and his body was forgotten in the dirty snow. They argued about who was stupid and who had the High-on's favor. The whisak was talking.

I could think of nothing but air.

I went back through the dark, out of Sckarline, and crept around behind the houses, in the dark and cold until I could come to our house without going past the fire. I took great shuddering breaths of cold air, breathed out great gouts of fog.

My mother was trying to get Bet quiet when I came in. "No," she was saying, "stop it now, or I'll give you something to cry about."

"Mam," I said, and I started to cry.

"What," she said. "Janna, your face is all red." She was my mam, with her face turned towards me, and I had never seen her face so clearly.

"They're going to kill all of us," I said. "They killed Da with a rifle."

She never said a word but just ran out and left me there. Bet started to cry although she didn't really know what I was crying about. Just that she should be scared. Veronique was still. As still as Harup and all the hunters.

Wanji came and got me and brought me to Ayudesh's house because our house is small and Ayudesh's house had enough room for some people. Snow was caked in the creases of my father's pants. It was in his hands, too, unmelted. I had seen dead people before, and my father looked like all of them. Not like himself at all.

My mother had followed him as far as the living can go, or at least as someone untrained in spirit journeys, and she was not herself. She was sitting on the floor next to his body, rocking back and forth with her arms crossed in her lap. I had seen women like that before, but not my mother. I didn't want to look. It seemed indecent. Worse than the body of my father, since my father wasn't there at all.

Bet was screaming. Her face was red from the effort. I held her even though she was heavy and she kept arching away from me like a toddler in a tantrum. "MAM! MAM!" she kept screaming.

People came in and squatted down next to the body for a while. People talked about guns. It was important that I take care of Bet so I did, until finally she wore herself out from crying and fell asleep. I held her on my lap until the blood was out of my legs and I couldn't feel the floor and then Wanji brought me a blanket and I wrapped Bet in it and let her sleep.

Wanji beckoned me to follow. I could barely stand, my legs had so little feeling. I held the wall and looked around, at my mother sitting next to the vacant body, at my sister, who though asleep was still alive. Then I tottered after Wanji as if I was the old woman.

"Where is the girl?" Wanji said.

"Asleep," I said. "On the floor."

"No, the girl," Wanji said, irritated. "Ian's girl. From the university."

"I don't know," I said.

"You're supposed to be watching her. Didn't Ayudesh tell you to watch her?"

"You mean Veronique? She's back at my house. In my bed."

Wanji nodded and sucked on her teeth. "Okay," she said. And then again to herself, "Okay."

Wanji took me to her house, which was little and dark. She had a lamp shaped like a bird. It had been in her house as long as I could remember. It didn't give very much light, but I had always liked it. We sat on the floor. Wanji's floor was always piled high with rugs from her home and furs and blankets. It made it hard to walk but nice to sit. Wanji got cold and her bones hurt, so she always made a little nest when she sat down. She pulled a red and blue rug across her lap. "Sit, sit, sit," she said.

I was cold, but there was a blanket to wrap around my shoulders and watch Wanji make hot tea. I couldn't remember being alone with Wanji before. But everything was so strange it didn't seem to make any difference and it was nice to have Wanji deciding what to do and me not having to do anything.

Wanji made tea over her little bird lamp. She handed me a cup and I sipped it. Tea was a strange drink. Wanji and Ayudesh liked it and hoarded it. It was too bitter to be very good, but it was warm and the smell of it was always special. I drank it and held it against me. I started to get warm. The blanket got warm from me and smelled faintly of Wanji, an old dry smell.

I was sleepy. It would have been nice to go to sleep right there in my little nest on Wanji's floor.

"Girl," Wanji said. "I must give you something. You must take care of Veronique."

I didn't want to take care of anybody. I wanted someone to take care of me. My eyes started to fill up and in a moment I was crying salt tears into my tea.

"No time for that, Janna," Wanji said. Always sharp with us. Some people were afraid of Wanji. I was. But it felt good to cry, and I didn't know how to stop it so I didn't.

Wanji didn't pay any attention. She was hunting through her house, checking in a chest, pulling up layers of rugs to peer in a corner. Was she going to give me a gun? I couldn't think of anything else that would help very much right now, but I couldn't imagine that Wanji owned a gun.

She came back with a dark blue plastic box not much bigger than the span of my spread hand. That was almost as astonishing as a gun. I wiped my nose on my sleeve. I was warm and tired. Would Wanji let me sleep right here on her floor?

Wanji opened the plastic box, but away from me so I couldn't see inside it. She picked at it as if she were picking at a sewing kit, looking for something. I wanted to look in it but I was afraid that if I tried she'd snap at me.

She looked at me. "This is mine," she said. "We both got one and we decided that if the people who settled Sckarline couldn't have it, we wouldn't either."

I didn't care about that. That was old talk. I wanted to know what it was.

Wanji wasn't ready to tell me what it was. I had the feeling that Ayudesh didn't know about this, and I was afraid she would talk herself out of it. She looked at it and thought. If I thought, I thought about my father being dead. I sipped tea and tried to think about being warm, about sleeping but that feeling had passed. I wondered where Tuuvin was.

I thought about my da and I started to cry again.

I thought that would really get Wanji angry so I tried to hide it, but she didn't pay any attention at all. The shawl she wore over her head slipped halfway down so when I glanced up I could see where her hair parted and the line of pale skin. It looked so bare that I wanted it covered up again. It made me think of the snow in my father's hands.

"It was a mistake," Wanji said.

I thought she meant the box, and I felt a terrible disappointment that I wouldn't get to see what was inside it.

"You understand what we were trying to do?" she asked me.

With the box? Not at all.

"What are the six precepts of development philosophy?" she asked.

I had to think. "One," I said, "that economic development should be gradual. Two, that analyzing economic growth by the production of goods rather than the needs and capacities of people leads to displacement and increased poverty. Three, that economic development should come from the integrated development of rural areas with the traditional sector—"

"It's just words," she snapped at me.

I didn't know what I had done wrong so I ducked my head and sniffed and waited for her to get angry because I couldn't stop crying.

Instead she stroked my hair. "Oh, little girl. Oh, Janna. You are one of the bright ones. If you aren't understanding it, then we really haven't gotten it across, have we?" Her hand was nice on my hair, and it seemed so unlike Wanji that it scared me into stillness. "We were trying to help, you know," she said. "We were trying to do good. We gave up our lives to come here. Do you realize?"

Did she mean that they were going to die? Ayudesh and Wanji?

"This," she said, suddenly brisk. "This is for, what would you call them, runners. Foreign runners. It is to help them survive. I am going to give it to you so that you will help Veronique, understood?"

I nodded.

But she didn't give it to me. She just sat holding the box, looking in it. She didn't want to give it up. She didn't feel it was appropriate.

She sighed again, a terrible sound. Out of the box she pulled shiny foil packets, dark blue, red, and yellow. They were the size of the palm of her hand. Her glasses were around her neck. She put them on like she did in the schoolroom, absent from the gesture. She studied the printing on the foil packets.

I loved foil. Plastic was beautiful, but foil, foil was something unimaginable. Tea came in foil packets. The strange foods that the teachers got off the skimmer came in foil.

My tea was cold.

"This one," she said, "it is a kind of signal." She looked over her glasses at me. "Listen to me Janna. Your life will depend on this. When you have this, you can send a signal that the outsiders can hear. They can hear it all the way in Bashtoy. And after you send it, if you can wait in the same place, they will send someone out to get you and Veronique."

"They can hear it in Bashtoy?" I said. I had never even met anyone other than Wanji and the teachers who had ever been to Bashtoy.

"They can pick it up on their instruments. You send it every day until someone comes."

"How do I send it?"

She read the packet. "We have to set the signal, you and I. First we have to put it in you."

I didn't understand, but she was reading, so I waited.

"I'm going to put it in your ear," she said. "From there it will migrate to your brain."

"Will it hurt?" I asked.

"A little," she said. "But it has its own way of taking pain away. Now, what should be the code?" She studied the packet. She pursed her lips.

A thing in my ear. I was afraid and I wanted to say no, but I was more afraid of Wanji so I didn't.

"You can whistle, can't you?" she asked.

I knew how to whistle, yes.

"Okay," she said, "here it is. I'll put this in your ear, and then we'll wait for a while. Then when everything is ready we'll set the code."

She opened up the packet and inside was another packet and a little metal fork. She opened the inside packet and took out a tiny little disk, a soft thing almost like egg white or like a fish egg. She leaned forward and put it in my left ear. Then she pushed it in hard and I jerked.

"Hold still," she said.

Something was moving and making noise in my ear and I couldn't be still. I pulled away and shook my head. The noise in my ear was loud, a sort of rubbing, oozing sound. I couldn't hear normal things out of my left ear. It was stopped up with whatever was making the oozing noise. Then it started to hurt. A little at first, then more and more.

I put my hand over my ear, pressing against the pain. Maybe it would eat through my ear? What would stop it from eating a hole in my head?

"Stop it," I said to Wanji. "Make it stop!"

But she didn't, she just sat there, watching.

The pain grew sharp, and then suddenly it stopped. The sound, the pain, everything.

I took my hand away. I was still deaf on the left side but it didn't hurt.

"Did it stop?" Wanji asked.

I nodded.

"Do you feel dizzy? Sick?"

I didn't.

Wanji picked up the next packet. It was blue. "While that one is working, we'll do this one. Then the third one, which is easy. This one will make you faster when you are angry or scared. It will make time feel slower. There isn't any code for it. Something in your body starts it."

I didn't have any idea what she was talking about.

"After it has happened, you'll be tired. It uses up your energy." She studied the back of the packet, then she scooted closer to me, so we were both sitting cross-legged with our knees touching. Wanji had hard, bony knees, even through the felt of her dress.

"Open your eye, very wide," she said.

"Wait," I said. "Is this going to hurt?"

"No," she said.

I opened my eyes as wide as I could.

"Look down, but keep your eyes wide open," she said.

I tried.

"No," she said, irritated, "keep your eyes open."

"They are open," I said. I didn't think she should treat me this way. My da had just died. She should be nice to me. I could hear her open the packet. I wanted to blink but I was afraid to. I did, because I couldn't help it.

She leaned forward and spread my eye open with thumb and forefinger. Then she swiftly touched my eye.

I jerked back. There was something in my eye, I could feel it, up under my eyelid. It was very uncomfortable. I blinked and blinked and blinked. My eye filled up with tears, just the one eye, which was very very strange.

My eye socket started to ache. "It hurts," I said.

"It won't last long," she said.

"You said it wouldn't hurt!" I said, startled.

"I lied," Wanji said, matter-of-fact.

It hurt more and more. I moaned. "You're hateful," I said.

"That's true," she said, unperturbed.

She picked up the third packet, the red one.

"No," I said, "I won't! I won't! You can't do it!"

"Hush," she said, "this one won't hurt. I saved it until last on purpose."

"You're lying!" I scrambled away from her. The air was cold

where the nest of rugs and blankets had been wrapped around me. My head ached. It just ached. And I still couldn't hear anything out of my left ear.

"Look," she said, "I will read you the lingua. It is a patch, nothing more. It says it will feel cold, but that is all. See, it is just a square of cloth that will rest on your neck. If it hurts you can take it off."

I scrambled backwards away from her.

"Janna," she said. "Enough!" She was angry.

I was afraid of it, but I was still more afraid of Wanji. So I hunched down in front of her. I was so afraid that I sobbed while she peeled the back off the square and put it on me.

"See," she said, still sharp with me, "it doesn't hurt at all. Stop crying. Stop it. Enough is enough." She waved her hands over her head in disgust. "You are hysterical."

I held my hand over the patch. It didn't hurt but it did feel cold. I scrunched up and wrapped myself in a rug and gave myself over to my misery. My head hurt and my ear still ached faintly and I was starting to feel dizzy.

"Lie down," Wanji said. "Go on, lie down. I'll wake you when we can set the signal."

I made myself a nest in the mess of Wanji's floor and piled a blanket and a rug on top of me. Maybe the dark made my head feel better, I didn't know. But I fell asleep.

Wanji shook me awake. I hadn't been asleep long, and my head still ached. She had the little metal fork from the ear packet, the yellow packet. It occurred to me that she might stick it in my ear.

I covered my ear with my hand. My head hurt enough. I wasn't going to let Wanji stick a fork in my ear.

"Don't scowl," she said.

"My head hurts," I said.

"Are you dizzy?" she asked.

I felt out of sorts, unbalanced, but not dizzy, not really.

"Shake your head," Wanji said.

I shook my head. Still the same, but no worse. "Don't stick that in my ear," I said.

"What? I'm not going to stick this in your ear. It's a musical fork. I'm going to make a sound with it and hold it to your ear. When I tell you to I want you to whistle something, okay?"

"Whistle what?" I said.

"Anything," she said, "I don't care. Whistle something for me now."

I couldn't think of anything to whistle. I couldn't think of anything at all except that I wished Wanji would leave me alone and let me go back to sleep.

Wanji squatted there. Implacable old bitch.

I finally thought of something to whistle, a crazy dog song for children. I started whistling—

"That's enough," she said. "Now don't say anything else, but when I nod my head you whistle that. Don't say anything to me. If you do, it will ruin everything. Nod your head if you understand."

I nodded.

She slapped the fork against her hand and I could see the long tines vibrating. She held it up to my ear, the one I couldn't hear anything out of. She held it there, concentrating fiercely. Then she nodded.

I whistled.

"Okay," she said. "Good. That is how you start it. Now whistle it again."

I whistled.

Everything went dark and then suddenly my head got very hot. Then I could see again.

"Good," Wanji said. "You just sent a signal."

"Why did everything get dark?" I asked.

"All the light got used in the signal," Wanji said. "It used all the light in your head so you couldn't see."

My head hurt even worse. Now besides my eye aching, my temples were pounding. I had a fever. I raised my hand and felt my hot cheek.

Wanji picked up the blue packet. "Now we have to figure out about the third one, the one that will let you hibernate."

I didn't want to learn about hibernating. "I feel sick," I said.

"It's probably too soon, anyway," Wanji said. "Sleep for a while."

I felt so awful I didn't know if I could sleep. But Wanji brought me more tea and I drank that and lay down in my nest and presently I was dreaming.

iv

There was a sound of gunfire, far away, just a pop. And then more pop-pop-pop.

It startled me, although I had been hearing the outrunners' guns at night since they got here. I woke with a fever and everything felt as if I were still dreaming. I was alone in Wanji's house. The lamp was still lit but I didn't know if it had been refilled or how long I had slept. During the long night of winterdark it is hard to know when you are. I got up, put out the lamp and went outside.

Morning cold is worst when you are warm from sleep. The dry snow crunched in the dark. Nothing was moving except the dogs were barking, their voices coming at me from every way.

The outrunners were gone from the center of town, nothing there but the remains of their fire and the trampled slick places where they had walked. I slid a bit as I walked there. My head felt light and I concentrated on my walking because if I did not think about it I didn't know what my feet would do. I had to pee.

Again I heard the pop-pop-pop. I could not tell where it was coming from because it echoed off the buildings around me. I could smell smoke and see the dull glow of fire above the trees. It was down from Sckarline, the fire. At first I thought they had gotten a really big fire going, and then I thought they had set fire to the distillery. I headed for home.

Veronique was asleep in a nest of blankets, including some of my parent's blankets from their bed.

"They set fire to the distillery," I said. I didn't say it in English, but she sat up and rubbed her face.

"It's cold," she said.

I could not think of anything to respond.

She sat there, holding her head.

"Come," I said, working into English. "We go see your teacher." I pulled on her arm.

"Where is everybody," she said.

"My father die, my mother is, um, waiting with the die."

She frowned at me. I knew I hadn't made any sense. I pulled on her again and she got up and stumbled around, putting on boots and jacket.

Outside I heard the pop-pop-pop again. This time I thought maybe it was closer.

"They're shooting again?" she asked.

"They shoot my father," I said.

"Oh God," she said. She sat down on the blankets. "Oh God."

I pulled on her arm.

"Are you all right?" she asked.

"Hurry," I said. I made a pack of blankets. I found my ax and a few things and put them in the bundle, then slung it all over my shoulders. I didn't know what we would do, but if they were shooting people we should run away. I had to pee really bad.

She did hurry, finally awake. When we went outside and the cold hit her she shuddered and shook off the last of the sleep. I saw the movement of her shoulders against the glow of the fire on the horizon, against the false dawn.

People were moving, clinging close to houses where they were invisible against the black wood, avoiding the open spaces. We stayed close to my house, waiting to see whose people were moving. Veronique held my arm. A dog came past the schoolhouse into the open area where the outrunners' fire had been and stopped and sniffed—maybe the place where my father had died.

I drew Veronique back, along to the back of the house. The spirit door was closed and my father was dead. I crouched low and ran, holding her arm, until we were in the trees and then she slipped and fell and pulled me down, too. We slid feet first in the snow, down the hill between the tree trunks, hidden in the pools of shadow under the trees. Then we were still, waiting.

I still felt feverish and nothing was real.

The snow under the trees was all powder. It dusted our leggings and clung in clumps in the wrinkles behind my knees.

Nothing came after us that we could see. We got up and walked deeper into the trees and then uphill, away from the distillery but still skirting the village. I left her for a moment to pee, but she followed me and we squatted together. We should run, but I didn't know where to run to and the settlement pulled at me. I circled around it as if on a tether, pulling in closer and closer as we got to the uphill part of town. Coming back around we hung in the trees beyond the field behind the shcoolhouse. I could see the stabros pens and see light. The outrunners were in the stabros pens and the stabros were down. A couple of the men were dressing the carcasses.

We stumbled over Harup in the darkness. Literally fell over him in the bushes.

He was dead. His stomach was ripped by rifle fire and his eyes were open. I couldn't tell in the darkness if he had dragged himself out here to die or if someone had thrown the body here. We were too close.

I started backing away. Veronique was stiff as a spooked stabros. She lifted her feet high out of the snow, coming down hard and loud. One of the dogs at the stabros pen heard us and started to bark. I could see it in the light, its ears up and its tail curled over its back. The others barked, too, ears towards us in the dark. I stopped and Veronique stopped, too. Men in the pen looked out in the dark. A couple of them picked up rifles, and cradling them in their arms walked out towards us from the light.

I backed up, slowly. Maybe they would find Harup's body and think that the dogs were barking at that. But they were hunters and they would see the marks of our boots in the snow and follow us. If we ran they would hear us. I was not a hunter. I did not know what to do.

We backed up, one slow step and then another, while the outrunners walked out away from the light. They were not coming straight at us, but they were walking side by side and they would spread out and find us. I had my knife. There was cover around, mostly trees, but I didn't know what I could do against a hunter with a rifle, and even if I could stop one the others would hear us.

There were shouts over by the houses.

The outrunners kept walking but the shouts did not stop, and then there was the pop of guns. That stopped one and then the other and they half-turned.

The dogs turned barking towards the shouts.

The outrunners started to jog towards the schoolhouse.

We walked backward in the dark.

There were flames over there, at the houses. I couldn't tell whose house was on fire. It was downhill from the schoolhouse, which meant it might be our house. People were running in between the schoolhouse and Wanji's house and the outrunners lifted their guns and fired. People, three of them, kept on running.

The outrunners fired again and again. One of the people stumbled but they all kept running. They were black shapes skimming on the field. The snow on the field was not deep because the wind blew it into the trees. Then one was in the trees. The outrunners fired again, but the other two made the trees as well.

There was a summer camp out this way, down by the river, for drying fish.

I pulled on Veronique's arm and we picked our way through the trees.

There were people at the summer camp and we waited in the trees to make sure they were Sckarline people. It was gray, false dawn by the time we got there. I didn't remember ever having seen the summer camp in the winter before. The drying racks were bare poles with a top covering of snow, and the lean-to was almost covered in drifted snow. There was no shelter here.

There were signs of three or four people in the trampled snow. I didn't think it would be the outrunners down there because how would they even know where the summer camp was but I was not sure of anything. I didn't know if I was thinking right or not.

Veronique leaned close to my ear and whispered so softly I could barely hear. "We have to go back."

I shook my head.

"Ian is there."

Ian. Ian. She meant her teacher.

She had a hood on her purple clothing and I pulled it back to whisper, "Not now. We wait here." So close to the brown shell of her ear. Like soft dark leather. Not like a real, people's ear. She was shivering.

I didn't feel too cold. I still had a fever—I felt as if everything were far from me, as if I walked half in this world. I sat and looked at the snow cupped in a brown leaf and my mind was empty and things did not seem too bad. I don't know how long we sat.

Someone walked in the summer camp. I thought it was Sored, one of the boys.

I took Veronique's arm and tugged her up. I was stiff from sitting and colder than I had noticed but moving helped. We slid down the hill into the summer camp.

The summer camp sat in a V that looked at the river frozen below. Sored was already out of the camp when we got there, but he waved at us from the trees and we scrambled back up there. Veronique slipped and used her hands.

There were two people crouched around a fire so tiny it was invisible and one of them was Tuuvin.

"Where is everyone else?" Sored asked.

"I don't know," I said. Tuuvin stood up.

"Where's your mother and your sister?" he asked.

"I was at Wanji's house all night," I said. "Where's your family?"

"My da and I were at the stabros pen this morning with Harup," he said.

"We found Harup," I said.

"Did you find my da?" he asked.

"No. Was he shot?"

"I don't know. I don't think so."

"We saw some people running across the field behind the schoolhouse. Maybe one of them was shot."

He looked down at Gerda, crouched by the fire. "None of us were shot."

"Did you come together?"

"No," Sored said. "I found Gerda here and Tuuvin here."

He had gone down to see the fire at the distillery. The outrunners had taken some of the casks. He didn't know how the fire had started, if it was an accident or if they'd done it on purpose. It would be easy to start if someone spilled something too close to the fire.

Veronique was crouched next to the tiny fire. "Janna," she said, "has anyone seen Ian?"

"Did you see the offworlder teacher?" I asked.

No one had.

"We have to find him," she said.

"Okay," I said.

"What are you going to do with her?" Sored asked, pointing at Veronique with his chin. "Is she ill?"

She crouched over the fire like someone who was sick.

"She's not sick," I said. "We need to see what is happening at Sckarline."

"I'm not going back," Gerda said, looking at no one. I did not know Gerda very well. She was old enough to have children but she had no one. She lived by herself. She had her nose slit by her clan for adultery but I never knew if she had a husband with her old clan or not. Some people came to Sckarline because they didn't want to be part of their clan anymore. Most of them went back, but Gerda had stayed.

Tuuvin said, "I'll go."

Sored said he would stay in case anyone else came to the summer camp. In a day or two they were going to head towards the west and see if they could come across the winter pastures of Haufsdaag Clan. Sored had kin there.

"That's pretty far," Tuuvin said. "Toolie clan would be closer."

"You have kin with Toolie Clan," Sored said.

Tuuvin nodded.

"We go to Sckarline," I said to Janna.

She stood up. "It's so damn cold," she said. Then she said something about wanting coffee. I didn't understand a lot of what she said. Then she laughed and said she wished she could have breakfast.

Sored looked at me. I didn't translate what she had said. He turned his back on her, but she didn't notice.

It took us through the sunrise and beyond the short midwinter morning and into afternoon to get to Sckarline. The only good thing about winterdark is that it would be dark for the outrunners, too.

Only hours of daylight.

Nothing was moving when we got back to Sckarline. From the back the schoolhouse looked all right, but the houses were all burned. I could see where my house had been. Charred logs standing in the red afternoon sun. The ground around them was wet and muddy from the heat of the fires.

Tuuvin's house. Ayudesh's house and Wanji's house.

In front of the schoolhouse there were bodies. My da's body, thrown back in the snow. My mam and my sister. My sister's head was broken in. My mam didn't have her pants on. The front of the schoolhouse had burned but the fire must have burned out before the whole building was gone. The dogs were moving among the bodies, sniffing, stopping to tug on the freezing flesh.

Tuuvin shouted at them to drive them off.

My mam's hip bones were sharp under the bloody skin and her sex was there for everyone to see but I kept noticing her bare feet. The soles were dark. Her toenails were thick and her feet looked old, an old old woman's feet. As if she were as old as Wanji.

I looked at people to see who else was there. I saw Wanji, although she had no face but I knew her from her skin. Veronique's teacher was there, his face red and peeled from fire and his eyes baked white like a smoked fish. Ayudesh had no ears and no sex. His clothes had been taken.

The dogs were circling back, watching Tuuvin.

He screamed at them. Then he crouched down on his heels and covered his eyes with his arm and cried.

I did not feel anything. Not yet.

I whistled the tune that Wanji had taught me to send out the message, and the world went dark. It was something to do, and for a moment, I didn't have to look at my mother's bare feet.

The place for the Sckarline dead was up the hill beyond the town, away from the river, but without stabros I couldn't think of how we could get all these bodies there. We didn't have anything for the bodies, either. Nothing for the spirit journey, not even blankets to wrap them in.

I could not bear to think of my mother without pants. There were lots of dead women in the snow and many of them did have pants. It may not have been fair that my mother should have someone else's but I could not think of anything else to do so I took the leggings off of Maitra and tried to put them on my mother. I could not really get them right—my mother was tall and her body was stiff from the cold and from death. I hated handling her.

Veronique asked me what I was doing but even if I knew enough English to answer, I was too embarrassed to really try to explain.

My mother's flesh was white and odd to touch. Not like flesh at all. Like plastic. Soft looking but not to touch.

Tuuvin watched me without saying anything. I thought he might tell me not to, but he didn't. Finally he said, "We can't get them to the place for the dead."

I didn't know what to say to that.

"We don't have anyone to talk to the spirits," he said. "Only me."

He was the man here. I didn't know if Tuuvin had talked with spirits or not, people didn't talk about that with women.

"I say that this place is a place of the dead, too," he said. His voice was strange. "Sckarline is a place of the dead now."

"We leave them here?" I asked.

He nodded.

He was beardless, but he was a boy and he was old enough that he had walked through the spirit door. I was glad that he had made the decision.

I looked in houses for things for the dead to have with them, but most things were burned. I found things half-burned and sometimes not burned at all. I found a fur, and used that to wrap the woman whose leggings I had stolen. I tried to make sure that everybody got something—a bit of stitching or a cup or something, so they would not be completely without possessions. I managed to find something for almost everybody, and I found enough blankets to wrap Tuuvin's family and Veronique's teacher. I wrapped Bet with my mother. I kept blankets separate for Veronique, Tuuvin, and me and anything I found that we could use I didn't give to the dead, but everything else I gave to them.

Tuuvin sat in the burned-out schoolhouse and I didn't know if what he did was a spirit thing or if it was just grief, but I didn't bother him. He kept the dogs away. Veronique followed me and picked through the blackened sticks of the houses. Both of us had black all over our gloves and our clothes and black marks on our faces.

We stopped when it got too dark, and then we made camp in the schoolhouse next to the dead. Normally I would not have been able to stay so close to the dead, but now I felt part of them.

Tuuvin had killed and skinned a dog and cooked that. Veronique cried while she ate. Not like Tuuvin had cried. Not sobs. Just helpless tears that ran down her face. As if she didn't notice.

"What are we going to do?" she asked.

Tuuvin said, "We will try for Toolie Clan."

I didn't have any idea where their winter pastures were, much less how to find them, and I almost asked Tuuvin if he did, but I didn't want to shame his new manhood, so I didn't.

"The skimmer will come back here," Veronique said. "I have to wait here."

"We can't wait here," Tuuvin said. "It is going to get darker, winter is coming and we'll have no sun. We don't have any animals. We can't live here."

I told her what Tuuvin said. "I have, in here," I pointed to my head, "I call your people. Wanji give to me."

Veronique didn't understand and didn't even really try.

I tried not to think about the dogs wandering among the dead. I tried not to think about bad weather. I tried not to think about my house or my mam. It did not leave much to think about.

Tuuvin had kin with Toolie Clan but I didn't. Tuuvin was my clankin, though, even if he wasn't a cousin or anything. I wondered if he would still want me after we got to Toolie Clan. Maybe there would be other girls. New girls, that he had never talked to before. They would be pretty, some of them.

My kin were Lagskold. I didn't know where their pastures were, but someone would know. I could go to them if I didn't like Toolie Clan. I had met a couple of my cousins when they came and brought my father's half brother, my little uncle.

"Listen," Tuuvin said, touching my arm.

I didn't hear it at first, then I did.

"What?" Veronique said. "Are they coming back?"

"Hush," Tuuvin snapped at her, and even though she didn't understand the word she did.

It was a skimmer.

It was far away. Skimmers didn't land at night. They didn't even come at night. It had come to my message, I guessed.

Tuuvin got up, and Veronique scrambled to her feet and we all went out to the edge of the field behind the schoolhouse.

"You can hear it?" I asked Veronique.

She shook her head.

"Listen," I said. I could hear it. Just a rumble. "The skimmer."

"The skimmer?" she said. "The skimmer is coming? Oh God. Oh God. I wish we had lights for them. We need light, to signal them that someone is here."

"Tell her to hush," Tuuvin said.

"I send message," I said. "They know someone is here."

"We should move the fire."

I could send them another message, but Wanji had said to do it one time a day until they came and they were here.

Dogs started barking.

Finally we saw lights from the skimmer, strange green and red stars. They moved against the sky as if they had been shaken loose.

Veronique stopped talking and stood still.

The lights came towards us for a long time. They got bigger and brighter, more than any star. It seemed as if they stopped but the lights kept getting brighter and I finally decided that they were coming straight towards us and it didn't look as if they were moving but they were.

Then we could see the skimmer in its own lights.

It flew low over us and Veronique shouted, "I'm here! I'm here!"

I shouted, and Tuuvin shouted, too, but the skimmer didn't seem to hear us. But then it turned and slowly curved around, the sound of it going farther away and then just hanging in the air. It got to where it had been before and came back. This time it came even lower and it dropped red lights. One. Two. Three.

Then a third time it came around and I wondered what it would do now. But this time it landed, the sound of it so loud that I could feel it as well as hear it. It was a different skimmer from the one we always saw. It was bigger, with a belly like it was pregnant. It was white and red. It settled easily on the snow. Its engines, pointed down, melted snow underneath them.

And then it sat. Lights blinked. The red lights on the ground flickered. The dogs barked.

Veronique ran towards it.

The door opened and a man called out to watch something but I didn't understand. Veronique stopped and from where I was she was a black shape against the lights of the skimmer.

Finally a man jumped down, and then two more men and two women and they ran to Veronique.

She gestured and the lights flickered in the movements of her arms until my eyes hurt and I looked away. I couldn't see anything around us. The offworlders' lights made me quite nightblind.

"Janna," Veronique called. "Tuuvin!" She waved at us to come over. So we walked out of the dark into the relentless lights of the skimmer.

I couldn't understand what anyone was saying in English. They asked me questions, but I just kept shaking my head. I was tired and now, finally, I wanted to cry.

"Janna," Veronique said. "You called them. Did you call them?"

I nodded.

"How?"

"Wanji give me . . . In my head . . ." I had no idea how to explain. I pointed to my ear.

One of the women came over, and handling my head as if I were a stabros, turned it so she could push my hair out of the way and look in my ear. I still couldn't hear very well out of that ear. Her handling wasn't rough, but it was not something people do to each other.

She was talking and nodding, but I didn't try to understand. The English washed over us and around us.

One of the men brought us something hot and bitter and sweet to drink. The drink was in blue plastic cups, the same color as the jackets that they all wore except for one man whose jacket was red with blue writing. Pretty things. Veronique drank hers gratefully. I made myself drink mine. Anything this black and bitter must have been medicine. Tuuvin just held his.

Then they got hand lights and we all walked over and looked at the bodies. Dogs ran from the lights, staying at the edges and slinking as if guilty of something.

"Janna," Veronique said. "Which one is Ian? Which is my teacher?"

I had to walk between the bodies. We had laid them out so their heads all faced the schoolhouse and their feet all faced the center of the village. They were more bundles than people. I could have told her in the light, but in the dark, with the hand lights making it hard to see anything but where they were pointed, it took me a while. I found Harup by mistake. Then I found the teacher.

Veronique cried and the woman who had looked in my ear held her like she was her child. But that woman didn't look dark like Veronique at all and I thought she was just kin because she was an offworlder, not by blood. All the offworlders were like Sckarline; kin because of where they were, not because of family.

The two men in blue jackets picked up the body of the teacher. With the body they were clumsy on the packed snow. The man holding the teacher's head slipped and fell. Tuuvin took the teacher's head and I took his feet. His boots were gone. His feet were as naked as my mother's. I had wrapped him in a skin but it wasn't very big so his feet hung out. But they were so cold they felt like meat, not like a person.

We walked right up to the door of the skimmer and I could look in. It was big inside. Hollow. It was dark in the back. I had thought it would be all lights inside and I was disappointed. There were things hanging on the walls but mostly it was empty. One of the offworld men jumped up into the skimmer and then he was not clumsy at all. He pulled the body to the back of the skimmer.

They were talking again. Tuuvin and I stood there. Tuuvin's breath was an enormous white plume in the lights of the skimmer. I stamped my feet. The lights were bright but they were a cheat. They didn't make you any warmer.

The offworlders wanted to go back to the bodies, so we did. "Your teachers," Veronique said. "Where are your teachers?"

I remembered Wanji's body. It had no face, but it was easy to tell it was her. Ayudesh's body was still naked under the blanket I had found. The blanket was burned along one side and didn't cover him. Where his sex had been, the frozen blood shone in the hand lights. I thought the dogs might have been at him, but I couldn't tell.

They wanted to take Wanji's and Ayudesh's bodies back to the skimmer. They motioned for us to pick up Ayudesh.

"Wait," Tuuvin said. "They shouldn't do that."

I squatted down.

"They are Sckarline people," Tuuvin said.

"Their spirit is already gone," I said.

"They won't have anything," he said.

"If the offworlders take them, won't they give them offworld things?"

"They didn't want offworld things," Tuuvin said. "That's why they were here."

"But we don't have anything to give them. At least if the offworlders give them things they'll have something."

Tuuvin shook his head. "Harup—" he started to say but stopped. Harup talked to spirits more than anyone. He would have known. But I didn't know how to ask him and I didn't think Tuuvin did either. Although I wasn't sure. There wasn't any drum or anything for spirit talk anyway.

The offworlders stood looking at us.

"Okay," Tuuvin said. So I stood up and we picked up Ayudesh's body and the two offworld men picked up Wanji's body and we took them to the skimmer.

A dog followed us in the dark.

The man in the red jacket climbed up and went to the front of the skimmer. There were chairs there and he sat in one and talked to someone on a radio. I could remember the word for radio in English. Ayudesh used to have one until it stopped working and he didn't get another.

My thoughts rattled through my empty head.

They put the bodies of the teachers next to the body of Veronique's teacher. Tuuvin and I stood outside the door, leaning in to watch them. The floor of the skimmer was metal.

One of the blue jacket men brought us two blankets. The blan-

kets were the same blue as his jacket and had a red symbol on them.
A circle with words. I didn't pay much attention to them. He brought
us foil packets. Five. Ten of them.

"Food," he said, pointing to the packets.

I nodded. "Food," I repeated.

"Do they have guns?" Tuuvin asked harshly.

"Guns?" I asked. "You have guns?"

"No guns," the blue jacket said. "No guns."

I didn't know if we were supposed to get in the skimmer or if
the gifts meant to go. Veronique came over and sat down in the doorway. She hugged me. "Thank you, Janna," she whispered. "Thank
you."

Then she got up.

"Move back," said the red jacket, shooing us.

We trotted back away from the skimmer. Its engines fired and
the ground underneath them steamed. The skimmer rose, and then
the engines turned from pointing down to pointing back and it
moved off. Heavy and slow at first, but then faster and faster. Higher
and higher.

We blinked in the darkness, holding our gifts.

ABOUT THE AUTHORS

MICHAEL SWANWICK is the author of one fantasy and three science fiction novels, including the Nebula Award–winning *Stations of the Tide*. His works have been frequently nominated for the Nebula, Hugo, Arthur C. Clarke, and World Fantasy Awards. Many of the best of these are collected in *Gravity's Angels* (Arkham House). *Jack Faust*, an information-age reinterpretation of the medieval legend, will be published by Avon in 1997. He lives in Philadelphia.

ANDY DUNCAN, a native of Batesburg, South Carolina, is a 1994 graduate of the Clarion West writers' workshop in Seattle, where he completed the first draft of "Liza and the Crazy Water Man." At this writing, he has stories upcoming in *Asimov's SF* and *Negative Capability*, a poem upcoming in *Asimov's*, and articles in *The New York Review of Science Fiction* and upcoming in *The Journal of the Fantastic in the Arts*. He lives in Raleigh, North Carolina, where he studied fiction writing under John Kessel.

JANE YOLEN is the author of over 170 books, most of them fantasy, fairy tales, and poetry for younger readers. Her adult novels *Cards of Grief* (Ace) and *Briar Rose* (Tor) both won the Mythopoeic Fantasy Award, and *Sister Light, Sister Dark* and *White Jenna* (both from Tor) were finalists for the World Fantasy and Nebula Awards. She is also editor-in-chief of Jane Yolen Books, an imprint of Harcourt Brace dedicated to publishing fantasy and science fiction for children and young adults. She lives in a small town in western Massachusetts, where in her spare time she writes lyrics for rock bands.

GREGORY FEELEY's first novel, *The Oxygen Barons*, was published as an Ace SF Special in 1990. His fiction has appeared in *Full Spectrum, Asimov's SF, Science Fiction Age,* Michael Stearns's anthology *A Starfarer's Dozen* (Harcourt Brace), Katharine Kerr's anthology *Weird Tales from Shakespeare* (DAW), and other magazines and anthologies. He lives in Hamden, Connecticut, and is working on a novel, *Neptune's Reach.*

ROBERT REED's most recent books are *Beyond the Veil of Stars* and *An Exaltation of Larks,* both published by Tor. He is currently working on a sequel to *Beyond the Veil of Stars,* again for Tor. He was nominated for a Hugo for his story "The Utility Man." Of late, he has had stories in *Asimov's SF, The Magazine of Fantasy and Science Fiction,* and *Tomorrow.* He lives in Lincoln, Nebraska, in part because of its unpredictable weather.

SUSANNA CLARKE lives in Cambridge, England, where she spends most of her time editing cookbooks and watching people take photographs of food. For her stories she likes to blend history with magic. Her other stories are forthcoming in Neil Gaiman's *Sandman* anthology (HarperCollins) and Ellen Datlow and Terri Windling's *White Swan, Black Raven* (Avon). She is working on a novel about the magician, Mr. Norrell and his pupil, Jonathan Strange.

SUSAN PALWICK's first novel, *Flying in Place* (Tor), won the Crawford Award. She is currently at work on a second novel, *Shelter*, also for Tor. Her recent short fiction includes "The Real Princess," published in Ellen Datlow and Terri Windling's *Ruby Slippers, Golden Tears* (Avon), and "Aida in the Park," forthcoming in Ellen Kushner, Donald G. Keller, and Delia Sherman's *The Horns of Elfland* (Penguin). Palwick lives with her husband, three cats, and two computers in New Jersey, where she teaches literature and writing at Stevens Institute of Technology.

MARTHA SOUKUP lives in San Francisco and writes short SF. She has published in magazines and anthologies, including Ellen Datlow's *Off Limits* (Morrow) and the young-adult anthologies *A Starfarer's Dozen* and *A Nightmare's Dozen* (both Harcourt Brace). She won a Nebula Award for a story reprinted in *Nebula Awards 30* (Harcourt Brace). "Waking Beauty" was written, in a slightly different form, at Neil Gaiman's request for the *Sandman* anthology, but was withdrawn by the author when DC Comics insisted on a work-for-hire contract. The story remains dedicated to Neil.

CARTER SCHOLZ was a finalist for Nebula, Hugo, and Campbell awards in 1977. His short stories were published widely in the 1980s, and he is the author (with Glenn Harcourt) of the novel *Palimpsests*, one of the latter-day Ace Specials. Following a hiatus from writing, his recent work has appeared in *Crank!* and Greg Bear's anthology *New Legends* (Tor). He lives in Berkeley, California.

JOHN M. FORD won the World Fantasy Award for his novel *The Dragon Waiting* (Avon) and the Philip K. Dick Award for his most recent novel, *Growing Up Weightless* (Bantam). He won a second World Fantasy Award for the long poem "Winter Solstice, Camelot Station." He has also won international awards for game design. He is presently at work on a new fantasy novel for Tor, tentatively titled *Aspects*. He lives in Minneapolis, in the reserve stacks of the Library of Babel.

MARK KREIGHBAUM has published short fiction and poetry in a number of anthologies and magazines. *Palace,* a science fiction novel by him and Katharine Kerr, was published by Bantam in 1996. He lives in Sunnyvale, California, and is currently working on a fantasy trilogy about art as an engine for social change.

MAUREEN F. MCHUGH's first novel, *China Mountain Zhang* (Tor), won the *Locus* Award for best first novel, the Lambda Literary Award, and the James Tiptree Jr. Memorial Award. It was a *New York Times* Notable Book and a finalist for the Hugo and Nebula Awards. Her short fiction has also been a regular feature of recent Hugo and Nebula ballots. Right now she lives in scenic Twinsburg, Ohio, with a husband who is a toy engineer, a son who is a Kung Fu fanatic, and a golden retriever named Smith. The only blot on this suburban bliss is the fact that they live next to a dairy farm, and when the wind is blowing in the right direction, everything smells like cows. She is working on a third novel, *Mission Child,* set in the world of "The Cost to Be Wise."